CLOAK OF FOLLY

CLOAK OF FOLLY

A NOVEL BY

BURKE BOYCE

HARPER & BROTHERS
PUBLISHERS / NEW YORK

To

Dwight Akers

for showing me the way to Vere House

NOTE

For readers who are interested in comparing Elizabethan money with the values of our own, the figure can be found, roughly, by multiplying by ten for modern pound sterling; by forty, for American dollars.

I am very grateful to Pauline Angell and Mrs. Frederick C. Mayer for books of reference which have been of great help to me.

B.B.

CLOAK OF FOLLY

PROLOGUE

I

The 31st day of August was buried in Essex the good Earl with three Heralds of Arms, with a standard and great banner of arms, and eight banner rolls, crest, target, sword and coat of armor, and a hearse with velvet and a pall of velvet, and a dozen of scutcheons, and with many mourners in black; and a great moan made for him.

John de Vere ended his life in honors. It was recorded of him that he entertained the Queen Her Majesty at his castle of Hedingham, as his ancestor had stood beside King Harry of glorious memory on the Field of the Cloth of Gold.

2

On an afternoon early in September, between five and six o'clock, a troop of horsemen breasted through the jostle at Aldgate in the walls of London. They were finely mounted, dressed in black livery slashed with tawny. Their caps were black, and their doublets; the bridles of their horses were hung in sable. They clattered under the gateway two by two, in a column that stretched beyond the cast of sunlight from the stone gate towers, from the grass-grown archers' walk, and the wallflowers and green fumitory and scarlet kiss-me-quick along the battlements.

Patches on their left shoulders bore a silver star, the mullet argent of the Oxford arms, and they rode with jaded buttocks and a thirst for small beer after hot miles in the water meadows of the Essex lowlands. They were seven score, a hundred and forty men and horses, out from Castle Hedingham since morning, jogging attendance on a new lord. The star and livery were badges of his service, the black trappings and rich array marked of the dignity of his state—seventeenth Earl of Oxford, Viscount Bulbeck, Lord Sandford and of Badlesmere, keeper of the lions and hereditary lord great chamberlain of England, ranked in precedence over all earls, and successor to one of the proudest titles in the kingdom.

The earl rode at the head.

He was a boy twelve years old.

He was a little below medium height, stocky, with brown curly hair and hazel eyes.

Like the rest, he wore black; black hose, black shirt, a slanted velvet cap tipped by black plumes. A silver dagger jingled delicately from a chain at his hip.

His name was Edward, and he was coming to the city three days after his father's funeral to become an orphan of the Queen.

His pageant moved into Cheapside, into a sweat of faces that closed about the horses' necks, parted, and closed again behind, giving way in currents and sluggish eddies like puddles splashed from the offal ditch in the middle of the street. Baskets swam in the eddies, bundles, faggots, buckets of oysters and shrimp and herring, quartered beeves and wine casks, leather jerkins and blue apprentice coats. The market seethed in the purple twilight, a teeming gash, its houses to the south high and well-built, framed in timber and heavily carved and gilded, its lanes on the north twisted narrowly between tradesmen's stalls kept by slattern women, the poulterers' shops in the Poultry, and the shops in Bucklersbury where apothecaries sold drugs and herbs. Over the tumult hung a stench of bodies and the shrilling of the street cries: "Cockles nye! New, new cockles! Brooms for old shoes! Will ye buy any straw? Pouchrings! Boots and buskins!"

A whisper ran down the line of riders, an expectancy like wind freshening over barley, and a young man riding by the boy leaned in his saddle.

"D'y' hear, my lord? London."

The boy nodded. His fair skin and sensitive lips were fine and drawn. He paid no attention, but kept his eyes fixed on the twitchings of his horse's ears. He looked small in the pomp and swirl around him.

The young man repeated his question, adding with a smile, "Don't be afraid, my lord. You'll soon know London."

"I know London," the boy said. "Our family were masters of Kensington once. In the time of the Conqueror. It was Chenesiton then."

They skirted St. Paul's in silence, past the old steeple, the moldering tracery, and the stonework smudged with smoke from the sea coal. Swifts flew crying about the west towers, and kites perched on the leads, beaks huddled in their breasts, scavengers of the city's garbage. The crowds here were hard and sinister, ravelings of town dandies, riffraff, harlots, beggars, servants waiting for hire, and public letter writers. Three men in capes and dirty ruffs dodged under the nose of the boy's horse and into a tavern door. The horse plunged. The young man beside him flung an oath and darted a hand for the bridle, but the boy was quicker. He rode the plunge like a cat, and gentled the animal down in an effortless ease.

"Players," the young man said angrily.

The boy lifted his eyes, his face lighting with a flicker of interest.

"Some company in the city. Or vagabonds. Y' can't tell with players." The young man scowled toward the group, who stood in the doorway, blinking a kind of forlorn but hopeful respect at the Oxford star and livery. "They can tell George Gascoigne, the poet, though. God's name!" He preened himself and looked pleased.

"We had players at Hedingham," the boy said. "They acted plays on feast days, and last year before the Queen." His eyes clung for a moment to the tavern doorway.

"Why not? They whore abominably and they sleep in barns, but they're poets' mouths." The young man was still pleased. He acknowledged the stares with a broad gesture.

"They were merry. The Queen praised them in Latin, and she and my father talked afterwards, in the evenings."

"Castle Hedingham was more than hounds and hawking," Gascoigne said. "It had wit and letters. Not all of them the worst." He coughed modestly.

"You are kind to ride with me," the boy said politely. They had dropped the tavern behind. The light faded from his face, and he returned to his own thoughts. He put spurs slowly to his horse. "I think it was at the Queen's visit I was made a royal ward."

He fell silent again.

Gascoigne waited, but he saw the boy had not spoken to him.

They came to Fleet Street, a clutter of alleys, jutting roofs, of filth and noise and booths where the latest monsters were put on show, the freaks of nature and obscene births, cows with fifth legs above their udders, and two-headed foals. Ludgate was beyond, and Temple Bar.

» 3 «

Gascoigne said, "This is for your good, my lord, to live here with the Queen's secretary. Consider your rank and your estates, the country stinking with plots and factions, and the venom from the old wars. Consider your uncle of Surrey—a poet, too, God's name—dead by the axe on Tower Hill; your uncle of Sheffield, killed in Ket's rebellion. These times swallow boys at a gulp. Or consider if your mother took a second husband—" He broke off, seeing the boy stiffen, and finished in a different key.

"You'll be merry, here, as merry as at the castle. Cecil House is rich. Sir William's padded himself fat. And he has a daughter, besides. Anne's a tender chit, and she'll be tasty when she comes to bloom. There's sport enough there to grow on." He dangled the morsel from another smile.

The boy avoided the smile indifferently. "I do not think Anne Cecil will make me merry."

Gascoigne, glancing sidelong, colored above the narrow starch of his ruff.

He let several minutes pass. When he spoke his voice was distant, and a little fulsome. "You've ridden far, my lord, and you're tired."

The boy did not answer.

Gascoigne paused. "We all knew your father," he said. "He was a true man."

"There never will be a man like him again," the boy said simply.

Gascoigne said nothing. He watched the street ahead. From Temple Bar another party of horsemen had appeared, a somber procession of velvets and brocades, and grave, dark beards. They came impressively forward in the leveling sunset. Nobles. Courtiers. Gentlemen pensioners of the Queen.

"Sir William's sent a welcome," Gascoigne said.

The boy looked up.

He looked at the procession, and on past them into the violet sky at their backs, past the great houses along the Strand. And past the Strand to Westminster and the palace.

He straightened in his saddle and rode toward them.

I | ANNE CECIL STOOD IN FRONT OF HER MIRROR, EMBILLOWED by silks and rejected petticoats, and indulged in a delicious uncertainty.

Below the mirror of her bedchamber was a litter of rouge jars and laces, pomander balls and winking enameled ornaments, the disordered casualties of her toilet. Her artless little mouth was pursed to a kittenish expression, and she primped at the glass, studying the effect as well as she could in the dimness that filtered through leaded windows. She had grown astonishingly pretty in the nine years since Gascoigne had called her a tender chit.

"I don't know, Meg. I believe the French cap was better."

Her dressing woman gave a finishing pat to hairpins and stepped back. "The pearl is most becoming."

She had been two hours with Mistress Anne, and she was tired. A lean, middle-aged woman in beaded stomacher and flowing wide skirts with rivulets of crewel embroidery, she carried the faintly hunted air Sir William Cecil's enemies said was natural in his household.

"Do you think so?" Anne considered, pouting.

"Becoming, and most suitable."

"But not elegant. The French is more elegant. Let me try the French one."

The dressing woman adjusted the folds of Anne's taffeta gown, spreading them apart over the silken kirtle. "The pearls are younger on you," she said.

"Younger! Younger! Who wants to be younger? You're a dolt, Meg!" Anne whirled in a burst of petulance. "Give me the cap!"

She struck the woman's hands away and snatched the French cap. She flung the pearl one off. It fell at her feet, a pale crumpled net.

"I'll wear what I please."

With a resigned sigh the dressing woman rescued the pearls from under Anne's heels. It took patience to prepare her master's daughter for the tournament, patience and a long humility.

"The Mistress Anne knows her own mind."

"Of course I do. There now, don't sulk."

The humility mollified Anne, who was like all pampered natures, sweetness in an instant when she had heaped her emotions on someone else.

She posed before the mirror, peering at her reflection. The French cap fitted tight to her head, giving her an elfin look, like a court page hooded in silver. From the glass, a brown frame of curls laughed back at her, a pair of slim shoulders.

"Oh, it's comely!" she cried, and clapped her hands with delight. "Isn't it comely?" She spun across the room to a girl who sat watching by the window. "Tell me it's comely, Eliza!"

The girl stirred among the velvet pools of her cushion. "It's beautiful," she said.

Her voice was lower than Anne's though her age was two years less. She had an oval, shy face, gentle in its contour but made piquant by a daintiness of line and the composure of her lips. Her hair was dark, braided plainly under a caul of tinsel, her eyes dark and very clear. Her childish body shaped to small breasts just rounding in the bud of adolescence; and she admired Anne's sophistication with a wistful awe.

"All your things are beautiful," she said.

"Ninny," Anne said, with a titter at such innocence. "What I mean is, will it catch my lord of Oxford?"

"I think it would catch any man."

"But my lord of Oxford?" Anne insisted.

The girl looked down, avoiding the question. "You've met my lord of Oxford more often than I have."

"Often?" Anne stopped her titter. "How often have you met him?"

"Only once. He stayed with us in Staffordshire last year, with the Earl of Sussex, on his way from the wars in the North."

"A hundred yeomen in Reading tawny behind him, and eighty gentlemen ahead, with gold chains about their necks." Anne filled in the details glibly. "I saw him that time, riding to his house by London Stone."

"He was kind to me," the girl said. "He told me about the Border rising, and the plot against the Queen."

"Was that all?"

The girl looked from the window across the sunlit gardens of Cecil House. "He read me some poems he had written."

Anne struck another posture. She tilted her head, holding her fingers at arm's length and admiring the petal tints of the nails. "I've known my lord of Oxford since he was twelve. He's always written poetry. That's because he's clever; he finished at Cambridge at fourteen, and can talk Latin as well as Her Majesty. Most courtiers try to write poetry when there's nothing better to do. But my father says they get over it later."

She dismissed the frippery with a shrug and took a subject more to her taste. "My lord of Oxford is the handsomest bachelor at court, and when I am old enough I shall marry him. That will be this year. I shall be fifteen this year. And all Her Majesty's maids of honor will cry their eyes out."

The girl sat motionless, her hands pressed in her lap. "I thought you were to marry Master Sidney."

Anne left off her posturings to survey the dark braids with a fidget of irritation. She was annoyed at being saddled with Eliza Trentham for the three days of the tournament. It was bad enough to have this child from the shires on her leading strings, someone to be endured because the Trenthams were wealthy merchants from the same class as her father and might be useful to him. It would be worse if Eliza were going to act like a simpleton and say what she thought. No one at court said what he thought.

Everyone took it for granted that the talk of marriage between Anne Cecil and Philip Sidney had come to nothing. Perhaps they laid it to the hostility between the Cecils and Philip's uncle the Earl of Leicester. Perhaps they laid it to the earl's preposterous debts and the rumor that Sir William Cecil did not trust the promised dowry payment. Sir William had a shrewd money sense, even for his daughter's wedding. But whatever they laid it to, people understood it was over and done with, and did not drag it out in public. Not in the same breath with the Earl of Oxford.

"Edward de Vere is a much greater match than Philip Sidney," Anne said loftily. "Her Majesty has given my father a title so that I can marry him. She has created my father Lord Burghley. We are nobility now." She tripped back to the mirror, where the dressing woman was selecting perfumes. "Edward has been a ward under my father's charge for nine years. He has nearly a hundred manors and estates."

"Your mother will be coming for you," the dressing woman reminded her.

"Oh dear—hurry, Meg!"

She forgot her irritation and prattled on in growing excitement.

"Edward's riding in the tournament today. You must hope for him to win, Eliza. He's not ridden a tournament before. Half the men would like to see him downed—Master Hatton and the new ones around the Queen. Edward's wittier than they are and they envy him. He hates their vanity and says biting things. But he's a marvelous rider, swift and strong. He's hunted and hawked all his life. And he's afraid of no one. I think he wouldn't be afraid of the devil himself. He killed a man when he was seventeen."

"Killed?" Eliza said. "What for?"

"How should I know?" Anne said. The dressing woman fastened one of the pomander balls and a long-handled, jeweled mirror at her girdle. "An undercook in our house. Thomas something. He ran him through the belly with his sword. Edward said the man was spying on him. He probably was," she shrugged.

"I think it's shameful to set spies on anybody seventeen," Eliza said. "It's shameful to make him kill." Her tone was strained, as though her throat hurt her, and the flush deepened in her cheeks.

"You child, everyone uses spies," Anne answered. "They're back of every arras. Edward is a great peer. What else can he expect but to be spied on? But the coroner's jury absolved him, so there was no harm."

She was shrugging again when the dressing woman said, "Your mother." The door opened, and Lady Burghley came in.

Anne broke her shrug in a curtsy. Eliza curtsied also. The dressing woman sank on one knee.

Lady Burghley ignored the curtsies, sweeping a glance at the untidy cushions and offering the Trentham girl a fretful pat on the head. Her lips were a compressed line in the starched circle of her ruff, her figure formidable in a dress of stiff blue satin. A managing mind and an irascible temper were Lady Burghley's armor against the world. That she wore the armor, in her private life as well as her public, was understandable. Her husband had trod the shifty road of politics through the reign of four sovereigns, and of two sons to carry on the Cecil fortunes, one was a wastrel, the other a hunchback. As wife and mother, as mistress of greatness and as a woman haunted night and day by the dread of the Tower, Lady Burghley needed hardihood and an unyielding will. But they did not make her any more agreeable.

"You are stayed for," she said.

"Yes, Mamma," Anne said meekly. She wilted in her mother's presence. She became docile, almost pathetically subdued. Fourteen years of dominance had shaped her mind in the habit of obedience. "I am sorry, Mamma."

"Be at more pains in your affairs. Everything is arranged. I have sent the message to my Lord of Sussex to keep a place for Eliza in the gentlewomen's gallery, and you will see that she is suitably entertained when you are not waiting on Her Majesty with the maids of honor. What are you wearing?"

"This, Mamma."

Anne revolved herself for inspection. Lady Burghley noted her critically, and with some satisfaction. The white, virginal gown, silver-dusted and glowing with Anne's vivid beauty. The slender waist, tapering throat, small exquisite chin; the lively profile, and the little flash of teeth that showed when Anne smiled. There was pride in such a daughter.

"The gown will do," Lady Burghley said. "The jewels are good, and the shoes. What is that cap?"

"It is my French cap, Mamma."

"I do not like it."

"It is in the latest style."

"Where is the pearl cap?"

Anne pointed to where it lay on the bed.

"The pearl becomes you better. Wear that."

"Yes, Mamma." Anne's mouth quivered, but she did not protest.

At Lady Burghley's nod the dressing woman came forward. She removed the French cap and began to pin the pearl one on, working silently with impassive fingers.

"The horses are at the stair gate," Lady Burghley said. "Join me there."

Anne's mouth was still quivering as her mother left the room. But she looked defiantly from Eliza to the dressing woman, and settled the pearl cap with a fillip of her head.

"Anyway," she said, "I shall marry my lord of Oxford."

The thought consoled her while they went along the corridors, in and out of the latticed sunlight that splashed through mullioned casements; past ornate panelings and under lofty ceilings where their footfalls echoed hollowly; by alcoves and embrasures, and glimpses of lovely terrace chinking the house walls with the golden arrows of spring. Chinking but not breaching, for the immensities of Cecil House guarded secrets of their own.

The great mansion on the north side of the Strand was labyrinthine, like its era. It encompassed an age that had never been before, and would never be again, so bold and turbulent, sly and crafty, so brawling and so brilliant, so paradoxical and so deadly. It had the lion's weight and the unicorn's whimsy. Its turrets were grim, its gardens pastoral, its stones massive, its Tudor windows lacy, and expediency ruled all.

From King Henry to King Edward, from King Edward to Queen Mary, from Queen Mary to Queen Elizabeth, Sir William Cecil had contrived his life to promote his country and himself, and the rooms and vaulted passages were webbed with policy. They were the plexus of every nerve of political movement. Intrigue wove through them like the thread of Ariadne. The word of an ambassador, dropped as he feasted among their tapestries, the babblings of a rag-looped Shoreditch beggar, out of his wits with running sores and the ague, were recorded with the same unwinking watchfulness.

They sucked whispers, and dockets filched by night, from conspiracies over half of Europe, from Spain and Scotland, from France and Flanders and the German principalities. They had an ear in every English shire. They weighed, and judged, and knew what things were spoken in castle closets. They gathered reports of the money rates at Antwerp, and hid muffled figures brought in the dun hour before sunrise for questioning after torture. They were inscrutable and alert. Nothing of force or displeasure ever marred their magnificent surface. But when the moment was ripe, an order would be signed, and a man would ride.

The corridors were commonplace to Anne. She accepted them as a normal part of her life, like family and clothes and fair looks, and did not trouble herself with them one way or the other. She never thought about them. But their atmosphere seemed to stifle Eliza. The younger girl followed Anne mechanically, staring at the twists and turnings as though she felt them closing in on her like a prison. Her feet dragged, and Anne had to snap at her to hurry.

Once Eliza asked, "Does my lord of Oxford live here?" in a voice so incredulous that Anne giggled.

"Of course. Though he'll live in one of his own houses now. Probably in London."

"I should think he'd want to. I know I would. But not London. Farther away than London."

"He wants to go to the Low Countries and be a soldier. But my father won't agree, and Her Majesty forbids him. Now stop chattering and come along. We've just time."

They had entered a balcony leading through a tall antechamber. The balcony was empty, but the rush-strewn floor of the chamber was clustered with groups of people, some talking, some pacing, some leaning by the walls, the daily petitioners, the seekers of favors and pardons and special grants, hoping for audience with Lord Burghley. Lady Burghley had descended from the balcony and was half across the floor, preceded by a wave of bows. Anne darted over to the balcony and pushed Eliza into a side passage. She motioned her to silence, and slipped around a corner.

"What?" Eliza asked.

Anne put her finger to her lips, pointing for answer. Below them, at the foot of a narrow flight of stone steps, three young men stood by a courtyard door, spurred for riding and drawing on their gloves. Anne paused, and fluttered down the steps in a sibilance of petticoats.

Two of the men bent low. The third looked up and smiled. Eliza, trailing after Anne, saw a laughing face, crisp hair, and a leap of scarlet. The breath went out of her and she stood stock still. Quick and tanned and vigorous, dressed head to toe in crimson velvet, the Earl of Oxford was twenty-one. Anne Cecil had said he was the handsomest bachelor at court.

"A marvel not to be looked for, to see May Day blushing indoors as well as out," he said. His tone was firm and sure, with a cheerful warmth like the color of summer fields.

Anne swayed on the bottom step, devouring the compliment with her eyes. "We're leaving for the tournament. Good fortune, my lord. I hear the challengers are to have a Red Knight."

"Not so red as a pair of lips, nor so soft for the plucking," he said. He caught sight of Eliza in the background. "God's blessing—Mistress Trentham. How do you come to London?"

"To watch the tilts, my lord," Anne said. "With her mother and father."

"I think the tilts will watch Mistress Trentham," he said.

He brought her forward, tongue-tied beside Anne. Eliza would have knelt, but he stopped her. "My audience of Staffordshire. Welcome to London, Eliza."

"Thank you, my lord."

"We're gay, here. I hope you'll be happy. But we only play at fighting. Tournaments aren't as real as wars."

"No, my lord."

"I should pray not," Anne said with a grimace. "Nor as dull as Staffordshire cowfields."

Eliza reddened, but the earl laughed. "We'll let her decide. Tournaments, wars, country meadows. Have you seen a tournament, Eliza?" She shook her head.

"This is her first," Anne said, bridling a little and edging closer. "Eliza is in my care."

"None better," he said. He smiled down at Eliza. "Anne keeps us all in hand."

"If I were a man," Anne said, "I would take tournaments. The pennons and the armor, and the horses galloping. And the whole court in jewels. Could anything be more wonderful?"

"Except love," he said.

"Oh, my lord," she said coyly.

He met her eyes for an instant and laughed again. "You hear what's in store for you, Eliza. Especially love."

"Yes, my lord. I have heard it before."

"So young, and hear of love? Where?"

"Not in Staffordshire," Anne said.

"In a poem," Eliza said. The reddening clung in her face, but she kept her look doggedly to him:

> Love's a desire, which, for to wait a time,
> Doth lose an age of years—

Her voice faltered and trailed off to stillness. He took the stillness up softly.

> —and so doth pass
> As doth a shadow severed from his prime,
> Seeming as though it were, yet never was.

The lines hovered like a phrase of music as he finished them. "Does that run true?"

She nodded.

"You remembered?"

"Your poem, my lord."

There was a pause.

> Seeming as though it were, yet never was.

He echoed it to himself, as though it were something fragile. "Would you lose an age of years for love, Eliza?"

"If I loved," she said.

He smiled.

Anne said, fidgeting, "We'll be late for the tournament."

"And if you were a man," he said, "would you take tournaments, too?"

"I will never be a man," Eliza said. "But whatever I was, I would choose to suit myself. Not for courts or for jewels, or people applauding from a gallery. I would decide my own way." His ease, the gentleness behind his smile, gave her courage. "I would even choose poetry if I wished."

Anne burst into laughter, and the two young men with the earl put their hands to their mouths. He smiled again, too, a little gravely. "Is that how you would choose for me?"

Her courage ebbed. She shook her head and could not answer.

One of the men said, "Barbary is ready, my lord."

He said, "Tell the grooms to wait."

They went out. He turned back to Eliza.

"I'll choose for us both," he said. "We'll be poets, Eliza, for our tournament. We'll honor poetry, and I will wear your token."

"Oh, no, my lord!" Anne gasped in dismay, but he waved the gasp aside. It was his prerogative to indulge moods, and his charm to do it disarmingly.

"Her first," he said. "Would you wish it, Eliza?"

Her look stayed on him like someone in a dream. Moving with a slow wonder, her fingers went to her throat, to the neck of her gown, down the stillness of her gown to her girdle. A small handkerchief hung there from a clasp. Slowly she undid it from its clasp and held it toward him. He took it in a courteous dignity that made her seem for the moment more than a worshipping and overwhelmed child. He bent to touch her hand. Suddenly, without warning, she lifted her arms, and throwing them around his neck, kissed him full on the lips.

Nothing was said. Only as he raised his head the gravity of his eyes shaded curiously with a faint, inexpressible stir.

He went quietly to the door.

Love's a desire, which, for to wait a time—

He smiled at Eliza, and stopped, leaving the cadence incomplete. The door opened and closed, and he was gone. Eliza stood.

"How dare you!" Anne cried at her. "Oh, how dare you!" Whirling with all her force, she slapped Eliza full across the face.

2 ‖ OXFORD RODE FROM CECIL HOUSE INTO A GALA CITY. May Day had dawned crystal, the weather clear and fine. Queen's weather, her subjects called it. The sun poured on London and London poured toward Westminster.

The Strand was crowded, the Thames from the Bridge to Lambeth a tangle of boats and barges, and from every fetid alley apprentices and tradesmen, butchers and soldiers, cutpurses and bawds, pushed out of the city hustle for standing room at the lists. Sedate merchants with wives and daughters, linen drapers, clerks, students of the Inns of Court, earringed seamen in off the Atlantic and the galleon routes of the Caribbees, elbowed in converging streams. Bakers sold sweetmeats on trays, fishwives peddled shrimp in willow panniers, burly scarred fellows lugged performing bears at the end of chains. There were tapsters and bailiffs and hostlers out of service. A Puritan preacher strode in the burly-burly, flailing his arms and calling the godless to repentance. He was mobbed under by a knot of journeymen tailors, beneath festive doublets and coats of goose-turd green. Beggars and vagabonds lined the ditches, and did brisk trade in sham epilepsies and fits and counterfeit ulcers. In and out among the skirts and hosen legs small boys frolicked like schools of dolphin. The huge, noisy, carefree, sprawling mass pulsed with the life and breath of Elizabethan England.

"That's young Sir Edward. Son to Sir John de Vere that was. He's in the jousts."

"A groat on him."

"You're a fool. He's newer to razor than spear."

"More fool, you. See his thighs. Oxford's a great name. He'd carry the canopy if the Queen should die. God save her."

"God save him from the spears. Yet he does have an air. Not so much an air. A kind of lustiness."

"Marry, he'll wear. Goodman caution, will y' bet?"

They gawked and pushed and trampled one another goodnaturedly. It was part of the sport: nobles and the Queen, pageantry, the horses' squeals and the brassy trumpets. For the price of twelvepence they could sit on a bench. For the price of nothing they could stand ten deep at the tilt-yard rail. They could have action and excitement and perhaps blood. They could stuff themselves on glitter and spectacle, and bandy gossip of the courtiers—their rank, their offices, their faults, their jealousies; who was in favor, and who out, who had been cuckolded and who begotten the latest bastard. They could whoop for Her Majesty and boo at the crash of knights from the saddle. They could have a day of hobnob with the great and go happily home afterward, full of sweat and ale and a neighbor's lice.

Their noise followed Oxford on his ride to the palace and washed around him as he swung from his horse and entered the challengers' pavilion. Inside he stripped to the waist while his squire rubbed him with lotion. His skin was a hard, white ivory, haired boyishly, ocher-colored, in unfleshed downiness on his chest and with thicker patches beneath his arms. The muscles ran along his ribs and down under his trunks as smooth as hickory. They would carry him today before

Queen and court and the citizenry of London for public trial of his manhood.

The pungent lotion made him blink. The pavilion rang with armor and the bustle of the challengers' squires and grooms. He braced his feet against the rubbing, flexing his legs and taking advice from the two who had ridden with him from Cecil House. One was his cousin, Lord Henry Howard, suave, scholarly, son of the poet Earl of Surrey who had been so close to the blood royal that he had paid for it with his life in the days of King Henry. The other was a gay, larking lad from the court, Fulke Greville.

"You'll be riding course with seven defenders," Greville was saying. He ticked them off on his fingers. "Lord Stafford's the best, then Tom Knyvet. Knyvet's dangerous. Take him at the throat. Then Tom Cecil, Mistress Anne's brother—drives a shrewd point—turn it with your shield."

"I've seen him run at the quintain."

"So. Then Tom Bedingfield. He'll bow to you at books, but he has more weight than you. Don't slacken when you charge him. Those are the roughest. The rest are nearer your match."

"Three Toms," Oxford said. "We'll make a pretty cat's brawl."

"And for a pretty token," said Greville, grinning at Eliza's handkerchief tucked among the loops of Oxford's belt on the stool by him. "D'y' note, Harry?"

Lord Henry smiled taciturnly.

"Hardly a token. Eliza's young," Oxford said.

"A fault time will cure," Lord Henry remarked.

"I'd have done the same, the way she looked at you," Greville said.

"There'll be many looking at him shortly," Lord Henry said. "He must show equal to these challengers. They're experienced in the lists."

He spoke silkily, without much hope, his voice drawing like a cautious thumb over the edge of his cousin's mettle. Oxford put on his shirt and doublet, and his squire began to buckle the pieces of his armor.

Another of the challengers came by: Christopher Hatton. Anne had mentioned him particularly to Eliza. He was decked out in the height of fashion. Like Lord Howard he was thirty-one, ten years older than Oxford. He had drifted to London from Northamptonshire to study law, but a good figure and ingratiating manners had made court life better for him. He paused obsequiously.

"I trust you will do well, my lord."

"As well as the next," Oxford said, busy with the greaves straps.

Hatton's eye ran over Oxford's corselet of mail, the boar's head on his crest, the pennon on his lance, with the De Vere star, and his scarlet livery. "Yes, we trust to do well in the joust, for Her Majesty's grace."

"In a joust or a jig either," Oxford said. "Her Majesty likes grace in both."

Hatton flushed at his temples. He knew the talk about him, that he had danced himself into the Queen's favor in a galliard. Yet there was expedience in cultivating this young lord, at least on the surface. He bared his teeth pleasantly. "We'll have hot work in the sun."

"Break your spears on the visor and a pox on the sun," Oxford said indifferently.

"And the jigs," Greville added.

"I can break a spear as it ought to be," Hatton said, with a fulsome solemnity. "I am for the charnel, the visor hinge. A spear broke from the charnel counts as two."

"Wondrous," Oxford said. But the irony was lost on Hatton.

"I lift powerfully at the point of shock, setting my back rigid and thrusting my weight. Just at the point of shock. Instanter. It sends a helmet flying."

"Wondrous," Oxford said again, and Greville drawled, "God's bones!"

Hatton gazed toward him coldly. "It is an excellent stroke, Master Greville. I do not carry a titled spear, but I can trust to gain me some small merit."

The trumpets sounded and the heralds began to clear the lists, and he strode affectedly away, trailed by his squire.

"There walks a boiled radish," Greville said. "Swollen with the water of his own opinion."

"One of the vegetables of the court. They sprout overnight, like weeds." Oxford said.

"Outsprout him, Ned. Wilt him down. Titled spear—Lord Christ."

The trumpets were sounding again. The pavilion was emptying. Oxford and his friends went outside. Grooms ran forward with horses.

Lances tossed, their pennons fluttering. Stately, with a slow swing of stirrup, the first challenger and the first defendant reined to the gates at opposite ends of the field.

The sun was higher in the sky by now. Its light struck gleams from steel and sent a dazzle along the Queen's gallery. Staring faces gaped around the enclosure rails, shifting in a kaleidoscope of colors, the yellow of dust and the tan of wood, emerald, vermilion, saffron, indigo, and gold. Greville and Lord Howard, with Oxford between them, watched from the pavilion as the constable of the lists opened the visors of the riders, at east gate and west. The constable identified them, measured their lances, and swore them to the oath of the joust.

Oxford's brown hair was damp at his forehead with his armor's heat. His hand gripped and ungripped with a restless movement on his lance haft.

The constable cried three times: "Let them go, let them go, let them go!"

The riders spurred, and crashed in the center of the list.

Another pair followed.

Hatton rode the third joust. As he passed Oxford on his way to the gate he reined in. "Perhaps you can set this tune to your jig, my lord." His voice was hollow in the depths of his helmet.

He closed his visor and went to the challengers' post. Plummeting across the turf, he broke his spear expertly above the charnel for a score of two.

"Now," Greville said in Oxford's ear.

Flecks of brilliance were beginning to glitter in Oxford's eyes. They looked like ice.

A plumed casque was on his head, slit narrowly for view. His body was in the saddle, feet on the stirrups, ash spear slanted at his toe. He heard Lord Henry Howard—"Aim for the shield, Ned"—heard the trumpets and the clang of the opening gate, and the constable announcing the Red Knight.

At the sight of him, riding into the glare in a smolder of carmine, the crowd hushed and the talk in the Queen's gallery quieted.

With a flourish he rounded the lists, dipped spear to the Queen, and wheeled into position.

He was smiling behind the grill of his helmet. The world he saw through the narrow steel slit was a good world. It was fair and beckoning. It waited for him to reach and take it for his own. He was rich in lands, wealth, and friends; youth and pride and the flush of confidence. Over his head his motto rippled on its pennon—*Vero Nihil Verius:* Nothing Truer than Truth. The star in his coat of arms had come with a De Vere from the Crusades, the boar on his crest blazoned the exploits of a De Vere in the forest of France.

There would be exploits for him, too; campaigns and wars and glory, fame won at the dykes in the Low Countries, or adventures on the sea with fighting captains, or battles against Spain in the storm that was brewing across the Channel. His family had fought at Agincourt, at Crécy, and at Bosworth Field. He would carve his way after them, and follow them to brighter fields than a jousting list. He was the Red Knight, riding in the springtime of a still-young Queen. May was new and the future boundless.

The constable cried the signal. He drove his spurs in and hurtled forward.

Tom Cecil charged at the same time from the opposite gate. He thundered toward Oxford, bending low. A hundred paces away, then fifty, then twenty-five—horse, man, shield. Tom Cecil was guarding wide; if he was dulled in wine, as he usually was, a shield hit would take him.

But Cecil had tricks of his own. At five paces he closed his guard. The shift was too late to counter. They met head on. Oxford saw his spear glance, snapping at the point, and his brain numbed to a deafening roar. His horse pitched on its haunches. His spine slammed against the cantle, a sharp bludgeon of pain. Reeling, he sensed Cecil's charger careen by him and slow at the farther gate; sensed the clean shatter of Cecil's spear.

He galloped to the challenger's pavilion, fuming while his squire undid his helmet.

"You sent me at the shield," he said passionately to Lord Howard. "He was ready for me."

"Tom is crafty," Lord Howard said with a dry shrug. "Like all the Cecils."

"God's blessing!" Oxford said. The flecks of brilliance were darting colder in his eyes.

The tournament swung into full action. It was a tumult of dash and splendor. The young courtiers who flocked under Elizabeth were picked for their daring, for their fire and recklessness. They were ambitious and eager, and rivalry for the Queen's favor fanned them to a white heat, tempering, testing them, forging them into the blade that was to hew an empire. They came from village and city and country town, from the Ridings of Yorkshire and the harbors of Devon, from the Midland hedgerows and the sheepfolds of the Cumberland lakes. Elizabeth and her older councilors were the anvil. Elizabeth and her young men were the sparks.

They pounded across the tilt-yard on foaming caparisoned horses, ripping clods from the turf and wracking bone and sinew.

Course after course they ran, to the din of the crowds and the galleries' cheers. Oxford met Tom Knyvet and Tom Bedingfield, broke on Knyvet's crest and flung Bedingfield from the saddle. His hair was matted wet, tight to his head. He tousled it with a damask napkin between charges. A lace of blood, started by a spear fragment, trickled from the side of his mouth to his collar.

"What score is Hatton?"

"Two helm thrusts, one body stroke. Better him, Ned."

"Give me a new spear."

Seven courses for each, seven catapultings down the lists, ribbons streaming, bodies taut. Lances splintered and steel rang. The ground was scattered with sheared plumes, broken harness and bits of armor. Heralds ran out to retrieve them and claim forfeit.

The riders knew how to spur and charge and stiffen their weight against the shock. They were veterans at this, their muscles were hardened from long practice. Hatton snapped his fifth spear to the haft, missed on the sixth, and on his last got in his charnel stroke, bursting the helmet fastenings and spinning helmet and collaret into the barriers.

Course by course, with a surge and gallop and drum of hoofs, Oxford matched his score to Hatton's. He tightened his saddle girths and flexed his gauntlets between jousts, waiting impatiently to mount, his face lit by quick excitement. This was like the days at Hedingham when his father was alive: the sport of the pikemen in the castle yard and the chase after a buck through Essex woods. He felt the plunge of his horse under him. His lungs ached, his mouth was sand. The sweat and blood were a tingle on his parched lips.

Four tilts. Five. The benches caught the drama. Their cheers swelled to a din, and in the pavilions the squires knocked each other's shoulders and set up a yelling. Hatton or Oxford, Hatton or the Red Knight. It would be one of the other for the prize.

"You're their lad, Ned. They're whooping for you."

"Look to Barbary. Sponge his flanks. Fulke, I'll win for a thousand pound."

He had trailed Hatton at the fourth tilt. He drew even at the fifth. He forgot the ache in his lungs. He forgot the blinding crash and the sob for breath. He reined and circled and reared, couching spear and riding with an ease and dash that made horse and rider and leveled lance seem all one piece. His body swayed as he charged, to spoil the aim of the point rocketing down the field at his crest. In the Queen's gallery Anne Cecil watched in a shiver of ecstasy. Farther off, among the gentlewomen, Eliza Trentham sat fighting back tears and twisting her fingers in her lap. The Earl of Sussex, seasoned in wars, smiled and bent to his sister's ear: "This jousting would have gladdened the old king. England can use such."

With Hatton's miss on the sixth tilt Oxford went into the lead. He ran his own tilt flawlessly, and at the last run broke spear cleanly on Lord Stafford's shield.

The squires cavorted in the challengers' pavilion. Fulke Greville pulled Oxford from his horse as he cantered in, and threw his arms around him. He and Lord Henry Howard poured wine down Oxford's throat. They toasted the Red Knight to the halloos from the benches and the screams along the rails. He was a man to their own hearts, and they had seen a sight.

"De Vere! De Vere! De Vere!"

"Oxford and the prize!"

"Ho, goodman, where's your groat now?"

"Paid, in God's name!"

"Marry, 'tis a lovely wight!"

"Cock and bones, the lad deals a blow!"

"Oxford and the prize! Oxford and the Queen! Oxford and England! Hoo!"

They swirled and clamored for him.

As his squire unbuckled his armor, Oxford laughed exuberantly at Hatton's sullen, vapid, wide-set face.

Then the trumpets blew again, and the court rose, and the day's jousting ended.

At night, after the jousts, there was feasting and music. There were fireworks outside the palace, and dancing before the Queen in the long audience gallery inside. Oxford danced with Anne. She looked radiant in her pearl cap and snowy gown, and when he came to kneel to Her Majesty his eyes caught hers among the maids of honor. Her Majesty saw, and nodded encouragement. Anne needed none.

She left her place and hung to his arm, chattering gaily with adoring glances.

"The whole court talks of you, my lord," she said.

"They must talk of something," he smiled.

"Oh, but it's true. Everyone praises you. You're the marvel of London. It was a magnificent tournament."

She was thankful the Trentham girl was too young for the dancing. She settled Eliza after supper in a side alcove between two sedate ladies-in-waiting, and crowded Oxford's evening with vivaciousness— "Will you fight again? I hope so, you'd be sure to win. How wondrous clever of you to ride as the Red Knight. 'Twas like some hero out of chivalry. Oh, they're playing a pavane. Shall we dance a pavane? Or shall we walk on the terrace for the fireworks?"

He danced with her often. She kept him to herself as long as she could, steering him adroitly from the alcove where the little Trentham girl sat with rapt and shining eyes. The Trentham girl's parents were in the outer circle near the Queen. Master Trentham spoke to Oxford as he and Anne went by.

"You have an excellent skill, my lord."

"And you have an excellent daughter, Master Trentham. You should let her stay in London."

"Staffordshire is more suited to her age, my lord."

"Of course it is," Anne said. "Eliza's a sweet child, but a mere baby. Come dance with Cissy Knollys. She's languishing for it." Cissy Knollys had a gallant of her own, and could be trusted.

The tournament lasted three days. On the third night Her Majesty awarded the prize. The challengers and defendants, in full armor, were escorted into her presence chamber by the maids of honor, and received chains, ornaments, purses and jewels from her hands. Anne escorted Oxford, and knelt by him, tingling with excitement, while the chief prize went to him—a brilliant scoring tablet for cards, crusted with rich diamonds. The fingers that slipped it into his paused imperceptibly as he kissed them, and the queenly, somewhat throaty voice spoke above his head: "We are proud of you, my Lord Oxford."

That night, before the dancing began, he left Anne and walked through the palace rooms. Eliza's handerchief was folded under his belt and there was an odd, casual, half-smile on his lips, as if he were amused at himself and yet drawn on at the same time by a certain pleasant impulse in his fancy. He walked between groups who bowed and flattered and admired him as he passed—Tom Cecil and the Carey sisters, Fulke Greville teasing with Cissy Knollys, the press of hangers-on around the Queen's first favorite, the Earl of Leicester; and Thomas Knyvet standing with his niece Nan Vavasour, a bright-haired girl iridescent as the Catherine wheels in the palace garden.

Tom Bedingfield stopped him. Tom was still stiff from his fall two days ago. Genial, easy-going, inclined to fleshiness around the waist, Tom Bedingfield was the sort whose qualities would never stand out in a crowd, but his smile was hearty. "Well won, my lord!"

"By a piece of luck," Oxford said. "I'm sorry you went down. Are you hurt?"

"Nothing that won't mend," Tom said. "My lord, if you've a minute—"

"A dozen."

"I've finished my translation of Cardanus' *Comfort.*"

"Good, Tom! Will you publish?"

"Gentlemen don't publish their writings, my lord. It's vulgar."

"God keep us from vulgarity. Bring it to Vere house tomorrow, Tom. We'll split a flagon on it."

Bedingfield grinned and limped off.

Someone touched him on the shoulder. It was Christopher Hatton. Fastened about Hatton's arm was a small golden bell and chain, the second prize for the tourney. He displayed it for Oxford's benefit.

"It rings," he said.

"The chain?" Oxford said.

"No no, the bell." Hatton said, and he tinkled it.

"So it does," Oxford said. "Like a boast."

He turned and went on with his search. He walked to the end of the rooms and back again.

But Eliza Trentham was not there.

The viols were tuning up. Anne would be waiting.

A gentleman usher whom he asked told him, with a bow, that there was no need to look further. Master Trentham had had a message recalling him to Staffordshire, and Mistress Eliza had left the city with her parents after the jousting that afternoon.

3

"IT IS A SOUND MAXIM," DECLARED LORD BURGHLEY, "THAT our sons should not be suffered to cross the Alps. They learn nothing there but pride, blasphemy, and atheism. And if they get a few broken languages, they profit them nothing more than to have one meat served up in different dishes. I doubt if Her Majesty will grant my lord of Oxford his license to travel."

Lord Burghley was sitting with his own two sons at Cecil House, eating sugar confections after supper and washing them down with an excellent Pedro Ximenes. Their discussion had led inevitably to Oxford. Since the week of the tournament the court had buzzed with talk of the Red Knight. Oxford was the wonder of half London, the delight of the Queen and the gossip of the foreign embassies. As Her Majesty's secretary, and as Anne's father, Lord Burghley had special reasons to be interested.

Lord Burghley did not approve of travel. He distrusted the lands beyond the Channel as sinks of iniquity that drained young men's morals and leached their common sense. He had never traveled himself, except for progresses with the Queen or shuttlings to and from his country house at Theobalds.

"Poor Ned," Tom Cecil said. "He's to be tethered, then."

"I do not think him tethered."

"He'll think so."

"Her Majesty," Lord Burghley said equably, "wishes him near her."

» 24 «

"So would I if I were Her Majesty," Tom said. "So does every palace virgin, and most that aren't. But how long can you keep him? He wants freedom."

"Your duty to Her Majesty should teach you a more respectful tongue," Lord Burghley said. "My lord of Oxford has come into great credit."

Tom shrugged. The argument was all one to him, part and parcel of the stuffy life at Cecil House.

"Well, it's as well. He'll fret, here. But he'd fret worse, being nosed after through the inns of Europe." He lolled back on his stool and squinted caustically at the ceiling. Tom had had experience with his father's practices. When Tom had been studying on the continent Lord Burghley's spies had reported everything.

"My lord of Oxford is what he is," Robert said. He was the hunchback, a youth with a sallow, pointed face. He had high temples and a mouth whose corners seldom moved, his words forming deliberately in the middle of his lips. He had been musing by himself. The shrewd qualities of his father had skipped his older brother and passed to him. "A wit and scholar, a mind that sees much and a heart that acts it. There would be value in him, properly directed. It would be to his good, as well as to Her Majesty's, if some outlet could be found for his hot blood."

"Oh, his hot blood," Tom said. "Leave that to Anne. She'll manage that."

Tom was amused at Anne. He thought of how certain things were done in Paris, and wondered if she were old enough to know what hot blood was.

Anne did her best. Her methods were artless and direct, and she did not need sophistication. Her guilelessness would have been cloying if she had been older, but it became charm and prettiness in a girl of fifteen. The shadow of Eliza Trentham was relegated to the background of Staffordshire, and she was radiantly happy, devising a hundred excuses to be with Oxford and fascinate him.

In the compact society of the court she had many opportunities. They met every day, in the palace galleries, at tennis and bowls, and among the rooms where they waited on the Queen. She would see him coming toward her, proud and gay and confidant, the center of a group of courtiers who milled around him in an admiring circle, and she would leave her friends and dart over to him, basking in his smile and her eyes glowing at being envied by the other maids.

"How splendid they all think you, my lord," she would say, and the flutter of her skirts beside him would show she thought so, too.

Or they would walk by themselves beneath windows that caught the sky in diamond panes as she listened to his ambitions to travel in distant kingdoms.

"I wish I were a man," she said.

"God forbid," he said. Then she would glance up and blush, feeling his look on her—on her throat and her breasts and her delicate, lissome waist.

He found himself attracted to Anne. He liked her spirit; it seemed to match his own. And he liked her vivacity and gayness. She was in the middle of every excitement at the court. She loved to dance, to laugh, to wear pretty clothes. He had not taken too great notice of her while they were growing up together at Cecil House, but now that they were both a part of court society he enjoyed being with her more and more.

Like Tom Cecil, he had been bored by the stuffy life at Cecil House. In the first flush of release from it Anne seemed to him like sunshine on April leaves, or the color of a rainbow through crystal glass, part dark, part bright, and all of it desirable.

He was many parts himself. Some of him was poet, some was courtier, some fighter. He had a venturesome mettle and a taste for all the experiences of the world. He had lost a father and a home when he was twelve. He wanted a son of his own body, and a family life. He wanted travel and the sights of foreign places, as Tom Cecil traveled, and Philip Sidney planned to do. His imagination, his love of books, his loneliness for his father and his acute sense of pride that grew from it, gave him complexities that were already, in his new manhood, chafing inside him. Anne was a stimulant to his restlessness.

Sometimes they would go on the river, in a boat hired at the palace landing, or at the foot of the steps below Cecil House, in Ivy Lane. The boatmen would arch over their oars, their minds on a fat fee, like cats purring for cream, and the boat would split the river surface in long silken ribbons. She would be merry and talkative, dabbling her fingers in the water and chattering gleefully. Then bit by bit her talk would quiet while the boat trailed its ribbons into the sunset; while he sat by her, his profile quick against the evening's iridescence and his breathing slow and deep, as though the river between its broad green banks were drawing from all the streams of England and washing them at his feet.

Once he kissed Anne.

They had been standing together on a terrace under the moon and she had been smiling at him, her lips parted eagerly and the pearls in her hair like childish stars. There had been a pause in what they were saying, and they had both known it would happen. He put out his arms and took her and thrust his mouth to hers. His whole frame tautened hard and violent. It was a kiss that left them shaken. He stepped back, and she turned blindly and ran in at the door. He started after her—"Anne!"—but Fulke Greville and the Vavasour girl frolicked by with a group and carried her with them, and the moment was gone.

He was uneasy that night. He tried to read, but could not. He tried to write, but his quill was stubborn. He settled himself with Tom Bedingfield's translation of Cardanus, which he and Tom were scanning together, but the words had lost their meaning. He gave it up, and went to a sleepless bed.

Early the next day he dressed quickly, breakfasted, and was at Cecil House by midmorning. He found Lord Burghley in his gardens. The Queen's master secretary was mounted on a little mule, indulging in an amble among the paths. Although the month was June, he wore a fur-trimmed gown and staid garments. His greeting to Oxford was deferential, it being an axiom with him that deference cost nothing and frequently bought much.

"This is my hour for exercise. If you will do me the grace—"

Oxford measured his step to the mule's plod, and they moved on together.

"Thank you," Lord Burghley said. He waited for Oxford to speak, who picked a stem of mint as he walked and twirled it impatiently.

"My lord," he demanded, "I should like permission to travel. If I am to go abroad, let me go now. You are wrong to keep me dangling. Let me go while the time is fitting, while I can go freely and in good will. Let me go before—" He broke off.

"Before what?" Lord Burghley said blandly.

Oxford evaded the question. "There could be matters that would interfere," he said.

Lord Burghley rode on a little, stroking the mule's neck and looking across the gardens. Without being tall, Lord Burghley was active and hardy, and carried himself very straight. Like all else at Cecil House, his gardens reflected him. Their paths were precise, their vistas and fountains and hedges correctly conventional, but boxed within their walls was a profusion of everything that flowered on English soil. The number and variety were richer than any of the noble houses along the Strand—great masses of blooms, rare single specimens, spicy shrubs, laid out by a master gardener with the finest care. Espalier pears and juicy apricots grew on formal trellises, gooseberries and hollies, marigolds and beds of herbs skirted around marble pools, and there were damask roses, and fleur-de-lis, and exotic pomegranates brought home by merchant captains. They were all collected and set in order. Lord Burghley derived enormous pleasure from them. In his gardens as in his politics, he kept close to the earth, and nothing was too large or too small for his attention.

"You have won eminence, and much renown, my lord," he said at length. "As your lordship's assured friend and servant I am much gratified. But since your coming of age, as well as your recent successes in favor"—he avoided the Queen's diamonds in a noncommittal clearing of his throat—"it would be meet for me to mention how matters stand with you."

"With my estate cleared out of wardship they'll stand fair enough," Oxford said carelessly.

"True. But foreign journeys are costly."

"I can sell lands."

"That would be unwise. Gentility, my lord, is nothing else but ancient riches."

"And honor and a fair name," Oxford retorted. "Let me go to France and Italy, or give better reasons. I'll not be put off with pat answers."

Lord Burghley guided the mule solemnly around a rosebush and surveyed Oxford before replying. He knew him so well after nine years of guardianship. A vigorous, supple, graceful figure. A fluted ruff. Glistening doublet, a cap plumed rakishly with pheasant feathers. Auburn hair, close-cropped; alert, bold hazel eyes, flecked with humor; and the springiness of an athlete. One of the sparks fanned upward by Her Majesty.

Burghley had misgivings about such sparks. He had already been nearly singed by Leicester, who would have made himself husband of the Queen, setting the whole country in a political blaze, except for Elizabeth's own inborn shrewdness. Here was another of them, scintillant, mettlesome, impetuously erratic, with a boundless energy and restless to whirl on any wind of life. There was courage in Oxford, power and vitality and imagination, but where they would carry him Lord Burghley hesitated to say. There was no way to foresee where this spark was bound. It might kindle to fame and stature, or it might burn itself out in its own fires, leaving only the ashes of disgrace. The possibilities were there for both. Lord Burghley sighed in his graying beard. He had seen men come and go.

He spoke sedately. "You are in poor means for journeying, my lord. Your estate is still in some delay."

"Delay?"

"Your father left a will, and debts, my lord. A matter for chancery. Your mother was to have probated. But after your father died she—"

"Skip my mother," Oxford ordered.

Lord Burghley adjusted his tone. "Afterward the matter was passed to me. Your mother married again while you—"

"I know when she married," Oxford said shortly. The hurt of his mother's second marriage had gone deep when he was a boy; it had never entirely healed.

He walked, frowning, studying the mint stem in his hand. "My father left debts?"

"Tangled and confused. There have been others since."

"What others?"

"The expenses of your wardship. You have not been thrifty, my lord."

"You've allowed me a thousand pounds a year. Is that extravagant?"

"Extravagance depends on the purse," Lord Burghley observed. "The tailor's bill for your first four years at Cecil House was above six hundred pounds. I recall other bills from last year. For a Geneva Bible, a Chaucer, and Plutarch's works in French, two pounds seven and ten. For Tully's and Plato's works in folio, four pounds more. Two weeks of board and lodging for you and your tutors and all your servants came to only six." He looked aggrieved.

"Shall I eat the books?" Oxford said.

"You may do as you wish. But Plutarch in French is not a diet money fattens on."

"I had not thought your lordship disliked French," Oxford said.

It was a cool reference to Burghley's politics, which Lord Burghley disregarded. "I do not argue the buying of books," he said. "A humble few have even been dedicated to me. Clothes, yes; they mark a man. And studies. I have given you law at Gray's Inn, as I have given my sons and other wards. But continual spending on frivolities wastes your substance. Your estate is not settled and cannot support it."

Oxford dropped the mint to the path, his face thoughtful.

"Nine years would seem enough for settling an estate."

"Not yours, my lord. Your father left—"

"God's my life, my father's in his grave. He can't stand here for accounting. He was just and admirable in everything he did. I loved him. We'll not speak of him again."

Burghley nodded sympathetically, his beard impassive.

"As for my debts," Oxford said, striding more briskly, "I can whistle 'em off. I'm no worse than others."

"I would not risk too far," Burghley said. "Debts are the privilege of those whose credit is secure."

Oxford spun on him. "Am I an earl or am I not, my lord?"

"Most certainly."

"Then leave it there."

"I would be willing. But I do not wish you to go amiss. A point has been raised at law—a little cloudiness."

"Law? More law? What point?"

The sunlight over the gardens gave a prominence to Lord Burghley's eyes over his spade-cut beard. He resembled a benevolent rabbit. "Your stepsister has a suit still pending from the time of your wardship, a claim to your office of lord great chamberlain."

"Ho—Kate?" Oxford's laugh scattered the chaff of his temper. "She's mad. On what grounds?"

"That your mother was not rightly married to the Earl your father. The claim is illegitimacy."

Oxford went ashen. "Illeg—" he choked, "Ill—!" His throat refused the word. He seized at the nearest thing to hand, the bridle of Lord Burghley's mule, and shook it with a fury that sent the animal straddling stiff-legged, yawing terror-stricken across the path.

"My lord—in conscience—" Burghley struggled with the reins.

Oxford shook the bridle wildly, unconscious of what he did, reckless of stamping forehoofs and the slobber from the bit smearing his hose. His face was white as his ruff. "Bastard! Foul-born! God's my life!"

"In conscience, my lord—a claim solely at law."

The mule jerked loose, half on the path, half on a garden crescent. Oxford stood panting.

Lord Burghley regained his balance. He guided the mule off the flowerbed and tried to speak composedly. "I believe the claim false, and weakly advanced. Patiently, my lord."

"False as hell!"

"My lord, I said patience. For your own good."

Lord Burghley had been jolted from his calm. His manner checked Oxford. For all his prudence there was an aura of force about Lord Burghley. It might have been his position, and his influence with the Queen. Or it might have been that he was aware of every motive and every secret of the kingdom.

"You have been pitched abruptly to ticklish heights," he said. "You are not able to twist the world to your liking. You were best to wear your new favors carefully. Spleen and violence could destroy them. Remember, also, you are blood cousin to my lord of Norfolk."

"Is it crime to be cousin to a duke?" Oxford said.

"Favor will not weigh in the scale with a throne," Burghley replied, unruffled. "You know the northern rebels. And chief among them is your cousin Norfolk."

"There is no charge against Norfolk. Her Majesty has pardoned him."

"On his oath of obedience. Which is as may be," Lord Burghley said with a dry cough.

The mule had completed its ambling around the gardens and brought them back to the house. A servant ran to hold the bridle. One steadied the stirrup. Lord Burghley began placidly to dismount.

"Be content to stay in England," he said. "Master the urge for travel, Her Majesty does not wish it. Will you come in, my lord?"

Oxford shook his head. He watched the long gown go into the house and disappear through the gloom of the doorway. It faded augustly and the doors closed after it. He heard the flurry of Lord Burghley's entrance dim away over the voices of the petitioners:

"Your lordship—"

"Worshipful sir—"

"Good Master Secretary—"

"Your gracious lordship—"

He heard another voice behind him.

"Edward—"

He swung around. Anne was standing there, poised on the gravel by the house steps, a question in her eyes. "I couldn't help listening," she said.

"It's no matter now."

"You're not to go?"

"No."

"Oh, Edward."

"I'm to dangle here till I rot," he said. He paced up and down. "What's the world? Nothing. What's the wind in a sail? What's France? Or Italy? The snow on the Alps or the sky over Venice? Nothing. Less than nothing."

The phrases tumbled from his lips. The gravel of the path crunched under his quick, restless strides.

"I'm sorry, Edward—"

"Dismiss 'em. Close eyes and be blind. Close ears and be deaf. Be deaf and blind and dumb and stay at home. God's blessing, we've a cure for fantasies."

She watched him dismayedly, not pretending to understand but awed at his outburst. "Why are you not to go?"

He stopped and faced her. "I'm too poor," he said. "I'm too spendthrift. And I'm too much my cousin of Norfolk's cousin."

"But you're not poor, Edward. You have castles and manors and huge lands." She put her hand on his arm with a consoling pout, sliding it along the gold knots on his sleeve. "And everybody spends too much, except my father." She gave a little laugh.

"A wry comfort," he said. But he could not help smiling.

"Besides, Her Majesty knows you're loyal to her. She's said so often."

She was tender and rueful and eager to bring him comfort. She moved closer to him.

He had never seen her prettier. She met his smile and her eyes lifted to his. He saw how ingenuous they were, and how they were lighted by a secret inner happiness. She would not be entirely sorry if he stayed. He felt a tug at his pulses. The happiness he saw was sweet and irresistible, betwitching in the perfume of the gardens and the spell of her nearness to him. It drove his heart to a tighter beat and made the world beyond the garden walls no longer real. He filled his lungs and remembered the heady magic of last night's kiss.

"I've never learned patience," he said. "You must teach me how."

She glanced sideways at the hand on his arm, the girlish fingers, the white skin barely veined. It lay close to his wrist. She could almost have touched his wrist. She did touch it, for an instant, lyrically. "What could I ever teach you, my lord?"

"Shall I tell you?"

She dropped her hand from his arm, laughing playfully, and skipped on in front of him a few steps. He laughed too, following her, his silver dagger sheath jingling at his thigh.

"Shall I tell you, Anne?" His voice was brittle, like fine transparent glass that would explode to bits at a blow.

"If you wish," she said.

"God's blessing, I think you know it already," he said.

"Do you, my lord?"

She stopped her skipping and came back to him, demurely, the sun delicious on her shoulders. "Do you think so?"

"I do."

"That I know it already?"

"Yes."

"I like you to think so," she said.

"Anne—" he said. He gripped her shoulders where the sun rounded over them, but she held him away.

"But you wished to tell me," she said.

He laughed again. "Make a lover of me, Anne," he said. "Teach me the honey words, and how to linger and play and draw the sweetness out till my brain faints with it. It's the art of a maid. A man's clumsy until she leads him."

She looked at him, amazed that he could read her so plainly and delighted that he cared to.

"Make a lover of me," he said. "Teach me to forget France and Italy."

His thumbs were a hard, unsteady pain in the flesh of her shoulders.

"Is there no more to life than France and Italy?" she said. She swayed toward him.

"Tom, I'm to be married."

"My lord—?"

Tom Bedingfield was at Oxford's house that night, polishing his translation of Cardanus, when Oxford burst in on him like a spaniel shaking water. He caught him by the waist and pulled him from his stool with a yank that sent the sheafs of foolscap sprawling.

"Tom, wish me Godspeed!"

"My lord—?"

"Take off that owl's look, Tom. I'm to be married."

"You, my lord?"

"God's life, have you ears?"

He put him at arm's length, grinning at the startled face and the short, plump, amiable body.

"I—my lord—"

Tom's mind wrested back from Latin syntax. He grinned, too, and thrust out his hand.

"Godspeed indeed."

Oxford seized the hand till the bones cracked. "With her father's blessing, Tom. And the Queen to be told tomorrow. You're staring at a bridegroom."

His jewels sparkled in the light of the tapers. His cheeks were flushed and vivid. Tom shoved the manuscripts aside with his foot and pushed the stool toward him. He ignored it. "I've been celebrating," he said.

"Who is the bride?"

"Mistress Anne, Lord Burghley's daughter. Would y' believe it, Tom?"

"There's none fairer in England."

"It's done. She'll have me—Tom, I've spilled your sheets."

"You'll work in rarer sheets than these, my lord."

"With a rarer will. Drink a health for me, Tom, I'm full to the throat. I'm cousin to Norfolk and son-in-law to Burghley. All things in one. Ho, Davy—wine!"

"It's late," Tom said.

"No no, you've waited for me. We'll read in the *Comfort*. I promised." He unbuckled his dagger belt and slapped it on the table. "Give me an hour. My eyes are locked."

"My lord—Ned—"

"Sit here. I'll tell you about Anne." He strode out, pitching his cap ahead of him into the next room.

At the end of an hour, having finished half a bottle of the wine, Tom tiptoed to the door of the room.

Oxford was lying asleep, flung at an inert angle across his bed. His doublet was unfastened at the throat, the toe of one boot hung limp to the floor. His arms were spread as he had dropped, palms upward.

Tom looked down at him. The sensitiveness of Oxford's face showed clearly as he slept: the handsome forehead and high, proud eyebrows, the lean, straight cheeks and nose, the slender fineness in the line of the young lips. His hair was rumpled from the sweat of riding, as Tom remembered it from the tournament, and his chest rose and fell with a slow and relaxed breathing. Oxford's face was innocent as a boy's in sleep, unworldly, tragically capable of being hurt.

Tom sighed musingly. He did not wake him.

4 'THE EARL OF OXFORD HATH GOTTEN HIM A WIFE—OR at least a wife hath caught him.'

Letters from court carried the gossip. It spread through England that summer, along with the news that the Queen was toying with the notion of marrying a French prince, and that the

Duke of Norfolk had been imprisoned on a charge of treason. The foreign embassies wrote busily to their home governments, linking reports and juggling chains of consequences. In the slippery balance of peace between Spain to the east of the Channel and England to the west, with France uncertain and Scotland split, the wedding of a premier earl, the courtship of a queen and the sedition of a duke had interlocking significance. The struggle was shaping, the lines were being drawn. Events larger than Edward or Anne flowed around them with the pealing of the chimes in Westminster Abbey the week before Christmas, and the magnificent feast at Cecil House.

His back to the merrymaking, Lord Henry Howard lounged in a window alcove. His scholar's cheeks, sallow beneath half-drooped eyelids, were pinched to a pallid wedge by his tall collar and the quilted shoulders of his maroon velvet cloak.

"Burghley has managed again," he said.

"This marriage?"

"This mummery. It is a score for the upstarts."

"That would seem a pity. We are told it is a score for love."

"Love, Charles?" Lord Henry turned a stare on the man beside him. The man had the suave elegance of the court, a weak mouth, and never confirmed with his eyes the lip-service he gave with his tongue. "What do you call love? Puddling fingers and boy's sighs? With Burghley artful and the Queen conniving? My cousin has been springed like a woodcock. He's snared."

"That would seem a pity," Arundel said.

"He's stooped for the bait. The Cecils were commoners until Her Majesty raised them. Now they snatch Oxford from us. And Norfolk is brought to prison. The nobles' party will be weakened by these losses. The Burghley faction will ride us roughshod."

Lord Henry's lips narrowed as he looked out into the great hall, across the blaze of festivity and the shifting, swirling figures of the dancers that crowded the great stone floor in the leaping torchlight. The old nobility could not forgive Burghley or Hatton or men like Leicester for pushing themselves into high place around the Queen. It was one of their chief grievances against Her Majesty that in her court and councils she infused the old blood with too liberal doses of the new. Lord Henry belonged to the ancient families that supported the old religion and the old ways. Their names read like a roster of the Conqueror's barons five hundred years before: Percy, Howard, De Vere, Fitzalan. They stood for feudal tradition, moated and enduring as their castles, and were loath to see that the sun of feudalism had set in a cloud of cloth-yard shafts under Henry V at Agincourt.

But Lord Henry had intellect, and a mind not too troubled by scruples. He bowed to the Earl of Sussex, who was walking by.

"A happy union for our friend and cousin, my lord. I hope it may last."

"Why should it not?" Sussex asked.

"I see no reason."

"Nor I." Sussex moved on with a nod to Arundel. A weathered soldier, he was blunt and outspoken, and impervious to the intrigues of court affairs.

Lord Henry, leaving the alcove, sauntered idly. He bowed to Hatton. "You bear the occasion well, Master Hatton. I congratulate you."

He spoke to Tom Kynvet and Nan Vavasour: "The winter season is opening joyously." Kynvet shrugged, and Nan Vavasour said, sloping her eyes, "For some. It will be a joy for Anne Cecil."

He spoke to Fulke Greville and Cissy Knollys, to Tom Bedingfield and Kate Carey, a word here, a phrase there, slipping into the group about the Queen, and came to Oxford and Anne. He bent over Anne's hand, and drew Oxford aside.

"This is a rare night, Ned. And a rarer prize."

"Better than diamonds," Oxford said. He laughed jauntily. His cheeks were flushed, his eyes gay. His wedding cloak and doublet of white velvet were matchless, embroidered with brocades of gold and set off by sparkling topazes. He seemed to focus in himself all the inexhaustible zest of youth, all its pride and glory.

"And more fragile," Lord Henry said, giving his cousin a silky smile. He lowered his voice. "You've not forgot Norfolk?"

"No. I'll send you word."

Lord Henry smiled again, and went forward to present himself to Her Majesty before he danced.

He was now at the heart of the brilliance and splendor that radiated through the great hall toward the Queen. In the spinning galaxy of her court she was the fixed center. Her nobles and courtiers were satellites who revolved around her. Beyond them was the firmament of England, and beyond England the outer darkness, where the shapes of foreign nations swung continually, sometimes close, sometimes far, but circling always in a dim and menacing limbo.

She sat among the revelry like an empress.

Her high, reddish cheeks were vividly rouged. Her eyes were bright, her laugh quick and spontaneous. Her russet-flaming hair was crowned with a diadem. Her skirts were sumptuous. Her jewels were exquisite. Her dress was cut low in the fair hollow between her breasts. Her slender, rather tall neck was collared by an immense ruff, the Tudor rose embroidered at its points, its pleats held stiff by silver poking sticks and by the starch newly brought from Holland by Mistress Dingham, called devil's liquor by the Puritans.

She flirted with the French ambassador, and waved a glittering hand at Spain's emissary. Leicester knelt at her feet, dark and saturnine, clothed with a fortune on his back, and threw sweetmeats to her dog Perrico. She was Elizabeth. She was Gloriana. The Virgin Queen, goddess of the moon, sung by poets and sued for by princes, a radiant Artemis bowered in the silvery dresses of her maids of honor, her stars.

English to her marrow, born with the Tudor flair for popularity, Elizabeth doted on such revels. After the bloody Wars of the Roses, after the bulldog rule of her father Henry, and her sister Mary's glum Spanish consort Philip, she reigned by relaxation. She loved England, and knew what it needed. She had tasted fear herself, she had been a prisoner; Tom Bedingfield's father was her jailer. Her mother had died on the block—Nan Boleyn the strumpet, the whore of Babylon. She could remember horrors from her girlhood, the dissolution of the abbeys and the hapless, persecuted priests, the fire and stake, the massed slaughters and the heads that rotted on London Bridge, and bodies swaying by the hundreds in iron chains. She had found England a scarred and blasted trunk, and it was her will and passion to make it bloom again. The splendid, joyous, carefree pleasures she lavished on the court and demanded from her nobles were suited perfectly to her temper and the course of her statecraft. Her pageants, her progresses, her tournaments and water carnivals and huge processions, gave assurance that the grisly years were done, and drew her subjects near to her, and her to them.

Pageantry lent a magic to the throne, and took minds from plots and schisms. She had already been seriously threatened—the Rebellion in the North had tried to depose her for Mary Queen of Scots. The rebellion had been nipped by Burghley's readiness and Sussex' generalship. The rebel earls had fled to the Low Countries. But the plot persisted around the Duke of Norfolk, who was letting himself be used as a tool for Spain and thinking of marriage with Mary.

It was a dangerous time to rule.

Elizabeth could watch the evidences of it about her. Behind the shimmering silks in shades of pease-porridge tawny and lusty gallant and lady's blush she could see the French ambassador, present for Catherine de' Medici. Catherine was cruel, ageing, a queen-mother whose schemings were bleeding France and setting her sons at each other's throats; she wanted alliance with England, or hostility. There was the ambassador from Spain, arrogant among the flashing buckles and gossamer scarves; from Spain's Philip, who had been married to Elizabeth's half sister and had once helped rule England. He wanted England again. He would have it by subversion or conquer it by force. Only the narrow seas lay between his Netherlands garrisons and London. And scattered through the dancers, English and foreign both, Elizabeth recognized the secret friends of Mary of Scotland, the passionate, vain, mercurial woman who as princess of France had quartered her arms with those of England and sent heralds ahead of her to cry, *"Place pour la reine d'Angleterre."* Mary still claimed herself, by royal descent, the lawful queen of England. A trail of deaths, assassinations, and wild battles had followed her across the Scots border to sanctuary on English soil; to half Scotland and to half the world she was a romantic martyr; to half a murderess.

Two women and a man. In Philip, Elizabeth had an adversary. In Catherine and Mary, the warning of what it was to be a queen.

Her nails scratched playfully under Leicester's ear. She could have had him for a husband, his wife Amy was dead—it was said by accident. But the country would have taken it badly. Leicester sulked, bankrupted himself on her entertainments, served as master of her horse and borrowed her money. She could have had Philip. Even now, approaching the age of thirty-eight, she was fending him off with the pretense of acceptance, though the pretense was wearing thin. She could marry one of Catherine's dissolute sons. Catherine was eager for it. They were all eager for something. Her eyes swept over the assembly, taking in everything and revealing nothing.

She tapped Leicester with her fan. She was extravagantly fond of him. "Go dance. Fénelon will tell Catherine you monopolize me. Who's here? Lord Henry, our scholar. My lord, if your brother Norfolk had half your wit and a quarter your dourness, Mary would never have him, and he'd be safe at home." She laughed, and beckoned the French ambassador. "*Vous nous voyez bien contents ce soir, Monsieur.*"

"*Ce qui contente Votre Majesté devient infiniment le plus aimable du monde—surtout à la question de mariage,*" Fénelon replied. She gave him the tip of her hand to kiss, and flirted with the Spanish ambassador over his back.

She was indeed pleased. This marriage was a good one. She did not always approve when a maid of honor gave up her maidenhood. It reflected on her own virginity and lack of children. She had handled poor little Mary Scudamore so roughly after her wedding that she had broken the terrified bride's finger—a fit of temper now forgiven, and Mary Scudamore was her worshipper. But this marriage had valid reasons. It lifted the Cecils socially. It increased their prestige, and Burghley's weight in her councils, to be linked to the De Vere line. And it would tie the dazzling and restless Edward of Oxford nearer to her side.

She was extravagantly fond of him, too. Her own restlessness was stirred by his energies and his physical attractions. He was an ornament to her court. But he was less manageable than Leicester—fine-drawn and fiercely independent. A wife like Anne was the best answer for him. He would never make a *cavaliere servente*.

Perrico jumped to her lap. She gave the dog to Mistress Blanche, her chief gentlewoman, and rose. The dancing stopped. The assembly knelt. She walked between bowed heads to Oxford and Anne.

"Take her to bed," she said. "It's a rude guest who drags out the wedding night. There are things that do not want waiting. God keep you both." Her majesty and bearing were inscrutable, but her tone was curiously soft. "Use her gently, my boar. She is young to be a countess."

They woke long after midnight. They lay close in the dark, throbbing intimately back to consciousness, dry-mouthed and with a kind of wild surprise.

"Edward—"

"Anne. Oh, my sweet."

"My dearest lord. My dearest, dearest dear."

Her head was cradled in the angle of his elbow, his lips were pressed to her hair. One of his knees curved across her body as it had sought for her in his sleep. The bed inside its heavy curtains was warm and tumbled, folding them in secrecy and hushed with their waking.

Their whispers twined like young tendrils, curling and caressing among the pillows. She moved against him, her voice smothered in the hollow of his armpit.

"Do I please you?"

"Oh God!"

He kissed her until she writhed for breath. His voice was hard and thick. "Never before—never since—not in all the world—" he said.

She shivered ecstatically.

He sat up, reaching through the curtains for the wine that stood on a table at the bedside. He poured the wine for her, and held her leaning to him while she drank. She drank in little sips, like a kitten, spilling drops from the goblet across his wrist. They could barely see one another, only the pale flesh of their skins and the rounding of the coverlet across their updrawn legs.

They lay back.

"The night's nearly done," she said.

"Not yet."

They nestled deeper. He pulled the curtains closed, shutting them away from sight or sound. He leaned on an elbow, his face above hers. She heard the swift intake of his breath, and his mouth drove against her lips.

The wine goblet, forgotten, toppled from the coverlet and rolled to the floor, clinking among the rushes that covered the stones.

Wrapped in his cloak and shrouded by December fog, Oxford walked stealthily through the maze of twisting alleys off Cheapside. He had none of the look of a three days' bridegroom. His step was

terse and strained, and the blurring shadows of the mist bit coldly
into his features. He was followed at several paces by a serving man,
wrapped in a cloak like himself and with a sword banging at his calves.

"Is she here?"

"By the next turning, my lord."

"And she will not—?"

"By no means, my lord."

"God's blessing!"

A figure loomed from the mist, a raw-boned woman, her deep eye
sockets rimmed with pink, and her head and blunt, sunken chest
huddled in a shawl.

"Kate Beggs, my lord, the prisoner's wife."

Oxford seized her by the wrist. "Do you know why I've come?"

"Aye, my lord."

"Speak low, stand by the wall. Would you have the Duke of Norfolk
die?"

"No, my lord, nor my husband neither." Her voice was a sullen
whine.

"He'll not die. He'll go free, and the Duke too. Have you been told?"

"Your lordship will bear me out that at the time his Grace the Duke
was removed out of the Tower to the Charterhouse, my husband being
a prisoner in the Fleet, your lordship came at my husband with these
dealings. Which I knew naught of till yesternight."

"There'll be a ship. She's ready to sail. Ralph Lane's paid you ten
pounds on her. You'll have five hundred for her price. Liberty for your
husband and two thousand pounds more, half here and half in Spain,
if you'll take the ship and carry the Duke away with you."

"No, my lord."

"It's as easy as winking."

"As winking at a hangman's noose. You'd bring my husband to be
drawn and quartered."

"And all of us if we fail. But we won't fail."

"It's a hare-brained doings. I'll none of it. I'm not to be cozened.
Yesternight my husband offers me nine hundred pounds for my share.
The poor poll, whispering and grimacing in his chains, and talking of
nine hundred pounds."

"Cock's bones, keep a civil tongue," the serving man said.

"I've seen hangings."

"You'll see throat slittings," the serving man said, hand on sword.

"Hangings aplenty. And I've a care for the duty I owe Her Majesty."

"There's no harm to Her Majesty," Oxford said. "Two thousand pounds to carry my cousin to Spain."

"No."

The serving man said, "Slit her throat. Tumble her in a ditch."

The woman retreated against the wall. Her eyes glittered at them.

Lights sprang up at the head of the alley. The torches of the night watch, wavering through the fog.

"Let her go," Oxford said.

He talked to Anne one night, lying beside her in bed. He asked if she knew what prison was like.

"Prison?" she said.

"Norfolk's prison," he said.

"My sweet lord, why do you think of him?" she said, pinching his ear.

"He is my cousin. I'd save him if I could."

"But Edward, you cannot."

"There are those who can. A word to your father, Anne—for my sake. Your father would listen. The Queen's party would listen to him."

"Oh, I could not. Truly I could not." She was appalled at the thought.

"So little a thing," he said. "For our love."

"I could not talk of state matters to my father."

He was silent. His hands had been on her, running and shifting over her. He drew them away.

"Besides," she said, "what is Norfolk to us?"

"Nothing," he said.

He was silent a moment more. Her breasts were palpitant, her skin tingled along his. She was naïve and eager and unashamed. He turned her to him, and his hands locked behind her.

But afterward, while he slept, Anne lay awake in the dark with a puzzled frown, wondering at the strangeness in his voice.

The Queen lay awake, too, in the winter nights. She longed for sleep, wooing it among the canopies and the gilt stars of the royal bedchamber, but it would not come. The thought of the scaffold shut it out.

She suffered for Norfolk. He had been tried and condemned. His guilt was treason, and the will of Parliament and the people called for his death. In January he was led from his judges with the broad blade of the headsman's axe faced toward him. All that was wanting was her name on the death warrant.

She understood the need, the dangers to herself and to her reign. Her ministers had warned her of the cost of showing weakness, and Burghley's agents reported that in Spain and France and Scotland her mercy would be taken as cowardice and an invitation to more plots. Norfolk had broken his oath and renewed his conspiring. But she sickened at killing him.

For what? For revenges, for murders, for children orphaned and mothers widowed; for the hacked and red-stained block, and blood from severed neck clotting the straw. Too much blood had been shed already. That was retreat, not advance. A return to the butcheries of the grandfathers, not the peaceful woman's reign she wished for her kingdom. There must be some other way to do it, to bind people into a single whole, knit hearts and minds and wills and a nation's loyalty. Some other way than by political executions and the lopping of heads.

Five terrible months she groped for the way. She tortured her conscience and harassed her council, for she had never before put anyone to death. She prayed for wisdom to find the secret, the mystery which she sensed but could not grasp, which would free her and England from the law of cave and jungle; an instrument of policy that would wield intellect instead of force. Twice, three times, four times, she signed the warrant and then revoked her signature. She pulled Burghley from his bed to fetch him galloping to the palace at three in the morning, and walked distracted in her room, shuddering with cold: "I cannot put him to death—God's Christ, I cannot!"

But in the end she surrendered. The secret was still locked from her. The old policies stood, and Norfolk died in June.

When the booming of cannon announced his death to the court, Oxford put his face in his hands and wept.

"Our new son-in-law is waking," Lord Henry Howard said, grinding down his own grief. "He will find he is in a bitter cage."

5 | Norfolk's death put a gloom over the court, and for diversion the Queen ordered a summer progress through the shires. Oxford and Anne took their place in the progress. It was part of the convention and their routine. There was, indeed, nothing else to do. The court was the focus of life and activity, and beyond its pale was only a void.

The Queen delighted in his dancing, and Anne thrilled in being his wife. It was all they asked of him. If he accepted the formalities, an obedient courtier and a model husband, they expected no more. He could spend the rest of his years that way if he chose.

The realization came to him slowly as the pattern hardened, and with it, even slower, the knowledge that he did not choose. He could not, yet. He could not harness himself into shafts, it was too early. The creativeness seething in him, of which he was still scarcely aware himself, was too strong.

Living with Anne, he began to find that the gay, frolicking spirit that had drawn him to her went no farther than social amusements and her girlish pleasure in court functions. It did not follow him into higher or wider or more open reaches. The first small rift had appeared when she would not plead for Norfolk. He had seen then that she was still controlled by her family. Had he married her, or had he married the Cecils? Had he got free of Cecil House to have it close in on him again?

He tried not to admit these thoughts. He tried to channel his energies into other courses. When at Warwick the Queen gave him command of a mock fort for a sham battle staged in the castle yard, he marched his troops as briskly as though it had been a real war. The sham battle, in fact, turned out to be a violent one. Fulke Greville commanded the opposing fort. Fulke was from Warwick and eager to make a showing, and he and Oxford were both young and foolhardy. Cannon and powder had been brought from the Tower in London; the troops were armed with guns and rounds of explosives. The forts shot squibs and fire-balls that blazed over the castle battlements and fell into the Avon, sputtered on the water, and rose again and whirled over the town. Oxford and Fulke led charges and countercharges, sparks from the powder hissing off their armor, and their men shouting and yelling through clouds of smoke. A dragon, all aflame, was set loose on the forts, and nine houses caught fire in the town. In one of the houses, by the bridge, an old farmer was asleep with his wife and, as the cry went up that they would be roasted alive, Oxford raced for the bridge, Fulke at his heels, and together, groping and sweating and coughing under the flaming thatch, they pulled the couple to safety. Oxford went back to Anne smoke-blackened, grimy, his face singed and his hair matted with soot, and she flung herself at him in a transport of joy.

"Oh Edward, what a wondrous thing. Have you taken hurt? Marry, I was sore afraid."

The excitement was a release for him, and Anne as entranced as if he had taken a city. They made up a collection to pay for the farmer's house, and finished the night in dances. Moved by the sport, by the exhilaration and sense of well-being that throbbed in his blood, Oxford recited them that night a poem he had written—standing with Anne and Fulke Greville, Tom Bedingfield and Kate Carey and Philip Sidney while they chattered in the torchlight on the castle lawn between the dances. The light struck at his quick face and sensitive lips as he recited.

> Were I a King, I might command content,
>> Were I obscure, unknown should be my cares,
> And were I dead, no thoughts should me torment,
>> Nor words, nor wrongs, nor love, nor hate, nor fears.
> A doubtful choice of these three which to crave,
> A kingdom, or a cottage, or a grave.

"An epigram," he said. "Can you solve the problem?"

Anne said the poem was very pretty, but too sad. "Why must all poems be sad?" she said. "They spoil the fun. Oh, the music's started again. Hurry, Edward, don't let's miss any."

A few days later Philip Sidney said he had the answer. He read it one afternoon as the Queen's procession was halted on a village common, brushing away flies and sampling the local small beer.

Wert thou a King, yet not command content,
　Sith empire none thy mind could yet suffice,
Wert thou obscure, still cares would thee torment,
　But wert thou dead all care and sorrow dies.
An easy choice of these three which to crave,
No kingdom, nor a cottage, but a grave.

When Sidney read his answer Anne burst into laughter. She said Edward had his deserts there. She considered it a marvelous clever joke.

The Queen declared that Oxford was not only a wit himself, but the cause of wit in others, and that she would never spare him from the court. She kept him at her beck and call all summer and through the winter. She had a gift of repartee that equaled his, and she traded quips with him at the courtiers' expense, and fondled him for his gallantry and his love of music, and tweaked his brown curls until Lady Burghley protested to friends that Her Majesty was taking liberties beyond the bounds of proper behavior with a young married man. The protest got to the ears of the Queen, who snapped at Lady Burghley, "My lord your husband winks at these love matters," and went on doting.

"If it weren't for your fickle head you could pass them all," Fulke Greville told him. "Even my lord of Leicester is on tenterhooks."

Oxford thought of Leicester, sleeping in the chamber next the Queen's and not able to make a move without her sanction. "I'll not put my head in that noose," he said.

He did not wish to be fickle. He had hoped his marriage would prove to Lord Burghley and the Queen and himself that he was no more wild or foolish or extravagant than other men—that it would win him leave to travel for a year and return to be happy with Anne and merit appointments and honors at Her Majesty's hands. He asked that winter for a license to travel, but neither Lord Burghley nor the Queen approved.

Behind it all he was conscious of his cousin Lord Howard's cold dislike of his marrying into the Cecils, whom Lord Howard looked on as raw and new opportunists, and of his cousin's pitying smile.

He did not wish to be fickle, but his nature was not the sort to let him trip his heels patiently in palace rooms and sit politely at long, dull supper tables in the great houses. His vigorous, healthy physique demanded action, his mind demanded to be put to work on problems to be grappled with or projects to be planned; and Lord Burghley's disapproval of his extravagances, and the ugly, unfounded charge of bastardry ate like a canker into his pride.

He was driven by the passion for Anne and the conflict within himself. It was not enough to spend evening after evening at the court, talking with the Earl of Sussex on military campaigns he would never see, or listening to Dame Parry tell fortunes by the fireplace. He needed something more.

In his need he turned to books and writing. They had tempted him from his childhood. His uncle and first teacher had translated Ovid into English, the best minds in the kingdom had guided his tastes in the classics and in modern literature. Poems, plays, histories, chronicles, especially fascinated him. For his first venture he paid for publishing Tom Bedingfield's version of Cardanus, putting his own preface to it in apology. Tom was reluctant, but Oxford overruled him—"an unpardonable error to have murdered the book in the waste bottom of my chests," he wrote, and followed that preface with another, a Latin preface to a Latin version of Castiglione's *Il Cortegiano,* done by one of his old tutors.

The two prefaces startled him by their results and by the pleasure he got from them. The London world of letters saw a patron in him, and authors began knocking at his door. Here was the relief he had looked for, the chance to whet his imagination and put it to work. He read what the authors brought him, hired rooms for some of them at the old hospital of the Savoy on the Strand, met them at nights there, or in the taverns. Their conversations were different from the court gossip, full of imagery, ideas, exuberance, plangent variety.

Robert Cecil had said he must have an outlet for his hot blood, and Lord Henry Howard had said he was caged. To Oxford, these men were a new and fascinating fellowship. They were scribblers, rhymers, makers of plays and pamphlets. They were the men who were catching the melodies of the Renaissance echoing from Italy, and singing them again in English words. They brawled, they fought, they wrote, they broke heads, they pumped quicksilver into the stream of the times. They could do their whoring, stab their rivals, or write their sonnets with the same gusto. In them English literature was beginning to live.

Oxford plunged in among them. They drank with him, envied his metaphors and rapier phrases, dedicated their books to him. Because he was a nobleman and paid for the printing of the books, they were respectful and flattering in their dedications. But in the taverns he was one of them, a companion, an adventurer in their craft. They welcomed him for himself, and protected the dignity of his title. In the taverns he was not my lord of Oxford. They called him Gentle Master Will.

"But Edward," Anne said, pouting, "Wyvenhoe's so far from London."

"The farther the better," he said.

"It's no farther than Castle Hedingham. Why can't we go there?"

"The castle has too many memories," he said. "I've bought a new home for us at Wyvenhoe."

"With the money for the new home we could have fixed the castle splendidly. We could have entertained Her Majesty."

"My father is buried at Hedingham. Let the past stay buried. There's time enough to talk of the castle when we have a son."

Anne patted her hair in place, glancing into the mirror above her table. "Of course we'll have a son. But I don't want to leave London at all."

They were dressing for a dinner at Cecil House—Lord Burghley was inviting a dozen lords and ladies—and afterward there would be cards and dancing at the court. Oxford had come into Anne's room as Meg was finishing with the hairbrush, and he went over and kissed the curve of Anne's neck.

"But I do," he said. "I've a new idea, Anne. A book of poems."

Anne spun around on her stool with a giggle. "A book of poems? Edward, people will think you mad."

"Oh, I won't sign them," he said. "You needn't worry."

She caught the irritation in his voice. "Edward, darling, I don't care what you do. I want you to be happy. But poems! Oh Edward, you're fine and gallant and foolish and plaguing and fantastical." She jumped up from the stool, and hugged him impulsively, snuggling as he kissed her again. "Can't you write poems in London just as well?"

"Have you ever tried writing poems?" he said, laughing. "They don't write themselves at dinners."

"The dinners aren't my fault," she said. "Besides, you waste most of your time on those lewd scribblers at the Savoy. You're out with them half the nights. You could give them up if you wanted to write. And my mother says you swagger through London with far too large a number of servants at your heels."

"The servants are mine," he said stiffly. "Not your mother's."

"But she sees them. Everybody does. If you really want quiet to write—"

"I'll get it at Wyvenhoe," he said.

"You will not," she said, backing away from him, stamping her foot. "You will not, you will not, you will not!"

He reached for her and drew her to him. "Anne," he said, not knowing whether to be angry or to laugh more at her tempestuousness. "Are you my wife?"

"If I am, I should think you would care for me," she said. "Edward, how can you take me away from London—the court, the excitement, the fun, all the things you know I like—for a noddy craving to write poems?"

"They won't all be mine. Some will be George Gascoigne's; he's at the wars in the Low Countries, but that's no matter. Hatton wants to come in, too. Hatton's for anything that will get him notice. He's been fretting at me to take up his poetry since Her Majesty's been smiling at Philip Sidney. It will be a collection, Anne. There's never been a collection of English poems."

"Then why have one now? Marry, who'd read them? I shouldn't."

"No," he said, letting go of her roughly. "No, you wouldn't." He stopped, perplexed and hurt at the tones of their voices, and that they should be quarreling like this. The rift had suddenly widened, like a crack in a bent bow, showing the grains pulled and at cross purposes beneath. Their love was the bow, and if it failed the arrows they fitted to it would lose their singing force. He spoke in a gentler way. "I don't ask you to," he said.

"You ask me to—to exile myself leagues away by the Channel, as if I were a seaweed at the edge of a damp tide," she said. "Then the Spaniards will come, and I'll be the first person to fall into their hands. Well, it will serve you justly."

This was so exaggerated that they both laughed. No one expected the Spaniards to come over the Channel. Their troop ships skirted close to the Flemish coast. The only danger on the Channel waters was from Dutch pirates.

"You're a sweet peevish chit," he said.

"Fie, calling me names before Meg!" She flounced her skirts, pretending to sulk, but the laugh had dissolved her temper. "Oh Edward, the true cause is that you still want to travel. You want to leave me."

"Not to leave you," he said. "To come home stuffed with what's new and worthy in foreign lands."

"In heaven's name, Wyvenhoe's foreign enough," she answered him. "Well, I'll go with you if I needs must. But I'll pray every day for London," and she whisked out of the room. He chuckled at her gamesomeness as he rode with her to Cecil House. Her spirits were a match to his own; he had married her because of her spirits, and when her eyes flashed they roused a swift response in him. But he was learning, in the intimacies of marriage, that Anne's rufflings were light and brittle, like ripples on a shallow brook, and that when the wind of her emotions had passed the surface was all docile. Anne would never be troubled by the intensity and searchings that he felt. A brook flowing over halcyon pebbles had no knowledge of deeper seas. It was beginning to be clear to him that she wanted none.

They went together to Wyvenhoe, where he settled in his new home and worked on his collection of poems. Some were by other poets, some his own, some Hatton's. He added an extra one for sport, an anonymous one that caricatured Hatton to the letter. The court caught the allusions in it, and roared. The collection came out under the title of *The Hundred Sundry Flowers,* and was a nine-days' wonder. This was the first time in England that such a volume of verse by living poets had been put between book covers.

In the court of Elizabeth even a volume of poems was tangled in personalities and politics. Many of the pieces were never meant to be printed. One of the authors was in Antwerp at the time, arranging the publication of a political satire against Lord Burghley written secretly by Lord Henry Howard. Hatton was on the Continent, so was Gascoigne. The book was certain to infuriate them; the unwritten law for courtier poets was that no work of theirs should be printed while they were alive. But Oxford was impatient, and his impatience flew in the face of custom. He veiled the authorship of his own pieces and

Hatton's, used only Gascoigne's name, and blamed the publication on a printer. But the device fooled no one very long, and his *Sundry Flowers* stirred a hornet's nest of praise and envy and hatred around his ears.

Added to that, three of his servants set on a pair of their fellows one day at Gad's Hill, on the highway toward Gravesend, and tried to rob them. The Queen's peace was broken, and Her Majesty called Oxford to answer for it. Lady Burghley, outraged for her family, for Lord Burghley was a high dignitary now—he had been made lord treasurer—pounced on Oxford like a hawk for the kill.

"Would to God you were dead," she cried, "or that I had been spared you for a son-in-law. Your wild ways have infected all your followers."

Oxford, who had hoped his book would win him some honor, perhaps the poet laureateship, which was vacant, answered that his servants were his own, and swung off in another direction.

Calling in Ralph Lane, who had been with him in the scheme to rescue Norfolk, he worked out a venture that would give him more action. They would form a company to buy ships and bolster the navy of Portugal, a country whose coasts lay along the sea route between Spain and the English Channel, and whose independence was being bullied by Spanish power. He tried to get the plan before the Privy Council, but nothing came of it.

Nothing came of any of his ventures.

Every way he turned seemed blocked. In the year after the Gad's Hill robbery, finally desperate at the shackles of idleness in the court, he broke away and took ship for the Low Countries, where English volunteers were fighting with the Dutch against Spain's tyranny under captains like Roger Williams. The Queen in a paroxysm of anger sent Tom Bedingfield to fetch him back. Tom, meeting him at Brussels, warned him his enemies at court were saying he had gone to join the rebel Earl of Westmoreland against the Queen, and in two weeks he and Tom were home again.

Anne did not ask him why he had gone. She gave him her smiles, her kisses, the passionate little mounds of her breasts, and their life went on as before. They rode with the court on a progress through the West

Country and visited the Cecil country estate of Theobalds for a long autumn of hawking and hunting.

But once, when they had returned to London, she referred to it casually with a small pout of curiosity. "Were the girls pretty in Brussels, Edward?"

"I didn't mark," he said.

"But you must have seen them. Were they?"

"None as pretty as you."

She rewarded him with a look. "Perhaps you were busier about the fighting."

"I was. The Spanish captains let me watch the siege of Bommel. I rode out through their lines. It was a sight to pale our tournaments. 'Fore God, I'd have liked to stay."

"Without me?"

He sat on a cushion and took her on his lap. They had finished supper alone, as the court was out at Hampton for the autumn, and the servants had left off clearing the table. "My honey Anne, what would you do in a war?" he said.

"Oh, I meant you ought not go to a war at all. You're much happier here. But I'm glad you saw it."

She hesitated, lifting her mouth. He brushed it with his lips.

"Did you see the Earl of Westmoreland at Brussels?" she asked.

"No. Why should you think of that?"

"I was worried that you might. They all said so at court. But we trusted you, Edward."

"We?" he said. "Who is we?"

"Why—" she said, "why—all of us." She pushed herself upright on his knees, and catching the sudden glance from his eyes began to talk with a nervous rapidity. "Even that little Trentham child was worried. They brought her to court, you know, to be presented to Her Majesty as a possible maid of honor, and she asked me what had made you go. I'm sure you'll be glad to know she was thinking of you. But everyone was."

"Your father most of any," he said.

"Oh, Edward!" she said, and stared at him, and broke down and covered her face with her hands.

He got up and set her on the cushion gently, sick that he had read her so easily.

"He's put you to spy on me," he said. "He'd sleep sounder if he knew whether his son-in-law had talked with the leader of the rebellion for Queen Mary of Scots."

"It isn't spying, Edward," she pleaded.

"He set you to find out," he said.

"Not for any harm to you."

"Because I've done none, by good fortune. I kept Westmoreland's messenger dangling for a week in Brussels. But what if I'd talked with him? You'd have kissed that out of me and tattled it. God's blessing, to make wifehood his damned agent!"

He strode to the door, looked into the passage beyond, closed the door quickly with the toe of his boot, and came back to her again.

"Have I married you, Anne, or have I married all the Cecils?" he said.

"But he's my father, Edward."

"Have I married you or him?"

She raised her face. Her cheeks were tear-stained. She saw that she had wounded him deeply, but her family's dominance was stronger than her love for him. She was blinded by it, and unable to realize, except dimly, helplessly, that any greater issue was involved.

"But he's my father," she said.

"Anne—" he said, and searched for words, but bit them off before they were uttered. He tried to remember that she was barely eighteen.

In the meantime there was the Queen to be appeased. She had received him coolly on her progress, looking through him as he knelt and apologized for going abroad without her leave.

"Perchance your journey will make you more content with our company hereafter," she observed.

She was gratified by his return, but not yet ready to accept him into her good graces, and he cast about for some means of restoring himself to favor.

He found it in the experiences of the past three years, in the latent forces the *Sundry Flowers* and the evenings at the rooms in the Savoy had set in motion. All that autumn, while he was at Theobalds, he had written constantly, and in the winter season of the court he presented what he had done. It was a play, his first effort, telling the story of the famous victories of Her Majesty's ancestor, Henry V. He knew it would entertain her and he hoped it would flatter her. He wrote more into it than bald history. He wrote his own repentance and his promise of good behavior in the future; the parallel between the wild Prince Hal and the wild Lord Oxford was obvious for anyone as astute as Her Majesty, and he pointed it plainer by having the Prince's men commit a robbery at Gad's Hill. The Prince's reformation and the victories he won capped the whole moral. Her Majesty, trained in reading allegories and scenting allusions, could not fail to see it.

She did not. She was wholly entranced. She sat through the entire performance, and turned afterward to Leicester and Hatton, who stood beside her.

"What think ye? Is this not a fair, brave piece? Od's my life, we've never had a better."

Leicester agreed, somewhat sourly, that it was well conceived. He did not like rivals.

Hatton said, bumptiously, "If the author did not call himself Master Will, to hide his shame, I would think my lord of Oxford was boasting of his men's robbery. Gad's Hill was his fame."

He looked at Oxford as he spoke, frowning. He would never forgive Oxford for the caricature in the *Sundry Flowers*.

"Oxford's name does not appear," the Queen said airily, charmed by the device that let her hide one meaning while she used the other. "The boar's tusks are covered."

"Do not trust a boar whose tusks may raze and tear," Hatton simpered. "Reserve it to the sheep, who has no teeth to bite."

Her nickname for him was Sheep, and she laughed, reaching from her chair, and patted one of his graceful legs and told him he was her beloved mutton and she would never desert him.

But a week later Hatton wondered about that, for in January Her Majesty signed Oxford's license for foreign travel.

Her Majesty was not aware of a letter Anne had sent earlier that autumn to the Earl of Sussex, who was acting as lord chamberlain and had the assigning of the palace rooms:

'My good Lord'—her letter ran—'Because I think it long since I saw

Her Majesty, and would be glad to do my duty after Her Majesty's coming to Hampton Court, I heartily beseech your good Lordship to show me your favor in your order to the ushers for my lodging; that in consideration there is but two chambers, it would please you to increase it with a third. . . . I shall think myself greatly bound to you, for the more commodious my lodging is, the willinger I hope my lord my husband will be to come thither . . .'

Anne was using the only stratagem she knew. Court life would be more attractive with three rooms. Edward would feel less cramped.

⌗⌗ **6** ‖ By nature lord burghley was methodical. By habit he was painstaking. Among the gaudy, full-blown world that surrounded Elizabeth these traits set him apart from other men and lent him the attributes of greatness. A man who will take pains can become great, if only for the fact of taking them. Beyond most of his time, Lord Burghley deserved the adjective. Yet he was passing a very uncomfortable morning.

He sat at his desk in Cecil House, stroking his beard over a paper that lay in front of him. More papers lay piled at either side. They were state documents, reports, secret intelligences that brushed at his fur-trimmed sleeves and waited his attention. There was the question of the Duc d'Alençon's pock marks. Her Majesty Elizabeth had raised objections to Alençon's proposal of marriage, saying she could never marry a face pitted by smallpox. Catherine was answering from France that a doctor had been discovered who could erase pock marks; the treatment had been administered to a court page, who had obstinately died from it; but Her Majesty could rest assured the means would be found. There was the question of the wool trade, hurt by the seizures and freebootings up and down the Channel; would Elizabeth arm her merchantmen and let them fight? Letters from the Prince of Orange pleaded for intervention.

He let them wait while he studied the notations on the paper before him. He had set down a list of dates in scrupulous sequence:

Anno XVI Eliz. (1574) 29th July. Lord Burghley went to London with his daughter, The Countess of Oxford.

3rd Aug. Earl of Oxford at the hunting of the stag.
1574. 16 Sept. Earl of Oxford at Theobalds from the Progress.
20 Sept. Monday Lady Margaret Lennox, Earl of Oxford, Lady Lennox, Lady Hunsdon.
21 Sept. Lady Lennox, Lord Northumberland, and my Lady.
October at Hampton Court. The Countess fell sick at Hampton Court. (Afore November)
7th Jan. The Earl departed overseas.

He checked the dates with his pen. Social engagements, dinners, the activities of the Earl and Countess of Oxford. Lord Burghley liked to think of his daughter as the countess, the title pleased him.

Lady Lennox was another question. She had rights as a joint heiress to the kingdoms of England and Scotland. The young King James was her grandson. Her husband had been slaughtered in the royal Scottish intrigues. Her eldest son, Lord Darnley, had been married to Mary of Scots; a blast of gunpowder in a house outside Edinburgh had mangled him, and he had died pitifully. Lady Lennox's sufferings, and her accusations against Mary, complicated English diplomacy. Born of Margaret Tudor, sister of Henry VIII, her blood combined the White Rose and the Red of the civil wars and involved her grandson in the succession if Queen Elizabeth should die. Beautiful, highly esteemed, she drew vivid tales of the horrors of murders done for ambition in the Scottish palaces.

Lord Burghley looked from the paper to the sheafs around him, the questions pressing for sifting and judgment. There was the question of money. No parliament had been summoned in five years, and some way must be managed to refill the treasury. Her Majesty had dissolved the last Parliament indignantly; she thought they meddled too much in church reform, hindering her in her wish to steer a moderate course, and she had scolded the extremists of both parties and arrested the most hot-headed reformists; Parliament might not reconvene in a money mood. There was the question of the Muscovy Company; Lord Burghley had been one of the first to contribute to the venture of opening overland routes to the Russian market, but Muscovites were not honoring their agreements and it seemed the shareholders would be finally certain to lose their investments. There was the question of Spain's absorbing Portugal, and doubling at one swoop her empire, her navy, and her merchant fleet; Lord Burghley's secret intelligence showed that probable.

But he had no heart for these this morning. He spread them away with his elbows and leaned over his list of dates. Being methodical, he distrusted mental logic. He could reason more exactly with his evidence visible on paper in black and white. He continued his checking:

6th March. The Earl presented to the French King.
17th March. The Earl departed from Paris and wrote to his wife and sent her his picture and two horses.
26th April. The Earl of Oxford departed from Strasbourg.
2nd July. The Countess delivered of a daughter.
24th Sept. The letter of the Earl by which he gives thanks for his wife's delivery. Mark well this letter.
3rd Jan. The Earl wrote to me.

Lord Burghley laid down his pen. He shook his head and frowned, unsatisfied, the frown of a man groping through an enigma. He knew his figures were exact. November. July. The months tallied. His son-in-law and the countess had been together at Hampton Court in October.

He scratched his chin and went back to a note, written at the top of the sheet:

Oxford confessed to my Lord Howard that he lay not with his wife but at Hampton Court, and that then the child could not be his, because the child was born in July. . . .

That was wrong. He counted the months again, ticking them off with perplexed thumb against his fingers. They certainly tallied. There had been ample time. As a matter of fact, the Countess's own physician had not discovered she had quickened until March. That could still give time, even if the earl had left in January. But he had the earl's denial in direct confidence from Lord Howard. What should he think?

The perplexity baffled him. It had the odor of ripening scandal. Lord Burghley could smell it. He trusted his daughter implicitly; he knew the earl did, too. Yet here was this denial, categorical, vouched by Lord Howard, and the tongue of rumor was beginning to moisten court lips. The physician, Dr. Masters, had told the same story, that Oxford had sworn publicly the child was not his. Was he, Lord Burghley, to believe he had?

He, Lord Burghley did not know. The deeper he pried, the more he was confused. Yet he would not put it past his son-in-law. Oxford was hasty and ill-judged and often made sharp, resentful answers to gossiping questions. To say the child was not his would be the common retort of a lusty courtier. Oxford may have wanted to hide the news from fear of losing his permit to travel. Or he may have thought his answer so obvious and shopworn it would stop the questioner. He may not have made the answer at all.

Lord Burghley's puzzling was getting him nowhere, and he was expected at the Privy Council that morning. He gave up the puzzle with a sigh, called for horses, and set out toward the palace, the sheet of dates tucked among the papers in his pouches like an insidious, smoldering fuse.

He entered the council chamber with deliberation, being too old a hand to betray any sign of the shortness of his breath or temper. The members of Her Majesty's Privy Council were sharp-minded, picked astutely by the Queen for the highest honor in the kingdom. The stakes they played for were their personal lives and the fortunes of the realm, and the game was dog eat dog. The weak went to the wall.

Lord Burghley looked at them.

They were somber and inscrutable, seated about a table in impressive dignity, figures against dark-framed windows with leaden mullions and a leaden sky, grave velvets and rich heavy stuff spangled darkly with gold and jewels. The *togati* of England. Sir Nicholas Bacon, the lord chancellor, self-made like Burghley and keenly acquisitive. Sir Walter Mildmay, chancellor of the exchequer. The Queen's secretary, Walsingham, nicknamed her Moor, and a synonym for gloomy, cold efficiency. The Earl of Bedford and Sir Francis Knollys. Leicester, magnificent, overweening, his beard beaked in his ruff like a moody falcon. The Earl of Sussex, England's ablest commander in the field. Burghley took a place between Sussex and Leicester, and knelt with the others when Her Majesty came in.

The Queen wore an umber-hued gown of French pile velvet worked in a filigree of silver threads, with a high circlet collar and pendant earrings that emphasized the lean, high angles of her face, and her manner was tersely stringent.

Elizabeth's evasiveness had run almost to its end. France and Spain, Scottish brawls and the Dutch deputies were driving her toward a decision, a thing she detested unless she was ready for it. She was irritable, contrary, and conciliatory by turns, confusing her councilors with tart replies and impatient quirks of gesture that threatened to explode in rage at any moment. They were her political guides, advisers of her national policy, but Her Majesty's mind was her own.

Events were hanging ripe to fall, but it seemed impossible for her to reach and pluck them. She drummed with her knuckles on the table, and snorted while Walsingham, in a steely voice, read long testimony, from secret correspondence, of the menaces stemming from Mary of Scotland.

"Menaces! Bugbears to fright children. We are cousins, she and I. Let me see her face to face. Let me talk with her. There will be no menaces."

"Your Royal Majesty's forbearance is Christian charity," Walsingham said, "but not wise for the safety of your throne."

"We have proposed such a talk," Sir Nicholas Bacon said. "Mary has refused to sit with Your Majesty except as an equal sovereign. A sovereign without a kingdom."

"And without scruples," Sussex said, scowling over the strong bridge of his nose. "Send her packing. She breeds woe in England."

"Packing to where, my lord? To France?" Elizabeth asked.

"God forbid," Sussex said.

"My lord of Sussex makes a pother for a pin," Leicester drawled, from the other side of Burghley. "Catherine will not have her in France."

Sussex shot him a look.

"To Scotland?" Elizabeth demanded.

Burghley spoke. "My loving liege, as we well know it were shaky policy to send her to Scotland. Since the Regent's assassination, Mary's son rules by Scots law. He has a father to avenge, and clamor would force him to try his mother for murder if she sets foot there. Should that be so, there is danger of risings and civil wars, which should not be fostered on our northern border. We should renew our attempts to bring her to trial here in England, with a jury drawn from English and Scottish nobles. Let them inquire into her case, her union with Bothwell, her taking up arms, her flight from her kingdom into Your Most

Puissant Majesty's protection. Let them render judgment whether or not she is still entitled to the Scottish crown."

Heads nodded in consensus, but Elizabeth stopped them peremptorily. "Mary is a queen," she said. "So are we, by God's grace. We'll try no queens in England. Bones of Christ, my lords!" she cried, "would you have us pillory the majesty of queenhood for every cart's-tail villain to flout at? We're not such a fool."

She was touchy, her eyes cowing them, and they said no more.

"What next?" she asked.

"Spain, my liege."

It was the lord admiral. He had a complaint from the Spanish ambassador, a protest against raids on West Indies galleons.

"Mendoza is always complaining," she retorted. "Are we raiding, my Lord Admiral? I had thought the boot was on the other leg."

"Who wears the boot depends on who is walking," he said cryptically.

"Or sailing," Leicester put in.

"Come come, then, who is sailing?" Elizabeth said. "Where are we complained on?"

The council smiled with relief. Everyone knew that Elizabeth's seamen were waylaying Spaniards homeward bound from the Caribbees. So did Elizabeth. This play was a better mood.

"On the high seas," Leicester said.

"Can'st see so far, my eyes?" Elizabeth rallied him. "Our kingdom does not reach into the high seas."

"Your Sovereign Highness has heard of Francis Drake," the lord admiral said.

"A Devon man. I've heard of a dozen. Rascally fellows, I make no doubt. Devon's a tough nurse," Elizabeth said.

"The tougher to do you service," the lord admiral said.

"Tush, we have no service. We've given out no commissions for freebooting. 'Twould be winking at piracy."

The smiles broadened. The council was relishing the humor.

"Singeing the King of Spain's beard," Knollys murmured.

"What's that?" Elizabeth said.

"They call it singeing King Philip's beard," Knollys repeated.

Elizabeth broke into shrill laughter. Her peals startled the echoes in the room. She rocked in her chair and flung back her head, shaking with mirth until her earrings spun, and slapping at her leg in the old trick of her father's. She looked like her father, bluff and uproarious and gusty. "God's love, for a madcap jest! The King of Spain can use a shorter beard. I smell it curl. Knollys, ye wag, ye'll split my belly." She stopped abruptly. Her gaze glazed, and she stiffened upright. "Check him," she said. "Check this roving barber. Let him look to his singeing. Philip could make him cause for war."

The council's smiles congealed, and the lord admiral asked uncertainly, "Drake, Your Majesty?"

"I know of no Drake. I know of no ships or seamen or Atlantic weathercocks. By'r Lady's death, my lord, must we con you the name of all tarry swaggerers that spit in the wind? We have larger matters." She glared.

The lord admiral bowed his head. By established fiction Elizabeth's left hand never admitted what her right was doing. She could shift from one to the other in an instant.

"Indeed, Your Majesty. Yet I am loath to forbid enterprise."

"Did I say forbid? I forbid nothing. Enterprise is an English glory, and should be nourished." She jabbed a sharp forefinger toward him, heavily crusted with rings. "You catch me at a word, my Lord Admiral. Give our seamen rein, we'll not shackle them in harbor for any king. But keep them within bounds. Beware of singeing. Look to it, my lord."

These were the changes, the contradictions, the swift veerings and tackings of mood that made the deliberations of her council so difficult.

It was the same with the French marriage, which Lord Burghley brought up diffidently. She would make no answer, though Burghley pointed out that Catherine was urging one and could not be put off much longer, and that the Duc d'Alençon was in Flanders, swearing that he burned with love and waiting to rush to England to throw himself into Elizabeth's arms. She listened stonily, while the council chewed its lips and Leicester glowered.

"Never ask me to bow knee to a Frenchman," Leicester declaimed. "England should have an English king."

"A king of factions," Sussex said, "to slice the country like a cankered apple. Some paltry earl, decked out in his party's trappings."

"What earl? What earl?" said Leicester, reddening and putting his fist on his dagger hilt.

"An earl by appointment," Sussex retorted, unmoved. "An earl of debts, acting the dog in the manger."

The jibe went home, for Leicester's earldom was new, created for him by Elizabeth; and all the court knew his jealousy. If he could not marry the Queen, no one else should. He half rose from his seat, choking back an oath.

"None calls me dog," he shouted in Sussex's face. "The dogs are those who would vassal us to France."

"Or deliver us to Spain. God's wounds, ye'd leave England alone and uncovered out of petty spite." Sussex was on his feet, too. His long nose and square, strong jaws were stubborn. "For our safety we must have an alliance."

"For your own safety," Leicester snarled.

"I'd not stir for yours," Sussex said.

Burghley interposed. "My lords, my lords, we must reason calmly. We must weigh and balance. For my part, I incline to the French marriage, it has the more advantages."

"Incline where you will," Leicester said. "And your pawn of Sussex with you. Cringe on a Frenchman. You were made for that."

"Now by God—!" said Sussex, lunging. He broke past Burghley, and flung himself on Leicester. Leicester met him, and the two earls grappled and swung blows. Burghley pushed between them, the table was in an uproar, and over the brawl and scuffle the voice of Elizabeth rang dominantly.

"Peace! Peace, on your allegiance! God's body! Are we a bauble, to be pawed for by a brace of schoolboys?" Her eyes blazed. "Mend your respect! We'll marry where and when we please! Leave be your caterwauling! Get you gone!"

She dismissed the council in a towering passion and with a hiss of brocades strode out of the room.

Greatly troubled, Lord Burghley waited on her within the hour. He felt guilty for sponsoring the French marriage. The Earl of Leicester was bitter against it, and Leicester spoke for many in the kingdom, yet there was sound policy in joining with France. There was tradition in a French union, provided the people would accept the match. The people, and the proud, incalculable woman who ruled over them. Lord Burghley felt the gloom of Her Majesty's displeasure on him, and with the gloom some exquisite twinges of the gout that was beginning to pain him more and more often when matters in the council went awry.

Barricaded in his cloak, he paced solemnly in the antechamber among the courtiers. A young man bowed to him, John Lyly, a London hopeful recently from the university, with what Lord Burghley considered a fiddle-faddle air. He had asked for employment at Cecil House, and been refused. Burghley shunted him with a nod. Strolling near by were Hatton and George Gascoigne, the poet. He was Sir Christopher Hatton now, captain of the Queen's bodyguard; Gascoigne had come back from the Low Countries and into favor by his story of the princely pleasures at Her Majesty's great visit to Kenilworth. They talked in low tones, their heads together:

"A new book, revised and new named. The malicious poem of *Fortunatus Infelix* changed—'twas a shrewd game to lay it to a riding tale of Bartello—Oxford's posies omitted, the whole presented as yours alone."

"The boar will rage. He will swear his *Hundred Sundry Flowers* is stolen."

"I care not. He printed my poems when I was abroad."

"Your garland of poetry is all Gascoigne. Your name to the stanzas, your likeness on the frontispiece. And the Queen has received a picture of yourself crowned with bays, like a laureate."

" 'Twill cut the earl to the quick."

Lord Burghley heeded them only vaguely.

Elizabeth's mood had changed again when he was admitted to her chambers. She sat amid her ladies-in-waiting, an enigmatic, queenly figure, her ringed and tapering fingers spread like pale ivory on the umber velvet of her lap. Her face was composed, dispassionate, curiously softened and reflective after the storm that had swept it. Its lines seemed indefinably blurred from their angular precision, and the sloping grayness that fell upon her from the window at her back revealed, under the lotions and the pomade, the creeping sag of age and the shallow, unobliterated hollows left by the smallpox. Lord Burghley approached her and went on his knee. He was in dread of a scene, for Elizabeth's calms could be preludes to terrible tempests. But she listened to his

» 64 «

reasons for the French match, to his apology for pitting himself against the Earl of Leicester, and to his wish to yield up his office if he had in any way offended; and as he finished she gave him a smile of wise and worldly perception.

"Don't be so silly a soul as not to regard her trust, who puts it in you."

Her voice was pitched gently, with knowledge and weariness. She leaned to him, stretching him her hand.

"God bless you, and long may you last. I am yours in all things."

Lord Burghley bent his shoulders. He could not speak. He took her hand and kissed it with a trembling fervor. His blunt beard shook, and there were tears in his eyes.

"In all things," she repeated.

"Your Majesty has ever been bountiful to me," he said.

This was more than play-acting. Between these two, the sage councilor and the regal, unmastered queen, there was a tenderness of understanding that spanned beyond the compass of gestures or mere affectionate words. The ladies-in-waiting were visibly moved, and Mrs. Thompson, Elizabeth's female dwarf, tugged her handkerchief from her girdle.

Elizabeth was the first to recover.

"Come come," she said more briskly. "Sir Spirit, if an ass kick you, you feel it too soon. I'll remove you from being my spirit if ever I see you do not disdain such a feeling. Serve God, fear the King, and be a good fellow to the rest."

Burghley forced a smile, "My enemies say I do not serve God when I would have you marry a Catholic prince," he said.

"Catholic? tush. 'Tis a true religion. I've heard the mass myself, to my soul's balm. There's no quarrel with Catholics. Our quarrel is with those who put France or Spain above the peace of England."

She seemed to think that was enough of the subject.

"Where is our young husband?" she asked. "When does he return?"

Burghley wondered why she should ask him about Oxford, but her features gave no sign. "Soon, I think," he said. "His last letters were from Italy. He comes from there to Paris, and so to the Channel."

"A full pilgrimage. We hear in Sicily he challenged all their noblemen to run a course of jousts with him, and none durst do it." She regarded him quizzically.

"I cannot say, my liege. His letters to me have been concerned with money. He has had to sell lands to pay these travels."

"He can thank God he has lands to sell. His Queen must go cap in hand to the Antwerp lenders."

"Yet I would he might have some grant or monopoly to bring him income. The Earl is very spendthrift."

She continued to regard him. "With his money or with himself?"

Burghley coughed. "Both, Your Majesty."

"It is a young fault. But he has enough for living. Our monopolies are needed for men who cannot bear the expense of public service."

"He spends for books, for publishings, for lewd literary companions that feed out of his purse—"

"Do not scorn them, my lord. Publishing and literary fellows speak for our times. They give a form and substance to events, and shape them for the common eye."

"A common sort of trafficking, my liege. Too common for an earl."

"If Spain launches her ships at us it is the common sort who will stand with us or let us fall."

"True, my liege. And yet—"

"And yet he is spendthrift. And yet he consorts with poetizers and rude players. And yet he scatters himself abroad when we would have our nobles around us here at home. And yet he is cause for gossip."

Burghley started.

"Oh, we've an ear. We should scold you for not telling us our little Anne is got with child. But no matter." She leaned farther forward, tapping his sleeve with a finger point. "France will not wait. Nor Spain. Action is crowding. And England must support us or we go down."

"England will support Your Majesty with its whole heart."

She smiled again, a thin, worn smile that seemed to pierce past Burghley, beyond the palace windows to where the smoking shoal of London's chimneys reminded her she was a queen. "I remember the play he wrote to gain my graces after he had run to Flanders."

"I recall it well. It contained certain buffooneries about the robbery his men did at Gad's Hill."

"I think you laughed at the buffooneries, my lord."

"For the moment, I confess. Though they were not to my taste."

"Well, well . . . He made us laugh, and we were lenient with him. We gave him his leave to travel. The play was about the wars of King Henry the Fifth."

"That was its story. Your Majesty was generous in finding merit in it. You saw it at the palace."

"I saw more than a play," she said. "Oxford has wizardry in his mind. He creates."

"My good liege—?"

Her smile pulled oddly at her lip corners. She brought her stare back from the distant London chimneys and fixed it on Lord Burghley. "I saw Englishmen winning a war," she said. "I saw Agincourt as it lived."

7   "MY LORD! MY LORD OF OXFORD!"

Oxford swung his feet from the bench where he had stretched himself. In the thick air of the cabin the cry had a frightened urgency. Behind it sounded a rattling at the door, and shouts and men running. Boots trampled overhead.

He stood up.

The steady, labored whispers of the vessel's timbers had given way to lurching creaks and strains. The deck beneath him was canted heavily, and through the cabin port the horizon swept up and down in a tossing line, dipping below a sky broken with April scud and rearing above waves whipped to an angry froth, their storminess matching the storm seething in his own mind since he had stepped aboard the ship, homeward bound for England.

"Pirates, my lord!"

Oxford flung the door open. The vessel wallowed clumsily. Like most of the coastal fleet, her length was only twice her beam. She was squat and bulgy, and she crowded her sail like a fishwife tucking her skirts above fat buttocks, and fled squalling for safety.

A half mile off, the triangular topsails of the pirate drove at her from the weather quarter.

He looked through drizzled sunlight and gray bursts of rain. The vessel's waist was a tumult that eddied around the mainmast and the brick and mortar of the cooking room: waving arms, oaths, baggy trousers and the panicky faces of the seamen who scrambled among the coils of cable, and knocked into each other as they ran, and shouted, and hauled on jeers and halyards. Oxford sprang up the ladder to the poop. The vessel's master, a suet-colored man in a long sea cloak, was alternately biting his nails and yelling orders.

"Can you shake loose?"

"No."

"Then we'll hold him off in fight."

The master gave him a pudding stare, bawling past his shoulder. "The Dutchman gathers on us. Brace—brace—and keep your luff! Handily there, midships!"

"Dutch?" said Oxford. "Or Spanish?"

"He's nimbler than a Spaniard. . . . Make ready to tack about! Yare at helm!"

The tumult doubled in the waist. With a slosh and roll the vessel came around. She lost on the maneuver.

"He's two hundred if he's a ton," the master said. "We're half that. God defend us, he spreads his cloths."

The pirate had tacked smartly, and the bone of spray at his bows drew closer. Oxford could see the canvas cloths slung along the length of the rail to prevent boarding, and the rope nets being rigged above his deck against falling spars and wreckage.

"Give them broadswords," Oxford said. "Will you be taken naked?"

"Two hundred if a ton. We're outweighed," the master said. He rubbed his hands agitatedly, striding by the bonaventure mast while the open water lessened between the vessels. "He expects cannonshot. We've no cannon."

"Let him grapple, and fight him to hand," Oxford said.

"I tried to slip him, but he knew the set of Portsmouth canvas. And the sun lit us, and he saw the green and white." He rolled his eyes upward at the Tudor colors stitched broadly on the sails. "He was too quick for me."

"Outweighed and outwitted both. God's blessing!" Oxford gripped him by the front of his cloak.

The master pulled free.

"Give them broadswords!" Oxford ordered. "Make a stand!"

His vehemence appeared to put courage into the master. He wavered, the suety cast of his face mottling with indecision.

Four men came up from the waist, armed in steel corselets and buckling on their scabbards.

"I've my servants," Oxford said, "and here's Yorke from the Low Country wars. We'll keep the sterncastle. Set the crew to the main-wales!"

Smoke puffed from the pirate, pennoning on the wind, and a ball skimmed over the wave crests. It cut the foam in widening splashes and disappeared. The master ran to the top of the ladder and cupped his hands.

"Sit close! In with mainsail! In with spritsail and mizzen! Bring her to!"

The vessel shuddered as the lines slacked off. The helm went over. Her speed fell away, and she yawed and nosed sluggishly in the seas.

"Get arms. Every man to his charge!"

Oxford shook him again. "Will you fight?"

"As God wills."

"Od's my life, heartily answered!" Oxford laughed and drew his sword. He was superb on the deck in the wildness of sun and rain, his large bright doublet, short cloak, rings at his ears and a flat cap aslant on his head.

The crew passed weapons to each other, milling about the waist in a confusion and rattling of steel. They clustered into bunches below the poop and peered up at Oxford and the master with slitted grins.

"They've no stomach for this," the master said.

The pirate bore in. He was close hauled, his dark sails slung and furled. His bowsprit loomed over the poop as if he would ram, then sheered and slid alongside. Some of the crew in the waist ran crouching to the bulwarks. Most stayed where they were.

"They've no stomach. Name of grace."

"Call to them," Oxford said. "Spur life into them!"

"You see for yourself," the master said, his voice a wail.

Oxford pushed him roughly aside. He bounded for the ladder and dropped partly down it above the waist.

"God's blessing, are you hares to a hound?" he cried. "This is an English ship! She wears the Queen's colors!"

The crew stared at him. He braced on the ladder, legs hard and stocky and straddled wide, his tones ringing.

"There's sailors in port would think proud to be in your shoes! Have you forgot who bred you? The blood in you was got by hardy fathers that dyed the name of English on this Channel. These were their seas! Will you lose 'em now? Will you knuckle to fear? Will you have it said in Spain and Flanders you've woman's guts? Who's up? Who's with us?"

They stared at the flash of his sword and the passion in his face. He was one man, and they were a score. But they were Channel born and his words were contagious. They shifted their feet, and their grins widened over their teeth, uncertainly.

The hulls of the two vessels ground together. Wood grated wood, and spars tangled with a ripping of canvas. The pirate's lateen sail raked the poop and bowled the helmsman from the wheel. The grapples were out. Billhooks, falchions and cutlasses prickled along the pirate's bulwarks and yonkers swarmed in the tops, yelling and firing muskets. Froth spewed up from the churn of water between.

"Come on, for cracked heads and bloody noses!" Oxford shouted.

Whoops answered from the waist. The crew were catching his fire, remembering the tales of old sea brawls told along the quays.

He sprang from the ladder to the poop, where the first grappling hook had clawed. He tugged to throw it off and his fingers tore on metal and plaited hemp. A one-eyed seaman slid from the pirate's rigging and dropped facing him. Oxford's sword went through his wrist and came out on the other side. The tendons jerked in a spasm and the man screamed. The whoops came fiercer in the waist, broken by the spatter of musket shot from the tops. Oxford climbed to the poop's rail. He stood an instant in view of them all, shouted again, and vaulted aboard the pirate.

It swept the crew with him. They tumbled after him pell-mell. The master was beside him, a spindly body, without the long cloak, thin shanks jigging like a bantam cock. Others were close behind. The helmsman laid about with a cutlass blade. The servants were there, and Yorke in dented half-mail. Forward, in the pirate's waist, the vessel's boatswain led a wild melee. The Englishmen slashed at the boarding cloths, hacking their fastenings and pouring on to the deck. They fought hand to hand in a packed mob that swayed and thrust and jabbed and cursed, wedged, back to back and chest to chest in a mass of bodies and the acrid reek of smoke. Arms rose and fell; swords, dirks, daggers, marlinspikes and belaying pins. Heads and shoulders rode through the turmoil, mouths that flung up, and gasped open, and disappeared. Feet trampled the planking with a leather drumming, and over the whole ship rose a high, throbbing, savage sound.

Oxford cut his way toward the pirate's wheel. He battled with a cold anger, as if the wrench of his blade and the fury of his attack were driven on by the wrench and fury he felt inside him. He was reckless of what he did, of himself, of the weapons aimed at him. He parried them on his hilt, warding and countering them with the skill of a fencer. There was a rash danger in his fighting, and the men in front of him gave ground.

The assault had been swift. It took the pirates by surprise. But there were three to one, and the English had no hope against such numbers. Their assault spent itself, and slackened. They were borne back, and herded to the rail, and began one by one to jump to their own vessel, carrying knots of pirates with them, like ants buried in mounds of their enemies. The yonkers, scrambling from the shrouds, joined in to bring reinforcements.

Oxford sensed the change. He looked around him. The pirate's decks were slowly clearing. The helmsman was dragging himself away. He saw the master pinioned, the thin shanks kicking, and Yorke bleeding at the mouth. He saw the pirate's captain, almost within his reach, face stolid as a Dutch cheese. The captain was signaling more men up from the waist. He saw the surge of them on the ladder. And then they closed in on him and bore him down.

Anne was waiting with her father when Tom Cecil came with the news that Edward was home. Tom galloped on a sweaty ride from Dover, and he was tired and his shrug cryptic.

Anne stood by her cushion as he greeted their father. The eighteen months that Oxford had been on the continent had made a difference in her. Motherhood had scarcely seemed to touch her, at least not outwardly. Her figure was still small and slim, her skin was fresh, and her breasts were delicate in a bodice of blue damask. But she had less of the eagerness that had flowed in her so vibrantly. The stories whispered of her in the court, the slanders about her and the birth of her child, made her like a person in a fog. She knew that she had changed.

But her eyes lighted when Tom turned to her. He would have a message from Edward, from Dover. Edward would have sent her some trinket, some pretty token. And in a little while Edward would be riding into London and would be with her again, and somehow everything would be well.

"Tell me," she said.

Tom spread his hands. "No Ned," he said.

"Tom," she said, "where was his ship?"

"No ship."

"But we had letters he was coming." A flicker of her mother's temper broke through. "Stop teasing me. You're a dolt."

"Anne," Lord Burghley said gravely, "speak in gentler fashion to your brother."

She sat down on the cushion again, and felt her legs suddenly weak.

"The ship didn't touch at Dover," Tom said. "It lay outside the harbor and put a boat ashore. I sent word back I was there with horses and servants, and the ship raised anchor and sailed for London. I never saw Ned. The coxswain said they were set on by pirates in the Channel, and that my lord of Oxford would not talk with any Cecil."

Anne could not believe it. She persuaded her father to take her to the dockside when Oxford's ship was reported making up the Thames the next day. She stood at the wharf, in a hurly-burly of sailors and dockmen as the ship was warped crankily in. She watched for a sight of his familiar figure on the deck. She found him at last. He came down the gangplank with a soldier companion, trailed by his servants. Her heart pounded with anticipation, and she called out and ran forward to greet him. His eyes met hers, but there was no expression in them. He went on by without a word.

The fuse Lord Burghley had tucked into his pouches had reached the powder, and the mine had burst under Oxford's feet.

His book was stolen, his wife public tattle, his name and honor bandied through the English court. He had heard it in Paris, and set out in a blind anger for London. He landed in England violent and embittered, with the looting by the pirates on the Channel as the last scalding humiliation.

Lord Henry Howard's malice had been adroit, and Lord Burghley's ponderous efforts to get at the truth had magnified the falsehoods. It did not matter that no one really accepted the story that Anne was an adulteress and he was a cuckold. The story had made the rounds of the court, and one way he was disgraced, the other way he was made a fool of; either way he was the butt of snickers and gossip.

He was helpless as Anne against rumors and cross-lies and the whispered insinuations.

Within a week the court knew one thing for fact: he was not living with Anne.

They all saw it. The talk buzzed in the palace rooms and corridors, and Arundel confirmed it to Lord Henry Howard as his lordship sunned himself on a window seat.

"He will not have her," Arundel said, "that's certain. He has broken with Cecil House and everything in it."

"I heard," Lord Henry said. "Burghley asked me why."

He shifted on the window seat and looked out to where the younger maids of honor were laughing around a fountain. The fountain had a device that sprayed water from a hidden spout when it was touched, and the maids were using it on a new lad from the French embassy, drenching him to the skin.

Arundel smiled. "Marriage is a risky business."

Lord Henry shrugged. "The maids will drown that Frenchman. Eliza Trentham and Nan Vavasour have doused him twice, and the simpering butterfly doesn't know how."

Lord Henry preferred to be reticent.

Others did not. Gascoigne called on his friend Yorke and took him walking among the crowds of Cheapside, where they were not likely to be overheard.

"Did he speak of his book?"

"Nothing else. He stayed at my house when we landed from Paris, and wormed me with questions."

"What did he say?"

"Raved like a madman. Would see no one. Would have his anger satisfied. He damned false friends and backbiters. Said you were loyal to him once."

"His chickens have come to roost," Gascoigne said. "His book is captured as the Spaniards captured us at Leyden. How are the wars? How is Sir Roger?" He strutted past the shops, patting at his mustache with a handkerchief to show the Queen's bauble dangling on his sleeve. "We do sweeter here. Turn in and drink to a laureate."

Conversations over card tables and the music of the virginals swung inevitably to Oxford and Anne.

"They say she is like to have been free with half a dozen."

"I'd swear not."

"Who'd name the half dozen? Not Anne."

"She's forbid to be with him at court."

"It's his anger against Burghley. My lord treasurer has pried too much into the tales."

"It's his anger against Lady Mildred."

"I think," said the Duchess of Suffolk, "that if the child could be brought to him unknowingly, he would soften. There's a tender mood in him. God knows my little lady of Oxford has proof of it." Kate Suffolk was a frank, kindly soul whose son was in love with Oxford's sister.

The court did not know how to take him, and friends like Tom Bedingfield and Fulke Greville stood off uncomfortably while Anne stayed in Cecil House and Lady Burghley scolded.

"Don't ask me to feel sorry, my lord," she told Lord Burghley, jabbing at her embroidery with her needle. "I foresaw all this. It comes of not keeping him in decent bounds. Running off to Flanders, trailing at the ends of Europe. He'd have gone to Greece if you and Her Majesty had not plucked him home. Coarse, rude company, rhymers, musicians —these shag-tail city scriveners who dedicate their books to him. Where is the dignity he was to bring to our family? He's beggared himself and put us to ridicule. How many lands has he had to sell to pay for his gallivantings? Not that he's arranged it. You've had to do it for him, handle his money and stop his agents from their thievings on him. I foresaw these fits and starts and this graceless conduct. Writing and poetizing and consorting with players. Don't talk to me of players!"

"Very true, my love, very true indeed," Lord Burghley said.

"Well then," Lady Burghley said. Lord Burghley did not argue. Lady Mildred was his second wife.

In the dormitory where the maids of honor slept, the girls chattered over the affair and shared its latest twists and turns while they undressed for bed. The fact that Oxford was not sleeping with Anne gave their own beds a vicarious thrill.

Nan Vavasour said that as long as Anne was out of the way there might be a chance for someone else. She sat on the foot of her bed, naked to her hips, creaming her full breasts with a lotion to keep them smooth.

"My lord of Oxford will be free now to pick where he pleases," she said.

The younger girls giggled self-consciously, all except Eliza Trentham, who unfastened her skirt and stepped out of it and neatly shook the folds. "I don't think you should say that," she said. "He still loves Anne."

"If she can't hold him, what's love?" Nan's pale blue translucent eyes laughed at Eliza in the taper light. "Love won't ease the itch in a man's private parts. My lord of Oxford is more of a man than most. He has needs. Anne can't answer them if she's at Cecil House."

"I think he will go back to her," Eliza said.

"I think he will not. Anyway, Anne's had him enough. Let him sport as he wants. I'd be quick to help him. Wouldn't you, Eliza?"

"No," Eliza said. "That wouldn't be helping him."

Nan laughed again and said Eliza was a fool, and after they were in bed set the girls so agog at the possibilities of what could happen that Sir Francis Knollys, who had the adjoining chamber, had to come into the dormitory in his nightrobe and stalk gravely through the room, reading passages from the classics to quiet them.

As in everything else, the Queen's was the final verdict, and the court was chary of Oxford until she gave it. She was in no hurry, and when she consented to see him at last she sent the maids of honor and her gentlewomen away and held audience with him alone. The patience of both of them was strained. She came down on him with a forthright bluntness, and his answers were cutting and arrogant.

"I am incensed with you, Oxford. Much incensed," she began at once.

"That is a two-edged word, my liege."

"How?"

"It can strike both ways."

"Mend your insolence, my lord."

"I know what I know."

"And are what you are. Oxford, you jar on our court with this quarrel."

"I am pulled to the perch like a jetted hawk. My wings clipped, my name a figure of scorn."

"I want my hawks beside me. They are my talons. Without them we'd have naught but weasels."

"Weasels indeed. Gnawers and suckers of blood."

"Put a curb on your tongue."

"As others are curbed."

"We will judge in that."

"Your Majesty has heard lies of me."

"Who tells them?"

"If I knew I would drag him here and stuff them in his throat. He's the greatest villain under heaven."

"You cannot name names, my lord? Then stop calling them."

He flushed, and bit his lip. She scrutinized him keenly. The lines of his face had matured since the last time she had seen him, before he had gone over to the Continent. His young look had disappeared while he was on his travels, as if the sights and sounds, the experiences there and the old arts of France and Italy had deepened his sensitiveness he had carried with him from London and shaped it to a stronger pattern. The splendid, dandified elegance of his doublet and ruff and crisp hair could not hide the thrust of chin and the broader angle to his jaw. The smirks and whispers, the spite against him and a black sense of injury, were written there too. She understood why, though not how. She knew the lengths people would go to break a marriage or glut ambition.

She frowned. "You think too much of these rumors. Anne is innocent."

"I never denied the child was mine. Anne is an innocent flower, but there are poisons under it. Is it rumor to set a block in every step of my way? Call me too young for wars and too extravagant for travel? Is it rumor that I was niggarded for the bills of my journeys, hounded by creditors, pinched and denied and cheapened until I must borrow Italian crowns at Padua?"

"Hah Padua! There were riots there. Brawls of students, and killings." Elizabeth eyed him down her high cheeks. "The bruit was *gentiluomini inglesi.*"

"Your Majesty knows I am spied on. It's his custom."

"Whose?" she demanded.

"My Lord Burghley." Oxford's tone was savage. "He has spied on me. He has set my wife to spy on me. He has thwarted and hindered me. Objected to the sale of my lands and peddled slanders about me. Shall I smile and be meek?"

"What's done is done," she said. "These angers mend nothing. It is vain *calcitrare contro le busse.*"

"Then he will have it thus: *ut nulla sit inter nos amicitia.*"

"Latin to my Italy," she said crossly. She did not like to be topped in her phrases. "Your friendship to Lord Burghley must be as it will be. Have we no English proverbs?"

"Yes, my liege—that it is my lot to starve while the grass grows."

The mask of her face quivered a moment, with the quick temper that resented temper in someone else.

"Oxford," she said, "what do you want?"

"Truth. And Your Majesty's good will."

She regarded him a long time, letting her temper cool. He had been cruelly wounded. Even if the whispers of his cuckoldry were false, the curbs Lord Burghley put to him had goaded him raw. Yet there was ability in him, great promise, too great to be thrown away. She remembered his play. She had heard how he roused the coastal sailors to fighting pitch, singlehanded on the Channel. She wanted to turn his brilliance to his own good, and to England's if she could. Her intuition told her that a gift of words and a power to catch men's emotions might be valuable one day. The moments lengthened, hung in the balance between that intuition and the pride in his eyes.

"Make your peace with Burghley and the court," she said.

"I'd as soon sleep with vipers. I know them all. Caterpillars. They feed on corpses and reputations. Not one of them but's meddled in this business. I'll not open my heart for them."

"They'll think you a fool."

"So much the better. It's no sport to destroy a fool."

"Write your poetry, and ride in my tournaments. You'll have fame from each."

"I'll never put my name in print again," Oxford said. "I'm taught my lesson there."

His voice showed how the wound rankled.

"I'm twice pirated, at home and on the sea," he said.

Elizabeth made no answer. She sat brittle and erect, plucking at her thoughts.

"What's left to me?" he said. "I am forbidden war. I am forbidden travel. I have no office under Your Majesty. My home is broken and my bed fouled with lies. I'll go my own way."

Elizabeth leaned forward and spoke more gently. "Write how you please, or ride how you please," she said. "There will come a time." Two spots of a dull, coppery color burned faintly under her rouge, and she rose abruptly. "My good will is easily had," she said. "But truth—" She lifted her shoulders.

Oxford dropped to his knees. From his belt he took a pair of soft silk gloves, Italian made, perfumed, and decorated with four intricate rose knots on the back of each. He offered them to her, and she accepted them. She was delighted. She admired them and fondled them, put them on and pulled them off again, and held them up and exclaimed at the workmanship, and the pungency they gave when she drew them back and forth in her palm.

"What is the scent?" she asked.

"From Italy, my liege."

"Our clumsy fellows here cannot equal it. I will wear none but this." She was in raptures, all smiles, and she patted his chin. "We'll name it the Earl of Oxford's perfume."

She gave him her hand to kiss, and dismissed him. As he went out at the door she stood by her chair, watching him speculatively.

 8 Through the summer after his homecoming the sense of injury gnawed in Oxford. The more he thought of it, the more it grew. He tried to overcome it, yet he saw it everywhere. It was in the looks of his friends, in the palace gossip, in the sly, half-hidden smiles of the whole court circle. People who had admired and fawned on him eyed him now a little

askance, and when his back was turned he felt how they were whispering and smacking their lips. Many of them had smarted under his quips and his quick, mischievous jibes at their vanities in the days before he had gone abroad. They were not sorry to see him down. Lady Burghley declared again that she wished he were dead, and Hatton said unctuously that he was being served with his own medicine.

This was partly true. He knew he was partly responsible; he had been heedless, restless, spoiled, extravagant, his intense nature fiery and impatient; he hardly yet knew himself. But the knowledge did not help. If anything, it quickened his resentment. Granted his faults, why was he welcomed back to England after a year and a half by slanders and titters? He, Edward, Earl of Oxford? He had done nothing to earn such disgrace or such treatment. He could not account for it, and in the first thrash of his anguish he acted by blind instinct.

He cut all his old ties, refusing to see Anne, or the Cecils, or to be involved in any way with the scandal, and went into bitter silence.

Lord Burghley, as baffled as he, wrote him pleading letters, asking him to say what was wrong between him and Anne. He answered that for his part he had nothing to say. In his black, desolate mood he wanted to be rid of all the Cecils.

It kept him from Anne, from his daughter, from the happiness he had hoped to have. But it kept him as well from Lady Burghley's scoldings and the stifling proprieties of Cecil House. He blamed these for most of the trouble, for the rifts and cracks in his marriage to Anne. Lord and Lady Burghley had thought they were getting prestige and a manageable son-in-law; he had thought he was getting Anne for himself, to share his spirits and to follow him with her quick, bright laughter into realms they could both share. Lord and Lady Burghley had been wrong. And he had been wrong. He loved Anne with his body, but she did not possess the depth that would have made him love her with his mind, and unless there is love with both mind and body the love is not secure. He broke with the whole past that summer, and sought freedom.

It was a wild, hectic, headlong freedom. He had told the Queen it was no sport to destroy a fool. Deliberately, mockingly, he made himself a fool.

In his boxes from Italy and France were the latest fashions of the Continent. He put them on and wore them, outlandish fashions that startled the court and set the good Londoners agape when he rode through the streets.

In his boxes were the newest poems and plays and stories from foreign writers. He took them to the taverns and to the Savoy, and flung them down like a challenge to English pens, and Lord Burghley sighed heavily in Cecil House at the reports of spies that my lord of Oxford had gone back to his old habits of consorting with lewd companions.

His rank had always hemmed him in. The post of lord great chamberlain was an honorary title that gave him nothing to do except at state ceremonies and processions. He flaunted his rank in irony and satire, as if it had been a jester's bladder, and hid his feelings under a cloak of folly.

He picked new friends for himself. The closest and the most sympathetic was Lord Henry Howard.

"Grip! Grip!"

"By the nose!"

"By the rump!"

"In and out! Hoo! Well snapped!"

"To the neck!"

"God's wounds! He'll be horned!"

" 'Ware horns, boy!"

"Round! Round! Get round!"

"Stand clear! Hoo!"

The body of a mastiff, snout slavered, pitched into sight above the circle of the crowd. It hung limp in the air, dripping crimson like a burst currant bag, and crunched to the earth outside. The crowd parted, the dog's master shuffled out to pick the body up, and the ranks closed again, ten deep. From inside the circle rose eddying dust and the snorts of an angry bull.

His elbow on the stockade palings, Oxford frowned in distaste. His face was flushed with wine and the heat of the Sunday afternoon, which shimmered the Thames to a dull pewter and drooped the flags of the Tower beyond the river. He did not like bull-baiting. He thought it useless savagery, a waste of good dogs and beasts. But it was a diversion for young magnificoes, and Lord Henry Howard had urged him to come.

Lord Henry's polished tact made acceptance of him easy. He was adroit and fluent, companionable and assiduous.

"You want new lads around you," he said, "who will question nothing and forget everything."

He supplied the friends from the list of his own—Lord Surrey, Charles Arundel, Francis Southwell, Walter Raleigh. They were there at the bull-baiting, wild spirits, like Oxford, ready with jibes and sophistries, setting the pace for speech and fashion. Lord Surrey wore strings of pearls; Arundel's shoe heels were three inches high; Raleigh pinned gleaming brooches on his hat and picked his teeth with a silver toothpick carried in a tiny silver box. Superficial, cynical, without illusions, they were an antidote to Oxford's pain, to the scandal that ate into him and the blasting of his good name. They lived brilliant days and riotous nights, and widened the breach between Oxford and his old way of life.

"Why do you suppose," Southwell was saying, holding a handkerchief to his nose, "our Sunday citizens cross to Southwark to look at this?"

"Appetite," Raleigh said. "They look at their Sunday dinner—neck of beef."

Oxford smiled mechanically. He did not care overmuch for Raleigh. A newcomer from Devon, in his early twenties, Raleigh was brash and cockily presumptuous, and spent too many efforts trying to attract attention to himself.

"Raze Bowes is bringing a mastiff from Paris Gardens," Lord Henry said. "He's the master of the game there. It should be a battle. Ned, are there such rich sights as this in Italy?"

"The cobblers' wives of Milan are more richly dressed every working day than the Queen at Christmas," Oxford said.

He winked gravely at Lord Henry, who returned the wink and said, "Do you hear that, Charles?" to Arundel.

"By'r Lady!" said Arundel, and hiccuped. He had drunk more wine than the others.

The crowd grew still, squeezed tight against the palings, shoulder to shoulder. Through the stillness the callings of the river boatmen for fares rose and wavered trailingly in the flat air.

Presently Raze Bowes led in his mastiff. The man was in leather jerkin and coarse woolen leggings, a giant of a frame. The dog was heavy, ugly, large for its breed, with a scarred head and powerful forelegs. They made a grim couple.

They pushed along to a stout, narrow gate and entered the stockade. The dog raised its muzzle, drool hanging from its jowls, and ran its tongue out, and settled on its haunches. Bowes crouched beside it and tested back and legs and chest with sure, hairy hands.

The bull was in the center of the stockade. It had fought three mastiffs already, and was slashed about the hocks and along the flanks. Flesh had been torn at the base of its neck, and its tail was cut and lacerated. All these gashes oozed, thickly, into red rivulets that twisted through its coat and dropped into small dark pools in the dust around its hoofs. But it was tough and wiry and still full of fight. It shook its horns at the crowd with short, jerky, scooping motions, and rolled its eyes toward the crouching man and the dog.

To bait the bull and win, the dog must bring him down. The nose was the best target. After that the throat, or a grip in the hind quarters, in the excruciating spot near the great testicle sac, below the base of the lashing tail. Against horns and hoofs there must be teeth and jaws, the quick hard in-run against the charge; against the bull's bulk and thrash, the instant timing, the spring, and the deadly, stubborn mastiff hold.

Raze Bowes straightened, slipping the leash, and took the dog by the collar. His fingers lay briefly along the cropped and battered ears. He looked about him and let go.

The dog trotted forward into the stockade and stopped.

It was the signal for the shouts again.

"Take him! Take him!"

"By the nose!"

"By the rump!"

"That's Bowes' best dog. That's Old Mustard!"

" 'Ware horns!"

"Hoo, Old Mustard!"

The shouts were gadflies to the bull. It snorted fretfully and lunged, bringing up with a whoosh and a sweep of horn at the dog's bristles.

There was a snap of jaws, and the bull wheeled to safer ground. The beast was wary. The first dog that afternoon had clamped it by the tail, a flailing of pain and terror that had ended at last in a splitting crack along the palings. It wheeled once more, short about, and backed away, fronting its adversary.

Raze Bowes had trained well. The dog had the skill of a killer. It followed the bull with a stalking gait, head sunk low in its shoulders. Its teeth were bared, its body hunched and ungainly. It measured distance with pale-rimmed eyes, and crept in step by step.

"Ho, brave!"

"Slow does it!"

"Wait for the grip!"

"That's Old Mustard!"

"Hoo! Hoo! Hoo!"

The crowd went into a prolonged roar.

Three dogs had died by this bull. As the white body edged closer it watched and shifted and then sidled abruptly, striking outward and downward with its hoofs. The dog sprawled clear by inches in a half somersault. The bull struck again.

It missed, bellowing.

The preliminaries were over, and the fight began in earnest.

The dog dropped its stalking tactics and commenced a series of feints and rushes. It worried at the bull, with nips and harries at hocks and legs. It slithered through the pools where the bull had stood, and its coat and paws were dabbled with gummy splotches. Dust from the bull's hoofs powdered the splotches.

They fought in a weaving circle, like country dancers, the dog on the outside, the bull in the center. The bull's nose was to the ground, its eyes walled. One of its lunges hit, a fling of the nose that threw the dog sideward, a furrow of horns gouging the dirt. The dog yelped, rolled, and doubled instinctively under the bull's belly. It ran heavily out on the other side, fresh blood spattering its muzzle from a rip in the bull's hide.

The bull swung to slobber at the wound, and the crowd clamored for more.

"Now, Mustard!"

"To't, boy, to't!"

"Shred him!"

"Bait him fair!"

They clamored loud and noisy, whooping their energies out over the half-chewed sweetmeats and nuts and wads of sugared bread in their mouths.

At the smell of blood the fight gathered speed. It grew faster and wider and covered more ground. There were no feints. The full snarling attacks carried half across the circle. The dog's lips, slimed with froth, drew back from its upper fangs like hoods, and its hackles stood on end. It drove viciously, snapped, growled, turned, and drove again. The bull's lunges held it at bay.

The bull charged in counter rushes, probing for rib or gut. It reared and whirled and stamped—two bloodshot eyes, a tail waving stiff—hookings rattling on the posts of the stockade. Another shred dangled from its hide.

An open crimson welt laid back a flap of skin on the dog's skull. Between attacks the dog lolled its tongue and licked the clots from its cheek.

The dust swirled and choked, the crowd howled them on. The bull spun, maddened and bawling; the dog shuttled in and out, front and back, trying for an opening. It wanted a death grip. The bull fixed it with a glazed stare, wanting death too, mashed and pulpy death to the smeared white coat and open jaws. Both animals were tiring. They panted, and their sides heaved. The dog's hinder parts trembled spasmodically. The bull's neck sank lower.

As their strength drained their rushes launched out blind; brute surges, like boxers drunk on one another's fists.

They tangled together in the center of the circle, and blurred in dirt and fury, and exhaustion threw them apart, the dog reeling to a squat by the palings, the bull spraddled, too spent to move except for the restless, interminable shaking of its head.

Stamina could not last it. A tension came over the crowd, a deeper note in the howls that showed the climax was mounting and that the end was near.

The dog maneuvered slowly around the stockade. The bull watched it but did not stir. Without warning, the dog ran in. The bull met it with a broken gallop and a check. The run was too wide, the check too soon. The bull's momentum carried it half around, and the dog's leap struck past the flank and landed between the hind legs under the tail. The fangs went into the loose skin above the testicles. They slit the skin like a knife slitting silk, caught, and hung.

The bull screamed. It pivoted on its fore-hoofs and kicked, and the dog dropped free, to the ground. It was unhurt, but the bull's blood spewed over it and it could not see. Still screaming, the bull caught it on the horns in a sidelong sweep.

The dog flung upward. It made a high arc, its ugly jaws clamped in a grimace, and a loop of its bowels trailing after it. The crowd scattered with quick yells.

Raze Bowes' shout lifted above the rest. He pawed his way through, and ran grotesquely around the edge of the stockade, stumbling and pushing and his arms stretched out.

He reached the dog as it fell. He caught it in his arms and broke the fall. It hit him full in the face and splashed him with blood—his beard, his jerkin, his great woolen leggings—and bore him to his knees with its weight. He stayed on his knees beside it, and the fight was over.

Oxford and his friends strolled off. Southwell said he was hungry, and Raleigh suggested anchovies and wine of Bordeaux at a tavern. He was very pleased; he had won five pounds on the bull.

But Lord Henry said they would come to his house. "I have a taste for pigeons stuffed with unripe gooseberries," he said, "and Ned can tell his tales of shining fights in the Low Countries. You told us last night how the Spanish general put you in command of a bridge, Ned."

"Did I?" Oxford said.

"But thickly. Your tongue was thick. We can hear it again," Lord Henry said. Oxford laughed.

"This was a sound fight," Raleigh said.

"These baitings seem prophetic," Lord Henry said. "I picture the English bulldog and the Spanish bull. The bull always wins."

"Not always, if the dog has courage," Raleigh said.

"No," Lord Henry said, "or the proper master." He said it so lightly that no one could have called it an insinuation against the Queen.

As they went by Raze Bowes, Oxford turned. "I am sorry, Master Bowes."

The gamekeeper looked up, his face stained. "Thank you, my lord." He bent again, and neither he nor Oxford said anything more.

Oxford sauntered on after his friends, running a fantastic story for them through the fingers of his mind; the more fantastic the better. It passed the time and made them all fools together.

The pigeons were excellent and the wine appetizing, and he slept late the next morning. When he opened his eyes and pushed aside the bed curtains the sun was streaming into the room. He blinked into the sunlight, trying to recall the night before, but he could not remember a word of his story. All he remembered was Charles Arundel's face, gaping at him in a comical seriousness like a sotted owl. He could see it still, a hazy form between the bed and the window, looking at him while he blinked. Arundel's face—or Raze Bowes'—or was it Arundel's? It focused finally into the face of Robin Christmas.

"Good morrow, your lordship," Robin said.

He was the agent for the handling of Oxford's lands, a man of meat-colored cheeks, strawy hair, Saxon blue eyes and an obstinate devotion. He regarded Oxford sorrowfully.

Oxford threw off the coverlet with a grin. "Is it, Robin?"

"What, your lordship?"

"A good morrow." He never could resist the mischief; the reproach in the look and voice was so apparent. He got up and began to dress. "Do you bring me one?"

"If your lordship means the weather—" Robin said.

"An acre of fair skies, bargained for and sealed and duly delivered? Robin, you'd traffic with God to turn an honest penny. But beware of blasphemy."

"My lord—"

"And of wit in the morning. It pules in the mouth like last night's wine."

"Aye, my lord." Robin endured patiently. As Oxford's lands had dwindled he had seemed to dwindle with them, but his devotion had not. He was thinking of the days of sevenscore horsemen and a hundred rich manors, when his young earl had been at the peak, before scandal had blasted him and before his fortune and his fair-weather friends had shrunk away, and he understood more than he showed. He said, "Your lordship has asked about the inheritance of your estate passing to your nephews."

"I want to leave it to them," Oxford said. "The thing is doubtful under English law, but Horatio and Francis are Veres. I'd sooner them than the tribe of the Cecils."

"Lord Burghley would raise objection," Robin said.

"He raises objection to whatever I do," Oxford said. "But bring me answer." He buttoned his doublet and took Robin's arm. "Robin, I need money."

"Not from the selling of your estates, if it please my lord. Your lordship has sold so many."

"Sell another. We'll get it back six times over. Players must eat."

"Players are bottomless pits, your lordship."

"We'll fill 'em with gold. We're buying in a venture, Robin. Come listen to Doctor Dee." Robin seemed to dwindle more, but Oxford set him on a horse and spurred him over the roads to the doctor's home.

Doctor Dee had a shredded gray beard and a forehead like an egg. He practiced the astrologer's art, read the stars and delved into the mysteries of earth and fire, the causes of thunder and the flux of metals. His Mortlake house held almost as many secrets as Lord Burghley's; the Queen consulted him on favoring influences, and the court sought his advice for suitable dates and the proper conjunctions of the planets.

Robin stood mute and apprehensive in the gloomy chamber while the doctor pored over yellowish clay lumps gathered around him on trays and weighing scales, his beard hanging wispily while he talked to Oxford in a sonorous voice.

"These are the samples, my lord. They are just as the expedition brought them. They have not been tampered with. Captain Frobisher fetched them to me with his own hands."

"What does Frobisher say?" Oxford said.

"He calls them gold ore, my lord."

"What do you call them?" Oxford said. He put out his finger and touched one of the lumps. It had come from the other side of the Atlantic, where Martin Frobisher had sailed on his second voyage to find a northwest passage to Cathay. Frobisher had not found the passage, but he had returned with this ore. It made an alluring prospect. "Are you listening, Robin?" Oxford said.

Robin nodded, twisting his cap.

"I make no claims, my lord. I must probe further in my analysis. But the signs are very hopeful. Other samples have been sent to the mint. In one of the reports they assay at seven ounces to the ton."

"Gold?"

"Gold, my lord."

"That would make us all rich. Robin, shall I be an adventurer for a thousand pounds?"

"If it is gold, my lord," Robin suggested cautiously.

"It may or may not be," Doctor Dee said, swiveling his eyes toward Robin, "but the determining of such things is a matter of ancient principle. Your lordship will have heard of the Syracusan Archimedes and the crown of King Hiero. I myself have obtained seven ounces of silver from two hundredweight of this ore."

"Master Frobisher has got him a treasure."

"The computations for profit are as high as forty pounds for every ton," Doctor Dee said. "A new voyage is in prospect to *Meta Incognita,* with more and larger vessels. Master Frobisher will bring back five hundred tons."

"That's a sound I like," Oxford said. "Robin, forget lands and look for a fortune. Sell enough to take us shares in this argosy."

He had never made much account of money, but the need for it was pushing at him more heavily. As he stood with Doctor Dee he had a dunning letter in his pocket from the landlady of one of the poets whose bills he was paying: "The grief and sorrow I have taken for your unkind dealing with me make me believe you bereft of all honor and virtue. Good my lord, deal with me in courtesy, for that you and I shall come at that dreadful day and give account of all our doings. . . ." He owed her for the first quarter rent of rooms.

He left Robin at the doctor's door, and an hour later walked into a tavern in the city near the old Blackfriars convent. The tavern was full of hangers-on, writers, actors, and men who had stopped in from a play rehearsal by the children of the Chapel Royal in one of the convent rooms. They sat at tables, talking and drinking. A viola da gamba was weaving out a tune, and they greeted Oxford noisily over the music.

"Ho, Ned!"

"Here's Will!"

"Well-a-day, Ned!"

"Welcome to your lordship."

He went in among the tables and sat down with them, and they crowded around him like a school of hungry fish, with prompter's copies, and bits of their verses, and the latest news of the theaters.

"Master Hunnis wants a new masque. I could write one—"

"Dutton's been committed to Marshalsea. Struck some gentlemen in a fray at the theater."

"They'll do the *Four Sons of Fabius* next. Before Her Majesty."

The tavern swam in words. He ordered sack and sugar and spread his knees relaxedly. He was happier here than anywhere else. They understood him for himself here. "A new masque? Say you stole it; Hunnis will pay you better— Those are fair rhymes, Tony; do you print the grimaces with 'em?— Larry'll have his fill of fray in Marshalsea. He'll be frayed like a whore's velvet. . . ."

Jack Lyly was there, the fiddle-faddle young man Lord Burghley had not employed, making notes for a novel and aping the dress and manners of Lord Oxford; and Bob Greene, fresh from the university, who wrote plays and songs.

"Mount up, Bob. Give us your new scene."

"He mounted last night. A fair wench. His scene's limp."

"So is his codpiece. They'll neither of 'em stand."

"His mount drained him. He pranced too much on her belly."

"It's a whoreson jealousy, Bob."

"Make liars of 'em. Read up. Work your hands between the lines for breath."

"He'd sooner work his hands between the legs. Don't prick him to it, Ned. He's unpricked."

"Seven nights in a week and no grace on Sundays, God's blood, a shotten bolt. A long spur at dark and a flabby fornicator at dawn."

The sack was strong, the laughter loud. There was freedom in the tavern, banter and exuberance and minds that sparked on one another. He spent the morning with them. They took him at his value, drank with him, joked with him, rode with him through the streets, following at his heels, bawdy and dissolute and boisterous, as he moved restlessly during the winter from his home to the court, from the court to the Savoy, from the Savoy to the theaters, from the theaters to the taverns, a fastidious, plumed, ruffed, showy spectacle, at the head of his motley troop.

Most of his evenings were passed with Lord Henry Howard and the circle of Raleigh and Arundel and Southwell. He drank heavily. When the wine had shuttled into his brain he spun them tales out of whole cloth, wild fabrics of his imagination, dyed in the color of his travels—great assaults beside the Duke of Alva in the Low Countries, where the Spaniards made him a general for his valor; sea fights in rich Venetian galleys; the pavements of St. Mark's glittering with diamonds, and Sicilian princes begging him to marry their daughters. His friends nudged each other and winked behind his back. The tales flowed from him endlessly. He could keep them up as long as he had an audience. He seemed to enjoy their preposterousness.

But once—he was more drunk than usual that night—he stared into his cup and his story was a different kind. He spoke of his father.

"It was in France," he said, "where my father was invited to the hunting of a wild boar. To this sport he goes. His dress was as when he walked in his own chamber—no arms, no steel, a dancing rapier by his side and horsed on a plain ambling nag. The boar was put speedily on foot. The beast was huge and fierce, and the Frenchmen made a long chase of it. At last my father alights to make water by a tree. Suddenly there comes the boar, down that very path all foamy at the mouth, his teeth whetted, his bristles up. The Frenchmen shout to my father to run and save himself, and halloo that he is lost. They cannot help him, or they dare not.

"My father does not change his pace. He does not swerve a hair's breadth. Finding his passage blocked, he draws his rapier and lays the boar dead with the first thrust. The Frenchmen quit their running, and crowd to him amazed, as if he had done the twelve labors of Hercules. 'My lords,' he says, 'every boy in my nation would have performed it; these beasts may be bugbears to the French, to us they are but servants.' And so he went back with them to dine in Paris."

The rest knew from his face that the story was true.

He stopped, and put the palms of his hands to his eyes. He took them away and looked at them. They were dry.

"My father was a man," he said. He got up from his stool, staggered to a couch and fell asleep.

9

Eliza Trentham was a maid of honor now. She was no longer an awed girl from Staffordshire, living with her parents in the seclusion of the country. She was a member of the court, selected for her looks and charm, one of the lively, decorative bevy in Her Majesty's train. She slept at the palace, sported with the other maids in the gardens, and was in daily attendance on the Queen. Nothing was hidden from this intimate, inner circle, and Eliza could not help but see and hear what was happening to Oxford while he was separated from Anne. From her cushion by the royal chair she watched the transformation that came over him. It was clear to everyone, as Oxford meant it to be, but to Eliza the clarity seemed tragic, and unreal, like those bright, false mirages the sea captains sometimes spoke of to Her Majesty. She could see the cynicism, the callousness, the feverish, nervous pace of his life. But she could see, too, in moments when he thought no one saw him, the look of emptiness in his face. She remembered how he had looked the day she and Anne had met him before his tournament. There had been no emptiness then. That had been a different image of Oxford, true and full, and Eliza knew that in her memory this other could never efface it.

Oxford did not live with Anne for two years. He spent his time with Lord Henry Howard and at the court, devising entertainments of plays and masques, and dancing with the Queen. And Eliza must keep her thoughts to herself, and say nothing of how she felt that Oxford was deliberately throwing away the best part of him. The Queen took him into superlative favor. His wild extravagances and wild friends amused Her Majesty. She was vastly diverted by them, and her sharp ears caught the fact that he was a great lad among the Londoners. She called Oxford her Turk, and said he was as fantastic as a sultan and brash as a grand vizier. She chortled at the court magnificoes he traveled with, and when Raleigh, in an impudent bid for more notice, spread his cloak for her in a puddle, she capped the impudence by treading on the cloak in her grandest manner. The court convulsed, and the Queen tossed Raleigh a captaincy for his joke, and a commission in Ireland.

The effect of Oxford's freedom on the young women of the court was a different matter.

This was particularly so in the case of Thomas Knyvet's blue-eyed niece, Nan Vavasour. Eliza's attention was first attracted to her in the dormitory. Nan sat in the dormitory at bedtime, brushing her gold hair and retailing the gossip about Oxford that carried into the palace from the city. The most red fullness of Nan's lips and the high, carmine roundness of her nipples were set like ripe fruits in her white skin. She giggled over Oxford's doings, and the talk of him in the long galleries. She would stand and stretch herself indolently, and let her loosened skirts fall from her waist, and run her nightgown over her head and droop her eyelids at Eliza over the other beds. Eliza would pretend not to notice. Nan would smile and shrug and after the tapers were out the girls would hear her twisting her body on her bed in soft and langorous contentment, humming a small tune to herself in the dark.

On Shrovetide Tuesday, the second year of his breach with Anne, Eliza spoke to Oxford at last. She touched him on the arm as he stood in a group of courtiers. He had been acting in a play for the Queen, and he was flushed with the applause, and the Queen's reception of two rich jewels he and the Earl of Surrey had presented. His eyes flickered over her in the gaiety of the torchlit hall, quick and facile.

"You liked the play?" he asked.

"There would be little matter if I did or not, my lord," she said.

He started slightly at the answer, and seemed only then to recognize who she was. "Eliza."

"Yes, my lord."

Eliza had grown very lovely. She was in her twenty-first year. Her oval face had lost its shyness, her figure was taller and more delicate. In the hubbub of court life she had kept her self-containment, her poise and her gift for sympathy. She was like a musk rose, fragile with bloom and the freshness of beauty.

He glanced around and led her to a window alcove, pulling the draperies partly shut. Dick Tarleton the London comedian was topping off the evening with his buffoonery—a flat-nosed, squint-eyed, roguish-faced man dancing his jig of 'a horse load of fools.' The draperies deadened the rattle of the clogs and the courtiers' laughter. He looked at her more closely. "My audience of Staffordshire."

"Once, my lord."

"Often, I hope. You didn't like the play?"

"I said my liking would be little matter. I thought it tragic."

"A play named *Murderous Michael* would have to be tragic. We wrote from the true tale—the steward who killed his master for love of the wife on a country manor between Gad's Hill and Canterbury. God's blood, I know that road." It was where his own servants had committed robbery four years before.

She lifted her eyes to him. "So many of the pieces you have shown have been: *The Cruelty of a Stepmother, The History of the Solitary Knight*—" She paused. There was no reproach in her voice, but only pity. "My lord, will you do nothing but tragedy?"

He frowned. "I write as I feel."

"It is a gloomy fare."

He chose to misunderstand her. "I keep them from being bored."

She turned toward the window. Below them the flambeaux of the palace guards flamed smokily, necklaced beyond by the lanterns of water barges on the river. The alcove where they stood seemed detached, suspended between the garish world they could hear and the ghostly soundlessness of the one they could not.

"And you?" she said.

His thumb ring glistened on his hand that rested against the draperies near her shoulder, shooting tiny darts from its facets against the window frame. He shifted his hand, and the darts stopped.

"That's another thing that's a little matter," he said.

She stared from the window. They had hardly spoken since he had come back from his travels. The Queen had many people around her and the court was large. They had rather avoided one another.

"You have gone far from Staffordshire, my lord," she said at last.

"Have I, Eliza?"

She made an involuntary movement at the sound of her name, the motion rustling the folds of her dress. "Very far," she said.

"So have you, Eliza."

"Not so far as to act my part on a stage, my lord."

» 93 «

She heard the quick suck-in of his breath. This time he could not choose to misunderstand. "What else shall I do?" he said.

He tried to see her face, but she kept her stare on the river. "Your audience is much greater now," she said.

"And more bitter." He jerked his arm in a caustic gesture. "Ask them why."

She turned to him again. Guffaws came from the end of the hall, where Tarleton was finishing the jig. The wavering shadows of the torchlight fell through the draperies across his face. His Piccadilly ruff was elegant, his doublet was sewn with precious gems, his manner was taut and arrogant.

Her eyes sought his. "You do not write of love any more, my lord."

"No."

The guffaws died. A babble of talk began. The courtiers broke into groups for dancing and backgammon and troll-madam. Eliza understood. He would be what he had made himself be, what others had made him. He would play this warped part until the lines were done and the theater emptied.

"My lord," she said, "you have a token of mine from long ago. I gave it to you at your first tournament. You wrote of love then, and poetry. You write of harsh things now. You have changed, and the token may seem wan and empty. You may wish to give it back."

He met her eyes. A flush of color darkened at his temples, and he shook his head. "No," he said roughly, "I'll keep it."

He pushed the draperies apart and strode away.

The court was caught up by a new excitement immediately afterward, and she was busy with her duties to the Queen and did not speak to him alone again.

The excitement was an envoy from the Duc d'Alençon, who sailed into Dover from across the Channel and posted up to London bearing the duke's unquenchable devotion, his miniature on ivory, and his passionate longing for marriage to Her Glorious and Peerless Majesty. The envoy's arrival climaxed a winter of arguments and guesses and angry rumors as to what course the Queen would take. London was in a furor, and Elizabeth intensely flattered. Her mind saw clearly that the mission was political. She had helped to prompt it, another gambit in the game of Continental power. The Flemings had put themselves under Alençon's protection against the Dutch; she was supporting the Dutch as openly as she could against Spain; the King of France was at present in league against England and was raising mercenaries for his brother the duke in Flanders; a Scottish Douglas was at the French court on secret business; Spain's shipyards were still expanding. The Duc d'Alençon was half her age and not of her religion, but he held a strategic position in Europe. The coming of Monsieur de Simier challenged her resourcefulness, and it tickled her woman's heart. She outdid herself in her welcome to him. She received him in formal audience at her palace like a languishing damsel, her dress cut so low that when he bent to kiss her hand he could see her navel. Her hair was piled with jewels, her yellow eyes were arch with coquetry.

She sighed over the duke's picture, pock-marked and huge-nosed, and as grotesque as Tarleton, and kissed it dotingly. *"Je vois vraiment que j'aime maintenant cette petite grenouille,"* she exclaimed. "How is my little frog, *Monsieur?"*

"Near dead with yearning for Your Majesty," Simier said. "I have letters for you from him ardent enough to set fire to water."

His foppery and mincing tone made Elizabeth's nobles exchange significant glances. Leicester belched, and she shot him a warning look. "My lord," she snapped, "if frogs stick in your guts you must make shift to go hungry."

She had never been gayer. The court moved outside with the spring weather, livening the days with battledore and shuttlecock, exercising in the tilt yard, and bowls and tennis. The Queen was in perfect health, which she declared briskly came from the fact that she never ate too much and did not have to take ten-day purges every few months as most of the court did. Except on state occasions she dined alone, and would have nothing to do with the nostrums and potions of the doctors.

Although she was nearly forty-seven she still had the figure of a girl, and a girl's delight in being pursued. The thought of marriage fascinated her. She toyed with it like a cat with a mouse. She kept Simier close to her, basking in his flourishes and phrases, called him her Monkey, flirted shamelessly with him in the gardens and by the fountains. She played chess and draughts with him at night, and lifted her skirts sprightly when she danced to show her silk-clad ankle.

She ordered feasts, entertainments, displays of wealth. The young courtiers jetted up and down in clothes that cost a fortune, fashionable shoes, fine hose, sumptuous doublets, plumed hats, and cloaks ornamented with tassels and bangles and silver bugles. City mercers and linen-drapers and the makers of ruffs grew rich on the sale of satins and lace and taffetas. Lord Burghley gave a dinner for Simier and his embassy at Cecil House. The guests sat down to two stags, two bucks, six kids, six shins of beef, four gammons of bacon; a swan, three cranes, twenty-four curlews, fifteen pheasants, fifty-four herons, eight partridges, and other meats, swimming in honey; sturgeon, conger, salmon, trout, lampreys, lobsters, prawns, gurnards, oysters, fresh-water fish. There were herbs and salads, thirty-three hundred eggs, three hundred and sixty pounds of butter, forty-two pounds of spices, and three gallons of rose water for washing the hands, and rinsing the mouth and spewing. Desserts came afterward—suckets, codiniacs, marchpanes of almond paste, gingerbread, florentines, tarts, conserves of fruit, and jellies of various colors molded into shapes of flowers, shrubs, animals and fishes. Forty-nine gentlemen and thirty-four servants waited on the tables, carrying beer and gascon, sack and hippocras over the floor rushes and the Turkey carpets. The Queen was immensely gratified.

Within a month it was being said that Simier was making love for himself more than for Alençon. The split over the French alliance widened in the council. Leicester swore the Frenchman had bewitched the Queen, that he had used sorceries or a love philter on Her Majesty. He threatened to drive him out of England.

When he heard it, Simier smiled.

He was an accomplished dandy, and his spies had been alert in the palace galleries at Whitehall and Greenwich and Nonesuch. He told the Queen what no one else had dared. The Earl of Leicester was secretly married again, to a third wife, Lettice Knollys, the former Countess of Essex whose husband had died three years before—some thought mysteriously.

The Queen exploded in a rage. She haled Leicester into court with his countess and lashed at him in a paroxysm of fury.

"Body of Christ, there is a sovereign in England! We'll teach you to your cost! A pox on knaves! You are suborned! You flout our will! Married in secret! Hell's fiends!"

"Madame!" Lettice Knollys said, bristling by her new earl.

"Be silent, you she-wolf!" Elizabeth screamed at her.

She turned on Leicester and cursed and stormed. "Married in secret! Cock's bones! I'll not bear it! To fawn on us and keep our grace, and all the while lie in her legs abed! A lecher would do more honest! A pander, a whoremaster! Blood of God, making our court a stews! Would to Christ you had got your fornication in a drabhouse!"

"My liege—" Leicester stammered.

"Roving your codpiece in her forest like a greasy poacher! Grunting and sweating and sliding of your manhood into privy sheets! Oh Jesus, that I should have laid nobility on a buttock-squeezing yokel! Damned sluttish lust! Strumpetry and wantonness! It stinks of itchy foreskins and friggings under haycocks! Get him away from me, my lords! Stir, some of you! Bed him in our fort in Greenwich park! Let him discharge there!"

Leicester tried to answer. He fell on his knees, but he could not stem the torrent. He owed the Queen twenty-one thousand pounds. He had grown stout, and lost the sharp insolent precision of his features. Leicester's beard and mustache straggled, and he was a little bloated.

"Get him away!" she shrilled. "Set him in the fort! Write me an order to the lieutenant of the Tower!"

She was vividly conscious of Simier, of the slight to her vanity, of the jangling note this struck in her own wooing. She poured out a tirade, swearing like a gutter-wife, and it was not until the Earl of Sussex braved her that she would listen. Sussex was Leicester's mortal enemy. He thought him dangerous to England, and distrusted him as long as he lived. "Beware of the gypsy," he was to say on his deathbed, "you do not know the beast as well as I do!" But he was honest and outspoken when speech was needed.

"My royal liege, this is no cause for the Tower. No man should be troubled for lawful marriage, which among all men has always been held in honor and esteem."

Elizabeth leaned back, gnawing at her upper lip. She looked at Sussex shrewdly, and waived the Tower.

But she banished Leicester from court.

His going left the anti-French faction without a leader. His nephew and heir-apparent, Philip Sidney, stepped into his place, but the graceful, polished, auburn-haired Sidney lacked age and experience, and all England was on edge over the question of the Queen's marriage to

Alençon. A consort for Elizabeth and a child from her blood were matters of national dynasty and the country's peace. Lady Catherine Grey, sister of the hapless Lady Jane, had been the nearest successor to the throne. She had been kept in seclusion, forlorn and neglected in the background. Lady Catherine had died last year, and the next in line was Mary of Scotland unless Elizabeth should wed. Tempers were brittle and nerves were short.

In August, Alençon came for a brief, dazzling visit, with bribes for the courtiers and a diamond ring worth ten thousand crowns for the Queen, provided by the foresight of his mother Catherine de' Medici. The Queen dined with him privately in Simier's rooms at the palace, and hid him behind an arras to let him watch her dance in her magnificent Florentine style before he sailed home again. The visit was supposed to be surreptitious, but everyone knew of it. Pamphlets flooded London and men fought at the tone of a word. Sidney and Oxford quarreled over the use of a tennis court; Sidney was as hotblooded as Oxford, they were both swashbuckling, still in their twenties. Oxford flung the name "Puppy!" at him, and Sidney demanded a duel. The Queen ordered Sidney into the country, and Oxford to her presence.

"Philip may cool himself at his sister's house," she said. "You will do the same here, my lord. I weary of these jars."

"I weary of men who do not know their rank," Oxford retorted.

"Master Sidney has been schooled," she said. "I have tutored him in the difference of degree between earls and gentlemen."

She searched him with one of her swift, acute glances and tried to be patient. She was aware of other differences, the feeling about Alençon, their old rivalry for Anne Cecil, their new rivalry in poetry and letters. Sidney and Oxford were her best court writers. They took opposite approaches, Sidney for the story, Oxford for the language, and each had his separate followers. It was as natural as young goats locking horns, and there was no real malice in it. But rank was an instinct with Elizabeth.

"Degree," she said, "stands between the sovereign and the people's unruliness. A gentleman who disregards nobility teaches the peasant to insult both. We'd not have that, my lord."

"Without degree," Oxford said, "the whole frame of state disjoints." He remembered Leicester. This imperious queen was an inextricable mixture of woman and ruler. It was impossible to tell where one left off and the other began; impossible, and unwise. "I was hasty with my tongue," he said.

"Nobility should be moderate in all things; it sets an example," she said. "You were wrong as a noble, he was wrong as a gentleman. The two wrongs cancel."

"Freely," he said. "Master Philip's of good will."

She showed she was pleased. Sidney's mother had nursed her through her smallpox and she had a tenderness for the family. She pinched Oxford's chin between her thumb and forefinger.

"So are you a good Will," she said, calling him by the name he went by in the taverns. She shook his chin affectionately and then dropped her hand. She tapped the arm of her chair and sighed.

"There are too many quarrels. The court will slice itself to pieces. We must wear a solid front against the world. My Will, weave us something to stitch us together."

"Something out of nothing?" he said.

"There is never nothing in that head of yours. Give us laughter and frolic. Shake us out of our spites."

She paused.

"You put Agincourt on the stage once," she said.

"Crudely, my liege."

" 'Twas crude enough," she said. "You had your Prince Hal buffet the chief justice for sentencing of him. That does not sit. It's counter to degree and our laws' dignity. Let it be changed if the play is played again."

Oxford nodded.

"But no Agincourt now. Put laughter," she said. "We want a brighter garment. We need liveliness and merriment, stuff of a cheerier dye. It will be a garment for both sides to wear; it will cover us all." She stared at him keenly. "Put laughter, Will."

"I am a poor weaver, Your Majesty."

"Tut," she said shortly. She rose.

"I would have these quarrels end," she said. She stared at him a moment more. Stepping forward from her chair she laid her palm against his cheek and raised his face as he knelt to her. "I would have all quarrels end," she said.

He knew she was thinking of him and Anne. She turned toward her ladies and signed to him to withdraw.

There was a round of picnics and autumn sports that fall. The flags flew from Hampton Court in the crisp October air while Her Majesty kept residence in the country. Trains of lords and ladies rode into the fields, past gaping beggars and the crossroads inns and the goodwives' linen drying on the hedges. The Queen rode with them, dressed in velvet of forest green, attended by gentleman ushers and halberdiers, and a falcon from the royal mews on her wrist. They lunched in woody glades and by the banks of streams. They drank nut-brown beer, huff-cap and dragon's milk, and listened to ballad singers chant the tunes of *Greensleeves* and *Babes in the Wood*. They nibbled watercress for putting the color in maids' cheeks, and looked for magical unicorns' horns as preventatives of poison.

Nan Vavasour was prominent on these jaunts. She seemed to love the riding, and when the court swung off the roads into the long, echoing alleys of oak and ash she took the lead in the impromptu races and the gallops under the trees. She made a bewitching figure in the saddle. Her body was graceful, her gold hair lustrous in her lattice cap. Her very fair face, rather sensuous mouth, and the fullness that sloped faunlike between her eyebrows and her ice-blue eyes, flaunted an earthy, playful mood through the shafts of sunlight and the tang of the woods. Oxford often noticed her. He smiled at her sometimes, and sometimes would spur his horse to keep even with hers while she cantered near him. They would ride to the next thicket, saying nothing, their horses' hoofs drumming rhythmically, and she would veer away to Tom Bedingfield or one of the younger courtiers.

They went on like this for two weeks, and then she approached him one day as the court halted for its picnic meal. He sat a little distance from the rest, his back against a forest beech, waiting for the food to be served. She came and sat beside him, leaning on one arm and doubling her knees comfortably.

"You're idle, my lord. What are you doing?"

"Listening," he said.

Her mouth teased at him. "Shall I keep you company?"

"You may have better things to keep."

"None, except my maidenhead, and that's kept as easily as lost." A trick of her nostrils gave her face a guileless look in the sunlight. "What are you listening to?"

"Talk," he said. He motioned to the groups around the Queen.

"Their talk?"

He nodded. "They paint themselves in words."

"And you sit and mock their colors."

"They choose their own," he said. "You can hear."

She tilted her head, listening with him. Sir Christopher Hatton was describing his favorite salad to Fulke Greville—capers eaten boiled, with oil and vinegar for garnish. His fussy, affected voice wheezed unctuously: ". . . these before the beef and mutton, very tasty, between sips of small wine, or a Charnico or Eleatica."

"Our Kit," Oxford said, "will thigh you a woodcock, chine you a salmon, lift you a swan, or unbrace you a duck, all with flourishes and by the card. He eats in as many posings as there are vanities."

Nan laughed, and skittered her feet in the leaves. "Does no one ever listen to you, my lord?"

"Too many," he said.

"I mean alone."

"Who would want to?"

"I would." Her mouth was teasing him again.

"You might be bored," he said.

"Perhaps twice boared. Your lordship wears a lusty animal on your crest."

A puff of wind blew the leaves over her skirt, and he brushed them off. Her legs lay capriciously quiet under the touch of his hand. Her skirt was smooth, and he felt the smooth undulant warmth beneath.

He put his shoulders against the tree trunk. "Then you could cry your virtue was crestfallen," he said.

She smiled airily. "I fear me."

The wind played at her hair.

Some of the leaves had wafted on to his cloak. She flicked her fingers at them. "Tell me what color I am," she said.

"What you choose," he said.

"No, you shall choose for me."

"Damask," he said.

"For blushes?"

"Damask and silver. The colors of a queen's maid in an autumn grove."

"Autumn is too cold. It brings winter and snow."

"Add the gold from your hair," he said, "and the snow will melt to spring."

"I can see why Her Majesty loves you," she said frankly, with another laugh. Her pleasure was open and unabashed. "You've studied women, my lord."

"Very little," he said.

She let her head slope back, peering up through the branches of the beech. "A man who has married has at least studied one," she said.

"They're not all the same," he said.

"We are in one way," she said. She glanced at him sidewise.

"The way that takes you to men."

"And men to us." She was not at all offended.

When the sun ran along her throat her skin had the sheen of milk. He could trace the swell of her breasts, firm and high in her bodice, rising and falling with her free, quick breathing.

"I think you know the way, my lord," she said.

"Plainly," he said.

Their glances held briefly.

The flicking of her fingers at the leaves made an insistent little whisper. He looked down at them. She saw the look. When he raised his eyes again her own were fastened on him with a bland, cool awareness. Neither of them moved.

She said, "The court will be going to London soon. Our rides will be over."

"Will you be sorry?"

"I like this. I like the fields and the horses and the sound of horns. But I like everything that's fun."

"London will be fun."

"It could be," she said lightly. She sloped her head back farther, and lay for an instant full length, her arms wide behind her, her skirts molded to her legs, and her breasts pushed upward, directly toward him. "What shame it is you have to live so much alone," she said.

10 A WEEK AFTER THE PICNIC, OXFORD DRESSED HIMSELF IN a soberer fashion than he had for two years, and went to see the Earl of Sussex.

The earl was in his chambers, studying the allotments of palace rooms for the winter season, but he laid them aside when Oxford entered. He was pleased at the visit; there had been few opportunities for visits from Oxford of late.

"Is something amiss?" he said.

"Myself," Oxford said. He drew up another stool and sat down while Sussex looked at him expectantly. Something was generally in the wind when Oxford appeared with that intense moodiness on his face.

"Her Majesty wishes me to go back to Anne," Oxford said.

"Indeed?" Sussex said. His training at court and in a general's tent kept his voice on an even level. He pushed the list of the palace rooms farther aside, with a casual motion. Since Oxford had served under him in the Northern campaign the relationship of the two men had developed a close mutual sympathy. The orphaned Oxford had seen in Sussex some of the image of his father; Sussex had seen Oxford's respect and admiration, and a tie of friendly affection, without display or sentiment, had grown between the older earl and the younger.

"Do you wish to go back?" Sussex said.

"I could answer two ways," Oxford said.

"That's not uncommon. What two?"

"If I go back to Anne I forfeit my liberty, my lord. When Anne is gay and merry I love her. But the shadow of Cecil House is always in the background. Anne wants a proper husband and a courtier. Cecil House wants a son-in-law who will be governed by its dignity. I cannot be both. One of them, perhaps, but not both. The hobble is too tight."

"And the other way?" Sussex said.

"I can stay as I am."

Sussex delayed his reply a moment, examining the wall behind Oxford's head. "Which do you prefer?" he said.

"I've hidden so long under a clown's mask, my lord, that to tell truth I don't know."

Sussex's glance returned to Oxford. He scanned him sagely. He saw that Oxford had dressed soberly for this interview, but it was part of his sagacity that he did not mention that the fact might be significant. He was aware that Oxford was quick and impassioned in his impulses, but that he could also be sensitive and reticent.

"Do you want my advice, Edward?"

"Yes, my lord."

"Then I will give it to you. Go back to Anne. Does that startle you? I would hardly think so. I've grown old in the court, and I can observe."

Oxford flushed slightly. He knew Sussex was referring to Nan Vavasour. He waited for her name. Sussex avoided it, however.

"You have been playing a character, Edward. You have your reasons—good ones in your eyes, I don't doubt—but the character is not true to you. It will end in disaster. Anne is your lawful wife. If you go back to her these rumors and scandals will stop. They will have nothing to nourish on. Your stepsister has charged you with bastardry; someone has lied that you are cuckolded. Such things are hard and degrading. But enemies are not conquered by running from them. Accept Anne as your wife again and outface scandal. It will gratify Her Majesty and set you stronger than before. Anne can give you repute in the court. She can give you herself; not a light matter, I should think." Sussex smiled. "And only Anne can give you a lawful son, as your father had one, and his father, and as you hope to have. Remember that, too."

"I do, my lord," Oxford said.

"Remember it before too late. Go back to her, Edward. You say you love her when she is gay and merry. Make her gay and merry, then. Keep her so, and love her so."

He smiled again. "Is that the advice you wished?"

Oxford stood up, raising his head. "I think it is, my lord," he said.

By the time the court moved into London he was sure of it. He told no one, and only Eliza Trentham suspected. She noticed his change of manner, and that he was not riding with Nan Vavasour as much as formerly. She stopped him one day as he was coming from tennis, and asked if he were looking forward to the winter.

"Yes," he said. "I want to be happy this winter, Eliza. I want to forget these last two years."

"Oh, I hope so," she said, "with all my heart." She did not say anything else, but he read the gladness for him in her eyes, and understood her meaning.

In London he sent a message to Anne at Cecil House, and on his first night in the city went resolutely to find her, hurrying through an early November fog along the Strand. As he entered the great mansion he felt the familiar leap in his blood and the old familiar tautness like an ache in his loins.

Anne had had his message, and she was waiting for him upstairs in her broad-ceilinged bedchamber that overlooked the garden.

Their meeting was passionate beyond anything he had imagined. It was not the place for upbraidings or raking out the past. It was the place for the memory of what they had been to one another. Anne's face was shining with tears, her mouth was trembling to his. The tapers threw a welcoming, caressing glow over the chamber and the deep, canopied bed. Meg the dressing woman sniveled and looked jocund by turns. The nurse fetched in his daughter Elizabeth for him to see.

The baby girl was much like Anne, and much like him. He held her on his knee while he fondled and petted her, and Anne fluttered over them like a child showing off an adored doll.

"She has your eyes, Edward, solemn and roguish together. And the quirk of your lips when you smile."

"My honey Anne, she's a mirror for us both."

The nurse's red honest features burst in a spate of weeping. Embers burned low in the chimneyplace, and the tapers were straight and tall beside the bed.

Then Meg folded down the bedsheets and bolted the corridor door from within.

The white linen of the sheets erased the picture of Nan Vavasour stretched indolent in a forest glade by the foot of a gray beech.

The nurse took the baby Elizabeth from his lap, and she and Meg curtsied and led her away.

Anne had put on for him a chamber robe of ruby-colored quilted taffeta, with high shoulders and gathered sleeves that narrowed charmingly to her little wrists. It smoldered like the chimney embers under her dark hair.

Going over to her when the women had left, Oxford stood in front of her and kissed her hair. He began slowly to unfasten the robe. She had no other garment underneath. Her body showed palely naked in a delicious slit that opened downward to his fingers, as if he were peeling an almond out of its skin. He parted the robe with his hands and pushed it back, sliding it until it loosened from her shoulders, where it hung for a pulsating instant, to collapse with a quick sibilance around her ankles. She drew her arms in front of her with an instinctive, startled gesture, and then, seeing the demand in his eyes, flung up her head, laughing with delight, and threw her arms around his neck.

She clung in absolute surrender, his strength hard against her. The jewels of his doublet were like sharp bites against her bare flesh. He made no sound. His fingers ran through her hair. They stroked at her temples, and up and down her throat. They dropped lower, and she tingled with responsiveness. He kissed her all over. He bent down on his knees, burying his face in the cleft between her breasts, pressing her breasts to his cheeks. He kissed her hips and sides and abdomen, and the two soft, sloping angles where her body slanted lusciously inside her thighs. It was as though secret, untasted dreams, hot images spinning through his mind, had whetted him to an intolerable tension. He picked her up and carried her to the bed and laid her on it. Her arms fell wide across the pillows, her slim bare calves were dainty against the sheets. He kept one hand cupped to her breast with a gliding, kneading motion while he looked down at her in the taper light and with the other hand undid his doublet.

They were both so eager that the climax was over before they were hardly aware. They could tell only by the sudden release of their throes and the long, slow drawing of their sighs. When he felt her lips relax under his he raised himself on his elbows and shifted his weight to the bed beside her so that she could catch her breath. He turned her to him and made a hollow for her in the arc of his body, and she crept into it as she used to do, curling as much as possible of her between his knees and chest. He kissed her on the mouth, tenderly.

They lay for several minutes. Presently she stirred.

"Anne—?" he said.

"I think I'm cold," she said. "It's silly to be cold, isn't it?"

"We'll mend the fire."

They got up. He put her robe around her again. She ran to an inlaid Venetian coffer by the wall and rummaged in it and brought one of his old robes for him.

"I've always kept it," she said.

He added a log to the fire, and they went and sat on cushions by the window. He took her head on his lap and she laid her cheek along his leg.

The fog muffled the sounds of the Strand beyond, the parties of horsemen and the far-off cries of the watch. Occasionally, through the thin streamers that licked at the sill, they could see the twinkle of stars.

After the wild onrush and spending of their love, the room enveloped them with a stilled, languid vacancy.

"Don't ever leave me any more, Edward," she said.

"Never," he said.

She looked contentedly from the window with half-closed eyes. The ache in his loins had subsided to a deep, gnawing, pleasurable sensation. Her ruby-colored robe spread at his feet with the quiet acceptance of a child's upturned palm.

He put his lips to her hair, and petted it in the same way he had petted the baby Elizabeth.

He looked from her to the window, trying not to be aware of the vacancy that lay around them, of a kind of blankness in the room and the wisps of fog, like sands washed flat and trackless by a receding tide. London was sleeping. Only an intermittent footstep in the corridor, or the creak of a distant door, showed that Cecil House kept its watchful vigil.

He tickled his fingers at her ear. The tide had ebbed, but soon it would gather itself to flow again.

Two men, crossing the Fleet bridge at Ludgate and following the westward jog of the city wall in front of St. Paul's, attracted as little attention as two fish in a school of herring. The city was intent on its own affairs. In the vaulted nave of the cathedral, known as the Mediterranean, the city gallants strutted, airing their finery and aping courtly manners. London's citizens paced through the streets, occupied with good business or bad, love or hate, greed or charity, friendship or spites, money to put into their purses or food to put into their bellies.

Porters struggled under boxes and casks and baskets, their hose bagged at the knees and knobby with the knouts of muscles in their legs; clerks, bargemen, morning shoppers, lawyers and their clients, carters, yeomen, army ensigns, wandering tinkers, all the thousands in the compact hubbub trying to get from where they were to somewhere else, twisted and joggled past each other at the narrow corners; and housewives swept their floors and shook out their curtains and threw their night's slops into the offal ditches.

In the kingdom's merciful peace under Her Majesty Elizabeth two men could walk London in honest liberty without question or even notice. It was doubtful if anyone troubled to recognize the land agent of England's premier earl, and the earl's private secretary whose two novels of *Euphues* had taken the court by storm.

Robin Christmas kept his same spry, dwindling, unpretentious air. John Lyly was a fluid, innocuous young man, with thinning hair above his forehead and a round, bright, almost diaphanous boyishness to his cheeks, which were set plumlike under the premature wrinkles around his eyes. His head was cocked a little to one side, listening to Robin while he walked.

"If he goes on as he is, it will be the end of him," Robin was saying.

"If he does not go on, it will be the end of me," Lyly said goodnaturedly. "Not to mention Tom Nashe and Tom Churchyard and Tony Munday and sundry others I could name. Besides my lord of Warwick's company of players."

"I could wish he had not taken over the Earl of Warwick's players," Robin said.

"Od's, Robin, what's the catastrophe? 'Tis as simple as wagging, like a sheep's tail. How else would we have our plays fitly performed, without the patronage of my lord of Oxford? How else would we point their excellences so well, the fine conjoinings of lines and scenes, unless we ordered the players ourselves, and rehearsed them as we want them, and fed them from our table? They'd blow our flame with Vulcan's bellows, otherwise. We'd be consumed with crudities and bombast. No, this is the way. The court is open to us. The Earl of Sussex is my lord's good friend. He's patron of his own company and chamberlain of the court. The plays for Her Majesty are picked by him, and he oversees their rehearsals. What more advantage could my lord have for setting up a company?"

"Money," Robin said.

"It's pity," Lyly said, dodging the contents of a bed pot that splashed into the street from an upper window, "so ugly a vice should lie in so pretty a word."

"My lord is ill off in funds," Robin said stubbornly. "He lost woefully in his venture with Captain Frobisher. The shares he bought of Master Lok. Three thousand pounds. And the ore brought home worthless."

"The ore was no *or*," Lyly said. He looked pleasantly surprised at his pun on the French word for gold, and grinned at Robin. Robin seemed unimpressed, and Lyly shrugged. "Doctor Dee was devious," he said, "and Lok shy."

"Not a shy enough Lok to keep out of prison. I was there when Captain Frobisher came to his house with forty men, damning him for a cozener. But my lord will not recover his pounds. I do not trust these argosies," Robin said. "They're one with my lord's unsubstantialness and flights of fancy. Ventures in ships, ventures in plays. Where do they lead? Into some airy dream where, like as not, most persons can't follow you. Look at Master Gascoigne; dead, and what's he got for it?"

"A grave," Lyly said.

"Land, now, will last you. Truth, Master Lyly, you can trust land. It's solid. You can measure it and buy and sell it. You can walk on it. You can eat from it when you're empty and piss on it when you're full, and it's always there. Land's earth, the stuff we're made of and the stuff we go to. There's a surety in land."

"And none in wind or wits."

"They blow with the seasons," Robin said. "You know how much money you've had from *Euphues*."

Lyly made a painful grimace.

"I don't trust 'em," Robin said.

"But you'll do as Ned bids," Lyly said.

"He's his father's son, and a rollicking, audacious lord," Robin said. "I wish he might not waste himself on trifles, and come into his true worth—into fame in arms or honor in Her Majesty's Privy Council. But I can never say no to him."

They had reached the neighborhood of the old priory of Blackfriars, a part of which had been parceled into halls and apartments, and where the boy actors, the children of Windsor and of the Chapel Royal, gave their play performances before they took them to the court. Lyly went by the performance hall and knocked on a door beyond. A servant, opening the door, said that Sir William was expecting them.

Sir William More owned that portion of the priory, and it was under his lease that the boys of the choirs used one of the halls as a theater.

His servant led Lyly and Robin Christmas to the main chamber of his apartments, and Sir William rose from a stool by a square framed table.

"His lordship has sent his best ambassadors, I see," he said. "The man of mind, and the man of money."

"His lordship hopes that one or both will persuade you," Lyly said. "He wants your good will toward the children's plays."

"It will take more than two voices to drown that clamor," Sir William said, with a blunt smile pulling at the corners of his beard. "However, gentlemen, sit down. I am reasonable."

He offered Lyly the single chair in the room. He and Robin Christmas took stools.

While wine was being poured, Lyly peered about with bland curiosity. Sir William More's room reflected the tastes and habits of a respectable and cultured London household. On its walls hung maps of the world, of France, England, and Scotland; there was a picture of Judith at the tent of Holofernes, a little chronicle, and a perpetual almanac in frames. The table where they sat held a globe, a slate to write on, a counterboard and cast of counters for making calculations and reckoning up accounts. Lyly met Robin Christmas' eye across the table and grinned again; no escape from money anywhere, his grin said.

Near the window a pair of scales and a set of compasses lay on top of a desk; a foot rule, a hammer, a seal, and a pewter inkstand with a pounce-box and pens of bone and steel. Around the room was a collection of a hundred or more of books. Among them Lyly could see the best chronicles of the time—he admired the choice as he studied them —Fabyan, Langton, Harding, Carion. He saw translations from the classics, and some originals; and lighter reading, such as Chaucer, Lydgate, and Skelton, in English, French, and Italian. He saw a volume of the statutes of Henry VIII, of Edward VI and of Mary, the *New Book of Justices* and other legal works. For medical use there was a *Book of Physic,* the *Glass of Health,* a book against the sweat, and a *Book of Medicines for Horses.* A pair of playing tables, a pair of virginals with white bone keyboards, and a base lute stood by the fireplace, the chimney of which was covered with a tapestry. The cushions by the fireplace were also of tapestry, and the curtains at the windows of sarcenet. Two more tapestry hangings kept the winter damp from penetrating the walls.

These were the surroundings, Lyly thought, of the people for whom he wrote his plays and novels, the people who attended the theaters with their buxom wives and daughters, and sat in the galleries next above the nobility, and munched nuts and pippins and sipped at ale during the scenes, and bought the latest popular books hawked by the booksellers' boys. They were solid, like Robin Christmas' land, rooted and hedged in fact, the ploughed fields of tangible comforts, and the practicality of next morning's breakfast; good, worthy, anxious, irremediably prosaic men and women, begetters of children and builders of homes, who lived respectably all week and ate neck of beef on Sundays, and forayed uneasily into pastures of lyricism and imagination they would never had dared to enter without the example of their Queen. Lyly looked at Sir William and his room like a deer from the wilds looking at a snug cowstall.

Sir William in his turn looked at Lyly with a benign and somewhat tolerant expression, as if he were more a butterfly than a deer—entertaining, beguiling perhaps, but with qualities of mind and sense that were a little embarrassing to a normal man.

He put down his wine and cleared his throat. "His lordship wishes me to drop my suit to break the children's lease," he said.

"Not only my lord, but the whole court," Lyly said. "The court gets much pleasure from the children's plays."

"The children are noisy," Sir William said. "They spoil my rest and disturb my work. The audiences are no better." He smiled agreeably. "Does my lord of Oxford want to take over the lease?"

Lyly was going to answer, but Robin nudged his foot under the table. "We are not prepared to say," Robin said. "But my lord of Oxford has a great interest in plays."

"I've seen them rehearsed at the public theaters," Sir William said. "I've seen my lord act in one of them. He is excellent at comedy."

"If you like plays, Sir William," Lyly said, "a trifle of noise now and then—" He waved toward the priory buildings visible through the window.

"I'd have no complaint if the noise were only a trifle. The theaters in London have been their own downfall, Master Lyly. You will admit that. You will remember the ordinance of six years ago that outlawed them beyond the city walls."

"Only public theaters," Lyly said. "Plays can be shown in private lodgings. You are private here at Blackfriars."

Sir William shook his head as a man not to be argued with. "I will read the ordinance to refresh your mind," he said. He drew a parchment toward him, and holding it to the light, frowned as he read:

The theater was become the occasion of much sin and evil; great multitudes of people, especially youth, resorting to these plays; and being commonly acted on Sundays and festivals, the churches were forsaken, and the playhouses thronged, and great disorders and inconveniences were found to ensue to the city thereby, forasmuch as it occasioned frays and evil practices of incontinency. Great Inns were used for this purpose, which had secret chambers and places, as well as open stages and galleries; where maids, especially orphans, and good citizens' children, under age, were inveigled and allured to privy and unmeet contracts; and where unchaste, uncomely and unshamefaced speeches and doings were published; where there was an unthrifty waste of the money of the poor, sundry robberies, by picking and cutting purses; uttering of popular and seditious matter, many corruptions of youth, and other enormities. Besides sundry slaughters and maimings of the Queen's subjects, by falling of scaffolds, frames, and stages, and by engines, weapons, and powder used in the plays.

He set the parchment aside and smiled again. "This was not all the fault of the Puritans, Master Lyly."

"It has the ring of their talk," Lyly said dryly.

"I do not hold with the Puritans that plays should be stopped altogether," Sir William continued, "though—"

"Though they'd do it if they durst," Lyly said. "Her Majesty's all that prevents them. Except for her they'd make roving beggars of us."

"There are evils that come from the theaters," Sir William said. "And the children players are fruit of the same tree. I gave a lease in the point of business, to make a few pounds and keep the hall from being idle. But the money is not worth the noise and uproar. I regret I did it."

"Then you will continue the suit?" Lyly asked.

"I have asked for a judgment at law to break the lease. The matter stands."

"You'll take away the last refuge of the theater inside the city walls," Lyly said.

"I want my own home as a refuge of quiet."

Lyly threw up his hands. "You'll get as bad a name as the Puritans," he said.

"I'll risk that," Sir William said politely.

"God's mercy," Lyly said, "a man could turn fishmonger these days. There's no respect for art."

"Art will survive if there is need for it," Sir William said. "Art is like business. It must make its way."

"No," Lyly said. "No, never. You cannot mix art and business. They're oil and water. Mix them, throw them in the same kettle, stir them with the same spoon; the shillings and pence will swim to the top and all you'll get will be business. Your art will be coated with the scum of money, and the people who look to it for nourishment will spew it out. Art with business is an unsavory brew no one should put lip to."

"I've not studied on the subject," Sir William said.

"Study it, sir. For if you make only a business of art, art will die cheap. If you leave it to its need, it will wither. What is need? What do I need? What do you? Marry, a bowl of gruel, a cloak, and four hovel walls, with daubs of mud to stop the winter chinks. But will you say so? No, nor I. We've been taught larger needs, and they've grown in us with the teaching. So our lives are lifted above the beasts. You should hear my lord of Oxford talk of this.

"The need for art and beauty must be taught with beauty and art, for how else can men come to what they have never seen? The poets and writers, the painters and singers and philosophers must carry it to men, for they bear the vision in them and see it plainer than most. But they must do it of themselves, not as a business. For a poet or artist to live on his works and eat their profits is like the pelican that devours its young; nothing is left to posterity but worms on a dunghill. The offspring grow feebler and misshapen. The pelican sickens of its own blood, turned inward on itself, and becomes grotesque, a mockery of its kind.

"Art must shelter under patrons who will nurture it as it is conceived and have the largeness and the wisdom to give it free birth. When Alexander the Great stopped long by the workshop of Apelles he did not think of money; but from his admiration alone the people came to know that an artist was among them, and bought all of Apelles' paintings. Wherever Maecenas lodged, scholars flocked, and learning went out from them. Study the subject, sir. It is as true as the Greeks, and it built the wonders of Rome."

"To a poet's eye, I grant," Sir William said. "But we are not in Rome. Will you take more wine?"

Lyly shook his head.

"I doubt if Maecenas had an eyrie of younglings screaming beneath his windows," Sir William said. "And Alexander could get away from the workshop of Apelles when he wished. I sympathize with my lord of Oxford and with your fellowship of players, Master Lyly, but I cannot withdraw the suit."

The wine glasses were empty, and Lyly and Robin Christmas got to their feet. Sir William had been courteous and affable, but they had wanted to feel him out.

"Well," Robin said, "the law is long."

"Yes," Sir William said, "you may see the children acting at Blackfriars for some years yet. Did you say my lord of Oxford will take them over?"

"I did not," Robin said. "I hope he does not. He had the cost of the Earl of Warwick's company this summer."

"They played in the provinces, did they not? That should have gained a few pence."

" 'Twas a vile summer for actors," Robin said glumly. "They were kept from Cambridge by the pestilence, and prevented in other places."

"Ah," Sir William said. "The tricks of fortune. Convey my good wishes to his lordship."

He went with them to the door, and escorted them deferentially through his courtyard into the street.

They went eastward, past the shadow of Lord Hunsdon's home— Her Majesty's cousin—and followed the alleys paralleling the river in the direction of Vere House. Lyly walked in silence, fretfully, thrusting at the street dogs and the trodden heaps of garbage with his boots. Robin moved beside him and kept his ideas to himself. If he would have preferred to be buying more acres for my lord of Oxford's estates than selling them piecemeal to provide the boots with which Master Lyly scattered garbage so cavalierly, he held his tongue. He had said what he thought, and what would come, would come. It was all in the day's duties.

How would a fanciful brain, like this young unprovident secretary's, know about dumping manors on the market for hard cash at ruinous rates? He was of the same stamp as most who flitted at the court— gauzy, nimble-worded creatures, spending their fathers' patrimony faster than the husbandmen in their fields could raise it for them. He would never run cheek by jowl with Sir William More, who was a man of another caliber, the sort who from the days of Her Majesty's grandfather, Henry VII, had been giving England a sound merchant trade and a good stability.

From his dealings in accounts and indentures and the handling of monies, Robin Christmas appreciated such men. It swelled his regard for Her Majesty that in her reign she somehow managed to combine them with the feudal nobles and the glittery courtiers, and bring them into her councils and around the woolsack in the House of Lords. They were new, as the poets and writers were new, and Her Majesty yoked them in double harness and got the best from them both. Robin Christmas could not have done it.

"We should have gone round by St. Paul's," Lyly said. "The alleys are too full for comfort."

The alleys were beginning to be congested with people. By twos and threes, men and women and girls and boys were coming out of back lanes and doorways. They came like twigs sucked by a stream, and washed against the house fronts in a slow, steady current, moving eastward with Lyly and Robin Christmas. The two men tried to push ahead, but their way was blocked. The faces were sober and constrained—not the city bustle of an hour before; they flowed among the twists of the buildings in a kind of bleak intensity, and the current caught them up and carried them along. When Lyly and Robin reached the corner for Vere House they were borne on by. They saw that the crowds had spilled over to the wider streets in the center of the city, that the streams were there, too, and that all the streams eddied toward Eastcheap and the Tower.

"By the mass," Robin said suddenly, "we've forgot the day. There's a punishment being done on Tower Hill."

Lyly went pale.

"The pamphlet," said Robin. "Against the Queen's marriage to a Frenchman."

"God's dines!"

"Master Lyly!" Robin said.

Lyly had wrenched around, his jaw cocked open like a fish on a hook and his mouth a rigid O, and he was shoving at the jerkin-covered chests around him.

"Break through! Break through, Robin! Come away!"

Voices beside him cackled protest, and voices behind him raised angry shouts—"What the good year! Cuff the rogue! Knock his head, i' God's name!"

"Master Lyly!" Robin said, pulling him by the cloak and putting his mouth to his ear. "Ye'll have us mauled. Ye'll not get out with a whole skin. Ye'd as well go along."

Lyly gaped at him and gave up, and allowed himself to be wedged forward by the weight of bodies behind him.

"Small blame to you," Robin said. "But you can close your eyes and stuff your ears. It's worse on you, I warrant, his being a writing man."

Lyly seemed on the point of retching, but he managed a nod.

"Well," Robin said, and he was pale also, "you've his lordship's protection for any follery you put to paper. You're safer fixed than this Stubbes."

Lyly's face was tragic. "I know Jack Stubbes," he said.

They came through Eastcheap and out into the space of Tower Hill. The mute, heavy mass of people was spreading sluggishly around a rough square walled on three sides by the narrow overhangs and pinched roofs of the London houses, and on the fourth by the great stone bastions of the Tower. In the center of the square, under a lowering sky, a broad scaffold of planking stood high, guarded by double lines of Tower yeomen, grim men in crimson coats emblazoned with the Tudor rose in gold, whose halberds glinted dully above the edge of the scaffold. The throng was already dense, and the streams squeezing from the streets were adding to it. There were no shouts or cries. But over the shuffle of feet and the vast quiet a low, inarticulate, murmurous sound, like the sough of wind on a sea heath, rose nervously from time to time and died away.

When they got to the square the crowd around Lyly and Robin Christmas broke and ran for places near the scaffold. Lyly and Robin were shouldered aside like apples in a chute. They hung back from being caught in front of the scaffold, and were shunted finally to the side next the Tower. The steps to the scaffold were here, and servants in dirty brown kersey smocks were carrying up bundles of straw. Another servant was fastening the block on the scaffold, and one was blowing on a brazier of hot coals with a small bellows. Handles of searing irons stuck up from the brazier.

"Oh God!" Lyly said.

Robin looked at the brazier and turned his head. He could smell the hot coals without seeing them.

"Stubbes and his publisher have a brave audience," he said. "Nobles and gentry beside the apprentices and townsfolk. My lord of Sussex is yonder, and Sir Christopher Hatton for Her Majesty. Master Thomas Knyvet; my lord Henry Howard. There's my lord of Oxford."

"Where?" Lyly said.

"By the steps. With Lord Howard, behind the yeomen. We can come to him with a push."

They wormed between shoulders to the line of guards. Lyly called,

"My lord!" and Oxford glanced around. At his order the guards let them pass.

"Jack," he said. "Robin. What brings you to this?"

"London," Lyly said. "Willy-nilly, like cats in a sack."

"It's a sickly business," Oxford said.

More smocked men came past, bringing jars of vinegar and cold water, basins, cloths, and towels. They took them up to the scaffold. The servant who had been blowing the coals put down his bellows and went off toward the Tower gate. He came back with two cocks, hooded and trussed by the legs, and carried them up the scaffold steps and laid them on the straw. The cocks threshed around and beat their wings a little, and then were still.

The smocked men moved with efficiency. They walked back and forth, making their preparations. The crowd in the square watched. The windows in the houses were crammed with heads.

The men brought two loaves of bread and two pots of wine.

"After blood, drink," Lord Henry Howard said, caustic beside Oxford. "A proof of Her Majesty's grace."

"There's mercy in it," Oxford said shortly.

"Englishmen must curry Fauvel, as the grooms in the old tale, or it's a mercy we'll all come to," Lord Henry said.

Oxford made no reply. His nostrils, his lips, the expressionlessness of his features, seemed to have been cut from marble.

A man in surgeon's gown walked between the files of guards. A pair of men-at-arms walked beside him. He was followed by a surgeon's assistant bearing a long, sharp dressing knife. The men in smocks clumped down from the scaffold, and the surgeon and his group mounted it. One servant stayed by the brazier to keep the coals flaming.

The crowd held itself morbidly still.

There was a stir at the Tower gate, and the procession began. The lord lieutenant of the Tower, master-at-arms, a chaplain, a clerk of Her Majesty's justice, the two criminals shackled in chains and flanked by yeomen of the guard, and a small company of yeomen behind. At the foot of the steps they halted. The lord lieutenant climbed to the scaffold; the chaplain, the clerk, the master-at-arms. The two criminals waited their signal. They were within touching distance of Lyly and Robin Christmas and the group with Oxford.

"Jack!" Lyly said hoarsely.

The nearest man turned slightly. He had a middle-aged, plumpish build, and an affable mouth. His cheeks were clean shaven and he was neatly dressed. His eyes were glazed and unseeing. Beads of sweat hung on his forehead.

"Jack Stubbes!" Lyly said.

A guard pushed at the man with a halberd staff, and he started, and went on up the scaffold steps.

Everything was ready.

In a resonant voice the clerk read the charge and the punishment to the listening, staring crowd. How one John Stubbes and his publisher had written and set in print a slanderous pamphlet attacking Her Majesty's gracious purpose to marry a foreign prince, crying the discovery of a gaping gulf between Her Majesty and the Most Puissant Duc d'Alençon, and boldly and insolently criticizing Her Majesty's just wisdom; how they had been judged guilty of sedition; and how, in penalty, the right hand of each was to be stricken off.

The deep, prolonged soughing repeated itself over the square when he had finished.

"We'll have martyrs next, dragged through the streets on hurdles," Lord Henry said between his teeth. He was looking at Oxford, trying to guess what he was thinking.

Then the shackles were loosened from the first criminal. He was the publisher. The guards led him forward. The chaplain moved beside him, murmuring a prayer. The chains fell from his wrists as the master-at-arms removed them, and fell rattling into the straw. He rubbed his wrists together and lifted his right one a little and stared at it with a dull, incredulous horror. He held it in front of him in a kind of ginger-liness, a stupefaction.

They fastened his wrist to the block with cords. The publisher's eyes closed, and he swayed. He was a wiry, hard-bitten man.

The surgeon took the knife from his assistant and stepped to the block. He bent over, and his arm and shoulders heaved swiftly.

The publisher gave a single piercing scream. The fingers of the hand on the block convulsed, jerked, and straightened out, curving upward.

in a quivering agony. Blood ran from the ends of them, and into the straw.

The publisher screamed a second time, and the hand suddenly went limp. It curved, like the fingers, then sagged, and plopped from the block, down among the blood. Thick red jets shot from the severed wrist, spraying the block and the straw and the surgeon's knife.

The surgeon handed the knife back to his assistant. The servant at the brazier passed him a searing iron, white-hot. The surgeon held it to the wrist. There was a hiss, a steaming, and the smell of scorching flesh. The publisher screamed a third time and his body writhed.

Using the same knife, the surgeon's assistant cut off the head of one of the cocks. He brought it to the surgeon, who discarded the searing iron. He took the cock, held the dripping neck, and clamped it against the wrist stump. The assistant tied it there securely.

A basin was ready, and cloths and towels. The surgeon washed around the stump, wrapped it and the cock in the cloths, and dried his hands on the towels. He stepped back and began to wipe his knife.

They undid the cords on the block, and a guard helped the publisher stagger away. He lurched to a corner of the scaffold and slumped to his knees, his body still writhing and twitching.

Not a sound came from the crowd.

They took John Stubbes next. He had seen it all, and as they bound his hand to the block, the sweat from his forehead was trickling down over his lips. The block was wet with the publisher's blood. Stubbes' hand pulled back spasmodically, and they had to hold it to bind it there.

The surgeon's knife gleamed. He bent.

Stubbes' teeth bit half through his lower lip. He rose up on the balls of his feet, his back a stiffening arc. When the last tendon had been sliced through and the plump, pinkish hand dangled and dropped he snatched off his hat with the other.

"God save the Queen!" he cried in a rasping shout. His eyes rolled to the whites, and he fainted.

The surgeon seared the stump and tied the second cock to it, and the guards brought him to with vinegar and cold water and led him over beside the publisher. The group at the foot of the steps could hear his moans.

"The fool," Lord Henry said. "Why did he shout for the Queen? Why not for vengeance? He might have had this rabble in his palm."

"Then it were better struck off," Oxford said.

"Faugh, read your lesson. England's not safe with this Queen."

"What lesson?" Oxford said abruptly. Lyly was retching with hollow, empty gulps that choked in the throat and brought nothing up. Robin Christmas was the color of lead, and Oxford's eyes had glinting specks in them, like ice. "What lesson, cousin?"

Lord Henry looked at the eyes. "Why," he said, "that this scribbler's truly named. He's Stubbes now, indeed." He passed the jest off lightly, but his own eyes were cruel.

"You've a wry humor," Oxford said.

"These are wry times," Lord Henry said. "They make English mouths pucker. How long will we endure it?"

"As long as England is the Queen's," Oxford said.

"A proper answer," Lord Henry said. "Just so long."

He gave a cold, sharp smile. "Be at my house tonight, Ned, and we'll make the lesson plainer." Tightening his cloak around him, he edged between the line of yeomen and disappeared in the crowd.

The people in the square were breaking up slowly, forming into subdued, whispering knots. Oxford glanced at the scaffold. The servant at the brazier had taken the loaves of bread and the wine to Stubbes and the publisher. The two men fumbled clumsily with their left hands. They broke the bread with their teeth and spilled the wine on their chins.

"Robin," Oxford said.

"My lord?" Robin's voice was a quaver.

"Wait here. When Stubbes comes down, take him in your care."

"Yes, my lord."

"Take him to my sister's house, Lady Mary Willoughby, at the barbican. Tell my sister and her husband I commend Master Stubbes to them, and ask if they can find some honorable employment to put him to. He has behaved well today. He is a worthy man."

"Yes, my lord," Robin said. His look was worshipful.

"Get yourself a mug of comfort on the way. I'll do the same for Jack." He frowned. "This sick business goes against the stomach. Come along."

A half hour later he and Lyly were downing great quaffs of ale in the tavern of the Boar's Head in Eastcheap.

11

LYLY HAD RECOVERED ENOUGH BY THE NEXT DAY TO keep on with Her Majesty's orders: to put laughter into the Queen's court.

He was at work with Oxford the following afternoon, rehearsing a play for the palace. He had a light, facile temperament suited to managing and directing the comedies he wrote, the pieces from Oxford's pen and from the tavern playwrights. He throve on quips and oddities and flowery expressions, and was happy as a May fly at rehearsals—

"Nimbly, nimbly, the clown's lines must go nimbly, Hugh; you croak like a raven. . . . Where are the wheat sheaves for the country scene? Get me sheaves from Master Tilney; and tell the master of the revels we require a device for the mouth of hell; something that gapes and yawns, which pray God Her Majesty won't do. . . . Come in, boy, come in, there's your cue. Lisp us the wife in your high voice. Ah—so. What the pox, my beardless Galatea, don't let it crack!"

The boys who took the women's parts winked among themselves and giggled, the men actors accepted him good-naturedly; his comedies were popular and he was their bread and butter.

Oxford lounged on a stool, putting in a word now and then, and describing the play to the Earl of Sussex, who checked it to see there was no offence in it before it was shown to the Queen. Tom Bedingfield and Fulke Greville dropped by. They and Oxford were friendly again since he had gone back to Anne. Sir Christopher Hatton strolled in, and looked around him with a fishy eye. He did not stay long but went on to his own apartments. *"Monsieur le Duc* will visit soon," he said. "I must ready my duties for him."

Monsieur le Duc would be visiting formally on his second trip to England. He was arriving shortly, confident of Elizabeth and of being England's king. Elizabeth was dubious about parading him in public. She thought it wisest to keep his pock marks and his big nose and gnomelike figure safe in Whitehall away from London's stares; but she wanted entertainments and festivities in the palace, and the court in a diverted mood. She had cut off two hands as a warning that she would have no criticism. Jousts and cock fights, bowls and archery, the plays of Oxford and Master Lyly and the tavern wits were to put a sheen over his coming, a bright glister. Lyly was glad to oblige. He remembered what Robin Christmas had said—he was protected as Oxford's secretary.

He stood in an azure doublet unlaced at the throat, his finger to his chin, and listened critically to a song. "Does it go, my lord?"

"Is it yours?"

Lyly nodded.

"The rhythm falters," Oxford said. He walked over and took the prompt book. "You weight the lines, Jack. Too many apples on the bough."

"It does sound lumpish."

"You can lighten it."

"I've no time. I've the costumes, and the morris dance to be practiced, and my prologue unfinished."

"The scene cries for a song. The Queen fancies them. I'll lend you one of mine."

He picked up a lute from an actor's lap and sang his poem easily, with a half smile. It seemed to have been made for the spot. He put the lute down.

"Copy it tonight," he said. "Hugh can learn it tomorrow."

The actors grinned through their beards.

" 'Fore God, if I had your skill. You write better than ever, my lord," Lyly said.

"Flattery, Jack."

"No, faith. You write like a man in love."

It was true. Oxford was in love. It was as though his marriage had swept back to the day when he was twenty-one, young and lusty and with his passions fresh and keen. The old exuberance flamed in him, the creativeness and the quick inventive spark. He hardly seemed to have crossed thirty. He was like the Oxford of nine years before. He poked fun at Sir Christopher Hatton and the foibles of the court. He danced with the Queen and tossed impudent jests. Raleigh returned from Ireland with a plan of campaign to meet the Spanish threat there, and argued it so well in the Privy Council that the Queen promoted him to higher favor and nicknamed him Water. Hatton, in a fright, sent the Queen a miniature bucket to plead that he would not be drowned out. She sent him back a dove—"that, together with the rainbow, brought the good tidings and the covenant that there should be no more destruction by water." Oxford slipped jibes at Raleigh into the plays.

He was in the audience chamber when the new Countess of Leicester flaunted herself in a dress more magnificent than the Queen's. The Queen rebuked her, but the countess went on appearing at court like an empress, in displays that outdid the royal wardrobe. Elizabeth, stung to a fury, boxed her ears. "As but one sun shines in the sky, so there is but one in the court, and that is the Queen," Elizabeth cried. The countess, in revenge, went about London in a great coach pulled by four milk-white horses, with footmen in black velvet.

"She is an insolent wench!" Elizabeth said.

"Order a coach for each of your ladies of the chamber, my liege," Oxford said. "Fourteen of them will silence her."

Elizabeth stared at him bitterly, then broke into mirth. He was versatile and imaginative and clever, and never greater in the Queen's esteem.

Anne, however, felt he was troubled. She could feel it in his kisses, and in the gaps of their talk when he lay beside her after his lovemaking. She did not think it was any lack in her. She gave herself to him readily, and their unions were full and complete. He spent as much time with their daughter as his writings for the court plays and the bustle over Alençon's visit allowed him. His plays were given a final rehearsal at the public theaters, with the courtier gallants sitting on the stage and chatting and cracking nuts, and the blue flag for comedy flying from the roof. They kept him busy and often away from Vere House. But her own troubles had made Anne more alert to the problems that might be on his mind, though not more able to help solve them; and she suspected he was worrying.

She spoke to her mother about it. "Edward does not sleep well at night," she said. "Something is wrong."

"A mistress, no doubt," Lady Burghley said. "I've been expecting it."

"Oh no, Mother. I'm certain of that."

"How are you certain? It's not for nothing some parts of a man are called secret. You can't prove by the spigot that the barrel has been tapped."

"Edward has no reason for a mistress, now," Anne said, blushing.

"Oh, reason," her mother said. "Hold men to reason and they run mad."

"But Mother—"

"And so will you. Well, find out who she is and your father will go with it to the Queen. We'll have satisfaction."

"I know there's no one, Mother."

"You're an obstinate child."

"I pray you—I would not be obstinate to you in anything. It's not a woman that's bothering Edward. It's a kind of—perplexity."

"Obstinate and giddy both. I've been married longer than you, Anne. There are only two things fret a man's sleep at night, a woman or politics."

"Perhaps in my father's case," Anne said, with a flash of spirit.

"Mind your sauciness. One man is like another as a pair of peas. Know one, you know them all—generally to your sorrow. I say there are two things fret their sleep."

She resumed her reading of a dinner list Lord Burghley's steward had left with her: bishops, earls, knights, privy councilors friendly to his lordship, and members of foreign embassies; an affair of State being readied for the French duke at Her Majesty's command, to further the exactions Her Majesty was making that on the surface at least everything must be harmony.

"Yes, Mother," Anne said.

"With your father, of course, it was politics," Lady Burghley said, and ticked off an ambassador's name starchily.

Anne was convinced it must be politics with Edward. The notion disturbed her. He had never meddled in politics; he had had too much of them as a boy at Cecil House, and in his conflicts with Lord Burghley, his debts, the lawsuit against his legitimacy and the slanders on his family life he had taken refuge inside himself. His futile efforts to serve as a soldier or in some office for the Queen had made him indifferent to state matters and resentful of the whole political breed. He seemed like a man living only for his own pleasures and enjoyments, content to be an ornament, a dancing partner, a privileged jester, and nothing more.

But now there was surely something. Anne felt his change of manner.

Once, during an evening at the palace, she found him talking to the Earl of Sussex. They interrupted their talk as she joined them, but she caught the drift of what they were saying. They were speaking of Spain. At Vere House Edward was having visits after dark from John Stubbes, his handless stump wrapped in a scarf, and coming from Lord Willoughby's. Lord Willoughby was Edward's brother-in-law, one of England's bravest fighters, a man with a meek face, a small mustache and the spirit of a lion, who had distinguished himself in the Low Country campaigns and come home to tame Lady Mary Vere for a wife; Anne wished she could have tamed Edward for a husband as thoroughly. Edward and Stubbes would be closeted for an hour. Then Stubbes would leave, and Edward would be a long time coming to bed.

A presentiment of dread began to grow in Anne. She tried to get him to confide in her, but he only smiled and kissed her.

"These things aren't for your ears," he said.

"Whose, then? The Queen's?"

"Anne, sweet, keep innocent of such things."

His evasion irritated her more. "You mustn't go to the Queen," she said. "You mustn't."

"Why not?"

"My father says you must never approach her unless she's ready to hear you. I don't know what this is about, but don't take it to her."

"Will you trust my judgment, Anne, or your father's?" he said.

She made a petulant gesture. "But he understands her, Edward. She will surely be angry. Don't go to her. We're happy as we are."

"She won't be angry with the truth," he said. "There's rottenness all around her."

"Then it is politics," she said. "Some kind of plot or intrigue. Edward, don't mix into that! Even poetry would be better!" She pouted and began to cry.

He put his lips to her forehead. "Politics is in the air," he said.

It was in the air like pollen in autumn. The winds were blowing shrewder, and the germs of events were seeding themselves. That same month Lord Burghley and Sir Francis Walsingham consulted in his lordship's chambers at Cecil House.

"If she holds him off another year we lose our advantage," Walsingham said. "Yet I think she means to do it."

"Will Alençon wait another year?" Burghley asked.

"As long as she sends him money. This Frenchman is a bottomless pit and Simier is his funnel. Between them they bankrupt us."

"Between them they will stand buffer against Spain," Burghley said. "You've read the reports from Portugal?"

"I have."

Philip of Spain had begun to tighten the screws. He had absorbed Portugal for himself at last, and in a single stroke added her ports and shipping to his power. The two councilors who best knew England's weaknesses looked at each other across Lord Burghley's somber table.

"How long?" Burghley said.

"He has his foothold over the Channel. He needs only an invading fleet."

Burghley stroked at his beard. Behind his bland, broad, impassive face his mind was fluent and rapid. "He will delay until Her Majesty gives him a cause. The King of Spain wants to be clear in the world's eyes. We must try to avoid rousing him. What have you from Plymouth?"

"What you know, my lord." Walsingham met impassivity with coldness.

"Has Her Majesty seen Captain Drake?"

"Not since."

Burghley's gaze rested steadily on the master secretary. Captain Drake's homecoming at this moment was unfortunate for English diplomacy. His ship was at Plymouth Hoe after sailing around the world, flushed with triumph and weighted down with Spanish loot. Those who had shares in his venture were eyeing the loot. Leicester and Hatton and powerful London merchants were among them. Walsingham was one. Burghley wanted the loot returned to Spain for the sake of peace. In the palace the Queen was trying to decide. There had been a stormy scene in the council.

"He has scoured the circle of his wake on the seven seas and left the Spaniards biting their cheeks for rage," Burghley said. "But what good to sail around the world if Spain takes the world?"

"Her Majesty could use the money," Walsingham said. "She would be rich from her share in the venture."

"To build protection against Spain with pirated Spanish doubloons would be a shrewd stroke. But Philip could strike a shrewder one," Burghley said. He sighed. "It is a hard service I work at for Her Majesty. Well well, she will answer at her pleasure."

"Do you flatter yourself Philip will be turned aside by soft words?" Walsingham said sternly. "Or the Spanish party in England? They are still plotting to put Mary on the throne."

"You have evidence?"

"Every day. Clumsy, crude machinations, but bad for Her Majesty's safety. Mary of Scotland is an endless conspirator. She plots like a maid in a romance—notes in the heels of shoes, in beer mugs, in packets of clothing. Schemes and layings of plans. She writes them constantly, and my agents pick them up. I have enough evidence to send her to the block if Her Majesty were not so tenderhearted."

"We will send her all the same," Burghley said. On this subject the two men saw eye to eye. "We are to have another push from her soon?"

"Very soon, I think. I've not uncovered the whole affair. Each one becomes more desperate and more dangerous. I get hints of assassination. Though as usual I suppose Her Majesty will do nothing."

"With every argument I can muster," Burghley said, "I still cannot persuade her to believe them or to take measure to protect her life. She does not wish them brought into the open."

"Particularly now," Walsingham said.

"Particularly now," Burghley said. "She is delicately involved with Alençon and France, and wants everything smooth. No plots or threats against her to frighten off a wooer. Say nothing to her, Sir Francis."

"Not I," Walsingham said.

"And keep me informed. We will let this new push lie quiet, and nip it in secret."

"That was my thought, my lord."

"And as for Captain Drake—"

"Her Majesty will keep us both informed," Walsingham said with a taciturn smile.

Burghley smiled, too. He held no rancor toward Walsingham. They worked together. They knew their Queen and their politics.

Lord Henry Howard also knew his politics. In the past few years he had drawn Oxford closer and closer to him. He had managed expertly to break Oxford from the Cecils, and driven the wedge between him and Anne. He had helped Oxford put on his cloak of folly and had encouraged his cynical barbs and his mocking of the court. It was a subtle process, craftily done, a slow disintegration carried on behind the masquerade of friendship. With every hurt to Oxford's pride, with every rebuff to his nature, Lord Henry had been at his elbow, pricking the wound a little deeper and offering consolements. He had followed his purpose like a tracking ferret. He would bring Oxford into the Howard camp and add him to the Queen's enemies.

When the Queen cut off the two hands for seditious writings he watched Oxford's face at the scaffold and felt he was ready. The time was ripe. "England isn't safe with such a Queen. Come to my house tonight if you'd learn more," he said.

Before the year was over Oxford learned. The mask came off at last. Lord Henry belonged to the Spanish party. So did Arundel and Southwell, the friends who had drunk with Oxford and slapped him on the shoulder and called him Ned. They wanted to be rid of Elizabeth. They would do it by any means, fair or foul, and set Philip of Spain on the throne. They expected Oxford to join them.

The reckonings of a stupid man are blatant and seldom fatal. A cunning man often over-reaches himself. Lord Henry had made the mistake of a cunning man. He judged Oxford by his own character. He had not made allowance for the loyalty and the hatred of treachery and scheming in his cousin's nature. It was the sort of mistake that is made only once.

Oxford could not sleep. The discovery jolted him like being jerked from a nightmare. His mind was staggered by Lord Henry's plans. Oxford's father, and his father before him, sixteen generations of De Veres had guarded the rulers of England with their lives and honor. Staring into the dark by Anne, listening to the night sounds of London and watching the stars wheel slowly across the window, he knew it was his duty to do the same.

The Queen must be told. But when? And how? And in what way? The court was full of spies. Whatever he said to her would be reported within an hour to the Spanish agents. The Queen had always had a scorn for cowardice and never thought of her personal safety. She would have to be convinced of her danger before she would listen. If he accused them in secret the Queen would only laugh and paddle her fingers on his cheek and thank him for his well-wishes.

He talked to Lord Willoughby and to the Earl of Sussex.

"We'll stand with you," Lord Willoughby said. "Her Majesty's soldiers want her rid of these vermin."

Sussex thought Burghley should handle it. "Let him tell the Queen," he said. "He swims better in murky water than you do, Edward."

"He swims too slowly," Oxford said. "The Queen is threatened."

Sussex regarded him with grave sympathy, not altogether displeased. "Take your own counsel," he said.

As Oxford began to question into Lord Henry's dealings, the whole story of his cousin's venom came to light. He knew at last that it was Lord Henry Howard who had tried to break his marriage. John Stubbes brought some of the story from the taverns, gathered from Lord Henry's servants. Oxford pieced some from his own suspicions. He had never talked of the scandal about Anne before; now he set to tracing the old rumors with a deliberate care. When he found they led to Lord Henry he was white to the lips.

"God's blessing!" he cried. "The Howards are the greatest villains on the earth!"

He twisted on his pillow until dawn, and even in his sleep Anne could hear him cursing between his teeth.

For a month or more he kept sternly to himself.

Then one day he broke in on Lyly at the rooms in the Savoy, and flung down a manuscript on the table.

"Get armor," he said, "and foils, and men who can act blood and anger. Here's your play for the Queen's Christmas."

"With the time so short, my lord?"

"Here's your play," he ordered.

They gave it before the entire court, in the pomp and splendor that collected around Elizabeth at the Christmas season like flies around honey; the Queen watching from her chair, circled by her maids of honor and her nobles, and Oxford watching the Queen.

It was a play taken from English history. Only a bold man secure in high position would have dared to show it. Its theme was the Wars of the Roses, wars not yet forgotten by the great nobles whose families had fought and hacked in them. It told the consequences of too much leniency, of blindness and refusal to face the facts of enemies in the royal household; it told of intrigues and uprising and armed rebellion, and a ruler dragged from his throne, and a king's murder. The history was so near to Elizabeth's day that the lesson was grisly plain. Elizabeth sat through the performance with a marble face, and left immediately afterward.

Ten minutes later Oxford was on his knees before her in her private chambers. Her face was not marble any longer, but twitching and contorted with anger. Her yellow eyes bored like gimlets.

"What is this, my lord?" she cried. "What is this?"

"Truth, Your Majesty."

"Body of Christ, what sort of truth? Every man-jack in the court can read me in it. The very lines clamor 'Elizabeth'! What's behind it, Oxford?"

"The truth of clear speaking." Oxford's eyes never flinched from hers. They were hard as her own, cold and daring.

"There is a time for speaking and a time for silence. God's my life, to take presumption on yourself and lecture me!"

"The play was only as it happened, my liege."

"Don't chew logic. The gall still tastes. What happened once can happen again. I'm not a fool."

"No, my liege. Nor I a traitor."

"Hah, a warning, then. Screaming at me like the bell of doom. Like the soothsayer at Caesar. Marry, I'll do better than Caesar. I'll probe. I'll get to the bottom of this. Where are the traitors?"

Oxford blanched. He had expected more subtlety from the Queen. He had hoped she would read the message in the play and reflect on it coolly before she acted. He had not intended to touch off a powder keg. He saw too late that Willoughby and Sussex had been right.

"Where are they?" she demanded.

"So near your Majesty could reach her hand and touch them."

"Who?"

"Men under Your Majesty's own roof," he said. "Here at court."

"Men! Men! Bones of mercy, would they be mice? Name them."

"Friends of Spain."

"Who?"

Danger gritted in her voice. The gimlet eyes were merciless.

He drew a breath. If it was to be this way, it must. At all hazard the Queen must be put on guard.

"Lord Henry Howard," he said. "Arundel. Southwell."

"Send for them," she ordered.

A page scurried off. Presently the three were brought in.

They knelt to her, and rose, and ranged themselves opposite Oxford to a tart wave of her hand. She wasted no time on preliminaries. "You have heard this play tonight," she said.

"We have, my liege," Lord Henry said. He bowed devotedly. The others followed him.

"A play of rebellion. Its point was manifest. I would know if you saw in it any meaning of yourselves."

They glanced at each other. "No, my liege."

"You are accused of being friends to Spain," she said bluntly.

A faint tremor darkened Lord Henry's face. "By whom, my liege?"

"My lord of Oxford."

Lord Henry looked at him. "It is a lie," he said.

Elizabeth broke in before Oxford could answer. She peered sharply. "You have been near companions, my lord."

"All the more cruel to be denounced by him," Lord Henry said. His voice held an infinite sorrow, nicely balanced with a hint of martyrdom, and subserviently respectful. "Your Most Gracious Majesty knows I am not friend to Spain. I have been foremost in commending your French marriage."

She nodded. She was well aware of that. The supporters of the French marriage were sure of her good graces.

"He commends it for a purpose," Oxford said hotly, "to cover his twists and turns. He's had dealings with Spanish agents."

"I deny it," Lord Henry retorted.

"So?" she said. "Well, Oxford?"

"Denial is a cheap word," he said.

"I am being set upon," Lord Henry said, "because I am not of Your Majesty's church."

"Tush, I know your church, too. Half our nobles are disciples of Rome. All religion comes of God. But do not put Spain above England."

"Never, my liege."

"Can you answer that charge?"

"I say it is false."

"Will he say it is false that he sent a man to the French ambassador to be smuggled out of England?" Oxford said. "The man was one of King Philip's kind. Lord Henry Howard hoodwinked the ambassador as he hoodwinks Your Majesty."

"The French ambassador, you said?" Elizabeth's questions came like gunfire.

"De Castelnau," Oxford said.

"You smile, Lord Harry," Elizabeth said.

"There's a dagger under his smile," Oxford said.

"Send for de Castelnau," said Elizabeth.

She sat without speaking while they waited, slowly revolving a great ring on her thumb. It had been brought her by Captain Drake as a gift, to placate her for the treasure stolen from Spanish ships. She was angry with Captain Drake that he had thrust his barnacled *Pelican* into the cross-currents between England and Europe. She was angry with Oxford for hauling his accusations into the open court and forcing her to take notice of them. She was not ready to do that. She was not ready to do it in front of France, or in front of Spain. God's life, what worth was a Queen when anyone in her kingdom could push a stick between the legs of her policies and trip her up? She stopped revolving the ring and sat staring petulantly.

The French ambassador was ushered in. Monsieur Mauvissière de Castelnau was ceremonious, urbane, and wary. He was a little annoyed as well, for he had been winning handsomely from Sir Christopher Hatton at the cards when the Queen's page had plucked his elbow and interrupted his game of primero. He entered with a Gallic conciseness.

"We have some madmen here, *Monsieur,*" Elizabeth said, when he had kissed her hand. "I think they be madmen, but I mean to find out. There are certainly plots being hatched, with their roots abroad. If they flower here, they will be cropped. Do you know of a foreign fellow sent you by my Lord Howard?"

De Castelnau was more annoyed. He wanted no part of plots, and his instinct was for self-protection. "Why, no, Your Excellent Majesty."

"No such fellow?"

"None, Your Majesty."

Lord Henry's smile drifted lingeringly over his lips.

Elizabeth turned on Oxford. "Where is the madness now?" she snapped. "You put me in mockery, my lord."

The four men turned with her. De Castelnau was between Oxford and Howard, the others a little behind. Oxford saw them, cold and calculating. Arundel's face wore a sneer. Southwell's was like a fox crouched to its belly in a covert. He saw he was alone, deserted by de Castelnau and answerless to the Queen. He threw himself on his knees.

"Swear him to it, Your Majesty. Swear him on his oath. He knows it's true."

"You still say so, Oxford?"

"By my father's honor. By my earldom."

Elizabeth seemed shaken. "God's life, I've loved you," she said.

"Ask him again, and hear it from him. Let him speak true."

She bent toward de Castelnau. The look of age she had been fighting off beat gauntly through the wrinkles of her neck and the tense web of crow's feet around her eyes. She spoke earnestly. "I beg you to tell me the facts, *Monsieur*. Not to injure these men, but to satisfy me. I wish to learn the truth."

De Castelnau raised his shoulders in a voluble shrug that said he would tell her if he could. "I have no knowledge of the business, Your Majesty. None at all. I have never even heard it talked about."

"Hah." Elizabeth sat back. Her face stiffened, and she drummed on her chair arm.

"I can remind you," Oxford said. He rose to one knee, the scarlet silk of his hose pulling taut across the other as he wrenched around to de Castelnau. "Did I or did I not, *Monsieur,* stand beside you when Lord Howard thanked you for getting his man safe away? You talked about the business then, and I was there. This is vital to me, *Monsieur*. God's blessing, come to my help."

"The incident is not in my memory," de Castelnau said.

"Oh God," Oxford said. He stayed on his knee, stunned.

The effect worked gradually on Elizabeth, like the creep of snow clouds over a winter sky. It was more terrible because of its slowness, because of the gray, sleety calm she maintained before the servant of the Medici.

"Well well," she said, "make an end to it. Things shall keep as they are. But we will sift further in this. My lords and gentlemen, you have my leave to go."

They answered in silence. Oxford rose. Lord Howard stepped coolly past him, advancing toward the Queen. "My liege, the Howards are your dutiful subjects. You have proclaimed a tournament next month to celebrate my kinsman Philip Howard's new earldom. My kinsman will ride in the tournament as a challenger, and prove his name."

"Well thought," said Elizabeth, who was always intrigued by such notions. "Tell the earl we are pleased he will challenge. Who are the defenders?"

"I do not know, my liege." He bowed and retreated suavely, slanting a hostile look at Oxford from the corner of his eye.

Oxford's voice knifed out at him. "I will be one."

Oxford sat his horse at the entrance to the tiltyard, cased in armor and listening to the roar of the crowd. His spear butt rested on his stirrup, his fingers flexed in the steel gauntlets, testing the grip and gathering the bridle reins for the constable's signal. His breath steamed curling from the grill of his helmet in the frosty morning, and his motto floated on the pennon over his head—*Vero Nihil Verius*. It was time for truth.

He frowned across the lists, to the mailed figure of Philip Howard at the opposite gate. He had not ridden a tournament since he had won his first prize ten years ago. The Howards thought him soft. They were waiting to see him beaten in public as they had beaten and humiliated him before the Queen. But they misjudged him. They had not troubled to look deeper than the follies and lightheadedness he put on for outward show. He had kept in practice.

He measured the course he would gallop, and spanned in his mind the difference between this tournament and that other. He had been green then, unfleshed in the world and brave with confidence. He had trusted to truth, and to the best that was in men. He had failed. Truth had crumbled and men turned hollow, and he had gone down in slander and disillusion.

He would not fail now. He had learned he must fight for truth with a courage from inside himself stronger than mere bravery, and that in the world of men he must take life by the throat. Well, he would take it. This time there was no airy vision, no boy's dream, but urgency and reality and the hard consciousness of his own vigorous powers. This time he would build secure. He bent and pretended to fix the bucklings of the girth. His heart was hammering.

In the audience gallery Anne watched anxiously. She could still not shake off the presentiment of dread. She knew that Edward had accused Lord Henry and Arundel and Southwell, that the Queen was provoked at the accusations, and that her father Lord Burghley thought Edward foolhardy and rash. The whole court knew it. This tournament was more than the spectacle and the cheers and the clanging shields. It was Edward's battle to establish his sincerity and gain a right opinion of himself. How magnificent he looked, trotting his horse through the gate and breaking into a canter, wearing his armor as lightly as a coat of satin. And what a shouting the people sent up for him. His comedies in the theaters had made them laugh, and his gallantry had caught their spirits. He was a great favorite.

Nan Vavasour, sitting behind Anne, whispered in her ear—"Do you think my lord of Oxford will win?"

"Oh, he must," Anne said. "He must."

"Marry, you seem afraid he won't." Nan's voice was spiced with a tiny malice.

"But he must," Anne said.

"I think Edward will win," Nan said.

"Edward?"

"I'm sure he'll win. But then I'm not his wife. Perhaps a wife can never be sure of a man like Edward." She gave a little laugh.

Color swept into Anne's face and drained out again, leaving it gray as glass. She turned the back of her head to the Vavasour girl with an angry fillip, as the trumpets began sounding for the charge.

The two horses thundered across the lists. The galleries rose. The two riders bent low in the saddle, swinging their shields to cover their bodies and crouching their helmets against the shield tops. They guided their horses with their knees and dropped their lance points in front of them.

They met in a cloud of dust and crash of splintering wood. Both horses were thrown to their haunches, and their hoofs cast out great clods of earth. Oxford forced his mount to its feet with voice and knees. Philip Howard did the same. Each rider was flourishing the broken butt of a lance, and a long jagged scar ran across the shield of each.

"Fairly broken! Fairly broken!" The cheers went up.

Each pair was to ride two courses. Oxford took a new lance and a fresh shield. The old shield showed signs that it might split. He had his squire tighten the girth. He looked across the lists to the figure of Lord Henry Howard, standing beside Arundel at the challenger's pavilion, and settled himself deeper in his saddle.

He heard the yells from the benches—"Oxford! Oxford!" He smiled to himself. He had come far from that first tournament when he was the Red Knight. He had not failed then. He would not fail now.

The trumpets sounded and they lunged forward again. This time Philip Howard's grip on his lance was unsteady. He tried to follow the agile, deceptive swervings of Oxford's course, and missed his target entirely. Oxford's spear went true. He charged with a desperate energy, eyes and nerves under perfect control. He drove Howard's body backward, inert over the high frame of the saddle, like a sickle cutting grain, and reined up at the far barrier untouched.

He rode back past Her Majesty's gallery to the whooping up from the benches and a shower of gloves and scarves and trinkets from the court ladies, and Lord Henry Howard spoke bitingly to Arundel. "He'll have the prize. The day's as good as his."

"Aye, my lord."

"We need better devices to keep him muffled. Where are your notebooks, Charles?"

"At my house, my lord."

"Bring them to me tomorrow."

The triumph collapsed in Oxford's hand. In the notebooks were all the wild talk, all the fantastic stories over the wine cups, all the jibes and the impudences and the tongue-in-the-cheek railleries that Lord Henry had prompted out of him. Arundel had scrupulously copied them down. . . . How the cobblers' wives of Milan were dressed richer on working days than the Queen at Christmas—that was from the bull-baiting; how a Genoa merchant boasted a chimney piece worth more than all the treasure of the throne; how the Queen had the worst voice for singing that ever woman had. ... The notebooks were sharper than a spear.

Lord Henry aimed them diabolically.

Within two months Oxford was in the Tower.

THE SUN, RISING OUT OF THAMES MIST, STRUCK THE gables of the houses on London Bridge. It coated the roofs and many-paned windows with topaz, and shone on the gilded signs of shops and alehouses. It whitened the turrets of London Tower and leveled slowly downward over the tracery of March rime on the damp walls. Its light cut blunt saw-toothed shadows along the battlements and the gloomy crenelations, in the squinting crossbow slits, the furrowed moat and the yawning arch of the water gate. The shape of the Tower's vast and stony antiquity loomed slowly into the daybreak, and with a clatter of halberds and a jingle of steel the Tower shivered and woke.

Oxford woke with it.

He was stiff from his night's fretting on a hard straw pallet. The little fire of coals in the chimney had gone out, and his coverlet was thin. He threw off the coverlet and stood up in his shirt and hose. At the outer wall of the room a stone coping was built over a hole in the floor for necessary purposes. He used it and came back to the center of the room, rubbing himself for warmth. A table stood in one corner, with a basin and a ewer of water. He poured the water into the basin and doused his face, bracing at the hurt to his sleepless eyeballs, and drying on a rough napkin.

He put on his boots and doublet and went over to the window. Square-set iron bars checkered the daylight that fell through across his head and shoulders.

He rested his elbows on the masonry and looked out. The dark, thick sides of the window were built at angles in the walls. They narrowed at the outside and shut off his view, but he could see enough. There were the chimneys of Eastcheap, and the flat span of the Bridge, like a crowded rabbit warren over the dawn-tinted opal of the river. There was the open space on Tower Hill, the trampled earth deserted and the scaffold silent in the middle as if cockcrow had caught it lurching across the hill among its ghosts and transfixed it there. There was a segment of sky, and a glimpse of an angle of the Bloody Tower, and the gate where the condemned were marched to execution.

Jackdaws twittered around their nesting-places among the lintels and the shelving crevices, and from below came the thudding of a mattock at work on the kitchen gardens in the moat. Beneath the level of the moat, hidden under the cold slab floors and ponderous Norman pillars of the Tower, were the donjons and question rooms and the instruments of torture; thumbscrew and rack, iron boot and knout and chain, and windlasses to spread-eagle agonized groins or pull arms from their sockets. A dank, rancid seep of staleness and putrefaction permeated everything.

Oxford stared a long time. He crossed his legs and put his shoulder against the window corner, running his hand back and forth over his empty dagger sheath. This was the Tower. The words drummed into his mind, and the gloomy walls and great hewn stones flung it back at him. He, Oxford, born to freedom and the open air, to wit and humor and lightness and unfettered life, in the Tower. What had brought him to this? Loyalty and speaking truth. He had tried to warn the Queen. He had tried to be honest. He had returned to Anne in love and good conscience. He had thrown off the disgruntled years and started over, fighting a new fight to hew to the lines around him. And how had he been repaid? With the Tower.

His ear caught the commands of the changing of the guard beneath his window. They carried to him hollowly from the paved courtyard, like voices from a tomb.

He shifted away from the window corner. The chill bit through his cloak and brought a colder reason to his logic. Pride and feelings aside, he could not deny that he was there by his own doing. He had known the chance he ran. He had made his choice, balancing the consequences against his duty.

Duty. It was a word he had read in books and heard from his father's lips—"An earl of England is not his own master," his father had said once. But the stones around him now gave it a rugged solidity. In the gaunt mass of the Tower he could see the symbol of a concept and a form over and beyond himself. Its walls were mute testimony that the weight of duty lay on everyone, on the guards in the courtyard and on the Queen in her palace. The guards' duty was to keep authority. The Queen's duty was to keep peaceable relations with Spain. Though they meant prison for a loyal subject she was bound to hold to them.

He took his hand from his dagger sheath with a frown and stared at the sunlight sloping down the outer walls. He had never much considered duty or politics. Here they were sudden bedfellows with him. The Tower, the barred view across river and city, the echo of voices in the courtyard, began to evolve a new pattern in his mind. Politics, to a queen who must bolster the law, was not for one man but for all; not for the Earl of Oxford alone but for the guards as well who marched stolidly down below. The irony was that he had had to be thrust into a Tower cell to see it.

The thought of Spain and England reminded him of the Spanish pikemen he had watched in the Low Countries. They, too, had their sovereign, their politics, their concepts. They had marched as the guards below him marched. But it had seemed to him they marched in a brute fashion, with scant idea of why or wherefore, little knowledge of causes or the shape of history. He wondered if the courtyard guards marched in the same ignorance. He remembered Lord Henry Howard's simile of the Spanish bull and the English mastiff; Lord Henry had said the bull would generally win. Lord Henry had spoken what he hoped. But did the guards, as Englishmen, have a deeper knowledge of causes, of duty and politics and history? They could not all be thrust into the Tower to learn it. They would not all learn if they were.

His hand moved along the window stones.

The Tower itself was history. The place had seen kings and felons die. In the Tower the two young princes had been murdered by Richard Third. The Duke of Clarence had been drowned in a butt of wine. The Queen's mother, Anne Boleyn, had spent her last night here. So had his own cousin, Norfolk. The damp that filtered from the donjons cried their thoughts, their sufferings and fears and pangs, the good in them and the ill, and the final scores they had reckoned of their souls in the racing minutes when the east began to pale. What senses, what searching, what cowardice or strength, what clarity of mortal vision in that ultimate instant had taken them all? The pure and the evil, the innocent and the guilty, men and women, craven or stout of heart.

He turned from the window impatiently. Even in the Tower he could not keep his fancies still. Bury his imagination in catacombs, it would riot with what it found there. He should have been thinking of himself, and he was thinking the thoughts a dead duke or a living man-at-arms might think. God's blessing, a bitter foolishness.

He strode across the room at a knock on the door. A jailer came in, bringing breakfast—bread and eggs and a flagon of claret. The jailer laid the breakfast on the table, and took a bag of coals and lit a fire.

"Good morrow, friend," Oxford said.

"Good morrow, my lord." His hands were cracked and gnarled among the coals.

"Is it 'my lord' yet?" Oxford asked wryly.

"Aye, my lord."

"It seems the title would be a little tarnished."

"Oh no, my lord. We're proper here. They're all rightful worships with us until they go." He had a warty face, stubbed with reddish bristles that stood out on his cheeks as he puffed at the fire.

"How long before they go?" Oxford said.

"Well, now, my lord, that's either one way or other. You can lay you there's no hard rule. I've known some poor noble wights, nor some not so noble neither, didn't go for years. Sometimes there's a trial, and your trial is a woeful dragger-on. Sometimes there's an order comes, and they go—'zick'—like that." He lifted a finger and made a slicing motion across his throat. "Yet not so many latterly. We don't get so many of those latterly. But the times are worsening."

"You look for more."

"What a man looks or don't look makes no account in the Tower, sir. But I put you this. You've got your Puritans. And where you haven't got your Puritans you've got your English Churchers. And where you haven't got your English Churchers you've got your Genevists. And where you haven't got your Genevists you've got your Romists. All very godly, my lord, and godliness is a great breeder of divisions and neck cuttings. And you've got your rebellions and your fornication. Cold plots and hot beds. The Queen hates 'em both. But they're too many for her. So I say there'll be a worsening." He got up and rubbed his palms on his smock, going toward the door.

"You know a great deal, friend," Oxford said.

"Aye, my lord."

"Do you know the Queen's orders for me?"

"No, my lord." The jailer's bristled face was uncommunicative. He went out, bolting the door.

Oxford sat down on the stool. He broke a piece of the bread, crumbled it in his fingers, and tasted it mechanically. He put it back on the platter unfinished. In the palace the Queen would be breakfasting now. She would be nibbling at an egg and sipping wine, and railing at him and calling him bastard. She always called him that when she was in a fury with him. She seized on the old claim that he was illegitimate and flung it at him like a lash. Bastard. The sting had burned all his life. Why had he been born with insights sharper than other men, with moods and sensitivities that drove him like a Wild Hunt?

"Oh God," he said aloud, "why wasn't I born a smug merchant, with nothing to my mind but bales and counters? It would be a happier lot."

He walked to the window once more. The court would be stirring. Eliza Trentham would be with the Queen—what made him think of her; her smile and her constant faith in him? Fulke Greville would be headed for tennis and Hatton for his morning's fawning on Her Majesty. At the Savoy Jack Lyly would be in bed, and at Signor Bonetti's Tom Knyvet and the more active courtiers would be lining for their dueling lessons from the Italian fencing master: *roversi! falso manco! imbroccata!* The latest modes in sword phrases. He could hear them. At Vere House Anne would be weeping.

The door creaked, and he faced around. It was Sir Owen Hopton, lord lieutenant of the Tower. Behind him were Lord Willoughby and the Earl of Sussex.

Sir Owen bowed. "My lord."

"Is it time for the mummery?" Oxford said.

"Not mummery, my lord," Sir Owen said.

"My sentence, then," Oxford said. He looked at the others. "What news?"

"Can't you judge, my lord?" Sussex said.

"No man can judge good news or bad by its knock on the door," Oxford said.

"Her Majesty releases you," Sussex said. "Her fit of temper is past.

But you must keep to your house until she gives you leave to come to court."

Oxford seemed to expand. His head went up. "And Lord Henry? And Arundel?"

"Under house arrest, as you are. Confined in the homes of gentlemen Her Majesty has named."

"As I am! God's blessing, are we treated equal? Am I made of a rank with knaves and liars?"

"Her Majesty promises to investigate," Sussex said. "You will have justice."

And Lord Willoughby said, "The Queen will believe you, Ned."

"I'll have justice or I'll trumpet it to heaven!" Oxford said. "Where is freedom in a state that makes no account between honorable men and villains!"

"Where honorable men set limits on their freedom out of respect to others," Sussex answered him. "Freedom is not libertine, my lord, either in tyranny or license. You might have wrecked our policies, and Her Majesty was obliged to punish you."

"Then I trust King Philip hears I slept in the Tower," Oxford said. "It may pacify him."

He fastened his cloak and started for the door, but Sir Owen stopped him with another bow. "Your fee, my lord."

"What?"

"Your shirt. Your lordship will remember prisoners in the Tower pay the lieutenant a shirt when they come to quit it."

"Condemned prisoners," Oxford said. "I'm not one, Sir Owen."

"You are a prisoner, my lord. It is custom."

"Plague on custom! Take the shirts of traitors and criminals. I'm none of those. I know my law. I know the ins and outs. There's no guilt judged against me. No shirt from my back, Sir Owen."

"I stand on my rights," Sir Owen said stubbornly.

"And I on mine."

"I am sorry, my lord. Then you cannot pass the gate."

"God's blessing, I can and will! You'll not hang this reproach on me. My lord of Sussex is a privy councilor. I appeal to the council."

"The argument may be allowable," Sussex said, as Sir Owen looked at him. "But it will take a special order."

"Then fetch it, my lords. I'll wait." Oxford unfastened his cloak and sat down doggedly on the stool.

Three hours later Sussex and Willoughby were back with the council's verdict. Lord Oxford could keep his shirt. He thanked them, and bowed to Sir Owen, and walked out of the door.

"By faith, my lord of Oxford is a violent nettle," Sir Owen muttered to Sussex as they followed him down the flight of circling stairs. "Another man would have been meeker after a night in the Tower."

Sussex shook his head with a grave sigh. "But he is not like other men, Sir Owen."

The Queen nursed her displeasure. Oxford was out of the Tower, but she kept him from the court and the theaters and let him chafe in Vere House. It was her punishment for her favorites, to curtail their privileges; and when they had suffered enough she relented. She had already taken Leicester back. Master Sidney would be next; they said he had written a novel for his sister the Countess of Pembroke while he was in the country, and Elizabeth was curious to see it, she liked the sound of its title, *Arcadia*. But Oxford must do penitence.

"We'll cool the Boar off for a space, eh?" she said confidingly to Hatton.

"The cooler the Boar the warmer the Sheep," Hatton said, delighted.

"Fie, you make pretty speeches," Elizabeth said, bridling and striking at him playfully with her fan.

"On honor, no. The speeches come from my heart," Hatton said.

"It's a dear Sheep. It's a dear heart," Elizabeth said. "We'll say no more of the Boar, and you can bleat content."

"Your Majesty is the soul of wisdom and the fountainhead of my being," Hatton said.

"Od's bones, my sweet Hatton, your ardor would take the maidenhead of mine," Elizabeth retorted, and Hatton puffed himself and smirked. He had a letter in his pocket from Lord Burghley begging him to intercede for Oxford with the Queen, but he had no intention of doing so. He hated Oxford and was jealous of Burghley, and was busy angling in his own benefit for the post of lord chancellor, a fat step beyond captain of the bodyguard and vice chamberlain of the royal household.

Elizabeth's ire at Oxford had calmed but her vanity was still hurt. Oxford had criticized her singing. She thought highly of her singing, and criticism, drunk or joking, was an affront. It would have to be atoned for. Vanity as much as statesmanship had sent Oxford to the Tower. But she was shrewd enough to hope, like Oxford, that Philip would hear of the night he spent there.

That would take care of Oxford's blurting charges of Spanish plots near her throne. That would reassure Philip that she was friendly and gain time, for she was not prepared, not prepared. She had sunk men and money in the Low Countries, she was tangled in French diplomacy, and she had few ships in her navy, not enough to beat off Spain. But it was humiliating that a foreign power could put its agents in her own palace and defy her to expose them under pain of committing a hostile act that might bring war and invasion.

She set out to know if Lord Henry Howard and other nobles leaned as strongly toward Philip as Oxford said. "Search. Probe these matters," she ordered. "We are still mistress here."

Burghley and Walsingham handled such things adroitly. Within a very short time they laid before Elizabeth reports that proved that in Lord Henry's case Oxford had told the truth.

"Spain has friends here," Lord Burghley said. "They are a continual danger."

"They spin a web with Mary of Scots at the center," Walsingham said.

"You spin a web equal to it, master secretary," Elizabeth said.

Walsingham bowed, and Burghley said with a sly twinkle, "His spiders are efficient."

"Would they were efficient enough to rouse Your Majesty," Walsingham said.

Elizabeth seemed disinterested. "I thank you for your reports," she said. She allowed them to stay kneeling while she twirled the great ring on her thumb. "Well well, keep watch, keep eyes. We have our affairs, and they theirs. What decision is made on our Devon pirate?"

This was Francis Drake. His ship had been moved quietly to Deptford, a few miles from London, and he was waiting the Queen's judgment. Elizabeth knew as well as Burghley and Walsingham that the question rested with her. No decision would be made until she made it.

With one of her inscrutable shifts of direction she announced to them then that she would visit Drake. She would go in formal state to Deptford and look into this piracy herself.

Her deviousness left Burghley and Walsingham floundering. The interview was not about Drake, but Lord Howard and the Spanish plots against her. They had given proof of the plots, and she shrugged them off to go and see a sea captain. It was impossible to follow her motives. But at Vere House Anne came running to Oxford with the tale.

"The Queen will take all her officers," she said, "and you will ride as great chamberlain. Oh Edward, that means you're in her grace again. I'm glad—so glad! We can go to court for the spring season."

He kissed her, smiling at the excitement on her cheeks, and when the royal progress started for Deptford he was in his place in front of the Queen.

He knew Her Majesty's humors better than Anne. Elizabeth had not restored him to grace. He was not forgiven, but he could wear his title. It was a grudging admission of his services.

They rode down to Deptford in massed, wild cheering. On lanes and in byways, along village walls and hedges, in tree clumps and farm wagons and on pasture gates and alehouse signposts, Elizabeth's liege subjects jammed themselves and yelled and shouted. They rode through the dust of the countryside, foot and horse, hauberk and plume, velvet cloak and satin gown, into Thames valley toward the ship of Frankie Drake.

Oxford, riding with his chamberlain's white staff in the middle of the pageant, caught the full roars for the Queen. The cheers began far ahead, where the men-at-arms marched, and reached to a din as Elizabeth passed, and died away behind. His ears caught a new note in them, different from the cheers at London or the summer progresses into the shires. Those were cheers of a crowd. These were the high, intimate cheers of men and women, of fathers of families and mothers of sons, chanting a faith out of their throats, a hope and an anxiousness, howling their encouragement to King Harry's daughter. A strident, raucous, surging noise—waves on a storm coast.

At Greenwich Palace the procession entered barges, and came by water to Deptford. Oxford found himself in a barge beside Nan Vavasour. She gathered her skirts to make room for him on the bench and he sat down. She looked at him out of cool, appraising eyes.

"You are a stranger, my lord."

"For a time," he said. "I've had strange dealings."

Her eyes seemed amused. They left his and settled on the long, heavy sweep of the oars as the bargemen rowed. "I don't think it strange for a man to go back to his wife. It speaks a sense of gallantry."

He was annoyed. He had meant the tournament and the Tower. At least had meant her to believe he meant them. It startled him that she put him on the defensive so easily. "Or a sense of love," he said.

"Oh, love, of course," she smiled. "But what most people see is the gallantry. Only the man who goes back knows whether it's love." She gave him a candid glance.

"If you wish it that way," he said.

"I've no wishes in the matter," she said. " 'Tis not my love."

She smiled again, adjusting the folds of her gown where it fell against his leg, and changed the subject. "This is a perilous day for Captain Drake."

"He's swum to the flood. He'll get a haven or a hanging."

"Her Majesty had the Spanish ambassador in yesterday. A dour don, full of scowls. I detest him. I'd gage Her Majesty does, too, but you could never tell. She had him listen to her play on the virginals, and her fingers skipped over the keyboard till the jacks danced. You'd swear there wasn't a burden on her shoulders, and that she never thought of the *Pelican*."

"*The Golden Hind*," he corrected.

She glanced at him once more. "I thought you'd like the old name better."

Oxford winced. Drake had rechristened his ship, calling it *The Golden Hind* in honor of Sir Christopher Hatton's crest. Hatton had bought large shares in Drake's voyage. If Drake escaped hanging he stood to win a fortune. Oxford, with just as good a risk in Captain Frobisher, had lost his whole stake.

"These argosies are the sport of fate," he said, "not flattery."

She saw his eyebrows knit in a frown, and saw how he was flicked on the raw by the spectacle of Hatton rich from Spanish loot and crowing over him.

"A man of spirit would make his own fate," she said.

He said nothing.

"He could if he chose," she said. "He wouldn't need argosies."

He met her eyes in spite of himself. She was looking at him with the look he remembered from the forest glade under the beech, her expression aloof and dispassionate, yet tantalizing in its bland sureness of the forces in herself and him. Then she turned away, and kept the talk to trivial things until the barge was docked.

The Queen went aboard the ship, leading her officers and maids of honor, and stepping gingerly on the tarry deck. Drake knelt to her, his sea dogs ranked behind him. The rails were covered with cloths of silver and gold. Silk pennons dripped from the mastheads and hung from the yards, and in the cabin a table for the Queen's dinner was spread with silver plate and rich goblets and furnishings torn from galleons' holds in the Atlantic and the Pacific, in the Spice Islands and along the coasts of the Spanish Main.

The ship was dark and sturdy and weatherbeaten. Her cannon winked brassy at the gunwales, her masts were seamy from rain and sun. She rode proud at her moorings above Deptford wharf and the green English fields, and beyond her bowsprit the Thames curved like flat smoke to the Channel.

The crowds were still cheering. They waved caps and fists and kerchiefs. They swarmed on the wharf and about the gangplank. Grinning men-at-arms shoved them back. They wedged each other. They fought for a view. They piled wherever they could see or hear. A hundred of them squeezed on a small creek bridge. The bridge crackled and broke.

There were screams. A hundred bodies thrashed in the water. The timbers of the bridge upended, like jackstraws, catching bellies and crotches and flailing arms. Black, sodden, clawing figures slewed and and sprawled through the creek mud, caked grotesquely. They mired in the suck like flies in syrup, and dragged their lives with them. Elizabeth exclaimed. Drake was on his feet. A company of archers thudded over the wharf and beat its way into the crowd. Boats shot out from landings. Sussex ran down the gangplank; Raleigh, Leicester. Oxford ran with them.

He tried to follow the archers, but in the confusion on the wharf there was nothing he could do. The wedged mob was too many. From the wharf the bridge was hidden by houses, and most of the people still cheered. An old woman snatched at his cloak. She was nearly toothless, her gums wrinkled and her head wrapped in rags. "Will they hang him, your worship?" "God knows," Oxford said. They weren't thinking of anything but Drake.

The Queen's luck held. When the screams quieted no one had been killed. The battered limped off to fence corners and the hale ones perched on the bridge skeleton and chattered their teeth and cheered as lusty as the rest. The ceremony went on. Elizabeth questioned the ship's officers, inspected maps and charts, rapped the brass cannon with her knuckles, and sat down to dine in the cabin.

If she realized the cheers were hers, she did not show it.

If she realized more than Spanish treasure and a sailor's neck lay in the noose it was in her power to tighten or slack off, she kept her own counsel.

If she knew the craftiest minds in Europe were watching for her to stumble, or heard over the shouting the low, reverberant sound of hammers driving the spikes for King Philip's navy, she never blanched.

If she smiled inwardly at the thought of how one stroke could answer England and the frayed schemings of men like Lord Howard who supposed her weak, no smile touched her lips.

If she understood history might be standing in the wings while she rinsed her mouth behind a napkin, she was too great a ruler of herself and her nation to cheapen its entrance with bathos, like a second-rate actor.

Her people were not children, and history could speak for itself. She dallied stiffly over her meal.

"They say mournful crocodiles cry and sob like any Christian body, Master Drake."

"To draw travelers to their distress, my liege, whereon they devour them. It has been my good hap never to see one."

" 'Tis a pity. We would have wished some confirmation for the story."

"They can be rendered harmless as doves by shouting at the top of the lungs, my liege, at the same time winking incessantly with the left eye while looking steadfast on the beast with the right."

"Tush, Drake. You've never seen one."

Drake's bold, rugged features were set with strain, and the men who had shares with him had gaunt and clammy looks. Leicester and Walsingham could not eat. Hatton was sweating cold into his ruff.

When the meal was over she went on deck again, and walked slowly to the ship's waist. Her maids and officers followed her, keeping a little distance and whispering behind their hands. Nan Vavasour slipped over to Oxford.

"Her Majesty is superb. Could you better this in a play, my lord?"

"This is no play," he said.

He saw Eliza Trentham through an opening in the group, on the far side of the deck. She did not see him. Then the opening closed, and he lost sight of her. Nan's hand was on his sleeve.

"Do you think we'll know now?"

"Her Majesty can't juggle it too long. She's supping at Greenwich tonight."

"Will you be there?"

"I'm forbidden the court."

"Oh, I'd forgot. I'm sorry."

"I'm here to parade my office in the public stare," he said, "and watch other men grow rich where I failed. Then I'm to kennel again."

He moved his sleeve. Her hand slipped off it unobtrusively. "What a vexation," she said.

She stood suddenly on tiptoe. There was a stir on the deck. "The Queen's calling for a sword," she said.

Elizabeth had spoken to Lord Burghley. He motioned to the Earl of Sussex, who stepped forward with a golden blade, unsheathed. The Queen took it from him.

"I can't see her face," Nan said. "She's turned toward the captain. God's wounds, will she strike him?"

"Not with a sword," Oxford said. "That's for the axe. I can see thirty thousand pounds for Hatton."

"Not yet, my lord."

But it was yet. The quick, high voice rang over the ship. "Kneel down, Drake."

There was no more cheering on the wharf. There were no more whispers on the deck. Drake and his whole crew knelt, and the silence carried the lapping of ripples along the ship's side.

The quick high voice again.

"Rise, Sir Francis. As God is in heaven thou art no pirate, but a true knight of England!"

And then the cheers let loose in a torrent. The thing was done. Elizabeth had answered England, and England answered her. The cheers were for her, for Drake, for her crown and safety, for pride and spirit and five hundred unconquered years, and the challenge flung to the teeth of Spain. They cheered the challenge again, and rolled it with the Thames down to the Channel.

Elizabeth stood a moment, looking around them all. Her sense of such occasions was masterful. She was a king's daughter. She took Drake's arm, and signed to Hatton that she would go ashore.

Hatton bowed to the ground and hustled down the gangplank to alert her bodyguard. He was beaming, and he shook like a well-fed poodle.

"There goes success," Oxford said. "Fat with thirty thousand pounds."

"You're bitter, my lord. Will we fight Spain?"

"If we must, we'll need Drake. I wish him well, he's valiant. God's blessing, to see favor all around me and not to taste it."

"There is a favor you could taste would be sweeter than any, my lord," she said.

"What favor?"

She smiled. "A cure for bitterness."

She stopped, for the Queen's eye was on them.

She laughed and moved away.

When she had left him, Oxford knew suddenly that her hand had been in his, and that his fingers had been sliding along her palm.

 13 WHENEVER SHE COULD, LADY BURGHLEY WENT INTO THE city to visit Anne. She rode from the Burghley mansion on the Strand and spent the day at her

daughter's home, asking questions and satisfying herself that things were as they should be there. Her visits caused flurries of nervousness and punctilio at Vere House. They demanded the respect due to a mother and the formality that suited her rank. They often sent Anne into tears, but Lady Burghley was firm. She was convinced she was doing her best. Anne was a child who had always depended on her, and in all possible ways she would continue to guide and shape her. She patted her little granddaughter Elizabeth on the head, probed stringently into household details, into family problems, and into the state of Anne's mind.

She was embroidering in Anne's chambers on one of her visits not long after Drake had been knighted when she brought up a point she had been wanting to discuss. "Have you learned the name of that other woman?" she asked.

Anne, seated at a sewing frame, looked up in surprise.

"Come, come, what have you done about it?" Lady Burghley said.

"There isn't any other," Anne said.

"My lord of Oxford is still inattentive to you, isn't he?"

"Not as woman," Anne said, turning red.

"As a wife, then."

"It's because of Lord Howard, and the Queen's coldness," Anne said. "He's much hurt."

"If he'd held his tongue he wouldn't have been hurt. He brought it on himself."

"Don't you think he knows that?" Anne said.

"I'm sure I don't know what he knows. And care less. I've given up trying to pin any sense to his antics."

Anne sighed. She was stitching a unicorn on buckram for a stool cover. She thought of the legend that these fierce animals were tamed by the sight of a pure virgin; how they would become docile, and lay their heads on the virgin's lap, with their priceless horns. She wondered if she ought to regret her virginity, and that she would never tame a unicorn. She could hardly think so.

"I had hoped your father would have taken note of this affair," Lady Burghley said.

"He doesn't need to, Mamma."

"The matter of my lord Howard has put him out, too. He's been fretted at it."

"Then please don't fret him more."

"Anne," Lady Burghley said. "Poor, blind, deceived Anne."

"But Mamma—"

"Don't you want my help?" Lady Burghley said, drawing a heaving breath.

Anne stopped sewing, the needle halfway through the buckram. She did not know what she wanted. She had never had any sanctuary inside herself where she could be alone to discover her wants. Her whole being had been a pale reflection of her parents. She only knew that ever since her wedding night it had been like this. Her eyes began to fill.

"There, now," Lady Burghley said, relaxing her tone and letting out her breath consolingly. Anne's brimming eyes seemed to comfort her.

"You should be grateful to me," she said.

"I am grateful, Mamma. I think it was Lord Howard that bothered Edward. That was all."

"If so, it's soon over and we've nothing to mend. Your father says none of the Howard faction is for Spain. The other nobles of Lord Howard's religion are sound English."

"Then Edward has done some good," Anne said. "He's showed who is loyal."

"Little good for you," Lady Burghley said with a sniff, "nor not so much for him, either. I must speak to your father again. We'll put a watch on my lord of Oxford's comings and goings, and we shall see what we shall see. I've had my suspicions since you spoke to me last month." She straightened militantly, settling her body to a more comfortable position in the steel hoops of her farthingale, and peered over the embroidery toward Anne. "Why are you so doting on him of a sudden? Are you with child again?"

"No," Anne said.

Oxford wanted Nan Vavasour. He had wanted her for a year. The want had grown ravenous in him, building stronger from his conscious efforts to stifle it. The more he had fought against it the fiercer it had grown, and her cool, mocking certainty of him had eaten into his marrow. After the events at Deptford he knew it was inevitable.

Two afternoons from the day aboard *The Golden Hind* Nan met him in his rooms at the Savoy.

They had decided to meet in the afternoons. Nan had to be with the Queen in the mornings and evenings, and could not run the risk of being out of the dormitory at night, but she had a few hours between dinner and supper when she was free.

Oxford sent Jack Lyly off to the taverns and a rehearsal in Shoreditch and waited for Nan's step along the passage. His throat was choked and his veins were like sand.

When she appeared at the door he stepped over and gripped her in his arms.

She had on a long hooded cloak over her dress. The hood had fallen back as she climbed the stairs, uncovering her miniver cap and smooth gold hair. He took the cloak from her and put his face to her breast.

He could smell the perfumed wash she used, a scent of rosemary clean and tantalizing like her. He felt a little nip of her lips and teeth on his neck as he bent, a quick, tart pressure.

When he lifted his head she was looking at him curiously. "Why have your waited so long, Ned?" she said.

The sun was streaming in at the windows. Spring over London. Spring over the Strand and the Thames, the palaces and the Tower, over the hall of Parliament and the homes of people. Spring over the noisome, twisted, offal-strewn lanes, the inns and shops, and straggled fields that led into the countryside beyond the old city walls. Spring in the month and the beat of the earth's deep pulse in the air. Oxford went to the window and drew the curtains, shutting out the light and leaving the room in a soft, luminous semidarkness. The city sounds filtered through the curtains lazily.

He kissed Nan again, this time on the mouth, and slid his hands to her waist. She let them stay a moment, and then leaned back.

"It might be better to bolt the door."

He laughed, and went to the door and shot the bolt. When he returned she was sitting on a stool, her hands behind her, still looking at him. She had loosened her bodice slightly while he was gone, and the top of her breasts swelled like white fruit.

He cupped his hands over them, and she moved pleasurably under the gesture.

» 154 «

"You're impatient," she said.

"God's blessing," he said, "do you suppose I'm made of stone?"

"I don't know," she said. "What do you want me to say?"

"Don't say anything."

She smiled. His cheek rumpled the small fur patch of her cap. It was held with jeweled hairpins. He took them out and brushed the cap aside and laid his lips on her hair, feeling it sleek and lustrous. The tassels lacing her bodice were crisscrossed in silk eyelets. Pretty things, but intricate to his fingers. She helped him with them.

"I've often imagined what this would be like," she said.

The bodice fell away and she dropped her arms to her sides. She gave him a moment or two before she stirred. She did not stop him or try to touch him. She seemed remote, as if she were no part of what he was doing, yet indolently sure of himself and her, and the tension that vibrated in them both. The passion was more keen to him than her bare breasts and the teasing, responsive lift of her shoulders.

"How often?" he said.

"Often enough. I was afraid I'd have to imagine for the rest of my life."

The teasing in her smile changed to a subtle, exquisite play of enjoyment. She brought his head closer to her and turned her body from side to side for his lips.

"Not any more," he said.

"No, faith."

Without warning she pressed his neck with the same sharp, fleeting sensuousness.

"You were very slow, Ned."

"The sweetest flowers bloom slowly," he said.

"That's nice. I've never loved a poet before."

Slipping away from him, she stood up. The suffused light in the room threw a glow over her skin, like a painting of Holbein, or a half-robed Danae showered with gold. She held her dress from falling with one arm and idly covered her breasts with the other.

She was all she had promised. "Nan!" he said.

She was smiling once more. "What color would you paint me now?" she asked.

"No color. Flame and sunlight. Who can see colors when he's blinded?"

There was a bed in the next room, partly in sight through the inner door and shaded by its canopy. She glanced toward it, and with a little silent laugh picked up her skirts.

"Wait for me," she said.

He reached across the stool and caught her arm. "No," he said. "Here."

Her laugh broke into a sharp fluting of sound. She shook her head, the glow of her skin darkening.

"You should wait."

"I've waited too long," he said.

"Fie, for shame," she said.

She stared at the mastery in his voice. His doublet was opened, and the strong flat muscular cordings on his chest strained tight as he held her. She pulled suddenly away and ran toward the room.

He rolled the stool under a table with a kick of his foot, and was at the inner door before she was. She swerved to dodge by, but he had her by the shoulders and spun her to face him.

His violence made her gasp. In her struggles the skirts escaped from her fingers, sliding to the floor, where she swished them aside with her ankles, holding him off and writhing for freer movement. He lifted her against him, and the force of his strength bent her backward.

"Ned!" she said. "Your doublet! Take care!"

He let her go at her cry.

"You scratched me," she said. She drew her hand over her arm and showed it to him. It was pink with a small drop of blood, and blood stood in a tiny beading like red seed pearls on her arm.

"A pox on doublets," he said. He threw it off, and his shirt, and tried to bring her closer, but she pushed nakedly against his skin.

" 'Twill leave a mark, Ned. Get me a kerchief."

She thrust away from him. Her eyes fell on a chest beside the door. Tugging it open, she rummaged in it and brought out an embroidered linen square. "This will do. Bind it for me."

She held the kerchief up.

He looked at it and his face went gray. It was Eliza Trentham's handkerchief, the one she had given him at the first tournament.

"No!" he said.

He seized it, snatching it from her, and threw it into the drawer.

"Take some other," he said. He gave her one of his own, and shut the chest.

She dabbed at her arm. "Help me, Ned."

He had turned on his heel and walked a few steps. He came back and wiped the cut, his fingers unsteady. He turned again and moved across the room and stood shakenly. "I'm a clumsy surgeon."

" 'Tis not bad," she said, inspecting the thin carmine thread below the shoulder. "The sleeve will hide it."

He said nothing.

She followed him to the center of the room, leaning smilingly while she ungartered her stockings and looking up at him sidelong. "I see I must needs stay."

"Stay or not," he said. "It's no matter."

He wiped the knuckles of his hand over his forehead. They came away wet, but he felt dry all through his body, as if the sand in his veins had scoured out of him, leaving him seared and hollow.

"Why, Ned," she said.

"Stay or not."

She gave another laugh. "Are you sick at blood?"

"At myself," he said.

"Marry, the prick of a pin. The prelude to a poet's. You've done no harm. I'll put the pomade thicker tonight and no one will notice."

"Yes," he said. He swung around to her. "Yes, cover your scars and your prickings till they can't be seen. Would God they never had been."

"Would God men were as skillful as women," she teased. "Can you cover your scratches at love, Ned?"

"God's blessing, if I could."

His tone was rough. She felt the wince in it and her eyes flickered toward the chest with its handkerchief. They came back to him, drifting down along his body. She lifted her mouth with a touch of mockery.

"I had thought you could do anything."

"I wish I might. But wishes die with what they feed on."

The same slow darkening crept into the glow of her skin. She had removed her stockings by now, and she stretched one foot in front of her, curling her toes languidly. "I must go at five."

Unclothed except for the short silk she wore under her skirts, she was still remote, appraising, taunting. Her words said they were wasting time, and her mouth gave him his choice.

He looked at her mouth.

He knew she would not come to him again if he let her go.

The knowledge hammered at the hollowness of his veins, and mixed with the swimming diffused radiance of the room.

"I'm not angry, Ned. Did you think I was angry?" She laid her hand in his.

His fingers stiffened. Along with the knowledge whirled memory of Deptford—Hatton's wealth, the Queen's disfavor, the sweets and riches loaded on others and dangling always beyond his reach; and Nan with him on the ship's deck and the hot realization of his palm along her wrist. And once more he saw Eliza's face, not seeing him, and disappearing in the crowd of courtiers.

"Lord Christ, how is a man to think?" he said.

"I don't know."

She moved nearer. The smell of rosemary at her throat was a tang in his nostrils. It bit into his mind and flesh.

"The bleeding's stopped, Ned," she said, and held her arm for him to see.

He circled it with his palm.

His palm was along her wrist, and on her arm, and at her shoulder. Desire had been whetted too sharp to be dulled. The craving in all his fibers rioted through him, redoubled in its second rousing. He turned without a sound.

He thrust his lips to hers. He pushed her lips apart, and crushed them like ripe cherries, and took her answering tongue. Full red mouth, gold hair and ivory breasts. Nan locked to him. No sound in the room but the wild, quick rush of their breath and the dreamy echoes of London beyond the window.

There was a carpet in front of the window curtain, rose and ocher and yellow-tinted green in the filtering light, like a forest floor in spring. He carried her toward it.

As he lowered her down, the short silk slid from her thighs. She laughed, and lay unresisting.

He tore at the buckle of his belt, and stripped himself of shoes and hose and breeches. He pulled them off, and slung them away, and stood naked.

Nan was lying on the carpet, laughing softly. She put her hands under her head and eyed him frankly. She was breathless from his kisses.

"You're certainly not made of stone," she said.

She was different from other women. She could yield herself while at the same time holding herself separate, and their moments together left him in a torment and an impatience for their next love-making. Her detachment had a provocative quality that acted like salt to his appetite. It was a reserve veiling the suggestion of infinite possibilities, behind which he was allowed to see but which he could never quite pierce. She was sophisticated, yet utterly natural; elusive, yet in a way that gave an endless sense of variation. In his experience at the court and in Europe he had learned that women were not alike. They all shared certain instincts and the necessity for being loved, but each one followed her own fashion. But they had one thing in common: the habit of pursuit. With Nan he had supposed the pursuit had been a little more clever, that he had wanted her and she had wanted him; that she had tormented him until she got him; and that when they had gratified each other she would be less clever and more demanding. It had always seemed to him that there were two steps to such affairs— pursuit and possession. He had expected her to take the second now that the first was over. Yet he discovered after a week of her that she was completely disinterested in trying to possess him, and that it was he who was doing the pursuing. He found her maddening.

They were equally passionate. They took a mutual delight in one another. In their periods of physical excitement she kept nothing back. Her body was as fervid as his, matching his in everything, straining with his toward the exquisite mounting tension they achieved together in the prolonged, delicious anguish before the final burst of relaxation. But when she lay in his arms while they waited for desire to kindle again she was remote as ever. The cool, impersonal veil drew around her mind, and the same faintly mocking smile tantalized him on her lips. She was like a woods animal that had stopped to frolic at the edge of a covert and then vanished into the forest without letting itself be caught.

Oxford stayed at the Savoy, seeing no one. He worked on plays with Jack Lyly in the mornings, and then sent Lyly away, and Nan came in the afternoon.

They ate wine and almond cakes. They sat in the window seat, her head on his shoulder, and talked. She told him the news from the court. Lord Howard was under close restraint for his friendship to Spain. Sir Francis Drake was the hero of the palace, and Her Majesty had ordered him to hurry the building of ships of war. Sir Christopher Hatton was strutting like a lord in pompous new clothes; it was said his venture had earned five thousand per cent.

"And my truth," Oxford said, "has earned me black ingratitude and the malice of cunning man. Nan, there's no honesty in the world. We're all rogues and knaves."

Then her spell would grow on him, and they would undress, and go to the bed in the inner room.

Once they made love on the window seat, with the pattern of the mullioned panes falling like lace on her breasts and the burn of the sun starting drops of sweat in the small of his back. But Nan thought this unwise. "The window's high, Ned, but we might be seen. We mustn't be careless."

She asked him the same day if he had any suspicions that her visits might have attracted attention. "The Strand's always crowded," she said, "and even if I wanted to I couldn't tell if I were being followed. I think I should come less often."

"One more week," he pleaded.

She agreed, but said that afterward it would be safer to meet at longer intervals.

Oxford laughed at her caution. In the Savoy men went in and out as they pleased, and had their women or not as they pleased, and a girl in a long cloak and concealing hood was too commonplace a sight to be noticed. He had no servants; the few he could afford were at Vere House, and he and Lyly ate in taverns. Lyly was the only person who could have guessed, but Jack was full of the plans for taking Oxford's theater company on a tour of the provinces that summer. Whatever he thought about the afternoons Oxford spent in the rooms—if he thought anything—he passed over with a wink and a grin.

"I'll send the Duttons for the bombast and some tumbling boys for the groundlings, if that concords with your notion, Ned," he said. "The rest of our young deer can roam with 'em, and graze on your shillings and pence. Lord, the items for expense! They'll do the Midlands, to Warwick and Leominster, I think, and by all means to Coventry. Actors are welcomed there, being apprentices to the old mysteries. Sir Thomas Lucy's company was to have played there, too, but his actor deer are too wild yet or his money too short, I don't know which. 'Tis no grief, our fellows will shine the brighter. Pray God they don't shine too bright on the wenches and get themselves darkened with the pox— those that aren't already. Well, the wenching in London is as fine as anywhere, hah, Ned? We'll do as brave staying here. Marry, I won't speak for you, but London maids don't shy from me, and 'tis known I'm a pretty piece of flesh."

Tom Bedingfield came in one morning. Oxford was glad to see him. He thought Tom was looking a little serious, but Tom had always been sober-minded. It was nearly noon when he came, and Oxford got him out of the rooms by suggesting dinner at a tavern.

Tom's talk was of books and scholars while he finished off a roast gosling and stirred sugar in his cup of sack. He asked if Oxford had read Cinthio's tales, which he said were not a match for Aristo's *Orlando Furioso* but solid and full of invention. He had been studying Montemayor's *Diana* and the Plutarch translated by Sir Thomas North and Amyot's French translation of the Latin.

"There are so many translations and so many excellent writings," he said.

"Give us more of your own," Oxford said.

"Oh, it's a harvest that puts my Cardanus to shame."

"*Scire tuum nihil est, nisi te scire hoc sciat alter,*" Oxford said.

Tom recognized the line from Oxford's preface to his work. "What use in knowing, unless you share it with another," he said. "I could say the same of you, my lord."

"I write," Oxford said.

"For the breath of actors' mouths," Tom said. "Breath isn't substantial. It would be good to have your plays in print."

"Never," Oxford said.

"You're too sensitive," Tom said. "But that's a curse of greatness."

"To be great a man must be sensitive," Oxford said, "but to be sensitive is not to be great. Thanks, Tom, we'll let things run as they are."

Tom poised a knife-point of gosling over his plate, the honey dripping from it. He seemed about to argue, but changed his mind and put the bite into his mouth instead. His round, friendly face was thoughtful. "We have that sort at the court," he said. "The ones that are hurt by your wit."

Oxford shrugged.

"You're very free with them," Tom said.

"I'm an allowed fool," Oxford said. "It's the only trade left me."

Tom's eyes grew more sober as he put down his knife. The tavern boy sidled up to the table on a pair of bandy legs and refilled his cup with sack. He waited till the boy was out of earshot before he said, "Have you considered that these men would be happy if you stumbled?"

"How can I stumble more than I have?" Oxford said carelessly. "These dancing chamberlains and carpet knights are an envious pack. They'll bark at any heels to hear the sound of their yapping. Drink up your sack, Tom, and we'll call for sweets." He liked Tom's friendship and soberness, but Tom's hints were too vague to worry him. He didn't see how they could have anything to do with Nan. If Tom knew anything definite he would say so.

He said goodbye to Tom in front of the tavern and walked along the Strand alone. Clouds were banking in the sky and there would be rain by night. He wondered if Nan would get wet going back to the palace. Perhaps if it were raining too hard he could persuade her to stay all night. His skin tingled at the thought of it. He could think up some excuse for her to give in the morning. Something, anything. If he couldn't, what was imagination for? The Queen was involved in politics and wouldn't be critical. He was hurrying a little as he turned in at the Savoy.

He climbed the stair to his rooms.

The door was open. He knew he had closed it when he went out. His hand dropped to his dagger. Drawing the blade, he pushed at the door with his boot, and stepped in.

Nan was standing in the room. Her eyes were red with weeping. Two men-at-arms were beside her, and a master-at-arms in the livery of the Tower stood at her shoulder.

"Nan!" he said springing toward her. "Nan!"

The men-at-arms blocked his way.

"Nan!" he said.

"Come in, my lord," a voice said. "And very welcome. You are under arrest."

From the window seat where he had been waiting, Sir Christopher Hatton moved forward and bowed, smiling banefully.

14 AT SIGNOR ROCCO BONETTI'S FASHIONABLE FENCING SCHOOL it was the unbroken law that personal feelings must be left outside. The men of Elizabeth's court who flocked to the *signor* understood that his practice floor was neutral ground. They came to learn his thrusts and parries, the tricks of Italian swordplay and the newest arts of fence. Their spites and grudges, their jealousies and the nursed insults, bred in the court air, were laid by in the *signor's* antechamber with their hats and cloaks, for otherwise the place would have been a bedlam with the working off of old scores and the settling of love affairs. As Fulke Greville said, "We are like the animals at a watering pool in those new Americas, we sheathe our claws at Bonetti's out of plain need." The only exception was the *signor* himself, who paraded among the buttoned rapiers with a flashing eye and a bellicose scorn, and heaped screaming abuse on every fencing master in London and every other method but his own.

Signor Bonetti boasted that he could teach his pupils to thrust two feet farther than any Englishman. He was contemptuous of the English downright blows and cutting play. Broadsword and quarterstaff were made for yokels, he said. He ridiculed the Spanish style and despised the French. His temper bristled at criticism of Italianized fighting, at what Sussex and the older nobles called "foreign foiners and frog-pricking button-butchers." Being a foreigner, he was excused for his temper, and his contempt of native boorishness had brought him notoriety and a good custom.

Signor Bonetti knew nothing of politics. He watched the courtiers perfecting their guards and toning their muscles in the morning exercise. He could pick out the swaggerers, those who held one shoulder lower than the other when they walked to call notice to the weight of their swords. He could tell at a glance which were the clumsy, the slow, the skillful and the timid. He corrected *mandritti* with a flourish, and beat a blade into proper line with a querulous stroke as he went by. He instructed them in the *passado,* the *lacuna,* and the elaborate use of the crosshilt dagger and the *main gauche* for warding blows, and when they were far enough advanced he sold them, for large sums, secret thrusts that were guaranteed to win past any defense.

He stood observing Master Thomas Knyvet in a bout with Master Greville. The two men panted and stamped, attacking and countering. Master Knyvet handled himself excellently well. He was adept at the pass; his crouching plunge carried him at a half run nearly nine feet and drove his point hard forward. His slips and side steps were well-timed in gaining place. He held his dagger guard somewhat wide, but that would improve.

Signor Bonetti was pleased with him. By the first of the year he would be ready for the *botta secreta,* and Signor Bonetti's purse would be the fatter for it. The *signor* considered that for this secret thrust he would give Master Knyvet the *coup de Jarnac.* With it, Master Knyvet could hamstring his adversary, leaving him the choice of surrender or of bleeding to death, as the Sieur de Jarnac had done some thirty years ago before Henry of France. It was a deadly trick, and infallible. It belonged to the Italian masters of the school of Marozzo. English masters did not have it. Once he had learned it, Master Knyvet would be formidably equipped. He would come to the *duello a la mazza.* He would answer anyone's challenge. "Will you walk in the field with me?" The secluded spot. The clash of blades. The shout. The thrust. The opponent collapsing like a punctured bladder. Signor Bonetti envisioned the scene with the rapture of an artist.

A sudden quiet interrupted him. A pause in the rapiers' slithering and the pleasant, noisy confusion in the room. The *signor* scowled and turned.

Lord Oxford was standing in the doorway. The earl was exquisitely dressed. He had on a deep blue cloak lined with tawny. His tawny doublet was slashed with blue at his sleeves. The Garter gleamed on his leg, jewels at his ear brushed the Flanders lace ruffling his collar, and jewels pinned the feathers in his cap. A solid-looking youngster just out of boyhood stood beside him in hose and shirt.

Signor Bonetti signaled impatiently for the bouts to go on, and the noise began again. The *signor* knew nothing of politics, but he was aware that Lord Oxford had been prisoned in the Tower for the matter of a mistress and that the Queen's court was closed to him. He was out of favor. Signor Bonetti sensed that the elegance of his dress smelled of heartbreak and defiance.

He hurried over and bowed. "An infinite honor, my lord. Does your lordship join us for a pass or two? *Dolce, graziemente, ma tutti con forza.* In the spirit of nobility."

"Not I," Oxford said. "For my cousin here, young Horatio. He's for the wars, and green at this man-scratching."

"In honor, in glory, in skill, in all things," Signor Bonetti said, looking at young Horatio's tough, phlegmatic build. "In the *passado,* in the *fendente,* in the *falso dritto,* the *falso manco,* the stroke *tondo,* the stroke *montante,* and the *guanto di pressa.* Give him a year at the school of Bonetti, and take away a swordsman."

"Stuffed with a hatful of names," Oxford replied. "Pray God they'll be more than sawdust."

"Your lordship may trust so," Signor Bonetti said, drawing himself up. "I have studied with those who knew Marozzo."

"A man could study with a dozen. Agrippa, Grassi, Viggiani. I read his book when I was in Italy."

"Your lordship is much accomplished."

"Do you follow Carranza?"

"He is a Spaniard and a theorist. They fence by mathematics. Philosophers."

"Horatio will meet Spaniards in the Low Countries," Oxford said. "It would be grievous to be stabbed by a philosophy."

"I can swear to your lordship—"

"Let him have a smattering of the Spaniard," Oxford said.

He had been roving his eyes over the room, and the noise on the practice floor had died away again. Signor Bonetti, looking for the

reason, saw that the sword points had dropped. The fencers were looking from the earl to Master Knyvet.

Signor Bonetti knew nothing of politics. That Master Knyvet was
distant kin to Lord Henry Howard meant little to him, but he had an
Italian's ear for intrigue. Master Knyvet was the uncle of the earl's
mistress, and the affair had cost Master Knyvet's niece a week in the
Tower. He moved his body to block the earl's view.

Oxford stepped around him. He strolled on to the floor, leading
Horatio among the swords and past the courtiers toward Fulke
Greville.

"My cousin wants to grow teeth," he said. "Will you help him,
Fulke?"

"We'll sharpen them," Fulke said, with a merry readiness that was
obviously forced.

Oxford smiled. He turned unconcernedly to Knyvet. They had drunk
together over Lord Henry's table. "You keep in practice, Tom."

"For my health," Knyvet said.

"Does your health trouble you?"

"No. My trouble is the health of others."

Oxford's shoulders raised in a shrug. To Signor Bonetti it seemed the
air in the room was like a pulled string. The courtiers were all staring.

"You take a strenuous medicine for others," Oxford said.

"What a man gets here will keep him well and sicken those he hates,"
Knyvet said.

"I don't question it," Oxford said.

Greville caught his breath and for a moment Signor Bonetti thought
the string would snap. But Oxford put his back to Knyvet and moved
aside.

Signor Bonetti felt himself indeed fortunate that his practice floor
was neutral ground.

He took up his parading again, and strode about in a nervous
vehemence. The bouts resumed. Rapiers clattered.

Young Horatio Vere fenced with Fulke Greville. Master Knyvet
picked out Captain Raleigh.

For the rest of the session Master Knyvet was very aggressive. He
went violently at Captain Raleigh, driving the captain back to the wall
with grim, ferocious tactics. Thick-wristed, with a heavy chest and

full neck and his eyes socketed deep above a pointed beard, he had re-doubled energy in his attacks. Signor Bonetti, watching him with satis-faction, decided that by the first of the year he would beyond a doubt be ready for the *botta secreta*.

To Lord Burghley's mind it was a question whether more had been gained or lost by exposing Oxford and the Vavasour girl. . . . Lady Burghley had been insistent, and Hatton had jumped at the oppor-tunity, but the Queen was in an irritable mood for such goings-on. The Duc d'Alençon was coming to London at last for the Queen's formal answer on their marriage. He could not be held off any longer. His coming set up mazes of design and intricacy more cunning than the maze at Hampton, like the carved ivory globes within globes that merchantmen brought back from the Levant, each locked inside the other and none wholly visible.

Alençon's private war in Flanders could be expanded to draw France and Spain into conflict. He was the lever on which Elizabeth depended and he was shrewd enough to know it. Now he was demanding money and men, looking to Elizabeth for aid and pleading for their wedding. His brother the King of France, his mother Catherine, Philip of Spain, the Dutch States under William of Orange, the Flemings, the Scottish court, and every noble in England, were all involved. The matter was vast and complicated, with infinite twists and facets that taxed Lord Burghley sorely. He was alone with Sussex in the council in approving the marriage. He thought it would provide an ally on the continent and let France take up the burden of keeping Spain at bay and pouring resources into the sinkhole of the Lowlands which had drained England almost dry. The Dutch, like Alençon, were begging for volunteers and money. But the rest of the council had fallen away from him. Even Hatton had gone over to Leicester. Hatton was much puffed up since the Oxford affair, and vaunted himself highly.

"I fear it was badly done," Lord Burghley said to his wife. "The chuckles are at my expense, and no one looks to me."

"Her Majesty will look to you when she needs you," Lady Burghley said. She was unimpressed by council troubles; they always fretted his lordship and always ended to his credit. "You should bemoan yourself more for the husband your daughter is yoked with. Who knows but what he may have got a bastard on this other wench?"

"God forbid," Lord Burghley said.

"I have brought our granddaughter to Cecil House," Lady Burghley said. "She and Anne will live with us. 'Tis known he cannot support them. I have talked with Anne, and she may see him if she likes. She is beside herself with doting on him."

"Love is a madness," said Lord Burghley, pursing his lips. "I see there will be more than chuckles at my expense."

"Your own granddaughter," Lady Burghley said. "We will rear her properly and marry her to an earl."

"We are married once to an earl already," Lord Burghley observed. "But they are welcome, my dear."

"Your own granddaughter," Lady Burghley said.

"Well," Lord Burghley said, "it's more than Leicester can do."

"All he can get is a stepson," Lady Burghley said. "And on three wives. Leave my lord of Leicester and think of Anne."

Anne did not ask to be thought of. She only asked for Oxford to love her, and for the nights when he came to her. He came sometimes, more and more often as the summer passed and the autumn turned to winter. She never refused him. They lay in each other's arms as they used to do, and felt the old quick fervor and surge of excitement for one another. But Anne never knew whether he was thinking of her or of Nan Vavasour. She had the pressure of his arms, and his strong, vigorous love, but she would remember then that Nan had the same— perhaps yesterday, perhaps tomorrow, perhaps next week. Anne didn't deceive herself that the Tower had killed Edward's infatuation. She knew that in her own case it never could. Prison stones thwarted passion, but they didn't bury it.

One day as she was playing with the little Elizabeth, her dressing woman Meg ushered in a visitor. It was Eliza Trentham. Anne sent Elizabeth away with Meg and stood up uncertainly. She and Eliza had not spoken together for years, except in the formal way at court functions. Anne had always been wary of Eliza, with her quiet smile and dark eyes. She had not encouraged a friendship that might bring her too close to Edward, and she wondered why Eliza had come now.

Eliza put off her cloak and kissed Anne's cheek, with the December wind still fresh on hers. Nothing in her voice or manner suggested there was anything unusual in her coming. She did not seem to see the pathetic contrast between herself and Anne, or to feel that Anne was a pitiful and forlorn figure.

Anne was grateful to her. She knew they were both thinking of Edward, but Eliza did not mention him. She talked about the court and the excitement there over the Duc d'Alençon, the plays given for his entertainment, the dinners and dances and extravagant festivities.

Anne was glad to hear them. She had been out of touch with the court since spring, when Edward had angered the Queen by exposing Lord Henry Howard and the Spanish faction in the palace, and as Eliza talked gently on she sat on the edge of her cushion and listened.

Before long she was asking questions. The court had always been alluring to her. Was Cissy Knollys still putting on airs as the Countess of Leicester? What had the Carey sisters worn to the dances? Had Alençon really a nose as big as his face?

"His nose is the size of two men's," Eliza said. "He is very ugly. His legs are bandy and his skin swart, and he scarce comes to Her Majesty's shoulder. I cannot believe she will marry him. Master Sidney wrote her a most pleading letter against it."

"That was when my father took to his bed for ten days," Anne nodded. "He was much distracted. I've heard little since."

"Leicester carries it all," Eliza said. "Her Majesty has publicly promised that she will marry the duke, but at night alone with us in her chamber she sometimes breaks into tears. We think she would be happy to be rid of him, but the duke wants thirty thousand pounds to go back to Flanders. She already paid him thirty before he came. Though it's said most of that stuck to Monsieur de Simier's fingers. *Monsieur* has been shipped home, sadly out of grace."

"Does he dress like a duke?" Anne asked.

"Oh, more. The costliest stuffs and the finest jewels. All bought, I'd say, with Her Majesty's money. He and his followers sparkle like painted birds."

"The court must be a brave sight," Anne said.

"We swim in gilt and glitter," Eliza said.

"I should love to see it. Oh, Eliza, I've missed it all."

"There's not much to miss," Eliza said.

"I was brought up to it," she said. "I've never known anything else. You had Staffordshire, Eliza. Meadows and country lanes, and nights under the moon with time to think to yourself. I've had Cecil House, and thrills and pastimes, and the court, and doing what my mother and father told me. Since I was born."

Eliza kept silent. She did not want to say she understood better than Anne knew.

"Now it's gone," Anne said. "I've lost it. I've lost everything."

"Perhaps you can get it back," Eliza said.

"How?" Anne said. She kept her face turned from Eliza, for she was aware they were both thinking of Edward again. She had lost the court because she had lost Edward, and she had lost Edward because she was too much a part of the court. How could she hold him to her? How could she keep the interest of his restless and unsatisfied mind? Her problem lay in a single word—how?

Eliza watched her sympathetically. "With poetry," she said. "With imagination."

Anne shook her head helplessly. "I haven't those."

"You could try."

"You mean Edward needs them." Her throat caught at Edward's name, but she spoke it. It had always been there, and it was out at last.

This was why Eliza had come—kindly and concerned and trying to show her what Edward needed.

She stiffened, still looking at the garden. "He's getting them somewhere else," she said.

"No, he isn't," Eliza said. "He isn't getting them, Anne."

"We won't talk of that," Anne said.

"Nan Vavasour isn't the answer he's searching for," Eliza said earnestly, leaning forward. "Lord Oxford has truer qualities in him than he's discovered yet. He's wasting himself, the better part of himself. He wants to find those qualities, and the freedom and contentment and fullness of mind to set them free. He wants poetry and imagination. Give them to him, Anne."

"I can't," Anne said.

"He's hungry for them," Eliza said.

"Don't you think I know?" Anne cried. "Don't you think I see? He wants so many things! Honor and glory, and dazzling fancies, and to be like his father, and to be no one but Edward. I'd give them to him if I could. His poetry, his imagination, everything. But I can't! I can't! We both know it. I can't save him. I can't even save myself. Oh, Eliza, you're the one who should have married him!" She twisted from the cushion and fell to the floor sobbing.

Eliza was still shaken when she got back to the palace. The Queen, sitting at the virginals while her ladies-in-waiting sewed, glanced up sharply as she entered the royal chamber. Though Elizabeth was teetering like an acrobat on the wire of the French match, with the diplomats of half the world breathless and the security of England balancing on her shoulders, she was alert as ever to the smallest details around her.

"What is it, child?" she said.

"Nothing, Your Majesty."

"You were at Cecil House . . . Our little Anne. My lord of Oxford."

"Yes, Your Majesty."

"Your eyes are wet," the Queen said. She left the virginals and stood up. "Weep for him, weep for him, girl," she said. "I wish I could."

It was after the first of the year, and the days were darkening early. The alleys around the Blackfriars convent were heavy in shadow as Robin Christmas started from the theater toward Vere House. He shivered in the raw, dank chill of the muddy stones under his feet and the stinking ice mist rising from the half-frozen offal ditches.

Robin wrapped himself warmer, blowing on his fingers while he hurried along. Young Horatio Vere walked beside him, and one of Oxford's men, a tall, stringy Cornisher named Brenings, followed behind, his sword skittering at his heels.

Robin had had a sour interview with John Lyly. As my lord of Oxford's secretary, Lyly should have been guarding Oxford's money; instead, as manager of his company of players he was spending it like water. Lyly wanted more actors, more plays, more jugglers, and another tour of the provinces that summer. Robin didn't know where the means were coming from.

"My lord your cousin," he said gloomily to Horatio, "will die a pauper." The effect of the interview put him in a snappish humor. A dozen great hulking clowns that would have done better as cobs or draymen had sprawled idle around the Blackfriars stage, rolling their eyes and muttering lines while Master Lyly discoursed airily of tours and projects. They were doing nothing, as far as Robin could see. But they would all eat like Gargantua at their suppers.

Horatio had no opinion one way or the other. He was an equable young man, and he knew that actors and stages were out of his sphere. But he liked his brilliant cousin Oxford and the occasional evenings in Vere House.

"I'd be sorry to think so," he said.

"For these bawdy players," Robin said. "When you are older, Master Horatio, use your influence with him. He bears a good love to you. You and your brother. His Horatio and Francisco."

"He calls him that," Horatio said. "Francis is the English of it."

Robin clucked approval. He had never known any harm to come from the English of things.

"Is it bad with my cousin?" Horatio said.

"He has sold twenty-four estates in five years," Robin said. "He's let go his lands at Wyvenhoe, he may lose his country manor on the Avon. We feed actors. I can remember when he had a hundred gentlemen, a hundred horses. Look at us now . . . Sirrah Brenings, keep to your duties, an't please you."

The stringy servant was dawdling with a pair of girls at a house window. They were leaning over the sill, their breasts pushed outward, and he had his hand inside the dress of one, squeezing her nipple, and she was squealing. At Robin's orders he took his hand out sheepishly and came on with a grin. The girls called after him.

"Y'saucy whoreson, to paw maids and make off. Stand to it. What d'y'do, longshanks? It's a bare night to sleep alone."

They spied Horatio, and called louder.

"There's juice. There's a snug one. Oh, a pretty lad. He'd be a stout push. Will y'house, pretty? How much has 'a there? A warrant 'a could show."

"I've enough for one man," Horatio said stolidly.

Robin chuckled, and the girls screamed, giggling, and rattled the shutter closed.

The men walked ahead, under the overhanging roofs that slitted against the sky, past squalid gutters and house beams gouged smooth by dray hubs at the alley corners.

"Stop," Robin said.

Someone ran after them. The figure held up a wrist stump, the right hand gone.

"John Stubbes," Robin said.

Stubbes smelled of cheap ordinaries and pot grease, but he was sober. He mopped his face with his left hand, sweating in spite of the cold, and with his right stump gestured them into a crosslane.

"Go round another way," he said, "and loosen your sword, Master Christmas."

"I? Sword?" Robin said.

"You're being hunted," Stubbes said. "Go round."

"Why round? Who hunts us?" Robin said, peering down the alley between the houses.

"We're for my cousin's," Horatio said flatly. "We'll not budge."

"They took at me," Stubbes said, "and I gave 'em the slip by the river stairs. I pray you, gentlemen—"

Shapes grew out of the ditch-mist in the alley. Four or five cloaks, low-pulled hats, and trampling boots. They turned the angle by the bawdyhouse and sent up a halloo.

"It's Master Knyvet's men," the stringy servant said. "It's his livery."

"For God's love, masters—" Stubbes said.

"What should they want of us?" Robin said.

"Stay and we'll know," Horatio said. He squared around in the alley, hand on sword hilt. Robin did the same. The stringy servant ranged alongside.

The men came up menacingly, spreading across the alley and blocking it. "Where's Oxford?" they said.

"Lord Oxford's at home," Horatio said. "Speak civil. We walk in the Queen's peace."

"Ye walk knaves. Ye're servers of Oxford."

"I serve no one," Horatio said. He stood his ground. "I'm his lordship's cousin."

The men glanced at each other. One of them laughed. Their blades clinked out of the scabbards.

"D'y' threaten us, sprat? Let be your sword."

"I give no threats," Horatio said stubbornly, "but I take none."

"Brenings—Stubbes—stand with us," Robin said. He swung his rapier like a bodkin. "Come, y'rogues, and we'll swash ye!"

The men bunched, and made a heavy, jostling rush. In the narrow crosslane there was no footwork. They bullied in by weight. They sprawled Stubbes against a wall, his stump thrashing useless. They knocked Brenings down. They veered from Horatio's guard, and battered past him and Robin. At the far side they turned to rush again. Horatio was still on his legs and Robin was shouting for the watch, and they changed their minds and ran on down the crosslane.

It was all over in a few seconds. Horatio and Robin were not hurt. Stubbes was mauled and torn. Brenings, the stringy servant, was lying twisted in the alley ditch, his doublet bloodied and his slime-crusted face staring up, dead.

When Oxford left her after his trips to Cecil House Anne never knew where he was going. She supposed it was to the theaters, or to Lord Willoughby's, or to Nan Vavasour. She was resigned to the idea that he was seeing Nan Vavasour by some secret means. What worried her was that he always wore his sword.

Since his man had been killed, Oxford never went unarmed. Anne was sure he was in danger. She did not believe he had put anyone to attacking Knyvet's servants, though it was said at court he had; Knyvet was at the court regularly, while Edward was not given a chance to be heard. But she was just as sure he would fight if Knyvet waylaid him. She would start awake from her pillow sometimes at midnight and listen terrified behind her bed curtain, thinking she heard Meg at the door to tell her Edward was murdered.

"Don't go abroad after dark," she begged him one night. "Stay close until mornings."

"Like a slug on a thorn?" he said, "reading my world in a pin point?"

"I dread your going," she said. It was March by now, and blustery. The wind slapped in gusts through the Cecil gardens and moaned down the chimneys. Anne shivered at its sound. "Wait until you're in Her Majesty's favor again. Then no one will touch you."

"Who's to get me into favor?" he said, and kissed her, and pulled on his gloves.

He went out into the street, and with a link boy to light his way, rode to Lord Willoughby's house for supper.

His brother-in-law lived near Cripplesgate beyond the Guildhall, with his wife and small sons. Lady Mary was as mettled and high-tempered as Oxford. She had fallen in love against the wishes of her brother and Lord Willoughby's mother, the Duchess of Suffolk, and her courtship had been stormy and the first years of her marriage turbulent. Lord Willoughby had taken her to his country house, away from London's effervescence, and kept her there like a jailed beauty until she learned how to wear the wedding yoke tractably and with patience.

She had a proud, gay, active temperament, a passion for her husband and her boys, and a love of show. She slept in a great chamber in a four-post bedstead with curtains of white satin designed with gleaming silk and mother of pearl, and bedspreads worked by her own hands, exquisite in color and texture. Rose petals covered the floor. Around the walls were tapestries and cabinets, with chased silverware and tinted china. Small tables inlaid with tortoise shell and silver carried jars of potpourri. She reigned here like a princess, received her friends, ordered her servants and managed her household. The combination of her spirits with Lord Willoughby's firm, steady humor made an ideal home.

Like Anne, she was worried about Oxford. As his sister, she knew his faults, but she was clever enough to keep them to herself. Before her marriage, she had not been in a position to criticize an older brother and a peer of England. Since her marriage, she had come to realize that a man's life must be his own. Her brother couldn't be changed a whit by her interference. Anne might have done it, if Anne had been a stronger character. But that was too late now.

There was plenty to talk of at supper besides Oxford. The Duc d'Alençon had finally gone traipsing to Flanders, with the Queen's thirty thousand pounds and an escort of nobles headed by the Earl of Leicester.

"Leicester would as soon escort the devil," Lady Mary said.

"Sooner," her husband said.

"Her Majesty is chastening him. It's said she wept all night for the duke."

"You've never done the like for me," Lord Willoughby said.

"In God's name, you're not a Frenchman," Lady Mary said.

"Fie, puss! Must a man be French for a lady to weep or sleep for him?"

"If I sleep for you, coz, I teem," Lady Mary flashed. "I can weep for a Frenchman without fattening."

"Help me, Ned," Willoughby said. "Your sister shreds my wits."

"A shred of wit will cover any of you," Lady Mary said. "You men are great rogues. You go in brave apparel that you may be taken for better than you be. You use bombastings and quiltings to seem fitter formed, better shouldered, smaller waisted than you be. You trim your beards and shave often to seem younger than you be; use perfumes both inward and outward to seem sweeter than you be; make courteous greetings to seem kinder than you be; and sometimes—oh, rarely sometimes—graver and godly communications, to seem wiser than you be. I know my 'seems.'"

"Then put seams to the shreds of your own wit in your 'seems,'" Oxford said. "To wit, it seems a shred of wit to seem unseemly."

"Oh, lord, I've done!" Lady Mary said, breaking into laughter.

"Nevertheless, when I go to Denmark, the wench will weep for me," Lord Willoughby said.

"And sleep with no Frenchman," Lady Mary said.

"Faith, no, that's out of mode," Lord Willoughby said.

"Will you go to Denmark?" Oxford said.

" 'Tis thought so."

"As ambassador," Lady Mary said. "To give King Frederick the Garter. Though I think Her Majesty would liefer strangle him with it."

"Diplomacy for our Baltic trade," Lord Willoughby said.

"The Garter is a way to the Queen's friendship with the Dane," Lady Mary said. "Where a woman cannot hawk, she must lure."

"Sprightly judgment, puss. Some man has schooled you," her husband said.

"A man who will school himself in Denmark, pray God, from the lures of Danish maids."

"There's better lure here. My heart's snared," Lord Willoughby said.

Lady Mary flung him a smile. "Ye goose."

"You'll stay at Elsinore," Oxford said.

"Yes, at the castle."

"I'd like to see it. The place is history."

"Oh, he'll tell you every battlement, every tower, every platform and bastion to the last scruple," Lady Mary said. "But not a breath of kirtle or petticoat, or what's in fashion there."

"She'd make me a milliner," Lord Willoughby said.

"It's woeful, being wed to a soldier," Lady Mary said.

"That he assaults cities instead of dresses," Lord Willoughby said. "Would you rather have me lay siege to petticoats?"

"No, we must wag as we can," Lady Mary said.

"Petticoat-wagging is always fashion," Oxford said.

"As men know," Lord Willoughby said.

He set down his wine-cup and would have gone on with that theme, for being married he enjoyed dwelling on woman's flirtatiousness and attempts to draw males into adultery, but Lady Mary gave him a look that silenced him.

Lady Mary said that petticoats were not wagged as easily as they once were. Styles were growing stiffer. In one of the dresses the Queen had worn for Alençon the stomacher had reached almost halfway to the knees. She described it—a forepart of white satin, embroidered all over with pansies, little roses, knots, and a border of clouds, pillars, and pomegranates, of Venice gold and some O's; immense wide, quilted sleeves worked in roses and pansies like the forepart, and a ruff with innumerable gauzy flutings and delicate starched spears of lace sweeping upward behind her ear jewels; an elaborate pendant showing Adam and Eve enameled in white, from Mistress Parry; a gold and diamond-studded mermaid from Mary Sidney; and a hair ornament of a heart set in a wreath of pearls, from Anne Cecil.

She was trying to be diverting. She said that if they followed the Queen they would be swaddled out of nature.

"And out of love," Oxford said caustically. "With hearts made baubles on the head."

His sister stared for a penetrating moment. "They're not so soon broken that way," she said.

She did not stay much longer, but left the men to finish their wine together. As she rose from the table and wished them goodnight, she smiled lightly at Oxford, in affectionate candor. "Be careful," she said.

Lord Willoughby suggested a walk in the garden after supper. His garden was smaller than the one at Cecil House, walled and secluded and protected from the March gusts by the London roofs around it, and he and Oxford could talk there more privately than in the supper chamber where the servants were clearing the table. Lord Willoughby wanted to ask what Oxford was doing to win back his place at court.

"Nothing," Oxford said, while they paced on the turf paths. The ground was softening with the first thaws of spring and their boots made no sound. In the light from the windows the vine tendrils on the house wall were a cobweb of shadows. "What can I do?"

"I had hoped the lord treasurer would have attempted something," Willoughby said. "He's friendly to you, after his kind."

"He'd patch matters if he could. But his shifts and jugglings are so gross and palpable. And he blistered his nose with Alençon. Whoever is to profit at court now must have Hatton's nod. Hatton will give me to maggots before he helps me."

"You've the knack of making enemies. Too keen a mind and too truthful a tongue. You speak out to your own harm, like your cousin Bacon. It makes you seem unmannerly. I'd have sworn when I courted your sister you were swearing my death."

"If I seem unmannerly it's because the race of man seems mad to me," Oxford said. "What dowry could I give Mary? I was dry of money from my travels. No appointment from Her Majesty, London calling me cuckold, and my sister clamoring to marry Peregrine Bertie. I could have sworn worse than death." He took a few steps in silence. "But that's come well in the end."

Lord Willoughby watched the rush of clouds over the garden in the wind and moon, their flying shapes spilling silver and jet on rosebeds and mulberry trees. "I wish all were as well, Ned. These court reptilia are poisonous. I've no love for good Master Vice-chamberlain Hatton."

"Nor he for me," Oxford said.

The wind whipped at Lord Willoughby's cloak, flipping down from the wall like an invisible hand. He turned back toward the house. "What action on your man being slain?"

"None. Hatton has Her Majesty's ear, Knyvet has Hatton's. They blame me."

"Stubbes says Knyvet wants revenge for his niece."

"He's free to want it. And I'm free to walk where I will," Oxford said.

"I'd beware of him."

Oxford caught the gravity of the tone, and knew Lord Willoughby was frowning in the dark. His irritation broke out in a laugh. "Must I beware of everything all my life? Must I hobble and scrape and pull my forelock to every fool who wants to play God and take revenge to himself?"

He began to walk faster. The night and the wind and the racing clouds seemed to stir responsive wildness in him, the recklessness that flared at the sense of difference between himself and such a man as Lord Willoughby, secure and happily married and riding his life at an even keel. He felt proud and arrogant in the difference, ready to plunge into a whirlpool of wilder waters, into a fury of action and self-escape. His empty marriage, Nan's enchantment, the ingratitude of the Queen, pushed him to a desperation.

"Let Knyvet be damned!" he said.

A voice spoke from the house steps. "Not yet, my lord."

He and Willoughby turned. Tom Knyvet was standing on the steps.

15 ‖ KNYVET CAME DOWN THE STEPS SLOWLY. His thick neck and deep eyes were lit by the orange glow of a torch. There were two men with him. One was the servant who had led him there. The other was a hanger-on at court, a man of his faction named Townsend. The servant held the torch aloft and gaped from Knyvet to Lord Willoughby. Townsend followed behind. The arching doorway outlined their silhouettes, and the torch threw their shapes in flickering patterns across the path.

Knyvet came down to the garden level. He lowered one foot after another to the three broad stone steps with the stalking fixity of a cat.

He said, "I'll not be damned till I smell hell fire. Good even, Lord Willoughby."

"Good even," Lord Willoughby said.

He nodded to Townsend and waved the servant indoors. The long patterns leaped and vanished, and the moon and clouds rolled back over the garden. Waves roll back the same way out of a sea pushed from under a cliff by a crashed boulder. Lord Willoughby went forward.

"You break in abruptly, Master Knyvet."

"Yes."

"The suddenness seems ugly."

"I crave your pardon for it. It cried urgent."

"So urgent it cannot wait on tomorrow?" Lord Willoughby said.

"An ugly sire begets an ugly brat," Knyvet said. "I've provocation."

He was approaching with the same rigid deliberation along the path. Townsend came down the steps truculently.

"None, I think, that can be answered tonight," Lord Willoughby said.

"By God, it will."

"Speak softer, Knyvet." Lord Willoughby felt under his cloak, loosening his dagger. He blocked the slow advance. "You are not welcome, and the hour is late. This will disturb my lady."

"I speak you peaceably, my lord. I've no quarrel with you. My quarrel is here."

He shot an arm past Lord Willoughby and shook it in Oxford's face. Lord Willoughby's features set. He would have knocked away the arm, but Oxford said, "Wait."

He undid his cloak and dropped it on the ground. The moonlight glinted on his sword hilt, and on the crosshandled dagger at his belt. He looked at Knyvet, and at Townsend by Knyvet's elbow, and at the taper's glimmer falling through the door on the garden steps; at the house's chimneys tall against the night in the London sky. Dregs of his laughter were still in his voice, the bitterness and anger. "Your quarrel, Knyvet? God's blessing, mine."

"You lie in your throat."

"Take your lie again. 'Twas my man murdered."

"With good riddance. You plot my life, and lay plans to attack me. You're a knave, a bastard villain." Knyvet's eyes, his back to the doorway light, were caved in blackness. "A rogue whose honor is a stink. It calls to be flayed from him."

"Death and Christ! I can defend it."

"Oxford! Knyvet! Let be!" A swirl of wind, spreading Lord Willoughby's cloak, showed his dagger half from its sheath. "Let be, for a pair of fools!"

He strode in, wedging them apart. His shoulder caught Knyvet's, sprawling him aside into Townsend.

"Draw, Tom!" Townsend said. "They'll spit you!" His sword rattled out.

Knyvet's sword flashed, and Oxford's. Lord Willoughby sprang back, clear of the blades.

"See to fair play, my lord," Oxford said. "This fretful porcupine would have his quills pulled."

He lost reckoning of danger, of any consequence to him. He felt only the malice in front of him, the deadly enraged hostility in the glare and the line of teeth like a death's-head in the black beard.

"Take Townsend," he said.

He knew Lord Willoughby had no weapon but a dagger, and that in such private brawls the seconds as often battled as not, as bloodily as the duelists. But he knew Lord Willoughby's repute as a fighter in the Low Countries, and that Townsend was not the man to match it. The issue was between him and Knyvet. Lord Willoughby would hold Townsend at bay. He watched Willoughby snap his dagger out and signal Townsend to stand farther off, and watched Townsend give way and lower his blade. Townsend's lips set thinly, and the moonlight ran along the steel like diamonds, spilling to the grass. Ice flecks danced in Oxford's eyes, and he swung his sword in a half circle. "Now, porcupine."

Knyvet flung off his cloak. "Pull quills if you can," he said. "Come on."

His dagger gleamed beside his sword. He crouched at the knees and sunk his head on his thick neck. A cloud that darkened the moon blotted his inky doublet and hose and left only the two points of steel and his grinning smile. The smile was set and murderous, scarred across his face in a baleful triumph, a white evil that conjured up the craft of Signor Bonetti and the specter of the Sieur de Jarnac.

He gauged for the opening rush.

Oxford was on him before he could move.

Knyvet parried with his dagger and they locked hilt to hilt, their bodies staggering together and straining like wrestlers. There was no hit either way. They broke, and sprang back.

In the pallid moonlight distances were treacherous, the long weapons deceptive. The fight would be grisly, by touch and guesswork. With that first parry Oxford felt Knyvet's thick strength. He must use all his own. He balanced in a quick recovery and braced for footing on the turf.

Knyvet had the advantage of the ground. He had Oxford on the path, while he fought at the edge of the open semicircle below the steps, with room to maneuver. Oxford was pinned between the flower-beds, cramped where he could go only forward or back, and facing Knyvet's thrusts head-on. He met one, turned it, countered another with a swerve of his sword. The pressure of the second forced him sideward. He shifted stance, and sank his boot heel in spongy loam.

" 'Ware!" Willoughby said.

Oxford saw the danger. Knyvet was inching in, attacking on his dagger side to take him at an angle. Knyvet wanted to drive him into the flowerbed and finish him there. He looked down at his boot. The mud stuck to it and caked. The thaw had made the flowerbed a mire.

Bending, he feinted toward Knyvet under the guard. Knyvet took the feint on his blade. At the same instant Oxford swung up with a spring of his body, leaping by Knyvet and hurdling the corner of the flowerbed. He landed on one knee in the open semicircle.

He was up when Knyvet turned.

They were on equal terms now. They held their daggers at the level of their hips, point forward, swords extended, and circled warily. A kind of exultation tingled in Oxford at the chagrin of Knyvet's face. Vindictiveness poured from Knyvet and his black beard was contorted.

"Where is your *passado?*" Oxford taunted. "Where is your school of Marozzo?"

"Spare your breath," Knyvet said.

He plunged in without warning. Oxford warded the plunge, taking the foible of Knyvet's sword on his dagger and cutting from beneath with his. The cut slithered against Knyvet's dagger quillions, and Knyvet's weight spun them both around and threw them wide.

They turned and plunged again. Oxford struck full at the black beard. It melted before his sword like a phantasm, and the shoulder of his doublet slit with a prickle of cold metal across his skin. Then the black beard was close to his eyes, grinning surer in the moonlight. He slashed with his dagger and it veered away.

He was not afraid of Knyvet. One of them or both would not walk out of the garden when they had done. But he had never been afraid of man or devil. He had learned the duello in Europe, its murderous, bludgeoning, rough-and-tumble tactics. He could be tripped, hacked, mauled, gouged or kneed, or thrown to the ground as a duelist in France had been, with Knyvet grappling on top of him, poniarding him in a line from neck to belt buckle while he battered in the back of Knyvet's head with his rapier pommel. By any means Knyvet would try to kill him.

His best defense was in attack. The weapons they fought with were four-foot rapiers, straight, double-edged, very narrow in the blade and protected at the hilt by a *pas-d'âne,* countercurved quillions, a knuckle-bow, and side rings. The grips were short, the pommels heavy, making the rapiers slow in the manage, and in the warding of a blow. The daggers were for warding, heavily forged as the rapiers, twelve inches long and sharp as razors. They caught the thrusts and checked the full-arm cuts, and stabbed and hewed in the in-fighting. But to catch a thrust aimed in the dark from nine feet distant was a chancy hazard. A miss would be the end of it, the rapier was too long for a close parry.

He studied Knyvet's guard. High rapier, low dagger, the point near the left thigh, a shade too wide. He would remember that. He could see Knyvet's thumb patting mechanically in the hollow of the dagger blade just in front of the quillions. The patting stopped. Knyvet's body settled imperceptibly. In the split second Oxford thrust.

Knyvet grunted with surprise. He crossed his rapier with his dagger and slid the blow off between them. He was almost too late. The blades crossed at the thickness of Oxford's rapier, at the forte, but he wrenched, lifting the thrust with his dagger and riposting with his sword. Oxford dodged, and slashed his dagger at the beard once more. Knyvet, doubling, ran out from under, beyond reach.

"Well done!" Willoughby said.

Oxford went after him. Straightening, Knyvet braced himself and launched a *passado,* his left foot past his right, a double stride that carried his point like a battering-ram. Oxford swayed, pivoted to avoid the charge, and leaped at Knyvet as he went by. Knyvet was not an amateur at rapier play. He was tough and seasoned. He brought up short and lurched around, and Oxford's wrist jolted against his. Their daggers quivered above their heads.

The ground grew slippery as they fought. The turf was slick and treacherous. Their boots slithered, and the squeeze of mud under their feet sucked wet in the chase of moonlight and shadow and the hard clink of their swords. Oxford knew the cuts and thrusts of the Italian style. He had skill at broadsword and quarterstaff, gotten from summer afternoons with the men-at-arms in the courtyard of Castle Hedingham when he was a boy. He countered Knyvet's feints and blocked his threats, and answered with threats of his own. He fought cautiously, alert for trickery, now facing the house, now with his back to it, weaving and parrying and rushing, his eyes on Knyvet's face and the grim-browed sockets above the beard.

Knyvet was taking his time. After the first violence he realized that Oxford was adept. Under the grace of a courtier Lord Oxford was powerful and sinewy, and dangerously at home in this work. Knyvet tried the *mandritti,* the *passado,* a *punta dritta,* a *punta revescia.* Oxford turned them all, and repaid them in broadsword strokes and swashing blows. He eluded Knyvet's efforts to seize his sword-elbow and disarm him with a twist and a bonebreaking hold, to grip his rapier or knife him in the ribs as he made recovery from an attack. Knyvet squatted lower on his legs, circling like a huge malevolent crab, and began to think of the *botta secreta.*

Sweat was running from both of them. In the moon their bodies stood out against the flowerbeds, tense, cold-etched, Gorgonesque in the fitful glitter of steel and the cold light; in the spells of dark they were interchanging blurs that rushed together murkily, and writhed and flung upward and broke away. Rips and scratches showed on their clothes. Knyvet's hose was torn, and Oxford's left sleeve hung tattered from his shoulder. Both were bleeding, Knyvet on the forehead, Oxford in the leg below his doublet. But neither had yet taken a crippling hurt. Blood was no matter. Blood or sweat. Steel must bury in solid flesh, to the stamp of a boot, a choke and a fall.

Oxford thought that for Knyvet this must be soon. Knyvet had begun to circle at more distance, beating at Oxford's rapier with his dagger with short, clawing movements to knock it out of line for attack, and when they braced face to face after a pass, matching will and muscle, Oxford could hear his panting breath. As Oxford pushed in harder he commenced to give ground. Feeling cautiously behind him with the sole of his left boot as he went, he retreated from the steps and the doorway light, along the edge of the flowerbeds and into a murkier part of the grass semicircle. Only his grin never altered. It remained stiff, scornful, as if it were a skeleton grinning, biding the moment to lift its coffin lid and start its jig.

In men trained to the sword there is a sort of sixth sense. In the encounter of the blades they receive, even if vaguely, perceptions and instincts of the measure of an adversary, like the encounter of ants' mandibles or the psychic impressions of the antenna of a butterfly. His sixth sense warned Oxford that Knyvet was getting ready for a final stroke.

It warned him not to follow too closely. He slowed his attacks and dropped his point slightly, chary of the black beard in a corner and trying to see the wide-guarding dagger and the nervous patting of the thumb.

Knyvet had retreated to the limit of the grass.

He waited for Oxford to come on.

Sidling along the house steps, Townsend was peering toward them, making inarticulate noises in his throat and giving little slaps at his boot with his sword. Lord Willoughby kept by him. The wind was broadening a field of sky above the garden, and the moon shone very bright.

It was the moment for the *botta secreta*. The memory of the money he had paid Signor Bonetti put a malignant joy in Knyvet's mind. He rehearsed the stroke rapidly to himself, crouching by the flowerbed. The feint obliquely down, to bring in Oxford's point. His own point outside, behind the left knee, the upward edge of the blade at the back of the thigh. The quick backward draw. Signor Bonetti had explained it all. They had practiced it in the *signor's* private chamber and the *signor* had pronounced it perfect. None in the English court could be able to meet it.

Oxford took a stride forward. He understood the chance of a secret thrust. Every swordmaster had them—grips, seizures, cuts, body-counters, fantastic evolutions guarded like treasures and impossible to foresee in combat—and Knyvet had coached with Bonetti for a year. But he was impatient to end this while Knyvet was sweated and scant of breath. He would give him no respite.

Knyvet's thumb stopped patting on his dagger blade.

Oxford struck.

Knyvet beat him off, thrust. Oxford recovered and came on again. Knyvet's hilt twirled in a polished arc. He feinted suddenly, obliquely down. Oxford swerved to the feint. Knyvet doubled low, and with a shout crouched and ran in under. His rapier snaked like a stiletto for Oxford's leg tendons in the deadly *coup de Jarnac*.

As the blade reached out, pale as venom in the moonlight, Oxford spun to the left and leaped. The action saved his tendons, but the blade sliced across the flat of his hip. At the same moment his point lunged inside the wide dagger guard and drove through Knyvet's side. Knyvet's eyes swelled in their sockets. He dropped his rapier, and took Oxford's with both his hands. He pushed himself backward, sliding off the steel. It came from his body reeking for a third of its length, and Knyvet fell to his knees.

"God's death," he whispered.

Oxford leaned on his rapier. Blood was gushing from his hip and soaking his hose.

Over the grass Lord Willoughby came toward him, with Townsend close behind, running to Knyvet. A cluster of servants who had been watching from windows and around the stone doorway arch trailed out of the house after their master in smocks and aprons and woolen-hooded caps. "Ned!" said Willoughby. "Ned, how is it with you?"

Oxford put his hand to his hip and held the hand in front of him, wet dripping off his fingers.

He tried to smile.

"A sharp quill," he said.

He stared down to Knyvet, who coughed hoarsely on the ground, and slumped against Lord Willoughby's chest.

They stanched the blood with napkins and carried Oxford and Knyvet into the house. They spread cloaks on the rushes of the floor and laid them on them at Lord Willoughby's orders, by the long supper table where the tapers glimmered. Silver wine mugs waited beside a platter of confections, left for the refreshment of the two brothers-in-law after their garden stroll. A servant brought wine to Oxford and tilted the mug at his lips. Faces pressed around him, breathing garlic, and curiosity, and avidness to see, and a gawking stupefaction, for the earl was a great favorite with the lesser folk of London and in Lord Willoughby's household: his kindness to Jack Stubbes had been a good Christian act; they had guffawed at his players and whooped at his tournaments. It was woeful to have him fetched to such a plight. With nudges and scurryings they shuffled in and out of the room, casting looks over their shoulders and loitering by the walls. One went for a surgeon. One brought quilts. One ran for a basin of water. Lady Mary's page darted in, squeaked, and went scrambling off upstairs.

Calling his bedchamber groom, Lord Willoughby had him cut the clothing away so the surgeon could get at the hurts. With Townsend he examined Knyvet's wound, a stab through the body, a palm's width below Knyvet's outer ribs.

"He'll live to call on his Maker in more brawls," he said to Townsend. "I've seen worse on the battlefield and the devils mended. Get him to his bed when he's had the surgeon. I'll give you men."

Oxford's wound was more serious. It had gashed to the bone, severing the flat muscles of his hip. When Lord Willoughby lifted the napkin to look at it the bleeding broke out afresh. But there was a thankfulness in Willoughby's voice as he replaced the napkin with a new one and wrapped it tight and rose from his knees.

" 'Tis God's luck you've your leg. That was a maiming thrust. I've never known the like."

"It comes from Italy, like sonnets," Oxford murmured. "I smelled it in the nick. I'd met it once at Padua, in the street riots."

"A plague on this villainous dueling. It will lame us all."

"Knyvet had forgot I'd been at Padua," Oxford said. His eyes went shut.

"A plague on it," Willoughby said.

He stood by the table. Evidence in the gashes and stabs and in the dark red splotches smeared among floor rushes made his curse genuine. A soldier, a patriot, a man whose views of life were shaped to tangible fact, he thought duels a mistaken folly. They were a canker in the common health. He felt when the nation was beset outside by force and aggressions, by guile and subterfuge, men were signing their own doom to weaken it by enmities and murderous quarrels from within. Neither strength nor peace could come from these divisions. And there were many of them. Many. Lord Willoughby listened to the groans behind Knyvet's clenching teeth and thought of his sons asleep upstairs. Would God the sins of the fathers would not be visited on them! Would God their homes would never fall to an invader's prey, that they would never hear the yells of a raping army!

A torch, flaming in the hall, lighted Lady Mary into the room. She wore her nightrobe, and carried bottles of medicinal waters and jars of lotion. Her page came after her, bearing the torch in one hand and towels under his arm. He put the torch in a bracket and gave the towels to Lady Mary.

After a quick glance at her brother, she went to her husband. "Can he be moved?"

"As the surgeon says. He's fainted from much letting of blood."

"How did it happen?"

Lord Willoughby told her. She looked once at Knyvet while he was speaking, and then turned away. Knyvet had been vomiting, and was not an attractive sight. "Nan Vavasour is old enough to be her own protector. An uncle should leave well enough alone."

"A brother, too," he said.

"And a brother-in-law," Lady Mary retorted. "You were three great children together. Could you not have stopped them?"

"At some risk," he said. "But to tell truth, I was not in the humor to take it. I fear I would have fain let some air into Knyvet myself." He looked rueful.

She regarded him, and her lips pulled in a little smile. She shook her head. "Gramercy for honesty. I'll say no more."

He smiled with her. Lord Willoughby had been raised in the Protestant faith, but he had learned that confession is good for the soul, particularly if made to an intelligent wife. He squared his shoulders a trifle and took charge again.

"We will nurse him here," he said. "He shall stay at Willoughby House until he's back in health. That will be some atonement."

"That will be no atonement at all," she said. "After this he will be deeper in disgrace with Her Majesty than ever. He shall go to Vere House."

"To be alone there?" he said.

"No," she said, with the pity of a woman for men's incapacity to get to the core of things. "To be with Anne."

So it was that Oxford lay at Vere House while his wound swelled and inflamed, while the surgeons bled him and applied their poultices and leaned over him ponderously with their beards, while he raved in a delirium of fever and pain, and mouthed scraps of poems and snatches of bawdy songs, bits of Latin and French and Greek, while he babbled of Ariosto and Chaucer, of courts of law, and men with legs like crabs, and flowerbeds, and gold hair, and lace-trimmed handkerchiefs.

So it was that his mind returned to him while Anne sat by his bed, soothing him and caring for him and looking to his wants, while the pain in his hip slowly lessened and the wound healed to an ugly scar, and the April rain whispered against the windows and a misty sun slanted a little higher each week along the bed curtains; while he watched Anne going and coming softly in the chamber, his eyes following her from where he lay propped motionless on the bolster, and lifted his head and touched her hand when she brought him his wine to drink.

So it was at last that they sat together in the window while the weakness of the long helpless days drained from him under the spring sunlight, while he cradled her head preciously against his shoulder and Anne told him that she was pregnant again.

16 ALENÇON HAD GONE, AND ELIZABETH, STILL UNMARRIED, had embarked on a progress the following year.

With hawthorn blooming in the hedges and larks singing from headlands of young wheat, the cheers of Suffolk villages came to her ears in a music that drowned the rumbling kettledrums of war. Through shires where the militia saluted and aldermen knelt to her in their robes of office, she showed herself to her people as the Virgin Queen.

Jouncing in her coach, in the lurches of the unwieldy vehicle, Elizabeth knew that she would never marry. The French match was ended, the private banquets and the public tensions and the ladies-in-waiting weeping in her rooms at night. Alençon had been insufferable at the last, Burghley and Walsingham had had their hands full to get him out of the palace apartments and back to Flanders. The pretence of marriage with Philip of Spain had raveled into transparency. There was no one else. She could not marry an English noble; her people did not want a foreign one. It was the spite of her times that she had inherited to a slippery and uneasy succession, too slippery to be secure in any but her own person. Her people were hers alone, and she must be theirs.

Her face twitched in annoyance as the coach bumped over a stone. Her courtiers who languished about her claimed even yet they were swooning for love of her. But her regrets were lean, like the leanness of her cheeks now, and the pinching of the lines around her nostrils with the passing of her fiftieth year and her climacteric.

"We find it not so tragic to be husbandless, Mistress Radcliffe, ha?" she said.

Mary Radcliffe, sitting in the royal coach for the company of a mile, had never married either.

"Faith, no, Majesty. I say straightly to men that their wit is like custard, nothing good in it but the sop, and when that's eaten you may throw away the rest."

Elizabeth smiled and nodded.

By putting aside the leather curtains of the coach she could see, around a bend of the road, the green-clad harbingers who were the spearhead of her train, trudging beyond flat fields where sheep and cattle would fatten in the summer; the yeomen of the guard in red coats with the Tudor rose; behind them the gentlemen pensioners, shouldering gilt battle-axes that flashed and twinkled in the sun.

The harbingers and yeomen and pensioners stretched in a great winding procession, splendid, commanding, marvelously colored, like a rich thread weaving through the tapestry of the countryside. Meadows rolled backward in ancient sweeps, tilled, sowed, their variant furrows softened by rain and by the first spearlings of crops still uneven in newborn growth, dusting the earth like powdered emerald, melting from shade to shade, bright and bold on the slow lift of the ridges and timidly sparse in the hollows, the trees bunched in copses or in squares of woods, or in willows by the banks of brooks, which twisted brown as the earth under a footbridge across a pebbled ford, by a farm cot capped by straw hair of thatch, or pools beneath a slope where the heads of ducks swam among the sedge tops.

Then the noblemen and the courtiers, proudly dressed, riding according to degree and followed by serving-men wearing their masters' badges on their left arms.

They jogged through a land made old by Briton and Roman, Saxon and Dane, by sea-rovers and the councils of the bearded Hengist and Horsa, the martyrdom of Edmund the Saint and the running of the silver shoes of Llanrei, King Arthur's mare. . . . On roads that had seen the housecarls marching toward Harold and the palisade at Hastings, the Norman knights in mail and the longbowmen home victorious from Picardy. . . . The mysteries of the Druids, the cleric scholars of the abbeys, and poets and troubadours from castle keeps. . . . And along their way the air shimmered dewy and crystalline as an aquamarine.

Next after the nobles came the Queen's coach. Although it battered her and stiffened her joints, Elizabeth used it out of vanity. It was lavish with paint and gold, upholstered in red leather, decked in ostrich feathers and studded by gilt nails. Six horses dragged it over ruts and holes, and in the worst spots serving-men heaved at it with their shoulders to hold it upright. Elizabeth, inside, clung to the seat in a grim determination. She was an excellent horsewoman, but the coach was an innovation and a mark of her prestige, and give it up she would not.

In the rear the maids of honor trotted on saddle horses, with riding masks to protect their faces, leading an endless line of riders, the lesser members of the royal household, tailed by two hundred luggage carts toiling along in dun swirls.

Elizabeth opened the curtains farther. They were nearing a village. The road was full of beggars, vagabonds who scoured the country lifting linen from the hedges and turning a shameless penny. The ears of most carried the brand of a hot iron for their offenses. They were of all kinds—fortunetellers, rufflers, basket women with laces, pins, needles and girdles for sale, priggers of praunces alert for a horse to steal, palliards of Clapperdogen whose shins were loathsome with false blisters raised by spearwort and that disappeared in a night, and Abraham men, the feigners of madness, wrapped in tatters and calling themselves Poor Tom. They grimaced and whined and groveled, limping, cavorting, waving crutches and shaking their rags like scarecrows.

"It's a sop of the same wit as a courtier's."

She leaned back, braced erect against bruises from the whalebone of her farthingale in the pitching coach.

"I wonder these people cry for me as Queen."

An acute percipience of England, a fresh awareness of the nation, was borne in on her from the sights and sounds of the May morning. She was of it, she was of all this. This country was her true husband. "I am mere English, my lords," was her boast in council, "English to the bone."

At the village she halted her coach by the common. She put back the curtains again and had the village folk brought to her. Among fly-swarmed cows and the braying of donkeys she spoke to them graciously. She heard their interests and listened to their problems. She praised the look of their cattle and the taste of their beer.

When she had finished she crooked a forefinger at Lord Burghley, who stood by with Walsingham and Hatton.

"Pray God this sort will sit in our new Parliament, Sir Spirit. It will go merrily."

"Pray God it will."

Burghley was less emotional than his Queen. The sights and sounds that kindled her enthusiasm on the edge of a village common in Maytime did not stir him. Though he had taken a defeat over the French matter he would follow her loyally. But he was a realist.

"If Your Majesty's rule could be brought so to every village, Parliament would be your slaves," Hatton put in flowerily.

"Tush, we want no slaves, but free men," Elizabeth answered.

"The Parliament will be heavily Puritan," Burghley said, gravely. "They're little like to be impressed by the bounden goodness of Your Majesty in talking to villagers between an ox and an ass."

"Why, 'tis the way the Blessed Lord came to the world, and they're a godly sect, Sir Spirit." Elizabeth was gay.

"They are severe and exceeding well organized," Burghley replied. "Your Majesty will have to take strict measures to them." He glanced with significance toward the middle of the common, where Leicester and Raleigh were urging the maids and courtiers to a country dance. "There is much they disapprove, and their necks are stiff."

"And mine wears a crown," Elizabeth snapped. She turned to Walsingham. "Do you gloom on the Puritans, too, my Moor? Burghley spoils my morning."

"No, my liege, on the Scots," Walsingham said.

Elizabeth glared at him irritatedly. Walsingham had told her about the Scots. King James, eighteen and beginning to assert himself, was falling under French influence, beguiled by Scottish nobles who had been in Paris; there was a plan afoot to recall Mary to Edinburgh, to reign jointly with her son, and to land an army of her partisans in Lancashire; through them, Spain might woo for an alliance with France. Elizabeth had ordered Walsingham to give her release from these worries while she enjoyed the progress, but Walsingham had a humorless persistence.

"God's death, I'm between an ox and an ass indeed," she exclaimed. "Here's a fair sweet day toward, and a joy o' sense, and ye compass me with gallstones and the gout." Walsingham suffered from one, Burghley from the other. "Make joyfuller talk," she said, waving a hand at the dancers. "Tell me what men the master of the revels will pick for my company of players."

"I spoke with Master Tilney before we rode from London," Walsingham said. "He will choose twelve of the best. Some will be from my lord of Leicester's company, one from my lord of Sussex's. Two or more will come from my lord of Oxford, the Duttons among them."

"Swear them to our service," she said, "and allow them wages and liveries as grooms of the chamber."

"That will be done, my liege."

"I must have Tarleton," she said.

"He is picked."

"I think London will gape at our advancement of actors," she said. "A troupe in the Queen's pay." She seemed very pleased.

"My lord of Oxford will gape at his finest players pulled from him,"

Hatton observed smugly. "His feathers will be plucked. I hear he goes about with a great retinue."

Elizabeth frowned and said nothing.

"Master Vice-chamberlain, these things are hardly charged," Burghley said. "My lord of Oxford is poorly served. He has no means for a great retinue. He cannot support his daughter, who must live in my care."

"Then your lordship will be glad he will lose a few of his lewd friends, at least," Hatton smiled.

"I am not glad to any hap that strikes him today," Burghley said. "My lord of Oxford's new son has died. The courier reached me this morning. My lord and his lady Anne buried the babe in Castle Hedingham yesterday."

With quiet dignity he faced Hatton, patting his beard. If he knew Hatton's jealousies and fawning lies to the Queen that had kept Oxford out of favor, if he knew his own shortcomings and well-meant blunderings in his dealings with his son-in-law, he did not show it. He kept his grief, and the stature of his respect. His fingers twitched a little, that was all.

"My lord," Hatton stammered, "if I had heard—. Your grandchild —a sorrow, a dolorous sorrow."

"Hatton, you fool, be silent," Elizabeth said. "Go bid them stop the dancing."

Hatton went away hurriedly in confusion, and Elizabeth looked deeply at Lord Burghley. She put a hand from the coach window and touched his shoulder. "My good Sir Spirit," she said.

Her hand with its rings rested on his cloak in a taut, human compassion.

"All of us who live are mortal," she said.

Turning to Walsingham abruptly and saying they would move on, she pulled the leather curtains closed.

For the rest of the day she rode in the coach alone. The curtains remained closed. The countryside joggled by, unnoticed, while Elizabeth sat thinking.

She thought of Burghley, and Oxford and Anne. She thought of the Puritans and their growing power, their preachers journeying tirelessly, spreading their gospel. They were fanatic for reform, and zealots in purpose. They realized the strength of the people's voice in affairs, and she foresaw already they would not shrink from a head-on clash with the crown. Unless she were prompt and resolute they might take control, with results that would shake the realm. She thought of Scotland, the simmering danger there, and how to keep the Frenchmen out, and the young James friendly. She thought of her own people, of the village she had left, peaceful on the surface and serene, but a prey to every wandering rumor that came through.

None of its folk had ever seen her before, none would ever set eyes on her again. The single royal sight of her, paused magical and beneficent on their common, would perhaps hold them steady, secure against the divisions and the clamors in the land; but how many such villages were there? Burghley had shaken his head at Hatton's notion she could bring her grace to each. She thought with a bitter smile of the serving-men who pushed at her coach, and what little they guessed of the troubles of a Queen who could not be everywhere and everything at once, who must be her own interpreter and her own best agent.

The progress came at last to the house of Sir William Cordell, the master of the rolls, and the Queen's coach turned in under the gateway, over the moat, into the courtyard where Lady Cordell waited to receive her.

When she had rested from the trip, Sir William escorted her to the turreted banqueting house overlooking the bowling green. Several of the courtiers had already started a game. The maids of honor, not in attendance at the moment, strolled round the garden where apricots blossomed on the sunny walls; they sat on the banks by the fishponds and watched the fish, and the shy water hens diving. Rooks circled overhead, leaving the rookery for their evening flight, and from the park came the thud of hammers as the tents of the retainers went up, and the grooms hissed as they rubbed down the horses in the stable yard.

Sir William and his lady spared nothing. These visits from Her Majesty left her hosts noticeably poorer, but Elizabeth wished it so. They were one of her ways of circulating the wealth, and shifting to her nobles some of the expense of her court, which devoured her substance like consuming grasshoppers. When Elizabeth, leaning on the parapet to see the bowling, dropped her fan in the moat, Lady Cordell with a trembling curtsy replaced it with the most elegant one in the house.

After she had supped she summoned Raleigh, and took him for a walk along the battlements. Raleigh was her most recent favorite. Since his fine arguments before the council on the handling of affairs in Ireland, she had put more and more faith in him. He belonged to no party, to no faction; he had no family connections at the court, and was grinding no man's axe but his own. She found him clever, stimulating, and very apt. She had her nickname for him: Water.

"Water," she said, strolling beside him in the dusk while she tapped her fingers on his arm, "where can a sovereign take comfort in her subjects?"

"In their devotion to Your Majesty," he said promptly, in his slurring Devon accent. "In their carrying of your name and glory to the four corners of the earth."

"We'd not be flattered tonight," she said. "We know what you're thinking. You're thinking of ships and expeditions. Later, later."

She walked in silence a short while.

"You've known my lord of Oxford," she said.

"Yes, Your Majesty."

"You've never pleaded for him since I sent him from court."

"I've not wished to set myself against Your Majesty's judgment."

"Would God there were more like you," she said. "But my lord of Oxford may have been wrongly reported. Certain things—and a sadness today— Tell me, Water, if it were not against my judgment would you plead for him?"

Raleigh considered swiftly. His mind raced to decide what was expected of him, and he spoke with care. "Your Majesty is witness to the love I bear my lord of Burghley. He is grievously discomforted by this matter. It would be honorable and profitable for Your Majesty to have regard for his health and quiet. As for my lord the earl, he has paid with long absence and many disgraces. I would be willing, my liege, to lay the serpent before the fire again, even though I might be the first to feel his poison and sting."

Elizabeth made no comment at once. Raleigh was afraid he had gone too far, but when they reached the end of the battlements she spoke.

"Send word to Oxford to wait on us when we return to Greenwich," she said.

The interview between Oxford and Elizabeth was stormy.

She had sent her maids away and received him alone, seated in an armchair in her chamber overlooking the royal park at Greenwich. The day was gray and hot and humid, thick with a hint of the plagues that swept periodically over London, and the fevers that carried off hundreds every summer, and she was in a disgruntled mood. Walsingham had been at her again with his continual tales of plots, and Burghley and Leicester were tugging in opposite directions in her foreign policy. She had not been able to shake her cares along the country roads; they had ridden back with her like an incubus.

The death of his son had worked a change in Oxford. He was more sober and mature than she had ever seen him. There was a look in his eyes as he met her chill yellow ones that warned her of a firm, tempered sureness shaped to a stronger self-possession, and told her at once that at thirty-three, after two years' banishment from court, he had broadened into the full scope of his manhood. When he knelt to her and she motioned him to rise the wound Knyvet had given him in their duel put a slight stiffness in his walk that added to his gallantry.

She began in a formal tone, saying she was sorry for his loss. He thanked her briefly. Both understood that the tragedy had been a cause for bringing them together, but neither of them wanted sentimentality. She spoke of Anne, of his players, of his health. He answered in the same way, showing no fear of her, no impulse to throw himself on her mercy. She felt herself becoming furious with him, and could have dismissed him in a rage. Yet her instinct knew that in the complexities of the events tightening around her she needed him. The instinct was unformed yet, vague and nebulous, but it was there. One day she would know the reason. She tired of the polite, fencing phrases and leaned brittlely forward.

"Oxford, why did you do it?"

"Which of my crimes does Your Majesty mean?" he said.

"Any of them, all of them. You are extravagant, wasteful, and improvident. You have behaved scandalously with Mistress Vavasour.

Incited brawls in our streets. Set our laws at nought. Charged treason in our court. I know not what else. Od's my life!"

"With such a list I were better in the Tower again. It would take the rest of my years to answer it."

"Peace! You're a saucy varlet."

"I'm a truthful one."

"A mad one. What do you say to Mistress Nan? Ha?"

"That I am the things I am, and that a man cannot live on promises. He looks for happier fare."

"Promises?" She picked up the word sharply. "What promises?"

"From the first time I knew Your Majesty I've been fed on promises. I've spent in hopes and sold my estates in expectations. The hopes and the estates are bankrupt. I'll expect no more."

"Christ's body, my lord, am I on trial here or are you? Do you put charges against me, too?"

"It is a charge that weighs my heart when my Queen credits lies about me."

A quick spasm passed over her features. She gave him a stiff piercing stare.

"I was promised favor," he said, "when I first came to court. I trusted in the promises."

She spun on him again, so violently that the frame of her farthingale crushed against the chair arm. "And how have I trusted you? And how has Anne trusted you? And how have you deceived us?"

"Which is the greater wrong?" he said. "The wrong of mind or the wrong of body? I've sinned in body, but I've been sinned against in mind. By my wife, and by my Queen."

"You console yourself with a mean substitute," she said scornfully. "Nan Vavasour is a light wench."

"She has a lusty uncle," he said, frowning at his hip. "I'll walk lame to my grave from that business. Does Your Majesty think I'd have brought it on myself? God's blessing, I had Nan, I'd have left well enough alone. Knyvet challenged."

"I was told not."

"More lies. Lies from Hatton, from Knyvet, from the Howards, and I am forbidden the court and cannot speak in my defense. I've served

Your Majesty. I serve you still. I'd looked for better at Your Majesty's hands."

"I'd looked to have you deserve it."

"You took me as a ward when my father died. I was raised in the extravagance of the court. I was taught to think you looked kindly on me. I was taught to think my path was open for me to preferment and some high office under my Queen. Instead I am slandered, lied about, abused, and thrown in the Tower unheard."

"The Tower was a lesson," she said.

"I cry your pardon. I thought it was the love Your Majesty once meant for me."

Elizabeth felt the smart of tears under her eyelids. For lone, long years her queenship had entangled her in one after another of cruel frustrations and the heartbreak of impossibilities. She could remember when Oxford was seventeen, remember with the throb and vividness of her vanished youth. She burst into weeping.

"Oh, my Turk, my Turk," she said, "let's have done with wrangling."

Oxford was at her knees in an instant.

"My liege—"

"A pox on it," she said. "It comes not between you and me."

"Never from my desire," he said, "nor from Your Majesty's," and kissed the fingers she held to him.

"I wished no disgrace for you," she said.

"If you smile there is none. It's forgot."

"Oh, my Turk."

She pulled out her handkerchief and pressed it to her cheeks. She fondled his face, and his neck, and his strong brown hair. He had not been at her knees in two twelvemonths. She had been too cross with him, too petulant. She would never be so again. She was as wayward and capricious as he.

"This is a happy sadness, Ned. It kills a hundred of my enemies."

"And blots a hundred Towers."

She blew her nose explosively and put away her handkerchief. Sniveling mottled her skin, and she had a horror of bathos. "God's death, we'll find sustenance for you. We'll keep you at court."

"Your Gracious Majesty." He kissed her fingers once more.

" 'Twill be a squeeze, like angels on the point of a pin, but we'll do it."

"Your Majesty has many demands," he said.

"Demands!" Elizabeth broke into a harsh cackle, the nervous reaction from her tears. "Y'speak sooth there. Demands, say you, Ned. D'ye know my revenues for a year?"

"No, your Majesty."

"Ordinary revenues, from crown lands, customs, and the like?"

"I do not, Your Majesty."

"Two hundred and fifty thousand pounds. With the which I must pay for my court, salary my government, fight my battles, and play godmother to half of Europe. I am crammed, Ned. My sister Mary left debts of two hundred thousand. To put the French out of Scotland and campaign in Ireland—'twas before you were a ward—cost six hundred and fifty thousand more. Taxes are rare and unwelcome and never up to the mark, assessments are hard and usually false. I sell crown land, and borrow from Antwerp, with London City backing the loans and the goods of my merchants under threat of seizure if I default."

Oxford answered seriously that it was a heavy load.

"It has grayed my Lord Burghley and made a shrew of me. I am called miserly and penny-wise," she said. "And my courtiers beg from me and my nobles berate me." She gave him a glance. "The count stretches till doom. For quelling the rebellion in the North, ninety-three thousand. For two Irish uprisings, half a million. For Alençon, to build his esteem in case I married him—ha, ask Burghley. How much does that come to?"

"I've not been reckoning," he said.

"No, that's laid on your Queen. The Netherlanders pay their soldiers only six months out of twelve, are always behind on their debts. Yet I must uphold them to block Spain. My own army is vile; wages are paid through the captains; their men disappear, and they lend one another their companies to pad their muster-rolls on pay day; and our court-captains parade at our revels in the winter seasons. There is tyranny and corruption in recruiting. I've set up inquiries, I've set up committees of appeal. Od's life, I'll have honesty to our common soldier."

Her voice was still harsh.

"To find sustenance. To meet demands. My expenses are never matched by income. I've no scheme of *rentes* as France or Spain. Philip can build a fleet, the Medici can maintain a soldiery. Elizabeth of England can do neither. I'm driven to haggle and bargain, to offer stewardships to the highest bidder and barter monopolies for the services of my subjects."

"But Your Majesty gets a full return," Oxford said, thinking of Burghley and Walsingham, Leicester, and the exploits of Sir Francis Drake. The men around Elizabeth had a free hand, and they were vigorous and full of enterprise.

"And a name for parsimony," she said. She was beginning to get angry again, her melting mood had shifted to an harassed sense of her grievance. "A name for parsimony and money qualms. I'm made a reproach for stinginess. They mutter against me and say I am greedy. Yet the protection of every soul in England, this realm, this island, from the least cabin boy in my ships to the proudest lord at Greenwich, depends on me. When the hour of mischief tolls, they'll lay all on the Queen."

She started up and strode back and forth in front of her chair, striking its arms with her fan. Oxford stayed silent, kneeling. What she said was true. Everything revolved around her—stability, money, the tensions of politics. When she seated herself again she was calmer.

"We'll find you something, my Turk. It cannot be the duties on wines, Raleigh must have those for building vessels and his plans for voyages. There are the wools and oils, but—. I granted you the Manor of Rysing once."

"It brings only part of what I need, Your Majesty. My players are like your kingdom. They cost dear."

"Aye, you have players; and taken a lease on Blackfriars, we hear. And you feed playwrights and city scriveners. You must be more like your Queen, Ned, you must scrape the pence. What service will you do me?"

"In war, if you'll give me leave. If not, in my plays."

"Your plays are entertainment. Are they service?"

"They've served you already," he said.

She looked at him quickly. "How?"

"They've told you the truth," he said. "And they've told London the respect due to kings."

"They've told acid jests about our courtiers," she said.

"Which are also the truth," he said. "But jesting acid will never burn honest metal."

"Well well, we have our pretensions at court," she said.

She leaned back, narrowing her eyes reminiscently. He had given her warning about Lord Henry Howard when no one else had dared to. He had done it so cleverly that few had seen it, but they had caught the pulse and fire in the lines. Londoners were catching them, and the country people who were seeing his players in the provinces.

Her mind turned to the village scene on her progress that spring, to Burghley on one side of her and Walsingham on the other, and to the village folk at a distance, watching, grinning, ignorant, innocent of causes, or the dangers of their own innocence. They were a fertile soil where weeds could grow, or the healthy roots of England. And she recalled her despair that a Queen could not be everywhere at once. She could not travel like bands of players, or speak to the villagers as the players could. She could not be chronicle and drama and tragedy and comedy, and make them laugh, and make them weep, and send them home with a moral in their heads.

Her eyes narrowed further, and the lines at her nostrils pinched tighter in the quirk of a smile.

"Write your plays," she said, "but without jibes at our courtiers."

Here was the answer to her instinct that said she needed Oxford. Here was the reason. She leaned forward again.

"Write your plays. We will provide for them."

She kissed him gustfully on the lips.

"You have our word."

17

"I MARVEL THAT YOU ARE SO CONTENT. BUT IT IS A GREAT comfort to me," Lady Burghley said.

"Oh, I am, Mother."

"I was remarking it to my lord your father yesterday."

Anne, seated at the virginals, smiled at her mother across the tune she was humming. One hand was fingering on the keyboard. The other was beating time for the little Elizabeth.

"I'm much pleased," Lady Burghley said.

"I'm glad, Mother. No, darling, faster on the 'derry, derry-down.' Quick and gay."

The little Elizabeth faltered on the words, and looked toward her grandmother and laughed. Anne laughed too.

"You are too pale. The city summers are not wholesome for you," Lady Burghley said. "You must be careful of the fevers. I wish we might have stayed longer at Theobalds."

"Not with Edward in London, Mother."

"You are a forgiving nature," Lady Burghley commented. "You pattern yourself on me. Well, that's all one. Has he been to the Vavasour girl lately?"

"I think not," Anne said. "Now again, darling, and mark the measures. Thou'st a sweet voice."

"There's never a certainty," Lady Burghley said. "I never could tell if my lord your father— Well, I marvel at you. But I'm much pleased."

"He's free to work with his books and players, and Her Majesty approves. I've never seen him as happy," Anne said.

She gave her mother another smile, and at the sound of horses in the courtyard jumped up and ran to the window. "He's coming," she said. "He'll be here to supper. And I've asked my Lord and Lady Willoughby. There's an end now, my precious. We'll learn *Heart's Ease* tomorrow and you shall sing it Christmas for the Queen."

She closed the virginals and patted at her hair, and began to straighten the little Elizabeth's dress, smoothing the rumples in the bodice and tweaking wrinkles from the skirt.

"The poor child, eight years to her name, and must be primped for its father like any stranger," Lady Burghley said. "Poor minx. Its grandam loves it."

"Indeed, we know, Mother," Anne said, pacifyingly.

Lady Burghley, hearing Oxford whistling on the stairs, gathered her needlework and retired, and Anne laughed and whirled toward the door.

Oxford met her as she threw it open. He caught her halfway through the whirl and swung her to him. He was in bounding spirits. "God's blessing, Anne, more pretty every day." Her toes scuttered the floor rushes like giddy weathervanes. He picked up the little Elizabeth, feet waving, and held her at arm's length above his head. She squealed and giggled. "Ah, you grow heavier, my lass, a man will long to do this one day and he won't be able. You sprout like a marigold in September." He kissed her and set her down, and took off his cloak and gave it to Meg, the dressing woman. "Good den, Meg." Meg curtsied, sparingly, and Oxford chuckled. Meg was dour and cronelike, a symbol of Cecil House, but she couldn't damp him.

He took Anne to the window seat and drew her on his lap. "We'll have a play," he said. "Such a play. To be done for the Queen."

"We have a song for the Queen, too," Anne said. "Our Elizabeth is for music, the same as her father."

"A song?" he said. "Marry, we'll hear it."

"No, tomorrow. 'Tis not perfect yet. What's the play, my lord?"

"A notion from Raleigh," he said, drawing Elizabeth beside him with Anne and pulling playfully at her brown curls. She sat in a blissful awe, quietly adoring him and satisfied not to sing. "He'll make a venture to the Americas, to put a colony there. He'll go himself, if Her Majesty will let him; if not, he'll send Dick Grenville. He's to make Ralph Lane the governor. You know Ralph. No, 'twas before we married. He and I had a plot afoot to rescue the Duke of Norfolk."

His voice was amused. He was struck by its casualness, that it was not hard or resentful. It proved how far he had come in breadth of approach since those days, that he could mention the old escapade with no more than a humorous shrug.

"The temptation's to exaggerate. Raleigh's abrim with stories, you can cull 'em out of any book. Tigers that halt to stare at themselves in mirrors; the Monocelli, the men with one foot apiece, but of such bigness it shelters them from the sun when they lie on their backs; the manticore with the head of man and three rows of teeth in each jaw, the body of a bear, legs of a lion, tail of a scorpion, and voice of a trumpet. Shall we have one of them for the nursery, Bess?"

"Oh no, and it please my lord," Elizabeth said.

"Nor for the play. I've been reading in Captain Best, Anne. He wrote an account of Frobisher's venture. An accurate man. He speaks of ice and white bears. I've recommended him to Lyly. 'Twill be a change from Ronsard."

"Does Master Lyly need a change?"

He cupped his hand under her chin, laughing into her eyes. She had hardly an idea who Ronsard was; French poets were vague to her, and most of the English ones. But he felt her interest, her delight in his enthusiasms and her wish to keep up with him. He felt how much she loved him. She would be having another child in the spring.

"We all need change."

His legs dropped from the window seat, where they had been sprawled. He stood up, and pulled her to her feet.

"We'll to court. We'll dance. Will you dance with me, Anne?"

"Oh, Edward—your hip."

"A pox on the hip. I'll stub your shoes. A pox on shoes, we'll buy you new."

"Edward—no—" She was laughing with him, struggling in his arms.

"Yes."

"You'll loose my hair."

"I like it loose."

"Meg does not. Nay, Edward, in front of the girl—" Still laughing, she broke from him and tried to run, but he reached after her and brought her back.

"Who'll teach her better than mother and father? Let her learn. Sing, Bess. Out with your song. Music for a dance."

All fall he had been like this. He had a sense of jubilance and well-being. His passion for life was unshackled. The fetters were struck off. He had the past and the future, good and evil, the teeming city and the glittering court, books and poems and plays to steep himself in and to be mastered and to fill his mind.

"*Heart's Ease,* lass. Pipe up."

Anne broke away again and he ran after her. She led him a chase around the room, past the virginals and around the tables and the cushions, until he caught her.

Lady Mary, coming early to supper, stopped in the doorway as he swirled Anne into a wild, breathless measure.

"I' God's name," Lady Mary said, after a startled look. "Next spring's babe is like to be a bouncing one."

In June the Earl of Sussex had died.

Oxford had gone to see him, at his house on Cannon Row, where he lay weakened by fever and by the consumption that had eaten into him after his military campaigns. He had been a sturdy prop for the Queen and the country. Lord lieutenant of the North, he had whipped the northern lords whose armies marched against Elizabeth. In the debates of the Privy Council he had held Leicester in check. As lord chamberlain he had devoted himself to Her Majesty's court. More than any other man, he had given friendship and encouragement to Oxford. He had been like a father to him. He was to Oxford what Leicester was to Sidney.

In the darkened room, propped by bolsters and with the curtains of his bed muffling the spasmodic coughs, he had greeted Oxford for what both of them knew was the last time. He had not spoken of himself. There were more important matters than dying. His wasted, gaunt hands had touched Oxford's and dropped back blue-veined on the coverlet.

"You are in regard again. Good, good. It will benefit you much, and it will benefit Her Majesty. Keep so, my lord."

"As God wills," Oxford said. "Though I can never benefit Her Majesty to match your lordship."

"Oh, more. These honors to the players are your witness. Men are right to give them welcome."

"Yes, my lord."

"You are of the fellowship of thought," Sussex said. "You ride in it as the companions of the old chivalry rode in arms. I envy you your time. I am of the castle, the sword and the ancient ways. You are of the young. In the sunrise of my day our minds were bounded by our moats; in the sunset of yours it can come to pass that yours will be bounded only by yourselves."

A fit of coughing seized him. Oxford offered him wine, but he waved it aside. Oxford put the cup down, and stood by the bed, silent and at loss for words. Sussex smiled and went on.

"I do not fear the sunset—mine or yours. The age is yeasting. The bubbles and excrescences puff to the surface. A wise man will not heed them, they burst to their own wind."

"Would God I could learn your lordship's wisdom," Oxford said humbly.

Sussex shook his head. "Learn yours. Your years are long yet. You must manage, you must travel the way." Although the effort weakened him, he seemed so anxious, so desirous to talk, that Oxford did not stop him; the moment was full of things that had to be said. "I will tell you that Hatton is an enemy. He is jealous of all you do. He will sneer and be insidious and hurt you where he can. Yet I think his pastry will rumble small in the belly of time. The court will for the most part sway with Her Majesty. Raleigh is ambitious, Leicester cantankerous. But treat them as bubbles, my lord. Mere swellings. Look to yourself, and to your fellowship. Your strength lies there."

"In books and plays, my lord?" Oxford said, for the old earl was a warrior.

"In the call to walk at liberty as thoughtful creatures. Plays are words, and words are thoughts in breath. Build them and let them have scope. In taverns or in palaces, the place is little important so it be where people live. Oh, I grant your inn brawls, your scribblers' envies, your addered venoms. No company is without them. The Holy Crusades against the infidel saw Christians stabbing Christians; yet the march pushed on. Yours will push, too. Let it go. Let it go until you have given men to reason, and ponder, and brought each one to the quality of valor in himself that stamps him a man. We shall have true freedom then. The prize of liberty is the worth of being governed.

"Her Majesty knows this. She allows these upstarts. She dresses them in pride and in incentive, and from them incentives and pride stem out to the kingdom. You are in the vanguard, and the vanguard is unruly. It is crude and uncouth. It hacks and tramples its fellows as hard as the enemy, for it is the vanguard that must thrust into the breach. It must take the brunt of battle. But what follows after can be brought smooth. To arts and delights and peaceful cultivation. You have the power for that. I have watched you."

"What power, my lord?" Oxford said.

"Your pen."

Oxford said, smiling gently at the dying man, "I have read so, my lord. The heathen Teutons believed their runes had magic. They believed that writing could stop a vessel in her course, divert an arrow in its flight, bring love or hatred, raise a corpse from its grave, or cast the living into a slumber like death. This would indeed be a power."

The gaunt hands moved on the coverlet.

"You have read well," Sussex said, and leaned back and closed his eyes.

Oxford saw Horatio and Francis off to the Holland wars, and pleaded for favor for his cousin Lord Lumley. His cousin was high steward of Oxford University and had the finest library of books and manuscripts in England.

He was sorry to lose Horatio, but he wished him Godspeed. He liked his young kinsman, his steady bearing and cool head.

"Go be a soldier," he said, "and cut your linen Holland fashion. I'd not have you stay home to rot your heart out." He gave Horatio and Francis each a corselet of mail. When Robin Christmas protested the expense he told Robin he would be richer soon; he had the Queen's promise.

In that same autumn the Spanish ambassador, Bernardino de Mendoza, received a letter from the Queen of Scots. It came to him by secret ways, delivered by a courier who slipped through London's dark alleys at night, flitting like a shadow and trailed at a distance by other shadows as noiseless as he. Mendoza read the letter by candlelight. The paper was crumpled and the ink splotched with tears; Mary was writing in tragic earnestness. Elizabeth had proposed terms for her release, with permission for her to go to France or Scotland. Mary was ill and old and needed peace. Should she accept? Mendoza penned his reply before morning. He folded it, sealed it, and picked up his quill again to report to his king.

"I have advised the Queen of Scots with the greatest artifice," he wrote, the nib sliding busily over the paper, "to refuse all offers of freedom or reconciliation with the Jezebel. Her release would do great injury to Spanish aims in England. Especially if she were in a place where the French could reach her. . . ."

In that same autumn the shadows flitted around Sir Francis Walsingham's house in Seething Lane. A man was taken for questioning. A knotted rope about his head. The rope tighter, the questions sterner. Blood squeezing from his skin. What did he know? Name names, give facts. He was a go-between for Mary and the Spanish faction. Would Philip invade? Would Guise join him from France? Was Elizabeth to be assassinated? Who was to do it? Come, come—details—details. With the opening of another year they hanged the man Throckmorton. They ordered Mendoza out of England. They moved Mary of Scots to a stronger fortress and a grimmer jailer. Lord Henry Howard was in Fleet Prison, and Charles Arundel was racing toward Paris for his life.

With another year a figure lurked in the dark at the foot of a Dutch stairwell many miles from London, raised a knife, and buried it in the back of Prince William of Orange.

With another year Sturmius, the great teacher and philosopher of the Rhineland and the Queen's agent on German matters, sent word to Elizabeth to put some faithful and zealous person such as the Earl of Oxford, the Earl of Leicester, or Philip Sidney, in charge of an army in the Low Countries.

With another year Sir Walter Raleigh's colonists set sail for Virginia; Anne's second daughter was born; my lord of Oxford's players were making the summer round of the provinces; and Lord Burghley, providing a loan of two hundred pounds to Oxford, told his steward Billet that catastrophe was near. Her Majesty had come to the end. Appeasement, compromise, leniency with her enemies, all her flirtatious policies had failed. King Philip wanted to smash England, and she could not possibly avoid war.

18

She did not avoid it. she met it head-on. In the summer of 1585 she sat with her Privy Council and prepared the declaration that would put her armies in the field.

She had retreated and temporized as far as she could. Now she would advance. The question was: how? In her council chamber she listened to the arguments. Leicester demanded a direct attack on Spain; Burghley advised her to fight in the Low Countries.

"It will be well to have your troops where you can bring them home with all possible speed if need be, my liege," Burghley said.

Burghley's reasoning won her over, for she did not want her soldiers thrown away on the Spanish coasts. She was not rich enough in soldiers to waste them. She gave orders to open negotiations with the Dutch, to take some of their towns as surety and to march to the aid of the Dutch States in their rebellion against Philip.

The proceedings pushed forward rapidly. In return for the towns of Flushing and Brill, Elizabeth would send five thousand horse and a thousand foot against Spain in the Low Countries. Enlistment officers began combing the shires, and Colonel Norris was summoned from Munster to lead the field armies. Her courage and decision set the wheels in motion. There remained only the choice of the man who would command and direct the campaign. He must be a man to represent her in the alliance with the Dutch, and a man able to pit himself against the wily Spanish Duke of Parma.

For a time she hesitated. Leicester wanted the post, he wheedled and cajoled. But he had been too brash in the Privy Council, and had opposed fighting in the Low Countries. Elizabeth felt it unwise to send him there, since the plan was not his. He might be lukewarm to it. She was inclined to the Burghley faction now, and she remembered the counsel from Sturmius, who knew his European politics. She gave the command to Oxford.

He left England immediately. He said goodbye to Anne and sailed for Flushing with Lord Willoughby. A westerly summer wind carried them fair, and he stood on the deck, filling his lungs with the salt air of the narrow seas.

"A month ago," he said, "I'd not have thought this would happen."

At Flushing, English ensigns flew from the ships already there, and under a glassy sun men-at-arms waited at attention on the quay, to salute him as he stepped ashore. His ship's cannon boomed. Smoke drifted up past the tile roofs, and the girls of the town flocked to see the famous and noble lord.

Oxford had expected to find the Dutch in a tragic way, but he was shocked at the difference between this visit and his last. While the girls and their families looked at him, nudging each other at his fine bearing and proud figure and rich, elegant appearance, he was looking at the soldiers in the streets, the wounded and the crippled hunched by the inn doors, and the starveling, dogged faces.

"Matters are much worse than when I was here last," he said to Lord Willoughby.

Misery rolled out to him from the town. It struck him full, as he walked ashore, like a blast from a furnace. It angered him to feel it, and he thought that Philip of Spain must be a stupid and stifling despot. The faces in Flushing convinced him.

He knew, as everyone did, that Philip's grandmother, the daughter of Ferdinand and Isabella, had died mad. Philip was hardly better. The rule of the Netherlands had come to him through his Burgundian ancestors, and for thirty years he had treated them like serfs. The Netherlanders were the most free and peaceable people in Europe, but Philip had despised and trampled on them. He had over-ridden the charter of Holland and the *blyde inkomst* of Brabant. He had broken his pledges to their liberties and vented his cruel, fearful instinct of cunning on them, and when they revolted he was savage in his revenge. His troops were blanketing the country, sacking and killing. Antwerp had fallen to him ten days ago, taken by Parma.

Oxford mounted, and rode toward the house where he would lodge for the night before going on to The Hague. "Tomorrow is the last day of August," he told Lord Willoughby. "It is the day my father was buried. I must do my best here, as he would have done it."

His responsibility sobered him. He firmed his thighs against the solid familiar feel of saddle leather.

"The ship should be unloaded before morning."

"I gave those orders," Lord Willoughby said.

"There are a thousand English on Walcheren without officers or arms. They were shipped so from England. They must be armed and officered. I want the rations from the ship for my staff. Put them in carts and start them for The Hague. And fetch the town's burgomaster to supper."

Lord Willoughby, writing to his wife that night, said she would be proud of her brother. "Ned is in his element here," he said.

Oxford went up to The Hague, galloping over the roads to a jingle of bridles. He inspected the English troops. He studied maps and charts. He talked to Norris, to Willoughby, to the captains and the superior officers. They laid plans and discussed strategies; he heard them all—approved or disapproved, and made suggestions of his own. He had always read history, the movements of armies and battles, and the reading was useful to him now. He went hours without sleep and seemed fresher for it.

The Hague was packed with soldiers. On his rides among them there were the smells of bodies and sweat, the stringy, starchy smells of the taverns, the armorers' poundings and the clang of anvils, straw and manure and the stable noises, trulls and camp-women screaming and laughing, spread-eagled in the soldiers' laps, dice rattling night and day, and the glint of sunlight on weapons. Reining his horse, he would sit and watch them, while his guard eyed the women and sniggered through tongue-wetted lips. The horny, bawdy, lustful, spraddling scenes drummed at his senses. They swam with life. They were more real than tournaments or bull-baitings.

They took him back to the love he had had for his father, and to the bristly men in Hedingham castle courtyard. He felt a new purpose when he watched them, not only for himself but for them. There was no moony vision here, no airy dreams or fantasies whispering insipidly to themselves and posturing to the mirror of their own conceit. This was the stuff hearts were made of. This was bone and sinew, and honest gut. He wished the Earl of Sussex had lived to see them. If the earl's ghost walked in The Hague it would be glad.

Sometimes he would get up from the council table, and while the others talked he would stand where he could look at the city. Its streets ebbed and flowed in a wash of troops. Its houses rose solid under a flat Holland sky. Beyond, the flat Holland country unrolled toward the horizon, ribboned by sluices and canals. It spread in front of him honest and vigorous, a thing of flesh and blood.

It made him think of a play while he looked at it, greater in human volume than man could create. He remembered the play he had been shaping, half finished when he had left London. Bob Greene and Tony Munday and some of the rest would finish it.

He wrestled with tactics, with baggage trains, forage for the horses and powder for the engineers. He used discipline on the raw levies and diplomacy on Prince Maurice and the Dutch leaders. They had been afraid that a man appointed by Her Gracious Majesty Elizabeth would be a spoiled and prating noble. They received him with ceremony at The Hague. He dined with them, and sent them away singing a different tune.

Colonel Norris found him one day on the balcony outside his rooms, bareheaded, his cheeks flushed, leaning on the parapet and frowning down intently.

"The matter of Arnheim, my lord—" Norris said.

"The matter of everything," he said. "The nub is there," and waved a hand at the picture below.

His headquarters were settled. He brought in his money and apparel and wine and venison. He rode through the city often. He steeped himself in it. The movement. The bustle. The vim. It quickened his capability for impressions and sent him back to the council table with an immense confidence.

Heat and dysentery dogged the troops. The men fell sick. They cursed and died and were buried. They lived and whored and longed to go home. But even in their dying, their cursing, their homesick idleness, their reality was prodigious.

Oxford called his officers together and spoke pungently. He told them what he felt as he rode through the city. "These men are strong," he said. "They have will, and wits to back it up."

"But green in battle, my lord," Willoughby said.

"And in handling arms," Norris said.

After Sussex, Norris was the best fighter in England. Balding, roundheaded, he had pleasant, tranquil eyes, a full, soft beard and mustache, and wore half-armor at the conferences, and a modest ruff.

"They have wit and will," Oxford said. "They move of themselves. They feel, and stink, and bleed, and love of themselves. What more do you want in men?"

He came from the window where he had been standing, walking to his place at the head of the table by Norris and Willoughby. He looked around at them one by one.

"Battles and arms may be the flourishes of war, but men are the frame of it. There are two sorts in this war we fight. The Spaniards are one sort, we the other. The Spaniards are strangled, sapless. Their frame's brittle, without juice. Their king's smothered them. He's called his subjects home from foreign studies, let none leave his kingdom to learn or read or teach outside his boundaries.

"You know his edicts. If priests disobey they lose their rights; if laymen, they are exiled and their property seized. His frontiers are walled with custom houses that question every traveler and sift every thought that passes through. No Spaniard can push an idea beyond his country or take hold of an idea from outside without the king's permission. Spain's locked behind a barrier. She's isolate, unpregnant, sterile to the seeds of the world. She rots in a void. Her soldiers carry the void with them and fight from a hole."

"Tough soldiers," Norris said.

"Brittle, Norris. I'll swear it. They lack roots and space and air. God's blessing, they don't grow. They're shriveled and stunted."

He talked with a swift, terse eloquence. The officers shifted on their stools and peered at him. He paused, and crossed to the window again, jerking his arm toward the casement, the clatter in the streets and the Holland blue of the sky.

"We've a different sort. Green. Raw. Stubborn. Wrangling and blasphemous. They offend our noses and they get the pox. But there's a base there, a breadth and surety. There's openness, and a place for winds to blow. Down in that street men walk as persons. The sound they make is the gabble of a headless mob, but each of them has a being in his own eyes. He can laugh or cry of his own will, argue of his own wit, and read the riddle in his own core of what he is or may be. Each man is rooted and stands of himself. We're a living breed.

"Draw these men to the Spaniards, and see your war. The living against the dead. That's your battle. Courage to speak and argue and pry out truth. That's your strategy and your feats of arms. God's blessing, it's plain. Look in the camps, look in the tents—look in the stews if need be—but look. You'll find marrow. In every Jack who trips on a musket, in every hostler kicking at horses' dung. Pushing and expanding in a thousand uncased souls, all questing, all in motion. It deepens like a well and flings like a host with banners. Either the living or the dead will win this war. But we build stouter than King Philip. The living can nourish on life, but not the dead."

Perhaps they understood him. He would never know. The gruff faces around the table were impenetrable. They were warriors, they thought in terms of skirmishes and deployment. But when he had finished Norris said, "Amen." And they sat in silence like the silence after a prayer.

He had his plans in order by the end of the month. Norris was to attack the fort at Arnheim. Men and supplies were ferrying from England. The Dutch were ready. He saw Norris off, marching toward the Yser, and began to get reports that the fort would fall.

In the middle of the week a courier arrived from London, sent by Walsingham at the Queen's command. Oxford strode into his rooms, hot from a gallop around the English camp, and read the message with the dust flaking from his boots.

He turned to Lord Willoughby. "I'm called home," he said. "Leicester is taking my place."

Nan Vavasour was still at court. She had made her peace with the Queen—an easy thing to do, she had always known, when Elizabeth's rages passed and when one was willing to be contrite—and she listened to the news about Oxford with half a smile.

She had nothing to say.

But on the afternoon when Oxford reached London she strolled down the long gallery of the palace and into the garden. She came on Eliza Trentham sitting on a marble bench by a fountain and sat down beside her.

"A pleasant day for thoughts," she said.

Eliza replied that it was. An early October coolness had driven off the feverish summer heat, and the gardens were colored in marigolds and Michaelmas daisies.

"I suppose," Nan said, "you're thinking of my lord of Oxford."

Eliza replied, a little lower, that many people were thinking of him at the moment.

"Thinking or wishing," Nan said, opening the fan that hung at her girdle and smiling at it idly. It had a picture of Venus and Cupid, drawn in lace. "But it will do you no good to wish, I'm afraid. My lord of Oxford will go to Anne Cecil."

"It's proper he should," Eliza said.

"Without a peep into the gardens, to see if a lady might be there," Nan said.

Eliza turned a steady look on her. "The garden is the least likely place where my lord of Oxford would come," she said.

"Possibly. But the most likely place to look for someone. I seem to remember he's fond of gardens," Nan shrugged. "He'll have enough of them now. I could have told you when he went away that he'd be back soon."

Eliza stared into the sparkle of the fountain. The talk was distasteful to her, but if she got up or moved farther along the bench Nan would take it as a confession of guilt. Nan would be sure she was trying to escape. She sat still and tried to ignore her.

"It's Leicester," Nan said, "and Hatton." Nan had a way of repeating something that was common knowledge in a manner that made it seem peculiarly her own, intimate and a little condescending. "They set to work on Her Majesty as soon as Ned had gone. Leicester can't endure anyone to be higher than himself, and he wants Sir Philip Sidney to have some honor. He'll take Sir Philip to Holland to polish his new knighthood. And of course Cissy Knollys has always hated the Norrises, a family squabble. And then Sir Philip has married Walsingham's daughter. It all comes out against Ned."

"So much has come out against my lord of Oxford," Eliza said, her eyes still on the fountain. "So many things he's attempted."

Nan shut her fan. "You're sorry for him."

"Yes," Eliza said. "Aren't you?"

"I don't know. Pity is very close to love. I've never said I loved him."

Eliza turned on her again. Her dark eyes were roused and angry, and black with scorn. "If you ever have, you should tell him now," she said. "He needs it now."

"Why should I?" Nan said, holding her look to Eliza's with a hard, insolent amusement. "Tell him yourself, if it means that to you. I can have him back any time I want him."

Over London, the shadow of war. Over war, the shadow of the Queen.

War hovered on its pinions like a hawk above a chicken yard, and Elizabeth spread her wings for her brood, a frightened and angry hen.

Timid, bold, dogmatic, vacillating, contrary, fitful, stubborn and indefatigable, Queen Elizabeth was one of the rare personalities gifted in the success of following while she seemed to lead. She had followed England as it roamed wider into the open, hesitant and scolding but giving it its range. Now she clucked it to cover and ruffled it under her with querulous squawks, with admonishings to the obedient and irritable pecks at the laggards.

Drake, Raleigh, Frobisher, Hawkins for the sea; Norris, Willoughby, Hunsdon, Sidney for the land; the lord admiral in charge of the fleet, Leicester in charge of the land troops; she arranged, ordered, juggled, and manipulated. One eye on her island flock, one on the sky toward Spain; the shipwrights mauling on the ways, the coast castles manned, the militia levies shambling in country lanes. Hurrying, hurrying, prodding, wheedling—Ireland to be garrisoned and James in Scotland to be dickered with—and when she could not hurry or prod or wheedle, temper and lightnings.

It had been half a millennium, five hundred years, since England had faced invasion, since such monstrous deliberate aggressiveness had been let loose on the Western World. The pillagings in the West Indies, the looting of Spanish galleons and the murders of English seamen, were side issues. Reason, diplomacy, compromise, were fatal illusions; Philip had expelled her ambassador years ago, she had kept his as long as she could, until her own life would have been the price for keeping him longer.

Philip wanted the conquest of England. He made fanaticism his excuse, but the fanaticism was self-born and a mask for his greed. Behind the bizarre façade of her palace of Nonesuch she bit her nails in impotence. Philip had few ports and a formidable coastline. England's coast was accessible and English ports lay vulnerable to the wide reaches of the sea.

Worse, she was vulnerable at home. Her grandfather had rolled the crown from the head of Richard III and ended the Wars of the Roses. But she had never had a unified country. Her flock were not all chicks of the same breed. Some were goslings, with belligerent pinfeathers that pricked and nettled her. Some would hunt with the hawk if they had the chance. The Puritans had preached themselves into a hate as fanatic as Philip's, and had so nearly got control of the last parliament that the thought of it still chilled her.

The partisans of Mary of Scots were scratching up another conspiracy, timed with the invasion and more desperate than before. It seemed to her that the nation was like her coach, full of stresses and strains. It took all her strength to keep it upright, and she wondered if it would hold together on the rough road ahead.

She moved restlessly from palace to palace—Nonesuch, Whitehall, Greenwich. Why wasn't Drake home from the West Indies, dipping his topsails in the summer wind off Plymouth? Why weren't more ships building? Why was Raleigh peevish because she had kept a cabinet of pearls from Sir Richard Grenville's loot? Why was she so distracted, at her time of life, by the legs and the ringing laugh of Leicester's young stepson, the dashing Earl of Essex? He was putting the court in a tumult with his thirst for glory.

She herself was in a tumult, chipped at, heckled, pulled this way and that. Leicester was feeding his vanity in the Netherlands, and doing little. The hotheads in her kingdom cried out for a sea thrust at Spain; she could send Drake to raid Philip's harbors. The older ones talked caution; where were her reserves, if Drake should fail? How would she get new ships if she threw away her fleet on a wild gamble? Her mind wavered between the two. . . .

And her people—alarmed, disjointed, aware of plots and treasons, delays and cross purposes and confusion. The villages she had seen on her progresses—shattered out of their peace and pitched willy-nilly into turgid, swirling currents that sucked their men away to war; the young men marching, the beds empty, the nights lonely in the warm spots beside the haycocks—how would they stand it? She stared over London and tried to pierce the distance with her thoughts, the Midlands, the Cotswolds, the Cumberlands, the Ridings of Yorkshire, how would they stand it?

Her mainstay in all this was Lord Burghley. He had never deserted her in any of her extremities. His age was weighing on him and he was crippled by his gout, but he came to her every day, with counsel and advice and occasional little presents to divert her mind. Long ago Lord Burghley had written down his maxim: "Keep some great man thy friend, but trouble him not with trifles; compliment him often with many, yet small, gifts." Elizabeth knew the maxim, but she did not find it cynical.

She made use of his friendship and respected his intelligence. She was quick to realize that a man who had enriched himself by her reign would not want to see it fall. For military and political purposes

Burghley was Elizabeth and Elizabeth was Burghley. She looked at his grave face, his patient beard, the careful fingers putting paper before her for her signature, the documents, the scrupulous, detailed orders, the sly twinkle of the eye that presaged one of his heavy flights of humor, and the thought was a consolation to her.

"Sir Spirit," she said—it was a day in June, and things had not been going well; the slowness and the delays were maddening—"we must do more."

The twinkle of the eye. "What imports Your Majesty? Import, that is, to mean. Not to be tedious, I do not think Your Majesty would import Philip." There was a chuckle behind the beard. Lord Burghley's gout was easier that afternoon.

"God forbid," Elizabeth said.

"Everything that can be done has been set in motion," Lord Burghley said.

"I mean our people," Elizabeth said.

Lord Burghley turned the chuckle to a tactful cough. One of the chief differences between him and his Queen was their attitude toward the people. Lord Burghley cared less for their opinion than she did. He attached less importance to what they felt—perhaps because he had risen up out of them by his own efforts. His prudent, circumspect nature tended to make him cold in popular matters. But he knew her concern about them.

"Our project has not succeeded," she said.

"No," he said.

She nodded with a frown. "You're a blunt Spirit. Well well, we've tried. We can try again."

"Yes, my liege. Though I would be at loss for the method."

"God's death, the people must be drawn together," she said.

She left the subject abruptly and went on to other problems. Leicester had inveigled the Dutch States into electing him their prince. He would have to be got out of it somehow, with Burghley's diplomacy. Did Burghley think Walsingham should go to Scotland? There were money questions, appointments, provisions for stores and naval bases. She sifted through them, the rings glinting impatiently on her fingers. She spent much time over a new design for a warship. When they came to the end she leaned back in her chair.

"I have been thinking of my lord of Oxford," she said.

"I will tell him, my liege, when we meet," Burghley said, gathering his documents with a sigh of fatigue and preparing to leave.

"You don't meet often."

"Your Majesty knows what hard case I am in with my son-in-law. No enemy I have could envy me that match."

"Master Secretary Walsingham," she said, "reports that our Boar is short of funds. It seems he's worn down his tusks."

"To the gum," Lord Burghley said. "Your Majesty understands already that I support his two daughters. He will have to disband his company of acting boys. What will become of him I know not. He took his loss of command in the Low Countries greatly to heart."

"Disband is a poor word for players," Elizabeth said. She pretended not to notice the reference to the Low Countries. That had been Leicester's influence, along with Walsingham, Hatton, and Sir Francis Knollys, and she did not wish to argue it with Burghley.

"Tell him we were thinking of him."

"Yes, my liege."

Over London the shadow of war. Over war the shadow of Elizabeth. And over Elizabeth the shadow of her country.

She examined Oxford closely as he knelt to her, searching for some indication of his feelings. Always before she had been able to read him. Now she could see nothing. His eyes were cold as stones when she peered at them. She tapped her toe under the hem of her skirt. She had sent for him in order to read his mind.

They were at the top of the water stairs at Greenwich, on the sunny terrace that led to the river landing. Below them the Queen's barge rode at the dockside, the oarsmen with the sweeps erect like a nest of spears, the palace guards presenting halberds, and the royal canopy red and gold against the water. Elizabeth and her maids, with part of her court, had been on their way to row in review past the ship works at Deptford when Walsingham had whispered that Oxford was come. "Bring him here," she had said.

At her sign the maids and courtiers and attendants fell back to a distance. Elizabeth, regal, spoke to Oxford alone.

"We've not had much of you since your return, my Boar."

"No, Your Majesty. I've been digesting a new game."

"Indeed? What game?"

"Double dealing," he said.

"I do not know it."

"Pray God you never will, my liege."

"Is it so tough a meal?" she said, with an edge of testiness. She did not like her decisions criticized.

"It sits in the belly like iron."

An indifference, an utter lack of interest, ran colorless in his voice. At other times his emotions had been quick-cut and apparent. But as he faced her, one knee on the terrace flagging, his hand on the other and his cap at his side, he knew that the spark was gone. He had been flung upward once too often and the heat in him had died. He neither wished nor cared to renew it.

"You're not the only soul, my Boar, who's had that colic."

He heard her without feeling. The sharp, stern tone, that would have been a whetstone for his wits once, did not stir him.

"I've tasted it myself," she said.

"I'm sorry if Your Majesty has suffered. But misery," he said, "makes empty company for an empty stomach."

"Empty? With iron in it?"

"Promise-empty," he said.

There was no energy to his words. No accusation or reproof. His face was like marble, stiffly correct as his cambric ruff, and he merely stated a fact. "Promise-empty."

He might have been a stranger. He felt as if he were. Behind her he saw the maids of honor and the court. He saw how they stood in groups, talking, admiring the river and making pretense of not trying to snatch some shred or guess at what was passing between him and the Queen. Hatton babbling to Lord Hunsdon, the Queen's cousin. Walsingham a little in front of the others, grumpish and taciturn. Nan Vavasour and Mary Radcliffe with Sir Henry Lee, master of the armory and the Queen's self-appointed champion at her tournaments. He saw Eliza Trentham in a cluster of the other maids, like a dark flower in a field of daisies. He looked away.

They were all there—the royal household. Lord steward, lord chamberlain, vice-chamberlain, comptroller of the household, treasurer of the household, treasurer of the chamber, master of the great wardrobe, captain of the bodyguard. All there, all to be promised something, all jigging for places and promotions. The gaudy lot would take a whole catalogue of promises. It didn't surprise him there was nothing left.

When he looked at the Queen again his eyes were not stone, but ash. "My duty to Your Majesty," he said. He would have asked leave to retire. But she motioned him to stay where he was.

"Your emptiness is your good fortune," she said. "It's spared you from painted counsels in the Netherlands. I brought you back from trouble, my Boar. Alençon went to the Netherlands, remember. He got the dukedom of Brabant with our help, and then the fool must make sack and slaughter of Antwerp. When the burghers trounced him out his mother snatched him to Paris for the laughingstock of Europe. Leicester goes to The Hague, and puffs himself like a clown's bladder, and Burghley must collapse him. You're well out of those ways."

He lifted his shoulders dully. "And in no other."

Her gown, sewn thick with pearls, gave off a crusty sound as she moved. She brushed past him, beckoning him to follow. He rose and went after her. She walked to a railing of the terrace. She stopped by it, still farther out of earshot from the others, and the sun grated on her reddish hair.

"We learn there is talk of giving up your players."

"I lack money."

She did not seem impressed. "A penny reason. My horse is of the same color. But I do not give up my kingdom."

"Your kingdom is yours, my liege, whether it eats or starves."

"Do you think so? That is a question that keeps kings awake."

"There's little offense to Your Majesty if I end my players."

"Yes, but there is," she said. A swish of her gown, the crusty sound again. Her long aquiline nose thrust at him. "There is, Oxford." Her look was almost a glare, a mixture of challenge and desperation and a demand for certainty.

He waited, but she did not finish the thought. She changed her tone, squinting at the brassy glare on the surface of the river. "In the Netherlands," she said, "you saw our army. You gathered it, watched it. What kind are its men?"

"A kind who will fight better than Philip's," he said.

"Why?"

"Because they are men."

"Do they know it?" she said.

"Roughly," he said. "Crudely. As the prisoner knows his fetters are struck off, but still moves rusty of his own volition."

"If they were taught to know more?"

"They could laugh at Spain."

"If all of us were taught to know more—men, women, all?"

"We'd be giants," he said.

She gripped him by the wrist. Her nose, her eyes, the thin lines of her face, sharpened in a glittering intensity. "Do it, my Boar."

She glanced around at the courtiers and dropped his wrist. She wanted no guesses. The value was in secrecy. "This is your way. I'll put you in it, as Pliny says, from the crown of your head to the soles of your feet. But do it."

"What way, my liege?" He was beginning to suspect what she meant, and his intensity was mounting, too.

"To teach," she said. "To open the mind, and medicine the rustiness from our joints. Slough away the fetters' scabs and give every spirit a reason and a motion. To show plays that will make all England one."

"God's blessing," he said fervently.

"I've brought you home from the wars to a command larger than ordering companies and the trailing of pikes, my Boar. No, not Boar. Will. Gentle Will of the taverns and the words, the playhouses and the laughter and the tears; the shape of truth and the forms of men and women compacted from his brain, that hold our own forms up to us and let us see our natures."

She drew a breath and went on more succinctly. "Spain hasn't such a Will. Our brother Philip would be afraid of him. That's Philip's weakness. It won't be mine. Our two nations are toe to toe. Our two peoples are locked. I want mine to have more in their heads than—" She paused for a phrase.

"Than earwax," Oxford said.

She laughed, her ruff quivering, and was serious instantly. "You were a friend of Stubbes."

"Yes, my liege."

"If I'd had answer to reach my people with, Stubbes would keep his hand today. We're not yet free, Oxford. When Norfolk died I had no other course. But I've sought one. Sought one. With the Puritans I must be strict. I've given them to my new archbishop. I may give you to them later. But Spain is a clearer matter, and immediate. The country must be with me. Willingly, not slavishly. By reason and heart and knowledge. Lord Burghley and I have tried to print a paper of news, to be spread in the provinces for folk to read. But there are not enough who read. And I cannot be an Epaminondas to all these thousands, leading them into battle as the Spartan general did, chanting poems of the old heroes. This is the only way."

She waved Walsingham forward.

"It's more than a task for one," Oxford said.

"Take a dozen—two dozen—a hundred. You've been shorn of glory in war. You've suffered slander, ridicule, disgrace. You've pauperized yourself for beggarly actors and got yourself a name for folly in the general mouth. In the world's book you're written as failure. But here's your own. Here's glory sweeter and richer, above pomp. Here is your testament."

She accepted a scroll from Walsingham and handed it to Oxford. He unrolled it, read it, the heavy stamped wax below the royal signature like a great jewel at the bottom. It was a privy seal warrant. His eyes skimmed through it. . . .

An order to the Exchequer . . . One thousand pounds a year, good and lawful money of England . . . paid to the Earl of Oxford . . . no accounting to be given for it, no reckoning to be asked from him . . . the grant to continue yearly, during the Queen's pleasure . . . At her Manor of Greenwich, the sixth and twentieth day of June in the eight and twentieth year of her reign. . . .

No mention of plays or players. But when he finished reading and looked up, Elizabeth was staring at him searchingly.

Oxford dropped to his knees.

She motioned Walsingham away, and smiled.

"Put Agincourt on the stage, my Boar. It's time."

She stood over him and he saw her face, brilliant in the gems of her hair, intrepid, rapt. And he saw that she expected him, also, to be a man.

» 224 «

19 | THEY PUT AGINCOURT ON THE STAGE. THEY PUT CHRONI-
cles and histories, tales of wars, stories of kings, rebellions, conquests, and heroes. They put plays to
stir patriotism, comedies for relief, and masquerades and gut-splitting
farces against Philip of Spain. Anything that would grip an audience,
rouse its capacities to think and feel and judge and do, and prick it into
wakefulness. In the theaters and in the tenements of the Savoy was a
hum of writing and rehearsing, of scanning lines, of learning parts,
of correcting, adding, cutting, of speeding scripts off to the touring
companies in the country towns.

Oxford met Eliza more often that summer and fall. The Queen's
vigorous support of actors and dramatic enterprises stimulated the
courtiers and the maids of honor to go to the plays, and Oxford's company at the old Paul's singing school was popular with the court
circle. He had moved his company to the singing school when Sir
William More had won his lawsuit and canceled the lease at Blackfriars. The school was more convenient to Whitehall than the theaters
outside the city, which were a horse-ride away in Shoreditch; it charged
fourpence a performance general admission instead of twopence as in
the public playhouses, and the spectators were less ribald and better
behaved.

Eliza would come with a party from the palace, rustling in silks
and grosgrains and settling like a covey of bright birds in the gallery
rooms. She would sit somewhat by herself, near Mary Radcliffe or one
of the older ladies-in-waiting, and Oxford would stroll by between
acts, or while the tumblers were vaulting and somersaulting, and stop
to talk.

He liked the few moments of talk with her. In the bustle and activity around them, the voices and the noise and the whirligig of excitement, the feeling of constraint that had been between them disappeared. He would lean by the railing, his hazel eyes lighted with
enthusiasm. The gallery room was raised just enough from the floor
so that he had to lift them slightly to look at hers. He could see the
firm, delicate contours of her mouth, the pretty texture of her skin, her

dark eyelashes catching the finespun reflected daintiness of her lawn ruff. He would ask her opinion of the play that was showing. She would tell him what she thought, the weak scenes, the forceful ones, the spots during the performance where her attention had held, the places where it had flagged; and he would purse his lips, and nod, and laugh as if she were a girl again, on her first trip to London.

It seemed very natural.

"What do you think now, Eliza?" he asked once. "Are we closer to Staffordshire?"

"Much closer, my lord."

"Good."

"It is, my lord."

"It's a happier pattern."

"It's truer to your lordship."

The play they watched that day was his own. It was a play of the Trojan war, the bickerings in the Grecian camp, and Ulysses' arguments that without free obedience and a willing respect for authority the Greeks would come to chaos. The court gallants who had bought seats on the stage at sixpence extra were shuffling cards and dicing, calling back and forth to each other and showing off their finery. Hucksters with baskets sold nuts and pippins to the audience, and in the gallery rooms booksellers' apprentices hawked books, pamphlets, collections of sonnets and favorite plays. The crowd in front of the stage shoved and laughed.

On the balcony above it the young Earl of Essex lounged in a promiscuous display with Fulke Greville and a slender, fair-skinned boy of fourteen, one of the Queen's wards, the Earl of Southampton. Lyly scuttered at the stage entrance, gesticulating to the callboy.

"There's more of yourself," she said.

He smiled with a mock gravity, letting his eyes wander over the scene. "A while since this would have been a miracle, to see me a teacher of statehood. Is the play still sound?"

"As sound as ever. I've always liked Ulysses' lines, they're strong and to the point. I suppose they're aimed at my lord of Leicester."

He grinned. "They might be. Or at any fractious noble."

"England is lucky you can write as you do, under protection. A city scrivener would have his ears clipped."

"And we'd have nothing said. Nothing but dumbness. Then we'd all jackdaw *'Señor'* to the Spaniards."

"I know the times are serious," she said.

"They must all be leaders, willy-nilly," he said. "God's blessing, there's an art in following."

"Her Majesty is concerned."

"We do what we can," he said. "These pieces are rough. But I hope to polish them sometime."

"I like your hope," she said.

"Is that all?" he said, laughing.

"No. I like your truth. And I like the way you're giving yourself to this. You might have forfeited everything out of spite—yourself, your writing. Everything."

"I could as soon forfeit my writing as my breath," he said.

"You might have forfeited your best talents," she said, "or sulked in your tent"—she glanced at the stage—"like Achilles."

The lack of flattery in her voice, the clear pleasure and understanding, made it easy to talk to her. He thanked her with his eyes.

Lyly dived toward them, pushing through the crowd. "My lord, the Cressida boy is took sick on a surfeit of apples, and I have put in another. And your man is here from Bob Greene wanting a prompt-book for *Henry V*. And are we to do our *Campaspe* on Thursday or the new masquerade? Good morrow, Mistress Trentham. Pray commend me to Her Majesty."

"Good morrow, Master Lyly," Eliza said. "You seem busy."

"What with a paltry this and a peevish that, I keep in a mortal frenzy," Lyly said. "Performances for Her Majesty, comedies for the players, and secretary for my lordship who has the energy of ten men. I'm a thing of little account. Will you come, my lord?"

"Presently."

"Commend me to Her Majesty," Lyly said, his plum-shaped cheeks agitated. "Bah, we go dismally today. My lord of Essex talks so loud the actors miss their cues."

Eliza smiled consolingly. "Her Majesty makes great account of you," she said. "His lordship depends on you, and you print your plays for London to read."

Lyly looked startled. He shot a glance to Oxford. "I print anonymously," he said. "No name. I get the pains and the players get the credit." He hurried away.

"Poor Jack," Oxford said. "A modicum more wit to suffer with would kill him."

"He needs someone to commiserate over him," Eliza said. "My lord—"

"Yes?"

"Master Lyly writes his plays as your secretary."

Oxford nodded.

"He prints them. Couldn't you print your own?"

He laughed again. "Anonymously," he said echoing Lyly's tone, and bowed to her and went to join Lyly backstage.

He was there the next day, and the next after that. When he was not at Paul's he was at the Savoy, when he was not at the Savoy he was at the public playhouses or some tavern. The clatter of the theaters, the dusty costumes, the squeak of the boys' voices, the long musical lines rising and falling over the audience in a spell like a magician's wand rang in his head in the days and in his brain at nights. They rang with purpose, exultant in the Queen's gift, in her faith, in the renewed faith she had created in himself. She had staked that he could weld the country, set it marching, free the heart and guts he had seen in the camps in Holland. He could put heads on the guts and pride into the hearts.

This was an instinct with him, a joy, a fierce conviction, for he had no time for philosophy. He rode through the London streets with his mind on words, on length of scenes and exits and entrances. He walked the byways around Paul's mulling the dialogue of the morning's rehearsal. Lyly had said he had the energy of ten men. More, he felt, like twenty—like the hour he had rallied the seamen from the poop of a cowed vessel in the Channel and carried them after him against the pirates.

He gathered playwrights for his project, quick, able fellows from the universities: Greene, Nash, Marlowe, Peele, Kyd. They brought him their plays; he guided them, directed them, goaded them to write, staved off their creditors, and put out ideas and topics for them to chew on. He drew from his books and learning, from Ovid and Plautus, from Plutarch and Montaigne, from the world of the Renaissance, and the world of the classics, from French and Latin and Italian and Greek, from Spenser and Sidney and Chaucer and Holinshed, from Lord Lumley's library and the new volumes that Lord Burghley's agents sent constantly from the Continent, and turned the rich storehouse into a bursting granary for the university wits.

He worked all that summer and fall. He worked over winegoblets at the Savoy, and over mugs of sack and the smell of fireplace smoke and damp rushes in the taverns.

He was working when the news came that Sir Philip Sidney had had a death hit from a musket ball at Zutphen.

He was working when twenty-five peers of England were commissioned to sit as jury at the death trial of a worn, stoutish, elderly woman, whose once-gold hair was fading now to gray. The woman was Mary Queen of Scots. And Oxford was one of the peers.

"Better, my lord? On the contrary, worse."

"Your lordship cannot think so."

"A deal worse."

Benign sadness tugged at Lord Burghley's face. He was paused at the doorway to Cecil House, where he had dismounted after a ride from the palace. Driftings of snow lay across his shoulders and collected at the fringes of his beard, and his body was stooped with the incessant pangs of his gout. The need for taking to his bed at intervals had become more genuine lately than when he had used it as a pretext to avoid unpleasant scenes with Her Majesty in the Privy Council, but he could still confront his son-in-law with a dignity and with the air of long-suffering reproach. Oxford was at Cecil House on a visit to Anne, and Lord Burghley had taken the chance to speak of his behavior.

"I am well informed, my lord. You have not mended your habits. Your companions are still madcaps, and a cause of sorrow to me and to my lady."

"I do not mean them to be, my lord."

"Nor do I mean to list your faults. A recital would swell them and be no remedy. But a listing could be made with brevity. The repayment of my efforts in your behalf—efforts, I remind your lordship, that have been laborious, unremitting, and not entirely without avail—

is a continuing neglect of your countess my daughter which puts her to much grief, a wayward inconsistency with moneys, a lacking of the forms and ceremonies appropriate to your station, and an occupying of yourself with persons of a low and questionable pursuit."

Oxford hid a smile at the brevity and controlled his annoyance. Burghley's nickname among the courtiers was Pondus, and he grew more long-winded with the years.

"I serve Her Majesty," Oxford said.

"I have also done some small service of late," Burghley answered, drawing off his gloves and preparing to go inside. His benignity as he surveyed Oxford frosted over imperceptibly, like the minute and glassy bayonets that stab from a pool's edge in a winter sunset. "But I have not weakened myself in merit thereby."

"No, my lord," Oxford said.

He understood the reference. The trial of Mary. Burghley had conducted it with a cool and triumphant enmity. The memory stood fresh in Oxford's mind, the jury of peers assembled in the high, dim chamber at Westminster, Mary without counsel, deprived of her papers, pleading her own defense with a courage and a spirit and an eloquence that should have moved the hardest heart to mercy. And opposed to her Lord Burghley's unemotional replies, fact piled on fact; the necessity for her death; the final damning proofs of the final plot.

Lord Burghley himself had been marked for assassination in that plot—Leicester, Hunsdon, most of Elizabeth's trusted men—and conviction was certain. It had been a victory for the vigilant, crafty, sleepless power of Cecil House, and Burghley had looked like a furred doomsman as he listened beadily to Mary.

Now Burghley was looking for some way to execute her without raising a clamor. He would like to avoid the responsibility. Elizabeth boggled at beheading Mary, and only fanatics wanted to see her head on the block. At present Burghley was counting on the Puritans for their backing. Oxford mused that there were many definitions of merit.

"Your annuity from Her Majesty could put your children to some good care," Burghley said.

"Your lordship knows that what I am, I am," Oxford said. "Her Majesty's money is not enough to care for my children and set the country in a frame for war. If we must have money, perhaps your lordship can persuade Her Majesty to restore my rights and revenues as steward of the Forest of Essex. Her father took the stewardship from my grandfather, and I've been kept from the inheritance. Our family has held it since near the time of the Conqueror."

Burghley's expression seemed to say that the time of the Conqueror was long past, remote from the possessions and privileges of a new age. He preferred more immediate interest. Besides, he and Oxford would never agree on money; Oxford on that question was incomprehensible to him. Oxford was incomprehensible to Lord Burghley on most questions.

"The frame of war," he said, "will be set firm, I think, by Sir Philip's funeral. You squander yourself too far on play-acting."

"Then I'll turn sexton and dig for burials," Oxford said, "if we're to make hearses our stages." He knew of the preparations for a public funeral for Sir Philip Sidney. All of London knew them. But he could hardly believe Burghley intended them as a show. Sidney had been dead four months. It seemed ghoulish.

"Sir Philip," Burghley said deliberately, "is much mourned."

"In God's kindness," Oxford said, "will you make a spectacle of him?"

"A sorrow," Burghley said. "Sir Francis Walsingham has spent six thousand pounds to contrive it. A pageant of sorrow. The whole city will walk in sable."

"His death is a sorrow. But his corpse hauled through the streets to the tune of six thousand pounds is a mummery. It's a shameful contriving."

"Events dictate contrivances," Lord Burghley said.

Oxford stared at Burghley in the falling snow. In spite of differences, Sidney had been a friend; chivalrous and kindly; a graceful writer, a symbol for poets and patron of a genius like Spenser; they had jibed and bantered but they had both loved books; and Sidney had given Lord Willoughby an honorable command in front of Flushing; a young, gay, generous spirit. Now his father-in-law had paid his debts, and was paying six thousand more to use his body for national policy.

"This is worse sham than play-acting," Oxford broke out. "Let the living talk to the living, and Sidney lie in peace. Walsingham is covering one funeral with another. He's drowning the tears for Mary of

Scotland with a trumped-up wailing over Sir Philip's wormy flesh."

"That is a matter of opinion," Lord Burghley said. He moved toward the hall where the servants were bowing him in.

"It is the end to which everyone must come," Burghley said piously, in a voice as bloodless as the February afternoon.

He continued to move into the house, sighing as he went and favoring his gout. The servants began to shut the doors, for they were nipped by the cold, but Oxford waved them back. He had paled with anger.

"I serve Her Majesty with life, my lord, and you parade death. I'm not away from Anne more than to do my duty. My companions are fit, and I wage war here as sure as in the Low Countries. Would I see Anne more often at Flushing or Zutphen? Good God, what an end to come to, to be pawns of politicians while we live and after we die! Sidney and I are the dumb show, and you and Walsingham sit behind and juggle us. Paint Sidney's skull black, dress him in woe, float his casket on rivers of hypocrisy, put him on exhibit along Cheapside like a hermaphrodite lamb or a penny monster in a booth. Whore his name for an emotion.

"I'm working honestly, and many with me, to bulwark England in a free and breathing strength. You may wish it or you may not, but I'll do it. And as there's a heaven above hell you'll not have my name to paw with when I'm gone!"

Burghley slid his eyelids over his eyes and resumed his long-suffering air of a man accustomed to seeing his advice disregarded when things went right and being railed at when things went wrong.

"I don't doubt it, my lord," he said wearily.

He went inside, and Oxford heard no more of the matter. When Burghley, however, sent quietly around among Mary's jury to get enough signatures to make certain of her execution, Oxford was one of those left out.

He was relieved. He knew he had provoked Burghley again, but that was nothing new. His conscience was clear of the axe that drove hissing into the block at Fotheringay, and he depended on Elizabeth.

The months ran quickly. A rush of preparing, of arming, drilling, storing supplies, drawing off more levies from the country and building warning beacons. A pressure on the court and London and the nation, an inconceivable dread that haunted the hours and lurked nightmarish in the clouds over the seas toward Spain.

Another summer and the theater companies were out once more, stuffed with plays and lugging their caravans from town to town. They went like surgeons carrying remedies for sickness, balms for fears and cures for the nightmare. Oxford and the London playwrights had mixed the cures out of sweat and blood, tired fingers and hot eyes and sleepless nights.

At the court at Hampton Anne said he needed rest. She was entering the early part of pregnancy again, when she was nauseated in the mornings and everything took on an exaggerated aspect. Her pregnancies had always been hard for her, her slight frame never seemed to be equal to them, and like most people who are exhausted she took it as a sign of exhaustion in someone else.

"You'll wear yourself out, Edward," she said. "Books and papers, papers and books, and riding back and forth into London. Stay and rest at the court."

"You stay for me," he said. "You're the one who needs rest. You like court better than I do."

"Not without you," she said. "And you're away so long."

"If Spain lands soldiers on our coast I'll be away longer, Anne. It's a work that must be pushed. We may not have more than this year. Perhaps in September we can go to Theobalds."

"I'd love it," she said. "Mother wants us at Theobalds."

"Your wanting would be the best reason, sweet," he said, and kissed her, and rode into London to ask Robin Christmas if the negotiations were finished about his ship.

He was buying a ship and outfitting it for the coming battle against the Spanish fleet.

He went down to Deptford, to the shipways where the great new war vessel was building, the *Ark Royal,* and watched the shipwrights pegging the beams and laying in the decks.

He talked to Raleigh about sails and ballast, seamanship and the proper size of guns.

He had a supper with his old friend Ralph Lane, who had been governor of Raleigh's settlement in the lands of the new world called Virginia in honor of Her Majesty, and who had been rescued by Drake

» 233 «

with the rest of the starving colonists. He tried to ask Lane about Atlantic storms, and how English ships were handled in a gale, though Lane was more interested in the colony, and in a weed that the natives smoked.

"We were too much cut off from our kind," Lane said, frowning at the recollection of the rich and lonely wilderness, "and since there was no hope of gain or advancement of anything beyond the bare necessaries of life, many of the colonists sat idle when they could and let the rest carry their share. As a result we lived at a mere common level, with no great enterprise in us. We brought back nothing but this tobacco. I was the first to smoke it in London, but I seldom try it, the apprentices hoop at me and call me mad. Well, we were once mad together, my lord. A pleasanter madness than now. Drake says the Armada is ready to sail."

But it did not. Elizabeth, listening to Drake, let him sail first. He caught the Armada in harbor at Cadiz, and in the flat, calm water his guns outmatched the galleys. It was a campaign without a flaw, that left Cadiz a shambles of thousands of tons of destruction, and delayed the invasion for one more year.

This was the time Elizabeth needed.

Oxford needed it, too. The theaters were in full swing. The plays were pouring from the pens of his playwrights' circle. Placards in London announced performances of his company every day. But the project was big. Very big. He had no way of judging how effective it was. Like Elizabeth, he could not be in every town and city. He could only call for plays, and more plays, for writing and more writing, and scan the faces of the audiences that crowded in, and tell Jack Lyly that tomorrow they would show a comedy, or a tragedy, or a tale of a King Edward, or a King Richard, or a King Henry.

He hardly noticed that May was in England again when his daughter was born, a tiny, pretty baby that Meg put in his arms while he bent over a pale and fragile Anne.

He hardly noticed that May had ended when he took Anne to the palace at Greenwich for the summer court.

He hardly noticed the heat, the stillness, and the unusually dank, feverish weather of June as he hurried through the gardens of the Savoy one day, wet and dusty from a long gallop, and Lyly met him on the path to tell him that Nan Vavasour was waiting for him.

20

SHE HAD SAID TO ELIZA, "I CAN HAVE HIM ANY TIME I want him," and it seemed desirable to her now that she should want him.

Poised coolly in the room that had changed so little in the summers and winters that had passed, she let her look drift around her with a pensive smile. The room itself was familiar. It was much the same, she saw, as when she had had him before. The stone fireplace, unlit in the June warmth and deeply smoke-blackened, the table and stools, the patterned carpet—her lips smiled faintly as she glanced at it—the dark, carved furnishings about the walls. There was the window casement, broad and sunny in the frame of curtains and throwing its checker of shadows across the window seat, and, beyond, through the doorway of the inner room, the canopied bed with coverlet drawn smooth over the impression left in the quilts by the weight of his body.

She regarded them silently, in a mixture of amusement and pleased reminiscence. She knew him so well. All these things told her how well she knew him. Edward's moods and ambitions, his loves, his hates, his passionate grasping at life and his quick, volatile intensity; they clung like an aura in the room.

On the table were his papers. Scattered notes, books, sheaves of manuscript, the scenes of a play he was editing with Kit Marlowe. These lay beside a packet of pen nibs and a pair of pewter inkpots, and were written in his clear, legible hand. Idly she picked up one of the sheets, scanning it without much curiosity. The part she read appeared to be a war scene.

Another part of the battlefield [it said]. Enter soldiers, fighting, and cross the stage. Alarums and excursions. Enter Duke and nobles, armed. The Duke speaks: Look up, my lords, the battle's cheerly won—

She put it down again with a disinterested pout, and traced her fingers over the back of a book: Watson's *Hekatompathia*. She shrugged and moved away; the book had been dedicated to Edward the year after she had come to him at the Savoy. These books and papers were the only difference in the room, the badges of his new activity and his new success. They were, she thought complacently, what had brought her there.

» 235 «

Nan did not deceive herself that she was growing older and must think of providing for her future in some permanent way, or that success made Edward more desirable than ever. The table with its purposeful, littered jumble, standing prominent in the middle of the room, as if he had been interrupted in a flight of fancy and it were waiting for his return, was witness to the higher honors he was holding, the richer favors, over and beyond the glittering title of Earl of Oxford.

For the risk of renewing their affair, she had considered it from every angle. The risk, she had decided, was not too great. The usual hum of court gossip had been buried in the excitement over the war with Spain; the Queen was immersed in the war, and would not be likely as strict as she once was; Sir Christopher Hatton had his attentions on military business, he working the crisis to his own advantage and whipping a froth about him like a spittlebug; and Lord Burghley was in something of eclipse for the time being, which would keep Lady Burghley silent.

Besides, other maids of honor were marrying, or forming attachments that might lead to marriage, or otherwise looking out for themselves. Nan had examined the possibilities. Young courtiers were more scarce than they had been. And the older ones were in the mood for glory and honor on battlefields, not romance. Of course, to be sure, there was always Sir Henry Lee, kindly and fusty and the Queen's perennial champion. . . .

It was at this point that Nan had gotten out her latest honey-colored taffeta and hung a fresh pomander at her girdle and had ridden from Greenwich over London Bridge to the Savoy.

Her arrival flustered Lyly, who had been taverning with Bob Greene the night before, and instead of going to Vere House had slipped into the rooms at the Savoy to sleep it off. He answered her knock after some delay.

"Mistress Vavasour," he said, alarmedly, and kept his face in the crack of the door, peering out while he fumbled to button his doublet.

"Good day," Nan said. She surveyed him with a humorous calm. "Pray don't trouble. Is my lord of Oxford awake?"

"He's not in bed," Lyly said, then blushed, fumbling more rapidly with his buttons. "That's to say, not here. Or wherever he is. He's not in bed, past doubt. I mean, he's past doubt awake. My lord's been at Plymouth."

"Has he?" Nan said. "What should he be doing at Plymouth?"

"His ship, Mistress Vavasour. He's fitting it to fight Spain."

Her eyes leveled past his face into the room, into the portion visible beyond his right ear and his fustian collar. "Must he live with his ship?" she said.

"Mistress Vavasour," he said pointedly, "King Philip's armada is looked for any day."

"It was looked for any day last year, and it didn't come," she said.

"Ah, true," he said, "true."

"So this year may be the same," she said indifferently. "When will Lord Oxford be in London?"

Lyly plucked at the top button of his doublet with his thumbnail. He was groping through the fog of his mind for some way to avoid an answer without being rude. But the fog was thick with last night's wine and he was a little dizzy, and the blue eyes had withdrawn from their scrutiny of the room and were resting on him. The button escaped from the buttonhole for the third time. "I think this afternoon," he said. "If you wish to come back—" He blinked hopefully.

"It's afternoon now," she said.

"Oh," Lyly said. He repeated the "Oh," and prolonged the pause after it as far as he was able. "How a pox did my man miss waking me?"

Nan smiled, and Lyly's face took on an expression as if he were gagged, like an actor who has lost his lines while the scene goes on without him. He said, "Or if you wish to wait—"

"I'll wait," she said.

She entered the room, Lyly trailing her. He took her cloak from her and folded it on a stool, squinting into the garden and chafing his hands to rub the clamminess from his palms. He saw no one down in the garden, nor any sign that she was being followed. He had an anxiety, however, to be away from the room as soon as possible. Pictures of the Tower flitted through his mind, very unhappy consequences on the heels of this, very unhappy for Oxford and the end of John Lyly.

Why had she come at this particular juncture, when fortune was riding high with them, when everything at the Savoy, at the theaters, in his career and Oxford's, was going so swimmingly? He had an anxiety to be away from the room, and greater anxiety to take her with him. It showed on him, and Nan laughed outright.

"Don't be afraid of me," she said. She accompanied the laugh with a placid nod toward the table. "Go on with your wit."

"I wasn't writing, Mistress Vavasour," Lyly said stiffly.

His chief dislike was people who assumed that an author of comedies was always a comedian. His next dislike was people who assumed a writer could turn the flow of his pen off and on like a spigot.

He excused himself and went out into the garden in front of the building, where he paced up and down on the paths, peering toward the Strand and starting at voices.

Presently Nan heard Oxford running up the stairs. She turned to the door. She could distinguish his step by the slight unevenness in it; the wound he had had from her uncle. He left Lyly below and came up alone.

Since the court's new interest in the plays she had seen a good deal of him, but always at a distance, and her eyes widened as he came in. A feeling of unexpected force and power came with him. He pushed the door open and swung it shut behind him, and put his back to it and stood looking at her.

His thick riding boots were grimy, his clothes powdered in dust; he wore a brown slashed doublet and plain unplumed cap, and trickles of sweat which he had not wiped off had dried on his cheeks.

"Ned," she said.

"Jack told me you were here," he said.

He kissed the hand she held out, and straightened again. That she should want to be there was something he was unprepared for. He had supposed the affair dead. He had thought her passion for him had spent itself in the occasional and almost desultory lovemakings after their experience in the Tower; that it had died of its own satisfying and been cut off finally by the duel with Knyvet.

"I frightened Master Lyly," she said.

"Jack has a memory."

"I could see he has."

She moved away with a smile, and went past the table to a chest by the wall, where a bottle of wine rested on a silver tray, spired six times in the shine of silver mugs. Her tone and manner, as well as her smile, conveyed to him a sense that she was perfectly at home, and aware of what she was about. He watched the shoulder of her gown lift as she poured wine in one of the mugs. She brought the mug back past the table and offered it to him. "You must be tired after your ride."

"I am." He had ridden hard and far, and the blood was pumping in his veins. He took the mug, hesitating as he faced her. "And for you?"

"No, thank you."

The smile toyed on her lips while he drank. He was thirsty, his throat dry. He finished the wine in long gulps and put the mug on the table.

Nan wandered to the window seat, settling herself among the cushions. She laid an arm along the sill and dropped a glance into the garden. "Master Lyly has disappeared."

"For the afternoon theater."

"How fortunate we have theaters," she said.

He came over and sat beside her. "You didn't come to talk of Lyly," he said.

His bluntness was abrupt, a protective screen thrown hastily up against the storm she roused in his mind. It did not seem to offend her. It seemed on the contrary to afford her a sense of enjoyment. He studied her as she sat there. He had always been intrigued by Nan. Her approach was frank and thoroughly apparent, yet she managed to flirt without flirtation, to offer herself assuredly and tranquilly, as she had offered the wine, without causing him the wry sensation of appearing gullible in his own eyes.

Even now, though both were certain why she had come, his knowledge of her told him she would wait for him to make the first move. She would sit in the window seat and smile, and look now and then at the garden in an absent, reflective way. But presently, if their hands were to touch. . . .

He got up again and went and poured himself more wine.

"How is Anne?" she said.

"Weak," he said. "The baby was too much for her. She's not well."

Nan said she was sorry. "Have you named the baby?"

"Susan."

"It's a musical name," she said. She said, "How did Anne let you go to Plymouth so soon?"

"I've my ship to look to. The Spaniards may sail next month."

"Will you really fight, Ned?"

"Yes."

She turned her head to the garden, the look he knew. "And in the meantime you're at Plymouth."

He set the second mug on the table beside the first.

"No," he said. "Not always."

A fleeting response in the twist of her mouth warned him that he had been wrong to say it. He came back and sat beside her once more, angry with himself for recognizing the warning, for not knowing whether he wished to recognize it or not. She kept her look on the garden, so that he could see only her calm, detached profile.

"June can be lovely in London," she said.

She raised her glance from the garden.

"Isn't it foolish to be afraid of memories?" she said.

"And if we're not?" he said. He had shifted his eyes from hers and he did not look at her, but he heard the stir of her body among the cushions.

She waited so long to answer that he had to look at her at last. She was laughing without sound, the crisscross pattern of the window panes lacy on her face and throat. "You never used to ask so many questions."

"I never needed to," he said. "I never wanted to."

"You were surer then."

"I was a fool."

"Ned," she said.

"What I wanted was you," he said.

The soundlessness of her laughter broke into a little fragmentary tinkle. "Yes," she said, "you made that evident."

The laughter drove him from the window seat. Springing up, he began to walk back and forth in the room, by the table, by the tall fireplace, past the chest and the bedroom door, and the splashes of remembered sunlight lying in mockery over the Turkey carpet at his feet. He was furious with himself. He was furious with her. He felt as if she were stripping him naked, sitting on the window seat and watching with a calm superciliousness the conflict that was going on in him. Then he swung to her, and caught his arms around her with all his strength. He thrust his lips down to hers, and held her until she cried out with pain.

He let her go, and stepped back.

She stared at him, one hand braced against the window sill, the back of the other across her mouth.

"I had to see," he said.

Gradually she recovered her breath. Her hand drew from her mouth.

"I had to do that," he said.

Her stare softened to the trace of a smile. "Why?"

"I had to find out."

She was not offended. She regarded him with the same amused tranquillity. "You take a rough way of discovery. What did you have to find out?"

"If it means anything."

"Am I as important as that? I should be flattered."

"Whatever you choose," he said.

"I hardly have a choice. But since you've given me one I'll choose to be flattered. I'm a woman."

"Nan—" he said.

The taffeta of her dress rustled as she smoothed its folds. "And after all, there have been a few years."

"Yes," he said.

She said, "We found out long ago, didn't we? We don't have to learn again."

"I had to," he said.

"If it means anything?"

"Yes."

"And does it?"

"No," he said. "It doesn't mean a thing."

She stood up, too. She didn't speak.

"Not any more," he said. "Not a thing."

Her gaze stayed on him, and he knew from her motionless face that she understood.

"It isn't Anne," she said. "I'm certain it isn't Anne."

"You're wrong," he said. "It's Anne. It's Paul's—the war—" He motioned toward the table, strewn in its clutter of plays and books, its manuscripts and fresh-penned scenes. The gesture told her better than words. "We aren't as we were," he said.

She took her cloak.

"Everything, then."

"Yes, Nan."

"Paul's," she said. "The war. A stage and a ship. I'm sorry I came."

"Don't be. I owe you a gratitude for coming. You've let me show myself that for the first time in my life I'm full and satisfied where I am, and to be doing what I'm doing. I don't need anything else. When we came together before I was at loose ends. Dangling, like a Maypole without enough dancers for its garlands." He made another motion toward the table. "The set's made up now. Good and evil, laughter and tears, madness, love, greed, beauty. A free, gusty dance."

"June in London," she said, with a stab of scorn.

"In all England," he said. "The fault isn't yours, Nan."

"What matter is it," she said, "whose fault it is?"

"None," he said.

"None in the least," she said. She was at the door.

He bent over her hand.

"God keep you happy, Ned. Anne won't," she said. She smiled. "I wish my uncle had killed you," she said, and her hair was a glister of gold, fading down the stairs.

Oxford closed the door and went over to the wall chest. He picked up the bottle of wine, unstopped it, fingered it. He did not pour any, and after a little he put the bottle down again. Going to the window, he stood a moment. From the window he went to the table. His eye fell on the scene he had been editing when he left for Plymouth. Mechanically he reached for a pen. "Another part of the battlefield. . . . Look up, my lords—" He added a line, and then another. At the end of the second line he stopped. He was surprised that he had let her go so easily. The thought occurred to him that Sussex would have been pleased. So would his father. He began to write again swiftly.

For a short time he wrote, standing at the table, and then realized that he had intended to see the afternoon's performance at Paul's. He dropped down the pen, and leaving the room, rode into the city. He watched the performance, and continued on afterward to Vere

House, changed his clothes, and cantered through the June twilight out to Greenwich.

Dressing for supper in the chambers allotted to her in the palace, Anne was in front of her mirror with Meg at her elbow when Oxford walked in. She caught his reflection in the glass as she was trying on a hair ornament, and jumped up with a little gasp, like a child's, tumbling the ornament to the ground. She had not expected him from Plymouth so soon. She looked like a child. Her face seemed unusually fragile, delicate and almost transparent in its whiteness beneath the dark frame of curls, and the glow of her cheeks was heightened by two feverish spots of color. Oxford felt that her body was trembling while he kissed her.

He had taken her to court somewhat against his judgment because she had pleaded so hard to go after the baby was born. Court had always been to Anne the delight that she cherished above everything else. The gallantry and sparkle, the songs and dancing and entertainments, were as necessary to her as sunshine to the daisies and violets in her father's gardens. She loved the opportunity to be gay, to have good times and wear jewels and pretty dresses. Her whole life had been centered around the palace world, and she had been a court beauty and maid of honor to Her Majesty at fourteen. Wifehood and motherhood had never quite replaced the fascination it held for her, nor had her troubled marriage or the problems of Oxford's volatile temperament. To be happy, with Anne, was to be at the court. So Oxford had agreed that she should go.

She was excited at having him with her, and in spite of his worry about her he was glad he could give her the happiness. She had had so little of it. She laughed and chatted at supper, taking congratulations on the new baby, and blushing, and patting at Oxford's arm. When he asked if she were well enough to dance she tossed her head and answered with her little pout that of course she was.

He led her to the floor as the music started. Her Majesty was not dancing that night, and the musicians opened with a merry cavolta. Anne bubbled with radiance. She spun through the skipping measures in a gay whirl, her skirts flew, her jewels gleamed, she swung and balanced, the tips of her shoes twinkling and the color climbing higher in her cheeks.

"If this could go on forever!"

"You love it, don't you?"

"Yes, oh yes. Edward, you dance so wonderfully!"

"My little Anne—you'd wear out every musician in the kingdom."

"All summer. All the lovely nights. Will they play a hey for us? I'd dote on a hey. Edward, you've always danced wonderfully. . . ."

He smiled at the fling of her curls, at her joy and animation. The music seemed to fill her with energy. It was like a tonic for her. She threw him little coquettish glances as if they were courting again.

"Isn't it odd to think we're married? I don't feel married tonight. Look at Her Majesty, wearing the pearls she filched from Raleigh out of Grenville's treasure ship. And Raleigh pretending he doesn't care. There's Leicester. He's supposed to be at camp, but he can't stay away. Oh, Edward, this is fun."

Tom Bedingfield came to talk, Fulke Greville and Sir Ralph Lane, and she gathered them in a circle around her, her eyes bright, her fan quick and playful in her fingers.

"The next jig? Why, Tom, to be sure. And Fulke must have a galliard. Fulke, do you remember the galliard at Warwick, when you and my lord played at sham battle? Sooth, I shouldn't remember, should I? It makes us old. Am I old, Fulke? Our little Bess is to be a maid of honor."

If sometimes the thread of her thought ran too fast, if her eyes were too bright or her fan too quick, Oxford's twinge of worry was put aside in the thought that she was having such a good time.

"Are you tired, Anne?"

"No, no, not a whit."

She seemed to want to crowd it all into that one night. She came back from her jig with Tom Bedingfield with the scarlet vivid in her cheeks, and laughed her way through a galliard with Fulke Greville.

"Are you sure you're not tired, Anne?"

"Of course. How could I be? Edward, you're sweet to let me have this. I'd like to dance with you again. You dance better than any."

He put his arm around her. They danced in the shadow of an alcove, and while their bodies swayed toward one another in the light, intimate figure of the steps, he bent and kissed her. They danced in the center of the hall, with the brilliance and glitter of the court packed about them, blending among the gaiety, melting in it, a part of it, and the musicians playing a wild, dizzying hey she adored. Exuberant. Giddy with pleasure. Faster. Faster.

"Oh, Edward, thank you—thank you with all my heart."

And then, after two hours, after three, the scarlet vivid not only in her cheeks, but at her temples, and over her forehead, and along her throat. Her eyes shaded suddenly with fatigue and a kind of protesting wonder as her hand went for security to his—a hand so dry and burning that he gripped it in a hard dread.

"I am tired now, Edward. I want to sleep."

And the long galleries that seemed endless in the midnight, and their apartments at last, and Meg's wrinkled face, haggard and frightening behind the flicker of the taper.

"She's so hot, Meg. So very hot."

The dark curls, the pretty hair ornament winking on the dressing table, the kirtle, the petticoats, Meg's speeding fingers. Her fan dropped by the bed like a child's toy, and her knees sagging as she leaned shivering against his shoulder.

"I can sleep now, Edward . . ."

21 JUNE ENDED. JULY CAME—JULY 1588—AND LONDON braced in the front line of the war.

There was no more dancing at Greenwich. The court-captains were joining their companies, and the Queen was riding out to hearten her camp at Tilbury. In place of plumed caps and pile velvets the fashion was steel morions and armor.

At Tilbury Leicester had a thousand horse and twenty-two thousand foot, the command of the army, and Norris as his chief-of-staff. The Queen's cousin, Lord Hunsdon, held a second army in London, twice as many horse and thirty-four thousand foot, for the protection of Her Majesty's person. Twenty thousand men patrolled the southern coast.

War was no longer at a distance, a campaign of remote names and foreign places. It was an immediacy, a reality. Distance had lost its security.

Burghley's spies and Walsingham's agents on the continent had made their reports certain. King Philip's Armada had left Spain. Dispatches from across the Channel sowed rumors in the city's streets and confirmed fears in the Queen's Council. Parma, in the Netherlands, had collected his garrisons and was massing transports in the Dutch harbors.

The Armada had sailed.

It had weighed anchor in the port of Tagus, turned northward, and disappeared. It had been at sea since late May. It was somewhere out there on the Atlantic, blowing toward England, blowing nearer every day.

From the waist of his ship Oxford saw the longboat shoot under the square stern and nose alongside. The crew of the boat struggled in the windy chop, their conical caps heaving forward and back with the pull of their arms at the oars, and spray slopped over their short, baggy breeches. The boatswain at the top of the ladder hailed them into the lee, fetching them up to row Lord Oxford ashore to Plymouth.

Oxford was standing by the black-and-white painted bulkhead that crossed the ship astern of the mainmast and supported the quarterdeck and the sloping poop above it. Forward, past a maze of lines and tackle, a smaller bulkhead rose to the forecastle. Between, in the waist, shipwrights were caulking deck seams in the second orlop. He caught the smell of pitch and the tap of hammers, the stench of tripe from the cook galley in the waist hold, and the rattle of gravel ballast being dumped aboard. He was wondering if his ship would be ready to fight if the Spaniards were sighted tomorrow.

The gravel came inboard in baskets from a barge moored alongside. Up full, swing, lug, tilt, and down empty. The shevers ran singing. Now and then he heard a shout: "Slack off! . . Pull! . . 'Ware below! . . ." Basket on basket until there was barely space for supplies, for water, for powder and shot, for the pikemen and bowmen and arquebusiers she would carry into battle. But the ship's master had called for more ballast. She was deep in keel and crank without it.

It was a blustery evening. The sun was setting in a wool of gray scud that drove from the southwest and scurried landward like a gallop of sheep. Over Oxford's head furled sails shook in the rope yarns that bound them to the yards, and the swifters bracing the pine masts vibrated in the wind. Except for the wind, Oxford thought, which had been wild and stormy all summer, Drake and Hawkins and Frobisher would have had the fleet out of Plymouth Sound and hunting the Spaniards before this. But that was a risk with the unsettled weather, and the Privy Council at London was still captious about risks. The council, in fact, had wanted to disband the ships. It would have done so if the lord admiral had not pledged his personal money and credit to keep them there.

Oxford turned from watching the longboat and glanced out over the Sound. The fleet lay at anchor in the red-streaked sunset, straining at its rope cables. Abeam of him to windward was the *Triumph,* he had gone aboard her yesterday to examine how Captain Frobisher placed his guns—a giant ship of eleven hundred tons, three decks and a ship's company of five hundred. Beyond her was the *Ark Royal,* the flagship of the lord admiral, fifty-five guns. Her painted and battlemented upper works showed clear in the sunset light; closer to the frothed slaty water her battened gunports looked like tight-lipped mouths, and her steeved bowsprit lifted sharp above her forecastle.

Oxford had admired her on the stocks at Deptford. So had the Queen, who had bought her from Raleigh for five thousand pounds and added her to Her Majesty's Navy. She was a fine galleon, massive and sturdy, with a length three times her beam that made her speedy and seaworthy. To leeward Oxford could see Sir John Hawkins' ship, the *Victory;* Drake's *Revenge;* the huge *Elizabeth Jonas,* christened so because she would save the Queen from her enemies as Jonah had been saved from the whale; the *Antelope,* the *Scout,* the *Golden Lion* and the little *Foresight.* They sat with the air of sea birds on the water —great ships, middling ships, galleons, galleasses, their masts and spars rocking against the sky, and in and among them the barks and pinnaces, the coasters and the volunteer ships, the merchant vessels, the victualers, and the small, bouncing caravels. Fifty-four there at Plymouth, under the lord admiral.

The men who sailed them were tough and seasoned, and knew the tricks of seamanship. Oxford was much impressed by the West Country fishermen, whose search for catches had led them year by year out past the Lizard and across to the Newfoundland Banks. They had been braving the Atlantic since the Cabots, and they could navigate and they could fight. He had encountered them in the town streets, outlandish fellows, strange almost to a Londoner as a Spaniard, blurred in speech by the broad weight they put on the *r*'s, and the public houses in the Barbican filled with the dank salt reek of their thick sea gowns. More and more were coming in, rounding past Rame Head before the fresh gale, mizzen lateen yard unparreled from the mast and launched out over the lee quarter for faster running, and bringing yarely to behind St. Nicholas Island.

Big vessels; brave, capable seamen. But how big against the Spaniards? How brave against the ram of a monstrous bastard galleass oared by three hundred slaves? When he scanned around him from the waist of his ship, Oxford felt as he had when he studied the faces at the plays. There was no way of knowing what the answer would be. In Plymouth Sound, in all England—ships—plays—stanchness or faltering of hearts—the Queen splendid on horseback exhorting her armies—the answer lay with each man.

Lyly's nose appeared at one of the round openings in the bulkhead used for small arms fire.

"My lord—" Lyly said.

His nose vanished, and after a minute he emerged on deck, walking in imitation of a rolling gait, not like a writer of court comedies but a private secretary to the owner of a fighting ship.

"My lord, I will make me a pomander and wear it about my neck, wench-wise. I have been to the lower orlop to count the cannon, and the stinking is abominable. We smell in the bilge as if the crew had voided guts there this month past."

"We do," Oxford said, nodding. "Like any ship. Bear up, Jack. You can fight in the tops where the breeze is sweet."

Lyly squinted at the fighting top on the mainmast, measuring the height to the lubber's hole in its elm floor. "A rarer idea," he said, "would be to get the wind of the dons and let them have the breeze from us. The rankness would blow 'em back to Spain."

"They may stink worse than we do," Oxford said.

"Impossible," Lyly said. "D'ye know what the sailors say? In fights we sling the yards in chains, for fear of the ties being cut by billhooks. Then if the yards are shot loose, the chains fall and mangle us. Marry, with shot and chain and arrowbolt and cutlass we'll be unlovely corpses."

"Stay in the cabin," Oxford said, "and don't talk to sailors. They feed your imagination. Are the cannon placed?"

"Twenty demicannon, ten to a side. Two cannon in the gun room as stern chasers, and the fowlers and light pedreros in the close-fights. It's done Frobisher's way. But the master gunner would like more powder."

"We have no more."

"He thinks the supply too short."

"There's no more in Plymouth."

The glibness of Lyly's phrases tempted Oxford to smile. Lyly picked up sea talk as airily as he had picked up the floweriness of his court writings. But this life was new to him, and he was doing his best. For that matter it was new to Oxford, and he didn't know that he was doing any better.

The boatswain was waiting by the mainwale, looking occasionally in Oxford's direction.

"Come ashore, Jack," Oxford said. "We're finished for today."

He started across the deck, circling round a shipwright who squatted forward of the mainmast, intent on his last few inches of pitch and oakum before the night set in.

"Faith," Lyly said, "if we'd not come down when we did we'd never have finished. A ship's as bad as a play for getting ready. It's a good thing—" He stopped. He had been going to say it was a good thing Oxford had not stayed in London for Anne's formal funeral.

Oxford walked to the mainwale and halted.

No, he had not gone to the funeral. He had attended the private services at Cecil House, but Lord Burghley had wished to have Anne buried in state in Westminster Abbey, and Oxford could not bring himself to be there. He had come to Plymouth, and left Lord and Lady Burghley to lay Anne in her tomb with official ceremony. Lord Burghley was acting according to his lights, but it was the tragedy of them both that his lights had never been Oxford's.

Anne had died four days after their dance at Greenwich. He and Meg had put her to bed, and she had not recognized anyone again.

It seemed incredible, and he was grieved and bewildered that he did not feel more sorrow. He would miss Anne—her pouts, her flashes of spirit, her childishness that had been so appealing. Yet their strange, thwarted marriage of friction and disillusionments had never given a true satisfaction to either of them, and its ending brought to him no great emotion or feeling of emptiness. Lady Burghley would take his daughters. Lord Burghley would take the mournful tomb in the Abbey. He, who had been Anne's husband, would take his regret that for both him and Anne her death must be a kind of release, erasing the troubles and distresses of her insufficiency for her, and leaving with him, at best, a sad and deeply pitying tenderness.

The sun had set, and the slaty tones of the water were creeping up the anchored ships.

He climbed outboard over the mainwale, and, calling Lyly, descended the ladder to the longboat.

Through July weeks they caulked seams, and stowed provisions, and polished their guns until the metal shone burnished. They drank in the taverns, drilled at boat practice on the Cattewater, and waited for the Spaniards.

Oxford champed with impatience, pushing the preparations of his vessel. The work was aggravating and slow. Salt to be laid in. Water in sweet casks. Hogsheads of wine. There were lead sheathings for covering the holes of cannon shot. There was ammunition for small arms. There were the upholsterings in the cabin, and replacements in the pavises that ringed the deck like a rim of shields. In the daylight hours he stayed aboard where he could watch the details himself, the items of inventory, the clews and garnets, spare whipstaff for the tiller, top armor for the mizzen top; where he could talk with the master of supplies still lacking, of extra bowlines, and kettles for the cook room, and length of cable for paying out if they lay at try off a lee shore. At nights he sat ashore and listened to the other captains, and learned how Her Majesty's far-sightedness had kept the coastal trade to British ships, so that Spain had no soundings of the harbors, and how she had encouraged a system of pilotage and buoyage, and how Sir John Hawkins had changed the designs of shipbuilding.

"Why, it's proved. More keel gives neater sailing."

"I grant you. And steadier for gunnery. But he's cut down the height."

"A shrewd move. Now take your carrack, your Spanish carrack—"

"—smooth as a swan she was, the whole way from Dartmouth. And mark—"

"I can tell the catechism of a good ship. Able to carry her guns in all weathers, be seaworthy and stay well when boarding and turning on a wind."

"You had that from Raleigh."

"It's sound catechism."

"—your carrack, as I say, stands high. High castles, fore and stern. Decks above decks."

"With Hawkins it comes to this, too much castle on a vessel is unwieldy."

"And the carrack's tubby, with great pitching in a head sea."

"Will we get the use of our close-fights? A tall poop filled with crossbowmen would riddle my quarterdeck."

"We'll get use of our guns."

Their speech had the ocean tang, the speech of traders to the Mediterranean and the Baltic, of Devon rovers and shipmen cradled in the Tamar and the Plym, the Dart and the Exe. Love of ships, skill of the sea, ran through it like a tide.

The new design of their ships, lower, longer, with less mass and bulk in the upperworks, was untested in battle or the maneuvers of a sea fight. Oxford thought, as the boisterous, squally days wore on, that unless the weather dropped it was likely not to be tested at all. The English fleet would be windbound in the harbor.

He heard that thirty ships and barks had been paid for by the City of London, that other coasters were gathering in at the ports, and that a squadron under Lord Henry Seymour was watching the eastern end of the Channel and the movements of the Duke of Parma in the Netherlands. He heard the total of vessels was nearly two hundred.

But he would look out into the Sound toward the *Ark Royal,* and then at the little caravels. And he would remind himself that many of the caravels only carried twenty men.

The Sound spread like an amphitheater under the broad, flat plateau of the Hoe, where Drake and the captains scowled at the wind and played bowls in the restless days. He could see it like a theater. Like the forestage of another Agincourt, and the actors waiting in the wings.

He had put his armor aboard, ready for sailing. His mariners lived on the ship. The fighting men were quartered ashore, to save provisions. In the ending weeks of July he joined the games of bowls on the Hoe. It was a fair spot close above the quay, fair for sport and for watching the horizon for a glimpse of sails.

The wind was still southwesterly on the day a merchant ship, her canvas bellying, scuttered into the Sound. The captains on the Hoe paused as she rounded in and sent her boat paddling like a water bug for the town.

"The dons?"

"There's no sign."

"She's running from someone."

Servants went down to inquire. It was not necessary. The news was plain. The watchers on the Hoe saw it leap from inn to tavern, from tavern to alehouse, from hostel to shop to chandlery to fishstand. Watched the streets filling with jostling, shoving figures heading toward the quays and sluicing overboard into the boats.

Drake, a bowling ball in his hand, let go a string of oaths. "Scabby whoreson bilge-lubber Spaniards! Pukers in beards, mangy pox-rump sweatshanks! Christ's bones! The devils take us backsides to the rocks, clewed to the bottom like spawning crabs. Hell scorch their guts and an onshore wind!"

Eyes to the Sound. The water quilted in whitecaps. The longboats pulling toward the ships. Confusion. Hurry. The edge of panic. The dons were coming, the dons. Sergeants and ensigns, gathering their men, yelled in the town.

"Cut sail, cut sail, Drake. We must beat out!" This was Frobisher.

There was a rush for cloaks. The buckling on of swords. Over the water came the shrilling of boatswains' pipes.

"God's death and wounds! Would ye bolt? Stay and finish our game." This was Drake.

The skeltering troops, looking upward and back while they jammed for room in the boats, could make out the steadying figure between sea and sky: Sir Francis continuing his bowls.

The wisdom was evident the next morning when Oxford reached the quay. Officers sorted the men, grouped them, and row-barges ferried them to the fleet. They moved quickly, alertly, without the strain of orders on orders and of making way for captains and their staffs. The panic had been averted. Time was less sharp if Drake could bowl, and the quays were nearly empty and most of the troops aboard. Oxford stepped into his longboat and was rowed to his ship. Lyly told him, as he climbed the ladder, that the Spaniards had been sighted off the Lizard.

The master had cut the ropes furling his sails and was breaking out the spritsail to get under way. To windward the *Ark Royal* had drawn ahead on her cable as her mariners chanted at the capstan. All over the Sound canvas was spreading, the crews aloft on the yards, boatloads of troops filing antlike up the sides, the ships beginning to stir.

With a slow awakening sluggishness bows fell off from the wind and pushed into the slapping whitecaps.

Oxford sent Lyly into the cabin for his armor and went to the quarterdeck. "Will we get into the open?"

"God knows, my lord. The wind's in a foul quarter. We'll gamble beaching if we sail. If we lie here we lose the dons."

Ahead, to leeward, the eastern arm of land that locked the Sound wove a rocky line between the whitecaps and the crested blue of the sea. A long tongue of creaminess licked at its base, breakers pounding in under the southwest breeze.

"Tow with the boats?" Oxford said.

"Not in a wind off the bows, my lord. The caravels, likely. But oars wouldn't hold the great ships."

"Sir Martin said we must beat out."

"Sir Martin Frobisher's a sailor. He don't take kindly to being bottled in here. We might squeeze it. We might."

He was eyeing the *Ark Royal* as he spoke. Her anchor was up. Pennons flowed from her mastheads, the royal standard and the flag of the lord admiral, Lord Howard of Effingham. She heeled slightly, her spars and battlements inching ahead, imperceptibly at first, then surer and at a quickening speed.

"Od's life, my lord, we're doing it. There's our orders. We'll gamble. Beach or fight, and the devil damn the wind . . . Close-haul! Tauten bowlines! In spritsail!" The master's shout rang over the deck.

One by one, at the signal of the lord admiral, the fleet got under way and stood close-hauled to sea. It was audacity. It was seamanship.

It was faith in their vessels and their knowledge of handling them. It was a feat never done before and never of a sort to be done after. One by one they skirted the headland, depending on draught of keel and trim of sail to keep them off the lee. No lagging, no hanging back. Agincourt again; the faces in the London theaters; the faces in the camp at The Hague. Faces of men who knew themselves, knew what they were and what they could be. Oxford watched the faces. Perhaps he had given them something. Some thought, some vision, some grain of daring, dropped from an inn stage or a platform in a town's moot-hall, to find soil and grow.

Drake was out, Frobisher; Hawkins was herding along the little ships. He watched the breakers against the headland—close—closer—creamy as milk and muttering in a long-drawn roar. They loomed forward, then stretched abeam, then fell slowly astern; and he turned and looked out to the open sea, and saw the Armada.

It came sweeping along the English coast in a great double crescent. It ran massively before the wind, and the spread of its sails covered the ocean in a cloud. Flaunting streamers and banners, trumpets braying, decks heavy with engines of war, ponderous galleons and lofty hulks, oared galleys, galleasses and steep, high-charged carracks rode enormously over the swells, trailing *pataches* and caravels on their flanks and pushing a squadron of small zabras out in front of them like spume in front of a tidal wave.

The sight was vast and gross and monstrous, more powerful than men had ever yet seen on a single ocean.

King Philip had squandered on his Armada.

He had wanted numbers, and his ships were a hundred and fifty. He had wanted weight, and the builders in his shipyards had launched him sixty thousand tons. He had wanted strength, and got it; the upperworks of the galleons would stop musket shot, the plankings and ribs of their hulls were five feet thick. He had wanted size, and he had got that, too; his galleasses were mighty fortresses, sea-going mansions, equipped with chambers and chapels, turrets and pulpits. The supplies he had lavished on them would have beggared Elizabeth: bacon, cheese, biscuit, fish, rice, beans, peas, oil, vinegar and wine. Twelve thousand pipes of fresh water; candles, lanterns, and hemp; ox-hide and lead sheathing to plug the holes from enemy guns. Great black-pitched cables twined the masts to buffer cannon shot, and bows and keels and sheathings were spiked for solidness with iron bolts.

He had put the hardiest seamen on the decks and the toughest slaves on the benches in the galleys. He had manned the fleet with picked fighting troops and sent it from Spain to sink the English ships or drive them off the Channel. No one but the English doubted it would be done, for by every reckoning the Armada was invincible.

The question was merely one of hounding down that sea-dragon, *El Draque,* and bringing him to combat.

The same storms that had held the English at Plymouth had delayed the Spaniards on the Atlantic. Their short, flat-keeled vessels tended to be leewardy in the open sea. But that would be of little moment in the narrow waters between England and the Netherlands, where fighting would be at close grips. With landfall off the Lizard they had the wind on their quarter, and they slewed into battle line and bore eastward. The Armada would scrape like a colossal seine the length of the southern English coast, netting up and crushing opposition as it went. It would proceed on to the Low Countries, cover Parma's crossing with his transports, and clear the lane to England for invasion. Its admiral, the Duke of Medina-Sidonia, had the plans in his cabin, outlined personally by Philip.

When, off Plymouth, a few thin ships began straggling seaward, downwind and pitifully single, the Armada unlidded its gun ports and looked as one would look at idiocy.

Oxford's ship, among the first out of Plymouth Sound, made a long reach into the wind. She cut ahead of the advancing Spanish fleet. Once away from shore she could slack off a point and wear more sail, and he was amazed at the way she handled, and the master's boldness in keeping her up. The master pressed her nearer and nearer to the cloud of the Armada's sails, pulling at his under lip with thumb and forefinger, measuring distance and course and the slip of her leeway.

He followed the *Ark Royal,* tracking in her smooth, curdled wake. Others followed behind, a dozen, a score. They crossed the Armada's path in a straight line, making for the broad sea and space for maneuvering. The strategy was admirable, even to Oxford's landsman eyes. If the lord admiral had let himself be pinned between the Spaniards and the shore he would have been forced to the beach. By running slant across the Spaniards' front he played for advantage in guns and sail. As the Spaniards veered to intercept him he slacked off farther. The margin was reckoned so tight that Oxford counted the men on the deck of one of the zabras.

Broadside, the English opened with their guns. While he buckled on his armor, which Lyly had brought him, Oxford felt the deck quiver under his feet, and the smoke rolled, curled inboard, and wisped out in the wind over the lee bulwarks. The Spaniards answered, but none but their bow guns were in range, and too light for damage at that distance. On the first orlop, below, the gunners of Oxford's ship sent up a derisive yell. They could see their shot smashing into the zabras and the high freeboard of the leading galleons.

By now the Armada was past the harbor mouth. The last of the English, streaming out, fell on their rear. The first half circled the far flank and got to windward. Both halves poured shot at the massed, steep targets. They found out at once that their guns had the longer power. Their ships were steadier and they made better aim. They stayed out of harm, on the weather gauge, and fired at will.

The Armada drove on eastward.

The English hung on the flanks, and battered.

And the Duke of Medina-Sidonia, in his ornate cabin, looked once more, a little more soberly, at the plans King Philip had outlined for him.

The sun through the netting above the decks reminded Oxford of the crisscross mullions in his rooms at the Savoy.

The memory was blurred.

Everything of memory was blurred in four days of battle.

His armor was dented and powder-burned. His throat was constricted and his eyeballs ached.

The netting was not clean, like the mullions. Things had caught in it. Broken arrows, crossbows, splinters from the yards and strands of rope. Jagged shadows over the deck. A leg blown off below the knee, raw and bloody, the shinbone spearing through. Greasy coils of human intestines dangling forward of the quarterdeck. Two shipboys, blood-slobbered, poked at them with billhooks.

A man ran by him, his left eye lying out on his cheek. Oxford grasped at him, but the man screamed and ran on.

"Go below. Get the surgeon," Oxford called after him.

Oxford turned and ran up the ladder to the quarterdeck. The ship heeled to a shock, and a billowing of smoke made it hard to see.

"He's rammed us! He'll try to board!" Oxford recognized the master's Devon accent. He would not have recognized the beard and the shouting mouth.

"Pikemen! Forward! In the close-fight! Stand to it!"

The carrack's figurehead crunched over Oxford's ship by the bow. She swung broadside with a slow momentum. Between decks his ship's guns belched. Pikes wadded and jabbed on the forecastle. Men on the carrack's yards, tangled above the English vessel, reached with sickle-shaped knives, hacking to cut the ties and cripple the sails. Steel champed on the sling chains.

"Clear me the yards, bowmen! Bring them down!"

The waist a splutter of musketry from the arquebusiers, and the glimmer of slow-matches. Ripped bulwarks, gear, sprawled agony and twisted bodies. Over the poop the carrack's towering sterncastle drifting nearer, the grinding of wood while spars and rigging snapped. Yards jammed among the canvas. Shot and arrows skittered on the deck.

Leaks in the carrack gave her a list. She was canted to the far side, white belly exposed. Her guns were angled high and the Spanish troops, unsure of footing, could not fire arrows or muskets except for those in the tops or the front rank by the bulwarks.

Thicker smoke. Guns blasting from between decks again. Cannon-balls jolting. Oxford's voice, wrenched as the master's face, and as unrecognizable.

"Jack! . . . Jack, stay here and bring word if they board by the stern. I want the master gunner. We can founder her."

Into the waist once more. To the lower orlop. Gagging powder reek, demons in a sulphurous pit, sweat-grimed and bare-chested, and the sour stench of vomit and suppurating wounds.

The carrack was yawing off.

Parched throat. Aching eyeballs. Memories that blurred and criss-crossed.

Jagged shadows.

Mullions in his windows at the Savoy.

Drake, in the *Revenge,* captured the flagship of the Spanish vice-admiral. She had fouled the neighboring ships and dropped behind. He sent her into Torbay. Another galleon blew out her stern. Sir John Hawkins went aboard her in a skiff with the lord admiral and sent her into Weymouth. The chase went on.

The fourth day the wind veered northeast and both fleets stood in toward the coast. There was a fight off Portland. The *Ark Royal, Victory, Elizabeth Jonas* had hot engagements. Oxford hammered at the carrack. The *Triumph* and five merchant ships pushed too far to leeward. The oared galleons of the Spanish fleet saw prey and set upon them. Drake and the lord admiral led a rescue.

The wind shifted to the southeast, and to the south-southwest, and died away. On a calming sea the ships lay within sight of each other. Losses and batterings had shaken the Spaniards. From the poops of their vessels they could observe that the English fleet had increased. The coast harbors were emptying out ships and men, more ships and more men. Small ships, but they threatened, and pecked, and added to the Spaniards' troubles. Their battle tactics kept the hulks and carracks turning to snap at them, losing seaway, wallowing, and turning again. Of the great English warships none was seriously damaged, and they clung like harriers.

Under the listless streamers that flapped from their mastheads the Spaniards pondered the dip and roll of their short, fat craft that made their gunnery so poor. They pondered the weaker range of their cannon, and the number of leagues yet to be covered before they could join forces with Parma, and the iron bolts in their hulls that were rusting in the salt water and beginning to leak.

The English pondered what to do about shortage of munitions.

That night, without wind, the sea was quiet.

The next day they fought off the Isle of Wight.

"My lord, if we live past this we'll have honor."

» 258 «

"It's likely, Jack."

"Great honor, I'd think."

"Very likely . . . Master gunner, how much powder?"

"From the victualer ship, my lord, enough to tickle Spanish bottoms till nightfall."

"Tickle sparingly. Save your shot."

"The scurvy fiends have bottoms like rock."

"It seems so . . . Must the wounded lie 'tween decks so close to the guns?"

"Aye, my lord Oxford. Where else?"

"It's bad for sick and hale both."

"Marry, my lord, come above deck. This is too foul here."

"Foul for what, Jack?"

"It stinks."

"Yes, and it groans, too. And bleeds in filth and tattered carcasses, and writhes out from under the gunners' feet, and prays that flesh will hold or that death will be merciful. Here's honor for you, Jack, in a wooden hole. It's bought here. Those that have motion afterward can tell how they bought it. They can show their stumps in country lanes and lie on their crutches at alehouse doors. They can pay for honor with running sores and paint it for eyes in blind and puckering sockets. They'll beg alms for the honor they have from mangled bones. God's blessing—honor."

"I thought you coveted honor, my lord."

"For myself, Jack. Not for these. . . ."

The mariners fished him out of the sea while they were bringing up the longboat to tow them into action.

His lips were blue and his olive skin the color of an eel's belly. He lay on the deck and vomited bile. They fed him water so he could talk.

He told them—the master had some Spanish and could break crumbs of meaning from him—that he had had no fresh water for a week.

"Your Drake," he said, "smashed our water casks at Cadiz last year. They were seasoned wood. We put to sea two months ago with new ones. The staves warped. The water seeped away."

They put him between decks, with the wounded men and the guns. He said he had a wife in Valencia.

There were few bodies in the sea; their armor sank them.

They towed into action for lack of wind. Oxford's ship crawled at the end of a cable, the mariners in the longboat straining. The effort convulsed their faces and gritted their jaws.

Oxford selected a galleass that had set her sails toward the Isle of Wight. She drifted limply, swollen with canvas. Her pennons hung down the sails, the ragged saltier of Burgundy flapping at her mainmast. She waited the approach of Oxford's ship like a fat sow, silent and expectant, but she began firing before he was in range.

The noise of cannonading from both fleets swung like a heavy pendulum over a long, slow groundswell. To windward the *Ark Royal* and *Golden Lion* were hidden by galleasses and a blanket of smoke. Oxford could hear the sharp pop of the Spanish guns and the deeper boom of the English. The *Triumph* was to leeward again, bearing in toward Wight if the Spaniards should try to land and set up a base there. The whole great cloud of the Armada rolled and heaved in the glassy swells, and a hundred English ships nosed and stung and prodded around it. On the rear of the cloud, where the English were, the edges broke into fragments; patches and puffs that billowed dense smoke and widened from the cloud in individual combats.

Shots from the galleass fell short. Oxford's own guns opened. He saw the sprays of water and hits on the galleass's castles.

"Bring the stern chasers from the gun room. They're heavier. Mount them broadside."

"We may be taken astern by a row-galley, my lord. We've no rudder in this wind."

"Bring them up."

Hauling, panting, coughing in the smoke. The cannon trundled to the lower orlop. Gunners scrambling outboard to load. Solid blasts out of the pair of forty-pounders.

"We're slowing."

"The longboat crew, my lord. They're spent."

"Put in another crew. Fetch us closer."

The master grinned, for they had lost the carrack in the other fight and the high galleass was stuff for slaughter. They sent fresh men into the longboat and slid closer. All about them it was the same—the English inching in, slicing at the Spaniards, their boats towing them to battle, oars dipping in the sun, and the white waterspouts of the Spanish shot. The sea a broad green platter rimmed by the horizon, the English coast cool with darker green and the sense of land. If the Spaniards had had boats for towing the English would have blown them out of the water. Oxford called for Lyly to follow, and ran forward.

On the forecastle were the bowmen and the arquebusiers, and gunners priming the light fowling pieces. It was the advantage of the lighter ordnance that it did not have to be loaded from outboard when there was close work; the men had the protection of the bulwarks and the steel shields of the pavises. As Oxford climbed to the forecastle a Spanish ball sheared half the bowsprit. The mariners scrambled to clear the mesh of lines, and Oxford saw that the space between the ships had lessened. He saw the Spanish bowmen in the fighting tops, the sheer sides of the galleass like a wall.

The shot from his ship knocked saucer dents in the galleass's planking, and embedded in the thick wood.

"God's blessing, Jack, how much do we have to pound her?"

In the longboat the crew were gasping while they tugged at the oars, and looking to the forecastle. Some of them were nicked, and crimson welled from their arms and smeared down the oars to the boat's thwarts.

"Open with the pedreros. Rake the waist."

A gunner, clinging outside the lower gun ports to load, wailed and splashed into the sea. With a quieter roll to their vessels on the smooth, almost windless surface, the Spaniards' fire was more accurate.

"Rake the waist. Pick off their bowmen on the castle. If we foul, stand by to board . . . Jack, find out what's left of our powder."

He went back to the quarterdeck, through the shadows under the netting, through ropes and tackle and groups of pikemen waiting for the order to fight hand to hand.

"She'll be ours, master. Bring in the longboat, we'll batter from here. When she flinches, we'll grapple her."

"My lord," the master said, "look to the *Triumph*. She's too far to leeward. We're nighest of the rest."

Oxford looked. The *Triumph* was wind-dead and slatting, two carracks spitting shot at her and a third sidling toward her in a ruffle of breeze. Frobisher was aboard the *Triumph*. He had lost three thousand pounds with Frobisher. But they were fighting together on one sea. In one fleet. He looked at the *Triumph* and then at the galleass that was to have been his prize.

"Tow us over, master. We'll help him recover the wind . . . Od's my life, what a pox are we to do to beat these Spaniards? Tow to Flushing?"

"Tow to hell, my lord, if we have to. Hola! Lord Christ! Guard heads!"

There was a rending noise and a mingle of screams. The galleass's cannonball struck square, and the mizzen topgallant—shrouds, spars, iron chains—avalanched to the deck.

Ships dropped out. Men died. They seared with fever and griped with dysentery.

But they clung to the Armada. They blocked it from the Isle of Wight, from the southern beaches and Dover. They pursued and hounded it and gave it no rest, and the Armada, its nerves frayed, broke for Calais.

Lord Seymour with his squadron joined the fleet at Calais. At night they sent fireships into Calais roads.

They drove the Armada out to sea again. They caught it off Gravelines, all hope gone of joining Parma, and battled it there all day, from nine to six.

This was the tenth day of the chase.

The Spaniards wanted no more. They were running aground on the French coast, and on the sand shoals of the Netherlands. They were dispirited, formations shattered. The wind was making up to a northeast gale. The Duke of Medina-Sidonia gave the signal, a beaten man in his ornate cabin. They turned and fled. Their vessels were high and shallow and cumbersome. Their rigging was too heavy, their keels too light, and the iron bolts that spiked them together had loosened with the battering and were leaking dangerously.

The English shipwrights used wooden pegs. Cut, hewn, crushed, wedged from its shape, wood still remains a living substance. It shrinks and expands, softens and hardens, but it endures with the resiliency of the human spirit.

The Armada was defeated by the things it relied on to make it invincible. Not the least of these were its iron bolts.

22

WHEN IT BECAME CLEAR THAT STORMS NORTH OF SCOTland and down the Irish coast had shredded the last remnants of the Armada, Her Majesty decreed a day of thanksgiving. On the last Sunday in November, in the fullness of peace and the rejoicing harvest season, she came in solemn procession through the London gates and rode to the cathedral of St. Paul's.

Trumpeters and a hundred knights preceded her, and the city's aldermen in scarlet gowns; the lord chancellor; the archbishop of Canterbury; the French ambassador and the English nobles; the lord mayor of London; the Marquess of Winchester held the sword of state. Gentlemen pensioners marched beside her with gilt battle axes. The Earl of Oxford rode ahead of her, and the Earl of Essex led her horse on a silken rein.

At the cathedral she walked up the long west aisle under a gold canopy, moving to her traverse in the choir while the clergy sang the Litany.

Walking beside the Queen, supporting the canopy, Oxford found his mind searching backward through time. He traveled reflective paths across the dimness of kneeling figures in the cathedral nave.

The thirty-eight years had been erratic, an endless shifting between calm and storm, like the battles with the Armada his Queen and his nation were commemorating. He had enjoyed the calms, and yet, perversely, the storms had brewed out of his own tempests.

He wondered if it could have been otherwise. His father's death, his wardship at Cecil House—these things had been past his power to escape. They had been thrust on him, patterning his life. What balm for an orphaned boy in the welter of public manners and public rearing? Where the haven, the remembered spot of refuge torn from him in Castle Hedingham? Only the image of a father, colored in a heartsick imagination, and the pang of bitterness at a mother's second marriage. He had loved his father.

Much of the fault had been his own . . . Anne, who had wanted him, borne his children . . . If her flashes of spirit had been stronger, more able to follow the soaring of his poetry and dreams. If his pride and self-will had been weaker. If . . . The fault was his. And others'. He and Anne had tried to play their parts. Their times and their natures had been against them. They had been tied by authority and cursed by spite.

Self-will. Pride. Words a man counted as part of honor. Even Lyly on his ship had talked of honor. This was victory, this was honor. But he put them aside. They were not what he sought.

He had thought so. He did not know. The concept had differing meanings. It was the opposite of a lie for some. For some, truth was the lies they lived by, lies so often repeated they became their truth, and falseness to their lips the only kind of lying. In between stood the cowards, the sycophants and hypocrites and the tellers of half-lies. All of them swore by truth.

Truth, if lived to the life, brought little honor and more loneliness. Truth fought the battles, and in the victory was left outside, a maimed soldier, while flattery and pomp went in at the Cathedral.

He frowned, seeming to feel his father's eyes on him reproachfully. Truth there was not quite true. Norris was no flatterer, nor Lord Willoughby. Sussex had not been. Raleigh and Essex were vainglorious, but not cowards. Drake was a hero—Grenville, Hawkins, Frobisher. The lord admiral. Sidney had been one. All these people kneeling to the Queen, jubilant with her, prayerful for their deliverance—they had rallied to her and stood around her. His faults had been that he was not like them. They saw his follies but not his visions. They knew his wit and tongue but not the heart that made them, and among them he was as lonely as when he had slept with Anne and his mind had cried to be twined with hers as his body was.

"Were I a king I might command content . . ." The line of his poem, whispering through the Litany. It had a vein of melancholy.

Why melancholy? That was the rest of his life, his joy in books, his plays and poems. That was the respite for his loneliness, as it was the cause of it, and the cause of his incomprehensibility to the court world, and the abyss between him and much he could have loved.

Melancholy, melancholy. Talbot, Earl of Shrewsbury, earl marshal of England, carrying his staff of the canopy up the aisle, what did he know of the beauty of a word, the beauty of a phrase, and the excitement of its creation? What did he know of freeing a language, shaping it, molding it, working it as a potter works with clay, bringing it to the

» 264 «

triumph of a living art? To see the perfect forms, the shades and deli-
cacies evolving, to grasp at them, and lose them, and spur the will
after them and grasp again until they were seized in flight and written
down? What did he know of that? Nothing. And nothing came of
his nothing. But Talbot was a worthy man.

He thought of his life. The best had been in his mind. The scenes
rough-hewn, hurried, the characters flung together. Tavern and court,
love and hate, thrown to the stage with extravagance and his impetuous
hand. Out of the conflict between himself and his world. Then out of
venom. Then out of the need of men for succoring. And always out
of truth.

He knew there would be more. The time was safe now, the stage in
full sun. The plays would go on, the play of his life and the plays of
his creating. They would be surer, and firmer, and nearer to perfection.
He had learned his lesson. He must make them so.

The Queen had paused at her place.

He looked around him. He saw his daughter Elizabeth among the
maids of honor. He saw Nan Vavasour. Eliza Trentham.

23 THE VICTORY OVER SPAIN ENDED ONE ERA AND BEGAN
another. To Oxford, during that year and the next,
it seemed that the fibers he had helped knit for the
war withered and dissolved. He watched new alignments in politics
and new scrambles for favor.

The Queen was intrigued by the open rivalry that was flaring now
between Essex and Raleigh and thought of little else. Hatton maneuvered to the post of lord chancellor. Lord Burghley groomed his son
Robert to fill the shoes of Walsingham, who was dying.

Leicester was taken off by a sudden cold. Though a story among the
courtiers said it was not the cold but a poison which he had had prepared for his countess; he had tired of Lettice and told her the poison
was a medicine to use in sickness; and Lettice, unwitting, had used it
as a cure for him. His death, and the story, put a final color to an
unscrupulous career, and the shock made the Queen more capricious
than ever.

Drake left court. The summer after the Armada he sailed against a second fleet gathering in Spanish ports. He crippled the fleet, but came back without loot. His enemies set on him in a wolf pack and he was deprived of further command at sea. Drake returned to Plymouth, to spend his time building fortifications and a water supply.

Oxford saw the ingratitudes, the bought honors and the cheap rewards. He was at the height of his powers in the public eye and his following of London writers; the leader of the theater as Spenser was the leader of the poets. He had never had more respect, and never had less sign of it. Except for his yearly gift from the Queen, he had no thanks, no offices, no plums from the tree the court sycophants were shaking.

His money affairs, as always, were in bad shape. His actors were expensive, and the settlement of his estate was clearing at last through the court of wards. Robin Christmas looked glum when he spoke of it.

He asked the Queen for the monopoly on fruits and wools and oils. The monopoly went to Raleigh.

He asked for the stewardship of the Forest of Essex, the lands that had belonged to his family. He got a browbeating, and angry refusal.

"You can have the lot, Robin," he said, coming home from the court one day. "You can have them for the measure of a verse. Or the ranting of a play. Her Majesty can give her kingdom where she likes. I've done with it."

"Your plays were most brave, my lord," Robin said loyally. "I saw them myself. Marry, my scalp pricked like a cat's back."

"Useless now," Oxford said. "All useless."

Robin's only answer was a sigh. My lord of Oxford had done his work well, and his payment was thanklessness. Robin's regrets were as much for Oxford's spirits as for the time and energy thrown away, and the hard cash.

It was at this point that Oxford thought of the Trenthams. He was still seeing Eliza frequently, at the theaters and in the court, and when she said that her father and mother would be in London for the fall season the idea occurred to him to invite them to Vere House. The idea was encouraged by Robin, who had grown ancient enough in Oxford's service to be privileged to speak his mind and who felt that life had been too solitary for his master since the Armada; he intimated that the house was large and empty and could easily include visitors, and Oxford sent the invitation.

The Trenthams accepted. Oxford found them delightful guests. He had known them, though not intimately, from the time he had stopped in Staffordshire when he was twenty, and he had met them now and then at court on their occasional journeys to the city. Sir Thomas Trentham was a discreet man, shrewd and capable in business matters but with an interest in literature and something better than the merchant's usual pitying tolerance for those who trafficked in it. Lady Trentham was charming and gracious.

Oxford took them to the plays, and to the masques at court. They complimented him on the books dedicated to him, the volumes of translation and the collections of poetry and music, and spoke highly of his own plays. They sat at family suppers and discussed the pamphlet battle raging in London between the Puritans and the English Church. Before a week was over Oxford knew he would be sorry to see them go.

He hardly admitted, even to himself, that this might be because of Eliza. She joined them at the suppers when she could leave the court. Oxford rode to the palace to fetch her, and they rode back together through the London streets in twilights like the one when he had first come to the city. She would sit at the table, across from her mother, the light of the tapers touching her dark hair and the firm, graceful lines of her cheeks, and the evenings she was with them seemed a special enjoyment.

Sir Thomas was surprised that the Queen had not given Oxford more honors. "You have performed a good service," he said once, pausing between bites of a dessert confection, "and you should have recognition."

Oxford replied with a smile that his plays would have to be his recognition.

"Not a very substantial one," Sir Thomas said, and Eliza said, looking up quickly, "But my lord, so few recognize them."

"Half of London doesn't know which plays are yours," Lady Trentham said.

"It's just as well. They don't satisfy me yet," he said. Lady Trentham answered that she had seldom heard of a true writer who was ever satisfied, and Sir Thomas cleared his throat.

"I'm only a business person," he said, "but if I had a property like yours in these plays I would want to establish it more solidly. I would want to publish."

Eliza laughed. "Father, all his friends have told him that."

"Has Eliza been talking to you?" Oxford said.

"No, the thing is obvious."

"For a business person, Sir Thomas. Not for a nobleman," Oxford said. "A nobleman poor in honors and that bubble, reputation."

"The lack of honors is no fault of yours," Sir Thomas said gravely. "And the lack of reputation can be remedied. I think you are more in the front of fame than you know. If there is ever a consideration of pounds and pence, my lord, I've been fortunate in worldly goods. I'd gladly be of service to you."

Oxford bowed his thanks.

"If the plays are not published, they'll be lost," Eliza said. "Even to publish under another name would save them."

"Or anonymously."

"My lord," Lady Trentham smiled, "such a thin disguise wouldn't hold a week."

"If it were done," he said, "it would have to be done more cleverly. Lyly would like to be my mask. Jack's itching to see his name in print."

"Your plays are too great to bloom under Lyly's name," Sir Thomas said.

Robin Christmas appeared at the door, and Oxford excused himself, saying that his settlement with the court of wards had come through that afternoon and Robin had been working on the figures of his estate.

He came back after a moment. Sir Thomas put down his wine glass and turned to continue the talk, but Oxford did not sit down. He stood behind his chair, his knuckles white along the headpiece. Sir Thomas looked at him, and Eliza and Lady Trentham. In the tapers' light his face was set and rigid.

"All my life," he said heavily, "I've been told I must be prudent. And all my life the settling of my estate has been hanging fire. How can a man be prudent who doesn't know what money he may have? When I'm dead, let them face my critics with that."

Eliza glanced at her mother and father. They were silent, being tactful. Leaning over the table, she reached Oxford's wine glass and lifted it to him. He took it from her, tasted the wine mechanically, and handed it to her again.

"I don't fear death. And if I live to be a hundred there will be critics. But face them with that."

"Is the news so bad, my lord?" Sir Thomas said.

"I am in debt twenty thousand pounds."

It was a staggering sum, and for an instant there was nothing said. The times were extravagant. Raleigh spent half as much in a year on his colonizing, and Essex on his showy grandeur. But Raleigh had monopolies and Essex had grants and commissions to dispense, and lavish presents from the Queen. For Oxford, with none of these, twenty thousand pounds meant catastrophe. In the white knuckles and set face the Trenthams saw the vanishing of his hopes that the end of his life would be able to crown the promise of it, would give him honor or the chance to shape his work to enduring form.

Sir Thomas rose, clearing his throat again. "My lord," he said, speaking gravely but pleasantly, "a man's money is a private matter. Yet so are his friends. I have said I was fortunate in worldly goods. I will think myself more fortunate if I can put those goods to serve you. Whenever and in any way that you will, I trust that you will call on me. Perhaps out of this we can make even better means to win your recognition."

He led Lady Trentham from the room.

Eliza would have followed, but as she was moving toward the door Oxford stopped her.

"Eliza," he said.

"Yes, my lord?"

"For the second time tonight I have to thank you."

"For what, my lord?"

"For your father's good will toward me."

"I don't ask thanks," she said.

He left the chair and came toward her. "You never have," he said.

"I've never been much aid to you, my lord."

"No," he said. "No, I've mired too deep, Eliza."

"And soared high."

A color stained faintly in her cheeks. It could hardly have been a blush, for it did not ebb and flow but clung there steadily. And he and Eliza by now knew one another too well for blushes. Yet as he watched her he questioned how well he really knew her. In the years of their acquaintanceship she had always been there, not demanding as Anne had been, or confidently possessive like Nan Vavasour, and he had thought of her simply as Eliza. But he wondered whether he had ever asked himself if the thought went further.

"The heights have scarcely balanced the depths," he said.

"That would be for others to judge, my lord."

"Don't bring me to judgment, Eliza. The purgatory has been enough for today."

"I mean you are wrong to judge yourself too harshly."

"Your charity is large," he said with a smile, "if it can condone my faults."

"I don't condone them. But I make a distinction between them and dissoluteness."

"You don't think me dissolute then?" he said. He felt that was perhaps putting things too simply, but he felt the compulsion to ask nevertheless.

"I have always thought you had honesty of purpose and a tender heart, my lord. They are qualities that mark very few men I have known."

"Even the knaves?" he said.

"If a man were a knave," she said, "he wouldn't be concerned with the thoughts of other people."

He accepted the correction with an inward chuckle. She phrased her answers so that he could accept them without embarrassment. A stronger glow of pleasure went through him that she had recognized he might be concerned with what she thought, and that she did not spoil it by a false show of coyness.

"Not other people, Eliza. One."

"The audit would be the same," she said.

"For you, perhaps."

"For everyone."

Oxford lifted his shoulders half-humorously. "All these sophistries from a word of thanks. Ripples speed from a word, like a stone dropped in a pond. They circle in all directions, to the uttermost compass, widening and broadening until far, dank sedge at the glassy distance sways its flag with their stirring. Deeds circle out like words. They strike and sink. The deed is gone, but the effect slips to an infinity.

"We try to believe we can be solitary, each soul a bright containment in itself suspended in time and circumstance like frozen droplets in a summer's hail. But we fall into the flood, and melt, and blend with other droplets in an indistinguishable sea. A bad deed falls so, or a good. It touches all else about it, and flows with all else to the end." His shrug as he stopped was tinged with an apologetic wryness. "What a pity philosophy only talks after its pate is broken."

"Why?" she said.

"Because I wouldn't be muddying tonight with these dredged regrets. God knows, Eliza, I never thought I'd be laying them before you, spilling them into the clear channel of your eyes."

"The philosophy is sound, my lord."

"It's long, like the tail of a comet."

"But I think with more substance. Dissoluteness and philosophy may go together. But dissoluteness and the faculty of sympathy do not. A dissolute soul is selfish."

"Can you say I've not been selfish?"

"I would say you have fires in you that have not always burned in control."

"Is that an excuse? Every man has fires. In some the heat eats slow and smoldering, hugging conformable wood on the domestic hearth, and families can warm fingers to the purr of a cat, dozing and nodding after supper while the log creeps to an ash; in some there is a leap and crackle of a flame that shoots up to set a blaze to the whole house. These fires have differences. They won't all stay in the sooted confines of a fireplace maw. The control of them is everything. A watchfulness, a foreknowledge. Yet when the logs are laid, who knows how fitfully they will burn? I've seen tough oak, fibered like a rock, spit with some wayward chimney gust as far as the eagerest birch.

"Chance lays the logs, and if the house is consumed we call it crime. What excuse for the crime, Eliza? None. The next house will blaze as high to the next spark. You say I have fires in me. That's common. You say they've not burned in control. That's common, too. I wish the wood in me were fat and pursy. It's not, and the sparks have flung. The happy men are those who have no sparks. And the rogues are those who blow the sparks from the hollow reeds of their own conceit."

She was smiling at him when he finished. "The night is too young to be spoiled," she said, "either with water or fire."

"The primal elements," he said. "You're right." He repeated his wry gesture. "What should I be doing with them?"

"They belong to you," she said. "They are a part of you. But I think they will hardly answer at the theater."

Her smile brought him back to the moment. Talking with Eliza freed his thoughts and gave them scope. He found himself wanting to say these things to her, she seemed to interpret them in the way he meant them, not warping them by pretense or self-consciousness. He liked the ease of sharing them with her because he could share them so easily. They made him forget the court of wards, his debts, and the fret and objectivity of the world.

He returned to the fact that he was taking the Trenthams to the play that night. It was a private occasion, a special device of Lyly's was to be presented. Most of the court would be there, and he was anxious for them to go.

He threw off his worries and gave his attention to the evening's entertainment; called for horses and a link boy, and escorted the Trenthams to the theater. Sir Thomas did not mention his offer again. He continued as if nothing had happened, urbane and genial, and did not impose himself on Oxford's reserve.

The place was crowded when they arrived. The women selling sweetmeats ducked and bobbed as Oxford entered, and the city gentry in the pit stopped their munching of nuts and apples and stared admiringly to see my lord of Oxford in the gallery rooms. His coming always made a stir in a theater. He had given London good laughs and salty tears, and the plays went better when he was in the audience. London had loved Oxford as a stout lad from the beginning. It loved him still. Whatever he chose to be called—Will in the taverns, Ned to his friends, Lord Great Chamberlain in the royal household—it took him as he was, and excused his whims and the cloaks he put over his nobility. Beneath the cloak London knew he was its own.

There was a stir of tension in the air, and Oxford explained the night promised excitement. Lyly's new device was an attack on the Puritans.

"I've not seen it," he said. "Jack's rehearsed it himself. I've warned him not to carry it too far, but Jack is angry."

"The Puritan pamphlets have been very fierce," Sir Thomas said gravely.

"If fierceness were all," Oxford said, "we can be fierce, too. Jack has a gun or two in him, and Tom Nashe is a battery. But the Puritans are as high-handed as the Spaniards."

"There is one in a town near us," Lady Trentham said, "who preaches that all the great houses must come down."

"And the church and the princes," Sir Thomas said. "I hope when they reach power they'll spare the merchants."

"You could laugh at them if they had humor," Oxford said. "But they have none. You're speaking *preter spem*, Sir Thomas. They think seriously day and night, and that makes them dangerous."

"It is a kind of distemper with them," Sir Thomas said.

"What can you do? Our politicians have made cause with them to be rid of Mary of Scots. It's like the lamb wooing the lion. Her Majesty's been alert to it. Except for her jailing them and thwarting them in the Commons they'd have us in chains as doleful as Philip's. She's kept them from our necks. God knows what will come afterward."

"I thought Archbishop Whitgift would have brought our country's churches to a conformity," Sir Thomas said.

"Her Majesty's black husband. A severe man, but he can't go down and bawl in the streets against Brownists. He can singe their leaders, but he can't stop pamphlets and their mouthings. Well, Jack swears this will be a pill for them."

"Master Lyly is doing a bold thing," Lady Trentham said.

"It's necessary," Oxford said, "and he has protection."

He drew his stool forward beside Eliza and sat down eagerly. The hum of voices had quieted, the court gallants were putting away their cards. The play was about to begin. The piece was Lyly's, but Oxford was as eager as if it had been his. In spite of the years at theaters the eagerness was the same. He felt it at every performance, new or old.

At the last minute, while the curtain over the entrance at the back corner of the stage was still closed, a young man came hurriedly from a stage seat and pushed across the pit to where Oxford sat. He was the

Earl of Southampton, Henry Wriothesley, seventeen by now, in fawn-colored doublet and hose, high ruff, and jewels flashing at his ears and collar. His eyes were a deep, limpid brown, and his curled brown hair hung to his shoulders, one lock carefully apart from the rest and falling with an elegant negligence on the flutings of the ruff. He had a fair, boyish face and a slender, virile body. His delight at discovering Oxford in the theater made him overlook the Trenthams, but he bowed to them quickly.

"My lord, I've good news for you," he said.

"How good a news?" Oxford said.

"Very, my lord."

Oxford smiled. Southampton had followed him in Cecil House as a royal ward, and Lord Burghley was trying to manipulate a match between him and Oxford's daughter Bess. Oxford hoped the marriage would go through. He had told Southampton so more than once. But the young earl said he was not old enough to marry.

"Will it keep, Henry? Or do we have it now?"

"Now, my lord. I've found a man your lordship should know."

"London's full of men."

"Not this kind, my lord. He's an actor. A fellow from the country, with a wife and child behind him at Stratford—the village by Sir Thomas Lucy's lands near Warwick. He's trying his fortunes here, and is much concerned with plays."

Oxford smiled once more. He knew that Southampton had more enthusiasm for plays and poetry than any of the newer crop of courtiers. He was much as Oxford had been at seventeen.

"So is every actor, Henry."

"Your lordship would have a special interest in him. I heard of him by the way, and spoke with him. His name is Shakespeare. I think he's the absolute man your lordship might be looking for."

He stopped then, for a sennet sounded on the trumpets and the play began, and he pushed through the pit and jumped to his seat on the stage.

Oxford looked after him, his lips twitching slightly. He was grateful to Southampton, as he was grateful for Sir Thomas's offer. He had thought at various times what name might fulfill his work. His friends knew his plays only in manuscripts. There were crude actors' copies in the theaters, but it was tempting to linger over the notion of re-writing them, perfecting them, seeing them in finished, poetic form as he wished them to be.

But the notion had withered and dissolved like everything else. He was not a young actor from a country village, not free in name or rank, he had to pay forfeit to circumstance. The rest of his life was mortgaged to his debts, the Queen neglected him, he had no son of his body to leave the last shreds of his honor to. He had learned that it was below contempt to be a dabbler in plays. Few, only a very few, had understood. It occurred to him that possibly he had understood as little as any.

A sixth sense brought his mind back into the theater. Lyly's device was started, and his feeling for audiences told him the pit and galleries were abruptly hushed and acute. He looked at the stage and saw the reason. An actor dressed like an ape was capering on it.

Oxford and the whole house were aware that the ape represented a Puritan. The actor left no room for doubt. He capered to the front of the stage, struck a bawdy pose, and screamed that he was called Martin. The pamphlets from the secret Puritan press had been signed 'Martin Marprelate,' and everyone there knew it; the caricature was plain.

The pit tittered. Someone laughed.

The ape mopped and mowed and went into a mocking dance, keep-ing time with a singsong verse. He jeered at princes, peasants, the clergy, the state. He fleered, whooped, hallooed, roistered, a mad, foul burlesque, coarseness with a bludgeon.

Laughter broke through the audience. The ape ran from the stage, came back with a piebald fool, and swung him in a reel. He trundled an ale tub in, sucked at the spigot, and rolled drunk on the boards. He ran from the stage again, pranced out, his arms full of church gowns and communion books, and, squatting lecherously, gnawed at them and tore them into pieces. All the while he kept up a patter of filth, and japes, and crazy snatches of gabble.

Here and there people got to their feet. Some started to leave, stalk-ing with rage. They clambered over the benches in the torchlight and knocked into their neighbors. The rest booed at them and catcalled. The ape flung leers after them. There were shouts and fists.

Half the nobles in the galleries were standing. The gallants on the stage were holding their sides, rocking on their stools and throwing back their heads in spasms of hilarity. The pit took its cue from them, and guffawed. Here was Puritanism with a vengeance, an ape fit for Bedlam, obscene, scabrous, noddy-witted.

A man, dourly dressed, wrenched a leg from a bench and started for the stage. They mobbed in on him and drove him back to the gallery rails. He struck around him, his face contorted, bleeding from the side of his mouth. A huge fellow reared up, whirling a cudgel. They threw him out. They ripped the bench planks and beat the dissenters into order. The back rows dragged them through the door. The front rows laughed till the tears came.

The performance went on and finished in an uproar.

Oxford had risen from his seat. He stood at the gallery rail of his room, in front of Eliza and the Trenthams. Twice he half-drew his sword. Twice he dropped it again into the scabbard. Once he seemed about to vault the rail and go to the stage. But he stayed where he was. His eyes were glued on the ape's antics.

He turned to the Trenthams when it was over.

"God's blessing," he said.

Sir Thomas had risen also. He took a handkerchief and blew his nose slowly, avoiding Oxford's look. "A strong pill, my lord."

"Jack's done it now," Oxford said.

The nobles were leaving the rooms. Essex. The lord admiral. They bowed to the Trenthams as they passed. Their stares at Oxford were curious, still wet from merriment but grave with a kind of awful speculation. Robert Cecil came by. He bowed, too, more to Oxford than to his guests, and spoke reluctantly. He liked Oxford.

"My lord," he said, "My Lord Chancellor Hatton asks me to say that he wishes to see you at the palace tomorrow morning."

Oxford started for the palace the next day. He breakfasted alone in his chamber—muscadel and eggs and bread, eaten quietly after he had dressed—and rode through Ludgate and Temple Bar and out along the Strand.

Partly because of last night, or because of Hatton, the ride made him think of the one that had first brought him into London. He had ridden the same route then—a boy, with a boy's wonder and a boy's grief, by Ludgate and Temple Bar and meeting, in the purple twilight, the solemn-bearded escort sent to greet him. The same route. He had ridden it often since; and with such difference. Twenty-eight years had tempered the wonder, had mellowed the grief to a controlled irony. London, for him, had touched life at every stop. It had sounded every note in the scale. If his father had lived, or his mother had not re-married, if he had had some other home than Cecil House, all this might have been otherwise. Yet he knew, truthfully, that perhaps it would not. That was speculation, like the looks of the nobles last night, a guess that could not be unriddled till the tune was ended.

Hatton was engaged in the Privy Council when Oxford reached Westminster, and he went impatiently into an anteroom off the council hall to wait. He had always hated to be idle, it was distasteful to him, especially the killing of time in an anteroom—the expectancy, the void, the flat vapid silence and the temptation to construct the interview in advance. He stifled his distaste and began to walk up and down under the impersonal stare of the guard on duty at the doorway, adjusting his cloak, flicking at the slashes on his doublet sleeves, and rearranging the hang of his dagger.

There had been a period in his life when the idea that he would wait while Hatton, the Sheep, the vegetable that had sprouted overnight, was sitting at a meeting of the Privy Council would have been a comic tragedy. As comic and as tragic as that he would not one day be sitting in the council himself. Events had spun into a tangled skein. The figure of speech was not the best, but his mind's eye filled in the picture. Clotho, Lachesis, Atropos. The three sisters. For perverseness he added the scroll of his family motto, like a banner over a portrait, *Vero Nihil Verius*. The Fates spinning, twisting, cutting, hunched at their dark trade under the aegis of Truth. An unseemly combination.

The minutes dragged. The guard at the door shifted from one foot to the other. His shoes creaked loudly. He looked at Oxford. Oxford looked at him. Nothing. The guard's stare remained blank. He shifted his weight back again.

Oxford was undecided whether it would be better to stay in the anteroom or to go downstairs for a stroll in the gardens, where from the windows he could see young Southampton flirting with the court virgins. He was listening for the creak of the guard's shoes again when white skirts slipped in at the doorway. A voice said, "My lord—"

It was Eliza.

"I was told you were here," she said.

She came into the anteroom and Oxford noticed—he had noticed it before—that an air of poise and gracefulness made her lovely to watch, even when she hurried. She must have run up from the gardens, he thought, for her breasts were rising and falling with a rapid little catch of breath, but her curtsy to him was soft and sweeping in its lack of haste. He thought of a mountain stream pausing in its tumblings at a shadow-flecked pool.

"Someone carries bad news fast," he said.

"Bad news carries itself, my lord. I came to see if I could help you."

For a moment it was hard to say that he was aware of any feeling except a conscious glow of pleasure at her presence there. She had come because he was in trouble, quite genuinely and without artifice offering to do what she could. For matters where Her Majesty took a personal interest there was seldom anything to be done, but in other instances a maid of honor could sometimes be an influence. He led her toward the window, away from the stare of the guard, which had suddenly become more blank than ever.

"I don't know what help I'll need until I talk to Hatton," he said.

"You've not seen him?"

"Not yet."

"The Puritans have complained of the ape," she said. "Their chiefs spoke with the lord chancellor early this morning."

"Is Hatton afraid of the Puritans?" he asked.

"They can bring great pressure," she said. "They act and think as a single group in the Commons. He is sensitive to pressure."

"He is sensitive to whatever thing will hamper me," Oxford said. "I put my hope in Her Majesty. I can remind my lord chancellor of that."

"Yes," Eliza said slowly. "Yes, you can."

"You don't trust it?" he said, seeing the doubt in her face.

Eliza considered her reply. "The last years have changed Her

Majesty. She has grown weary, and her interests have narrowed. The Armada was a great strain on her. She is worried about her successor, she will not name one for fear of civil war. And she has Raleigh and my lord of Essex. When Essex is angry with her he goes to bed and sulks, and she brushes everything aside, sends her own physician to him and is disconsolate till he chooses to be well again. We've seen it at court." She raised her eyes, shadowed by an unwillingness to hurt him. "It may be that she will be indifferent to protecting you."

To his surprise, he did not feel hurt. He was thinking, as he looked at her, of the unwillingness, of her loyalty, of the growing unspoken sense of things that might be said between them more important than a Queen's support, and the shadows in her eyes.

He said, "You mean that she won't."

"Yes, my lord."

He gestured impatiently, as if on an impulse he could throw off the whole sick business, all the work and aspirations of his life, fling them away as not worth the struggle to keep them any longer.

"God's blessing, when we have to depend on favor!"

He stopped, for he saw in her eyes not only an unwillingness to hurt him, but the admission that he could hurt her equally as much. She expected him to know that he had more than favor. He had himself.

The guard straightened to erect attention while the door at the end of the anteroom opened. Hatton came out of the council hall, walking rapidly.

His face was clouded by an expression that implied a weight of questions on his mind and an unpleasant morning for his dignity with my lords of the Privy Council. His astute, rather bulgy eyes and features florid with too many years of wine and sweets looked as if the meeting had not gone well for him. As he caught sight of Oxford he stared heavy-lidded, and the clouds on his face broke in a slow dawning of porcine satisfaction. Chance had delivered Oxford to him at a moment when his self-esteem could do with a little bolstering.

"Ah, my lord," he said, "I was meaning to have spoken with you."

"And I with you," Oxford said. "But I have suited more action to my meaning. I'm here and ready."

This was not the method for making an approach to Hatton, but he had never been able to swallow his disgust for the man. Hatton had always seemed to Oxford pretentious and a sham. Against the integrity of even the other adventurers at court he rang hollow.

Hatton merely blinked at him, the satisfaction on his face showing more relish. The higher Oxford talked, the farther he could bring him down.

"My speech can be short. The Puritans have heaped much blame on you."

"I could do the same with the Puritans."

"Your actors," Hatton said, "have played a scandal."

"An ape."

"An ape to mock the Puritans, which is a scandal. A scandal for them, and, being true and devoted subjects of Her Majesty, by logic and consequence a scandal for us. The manner of the malefaction is all one."

"For God's sake," Oxford said, "leave off logic-snipping and come to the point. The Puritans have been aped and they want payment."

"Yes, my lord. From those who did it."

"They should follow their own precepts and give an ape for an ape. They've talked to you, then."

"The question has come under my authority as lord chancellor."

Oxford said more quietly. "Since when does a lord chancellor bother himself about a troupe of players? Aren't there meatier problems?"

"We will decide what the problems are," Hatton said, staring harder and drawing himself up in official pride. "I will tell you, my lord, that if you were not the patron of the players, this could be a star chamber matter."

He scowled, padding his hands against his velvet doublet. His new honors had bloated his pompousness, but beneath his fatty layers of vanity he had a dangerous spite, and the power to wield it.

"The players must be disbanded," he said.

"You're jesting," Oxford said.

"I am not."

"My players were defending the archbishop."

"The archbishop can defend himself. Her Majesty has spoken with him."

The effort to control his temper made Oxford blench.

"I will promise their behavior, my lord chancellor," he said stiffly. "I will tell Lyly."

"You may tell Lyly what you like. He has done you poor service. But your company must go."

"My lord—"

"I have no time," Hatton said.

He turned to move away. As he did so he came face to face with Eliza. She had been listening to him incredulously, and the carmine was as vivid in her cheeks as Oxford's were white.

"I cry your pardon, my lord," she said, "is this all? Is there nothing more?"

"Nothing," Hatton said.

"Eliza—" Oxford said, and started forward, but her eyes looked at him so eloquently that he stopped. He fell back.

Hatton observed them with a smirk. "This will be an end to his vaporings," he said, and moved on again.

But Eliza, putting herself in front of him, blocked his path. "I beg you to consider, my lord. Is the price great enough?"

"Price, Mistress Trentham?" Hatton said. "I am not aware of any price."

"The price for losing these players, my lord. What can you gain from it?"

Hatton's smirk broadened. "Silence from my lord of Oxford," he said.

"Oh, you're cruel!" Eliza exclaimed. "Cruel and vengeful! What right have you to keep my lord of Oxford tongue-tied? These plays of his, these writings you call vaporings, are vision and beauty, greater vision and finer beauty than you or I or any of us have seen before. You can't silence them!"

The color had swept from her cheeks into her temples, transforming her from the gentle, self-contained Mistress Trentham to a bladelike, defiant figure that flashed on him in a courageous scorn. She was not afraid of him. She confronted him in the security of a wealth and family that put her beyond the reach of the lord chancellor. Hatton gaped at her and then at Oxford. Oxford's eyes were fastened on her.

"The affair is not for you to meddle in," Hatton said loftily.

"Silence?" Eliza said. Her breasts were rising and falling as they had when she had run up the stairs, but now there was no catch in her breath. The words poured out of her in self-forgetfulness, intent only on her determination to have her say. "As well try to silence the wind or the beat of the sea, or the larks that sing in Staffordshire. You'll never silence him. If ignorance and authority stoop to such shame—never.

"How can you understand my lord of Oxford? You cannot and you will not, and so you must throttle him for an art that touches all human life, the glints and facets of joys and melancholies, and human triumphs and human weaknesses. You must throttle the man who's unlocked our speech and made it leap, set our minds free and braced our hearts with his turbulent spirits. You'd put him forever under shadow. I swear you will not."

"The judgment stands," Hatton said, commencing to puff.

"Keep your judgment, my lord. Its foolishness will condemn you."

She looked at him steadily until he plucked at the tasseled edge of his cloak and said, "Well well, step aside."

"You say this is the end," she said. "I say it is the beginning. We'll make it so, my lord chancellor. We'll make it the foundation of a greatness that will grow so high your malice will be a dwarf. How small! How poor! You've not stopped Lord Oxford. His plays are written. He doesn't need London, or the court, or you, to bring them to perfection. We can hire other actors. There are other theaters to be rented. There are friends to stay by him and printers to trumpet his lines to the corners of the earth. You've misfired sadly if you think this is the end. Out of this leisure your envy's given him he'll bring fame and glory past anything a lord chancellor can imagine!"

Then she swung away from in front of him, and with a low curtsy left the way clear between him and the door. Her outburst had been amazing. Oxford stood tense. The guard at the doorway had glued his stare rigidly to the ceiling. Hatton, hissing through his mustache like a gander, blinked again twice and stalked in a dudgeon out of the room.

Oxford went over to Eliza. He raised her up. Her defense of him had driven tears to her eyes, tears of indignation, of brave assurance and utter trust in him. He saw them there and took her in his arms.

It seemed such a natural thing to do.

He held her in a long silence, his lips to her dark hair.

After a few moments he said, "Eliza—"

"Yes, my lord?"

She expected him to be angry with her for interfering, for pushing into his life and having the audacity to speak so wildly about him and his plays and his work. She twisted her head from his shoulder and tried to move out of his embrace, but he kept her from drawing back and said, "Do the larks still sing in Staffordshire?"

Her face lifted at the tone of his voice. "Exquisitely, my lord."

He nodded, and laid his lips against her hair again, a peaceful movement, restful and content.

Neither of them stirred for another while.

Eliza was soft in his arms, and he was listening to the fresh catch of her breath.

"You came to my rescue," he said.

"Yes, my lord." She looked at him, hesitating. "Was I wrong?"

"You've always been ready to come to my rescue, Eliza."

"Because I believed in you," she said.

"Yes, you have. From my first tournament—when you kissed me. You were a girl then—a baby to me—but I knew then that you believed in me. Eliza, if our lives had been different."

"You still have your life," she said. "It's your own."

Putting his fingers under her chin he tilted it gently upward. The tears had dried from her eyes and left them dark and shining.

"Is it mine," he said, "or yours?"

"I've never wanted your life to be mine," she said.

"I know that, too. You're the only woman who hasn't."

"I think you've made your life a victory, my lord. You could have been spoiled and squandered, a loss to yourself and to the kingdom, worst of all a loss to the truth of your own being. But at the hardest crises, at the roughest shocks, you've turned back instinctively to the qualities in yourself. You've drawn on them as the sun draws water. You've distilled them, and they've fallen like rain from heaven on the parched, stunted souls around you." She broke off, seeing him smile. "Water and fire again. I seem to talk of elements as well as you."

"I wasn't laughing," he said. "I was thinking what solace you are."

She smiled with him, not trying to answer.

He tilted her chin farther. "And now—?"

"I expect bigger things, my lord."

"What things?"

"I don't know. But I expect the victory to go on to greater accomplishments. You can achieve them."

"Alone?"

"I hadn't thought," she said.

"Together," he said.

Before he could say more the door to the council hall flung wide with a rattle of bolts. Essex and Raleigh knelt inside, the other councilors ranged behind them in order of precedence, and Her Majesty Queen Elizabeth passed at a stately tread between them to emerge into the anteroom.

Oxford and Eliza sprang apart and fell to their knees.

Her Majesty's oblong face was wrinkled. Her nose was a little hooked. Her lips were narrow and her teeth black. In her ears she wore two pearls with very rich drops, false red hair on her head, and a small crown. Her bosom was cut extremely low and she had on a necklace of fine jewels. Her hands seemed smaller and her fingers longer, spread as she walked over the fullness of her dress, which was white, and embroidered with pearls the size of beans. From her shoulders hung a mantle of black silk, shot with silver thread. She moved over the floor in a magnificent manner, the councilors rising and following after her, but her eyes darted around the anteroom as she went forward, stabbing at the guard and peering suspiciously at the thick folds of the window draperies.

When she saw Oxford and Eliza on their knees she threw them a searching look and halted abruptly. Essex and Raleigh stopped in their tracks, and all the councilors halted. Her eyes caught the traces of tears on Eliza's face, and the sudden confusion in Oxford's, and her brows went up.

"What have we here?" she said. "More bawdry about players?"

Oxford met her look directly, his brain racing to formulate an answer. Her Majesty was shrewd, and her questions demanded instant reply. She could not be put off, and her instinct told her something was afoot between him and Eliza. He wondered if he should try to temporize.

"Come come, my lord, speak up."

"No, Your Majesty, another marriage."

The rashness of his answer piled everything in one stake, risking it all on a gamble for the future so close to his grasp, for himself and Eliza, and the strength and love they had found in one another, for Her Majesty was more jealous than ever of her maids, and her old woman's wrath more terrible against those who thought of marriage without her sanction. His reward was Eliza's smile, and the quick, fearless slipping of her hand into his.

They waited for what Her Majesty would say.

The arched eyebrows remained lifted. The yellow eyes, flecked by troubles until they seemed almost black, regarded them unwinkingly. The narrow mouth tautened, and the wrinkles that rouge and powder could no longer hide puckered at its corners.

"God's bones, Ned," Elizabeth said, "we think it time."

EPILOGUE

On a morning in early September a company of riders breasted slowly toward the gates of London from the suburb of Hackney, two miles beyond Shoreditch.

They were a small train, riding two by two, elegantly dressed in the black and tawny livery of their master. Their clothes, their bearing, the rich trappings of their horses, were suited to the dignity of his rank and honors—the seventeenth Earl of Oxford, Lord Bulbeck, Sandford and Badlesmere, lord great chamberlain of England and newly appointed steward of the Forest of Essex.

Oxford himself rode at their head, with Eliza beside him.

He was in his fifties now, erect and sturdy. His face showed the fever marks of the plague that had ravaged the city that summer, but he carried himself proudly. Twelve years wedded to Eliza, he was coming up to London to take his place as a member of the Privy Council.

It was a mellow day, a rare, pale, cloudless sky. Queen's weather. But the Queen was dead that year.

Many were gone with her. Lord Burghley. Hatton. Essex beheaded for rebellion, Raleigh in the Tower for the failure of his colonies.

King James sat on the throne in London. They had put the question to Elizabeth at last, when she had one more night to live; Master Secretary Robert Cecil leaning over her shriveled form, above the rusty sword she had used for plunging into arrases and behind curtains in her final spasms of terror, straining his ears for the croak of her reply— "I will that a King succeed me, and who should that be but my nearest kinsman, the King of Scots?" The messenger waiting below her chamber window had watched for the signal of her dying and galloped headlong to the North, as if outstripping her soul on its flight into eternity.

Eliza's eyes shone with happiness. Behind her and Edward their young son, Henry, rode with Edward's cousin, Sir Horatio Vere. Ahead of them the road ran toward London smoothly and peacefully. Ran as the years of their marriage had run, bringing her beloved lord and husband to his just deserts.

As the company passed through Shoreditch the flags were flying from the playhouses, opened again after the plague. Three actors, strolling by the roadside, stood out of the way, doffing their hats respectfully. Other actors crowded the porches of the playhouses and clustered from the doors to see Oxford go by. They stared in admiring reverence, waving greetings and bowing homage to the man who by his high imagination, by pen and purse and boundless efforts, had done more than any to set their profession on its path toward its present glory.

Oxford returned their greetings.

He was conscious of fulfillment in their stares. He was conscious that the stage had never been in more esteem. The King and Queen were patrons of the players. The young Prince had taken over a company. The playhouses were flourishing. Beyond the city, across the Thames, the Globe Theater blazed with the luster of the name of Shakespeare. In all this he had had a part.

These were the spiritual rewards, 'the years with Eliza, the freedom and delight, the knowledge of accomplishment in his own and others' hands.

"They love you," Eliza said.

Oxford smiled, laying his fingers over hers on her saddle bow. It was sweeter that Eliza loved him; that he loved her.

Spiritual rewards, and material. All had come to him. The King had renewed Queen Elizabeth's grant, her payment of a thousand pounds a year. That was a token of His Majesty's regard. His suit for the stewardship of the Forest of Essex was allowed him. That was pride and title for his family, an inheritance to be passed to his son. Greatest of all, he was raised to the Privy Council. That was the utmost favor he could hope to have, the goal of every ambition in the English realm.

"They will remember the councilor when they've forgotten the poet," he said.

"They will never forget the poet, Edward," Eliza said. "I'd never wish them to."

He repeated his smile. "Let them only remember that I won my recognition," he said. "The Privy Council is monument enough. I will be satisfied."

Behind them they could hear Henry's boyish voice, laughing as they came nearer to the bustle and excitement of the city.

Oxford turned to her more fully, his fingers still on hers. "I've not done wisely always, Eliza, nor always well. My work is unfinished. But some of it has rooted, and some borne fruit. If the fruit has any wisdom, these laurels are the testimony."

They rode a little farther. The road was filling with its morning business, the carts and baskets, the blue-clad apprentices, peddlers and trudging farmers and beggars, thickening about the horses' flanks. The great spire of St. Paul's rose over the city walls.

"They are the laurels men understand best," he said. "They are my triumph over spite and folly, the prize we have both longed for. I am content to let them be my epitaph."

"Epitaph?" she said. "With the whole world before you?"

"As it was when I rode first from Hedingham." His smile was affectionate. "You are very dear to me. You know the truth. I have served England. I have served my Queen. I have brought myself to honors, like my father. For the rest—" He paused, and his eyes went for a moment to the playhouses, which were dropping gradually away among the roofs of Shoreditch.

"The rest is silence," Eliza said.

He nodded equably. "It's a good line," he said.